FAR AND NEAR

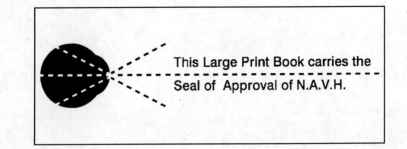

This Large Print Book carries the
Seal of Approval of N.A.V.H.

HAVEN SEEKERS, BOOK 4

FAR AND NEAR

AMANDA G. STEVENS

THORNDIKE PRESS
A part of Gale, Cengage Learning

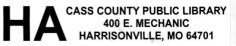
GALE
CENGAGE Learning·

Farmington Hills, Mich • San Francisco • New York • Waterville, Maine
Meriden, Conn • Mason, Ohio • Chicago

GALE
CENGAGE Learning

LIBRARY OF CONGRESS CATALOGING-IN-PUBLICATION DATA

Names: Stevens, Amanda G., author.
Title: Far and near / Amanda G. Stevens.
Description: Large print edition. | Waterville, Maine : Thorndike Press, 2016. | © 2016 | Series: Haven seekers ; book 4 | Series: Thorndike Press large print Christian mystery
Identifiers: LCCN 2016003833 | ISBN 9781410486981 (hardback) | ISBN 1410486982 (hardcover)
Subjects: LCSH: Large type books. | BISAC: FICTION / Christian / Suspense. | GSAFD: Suspense fiction. | Christian fiction.
Classification: LCC PS3619.T47885 F37 2016 | DDC 813/.6—dc23
LC record available at http://lccn.loc.gov/2016003833

Published in 2016 by arrangement with David C Cook

Printed in Mexico
1 2 3 4 5 6 7 20 19 18 17 16

Now unto the King
eternal,
immortal,
invisible,
the only wise God,
be honour and glory
for ever and ever.
Amen.
1 Timothy 1:17, King James Version

[. . .]

Whereas the behemoth of federal power has forgotten the responsibility that it carries to protect the liberties and autonomy of every citizen;

Whereas a corrupt federal government, drunk on control, has invaded our state, our police, and our people's last refuge of liberty — the freedom of thought in their own minds;

[. . .]

Whereas these actions constitute a direct attack on the sovereignty of our state and of our people;

Therefore, let it be known that we, the State of Texas, hereby reject the power of the Federal State and will henceforth no longer be subject to the authority of the United States of America;

Therefore, let it be known that we, the State of Texas, hereby reestablish our independence as the Sovereign State of the Republic of Texas.

[excerpts, Republic of Texas, Declaration of Sovereignty]

1

He owned a sweetgum tree.

A house, too. Land — two acres. But for some reason, the star-shaped leaves of that tree stood out today, as his truck coasted to a stop in front of his house. His. Marcus parked. Gave himself a few seconds to gaze at it, the two peaks of the roof, the covered porch, the windows. Ten windows in all, every room full of light. The house was almost fourteen-hundred square feet of needed work. But it would be home. He wished he could get his own loan now, put the deed and the mortgage he was paying in his own name instead of Walt's, but he could be patient these days. Mostly.

Lee reached down for their cooler on the truck floor. "Shall we?"

"Yeah."

He shut off the ignition and got out. The blue Chevy S-10 was thirty years old, but the engine and transmission weren't. Somebody had even taken care of the body, keeping rust to a minimum. The height was doable for his knee, and the price had been doable too. He clapped his hand once on the truck roof before he moved to join Lee.

They headed up the concrete walk, and he motioned to the porch. "Picnic?"

"Of course."

No chairs or table inside. Might as well sit in the sun. This late in the afternoon, it poured onto them despite the awning.

Lee sank down on the porch, feet on the top step, and opened the cooler beside her. Marcus gripped the white railing and lowered himself next to her, the cooler between them. He stretched his right leg out.

The sun warmed the top of his head. Add another item to the thankfulness list alongside his house and his truck — spring in Texas. Locals said summer would be warmer, and they'd hardly had a winter. He'd missed Michigan snow, the personality of its different forms — spiteful sleet, patient flakes, persistent drifts that froze into walls of ice and refused to melt.

By the end of February, Texas spilled sunshine and warmth, and summer began in April. Now, with the calendar flipped to May, Marcus was ready for the heat Texans promised. This was good country. His country soon. He leaned his head back and closed his eyes, and the sun soaked into his eyelids until he saw pink stars behind them.

Sandwich wrappers rustled, and Lee set his in his hands. "Italian sub."

"Mmm." He opened his eyes.

For the next few minutes, both of them focused on the food. His foot-long was gone before her six-inch flatbread with vegetables and roasted chicken. One of these days, he'd convince her to add cheese and dressing. And salami.

Nah, he wouldn't.

When they'd finished, Marcus balled up their napkins and wrappers and shoved everything into the cooler. No trash can here yet.

Austin's little green car turned at the end of the street, pulled up the driveway, and parked. Violet hopped out of the passenger seat and bounded up onto the porch.

"So this is it. It's gorgeous, Marcus."

Not yet, but the smile wouldn't stay off his face. Marcus got to his feet and tugged out his keys. "Thanks. A little rough on the inside."

"Oh, whatever. You'll make it awesome."

He and Lee. She caught his eye as he turned on the crowded porch. Austin ambled up and stood on the grass, eyeing the house up and down.

"Nice," he said.

"Have to paint this." Marcus gestured to the ridiculous orange door. "Brown or something."

"Or green," Lee said.

No, not green. Against the pale yellow siding, a green door would make his place look like a dollhouse. He motioned everybody ahead of him, shut the door, then took the lead.

"Stairs go down to the basement. It's unfinished." He led them to the south side first. "It's a three-bedroom, so here's the first two. Bathroom in between. That sink'll have to come out, and something ate the finish off the faucet."

"You have a pink shower curtain," Violet said.

Marcus motioned them to the first of the bedrooms. "Lot of stuff left behind. All the curtains, magnets on the fridge, towels in the linen closet."

"Um . . . curtains?" Violet cast a meaningful gaze at the bare bedroom windows.

"Well, I threw everything out. Old and stained. Keep forgetting the shower curtain."

"How can *you* forget to throw out something pink?"

She walked into the bedroom and turned a circle. Lee stepped in farther too. Lee's slim neatness, the blue crewneck T-shirt and trim jeans, the composed lacing of her fingers behind her back, only emphasized the room's stains and smudges.

"Yeah," he said when Violet turned her frown to him. "It's all like this."

"The carpet may not come clean," Lee said. "We haven't attempted it yet, but it will be replaced as soon as possible, and the walls will be painted soon as well."

That Lee liked his house mattered a lot, of course, but this was something else. She joined the house-showing as if she owned it along with him. Comfortable in this space, though it was still technically only his. His chest filled with something light and . . .

His throat tightened. A home and a project. Work for his hands, the best kind of work. Open space outside, safe space inside. Austin and Violet. And Lee. Behind his eyes, a burning started.

No.

They went back through the entryway to the family room, and Marcus enjoyed the memory of Lee's first time through the house, how she'd praised all the things he loved about this room. The ten-foot ceiling, the light from the double windows, the openness between the living room and kitchen. In this room, the house felt bigger than it was.

"Who would paint their whole house ivory?" Violet said as they crossed into the kitchen.

"Exactly what I said." Lee stood with her back to the wall, giving Violet and Austin space to explore. "It's impractical, given these people's lack of cleanliness. Not to mention monotonous."

"Easier to paint over, though," Austin said.

"We're going to paint the kitchen first."

As if the house were still new to her — well, it kind of was — Lee meandered through the kitchen. She ran her fingers along the white builder's-grade countertops — either side of the stove, the island.

Violet opened the oven door and peered inside. Her nose wrinkled. "Gross. Can't you throw this out and get a new one?"

"Not now." Marcus leaned an elbow on the island. "This stuff is solid. And the sink's in good shape. I'll have to hire somebody for the floor."

Even if he could run again someday, he'd never install flooring again. Lee glanced at him, maybe picking up an edge in his voice.

"It's a great place, really," Austin said.

"The potential is obvious, and it's close to town."

They wandered to the master bed and bath, vacant and dirty and ivory like every other room in the house.

"The vaulted ceiling is great," Austin said. "Ten feet, like the living room?"

"Yes and yes," Lee said, and Marcus stood in the doorway and watched them all. He couldn't help smiling again.

Violet turned a circle in the center of the room, as she'd done in every other room. "You should paint it mauve."

"Interesting," Lee said. As if she didn't hate the color mauve.

Marcus took them into the garage last.

"Yes, the garage is cleaner than the house," Lee said.

"Huh." Violet turned a circle out here too. Then grinned. "Well, you'll want to have a workshop out here right away, so that's a win. Or will you use the shed thing? It's almost as big as the house."

"Probably use both." Marcus's phone buzzed in his pocket. He pulled it out and frowned. Walt. The others watched him take the call. "What's going on?"

"Marcus, I need you at the office."

"Now?"

"This information can't wait, and I can't

share it over a phone line."

"Okay."

"Are you with Lee?"

Reflex pulled his gaze to hers, to the concerned lines of her face. "Yeah."

"Bring her with you."

"Walt, is there danger?" At least tell him that. Let him take precautions.

"Not right now. Just come to the office as soon as you can."

"Okay." He hung up.

Across the room, all three of them were staring at him.

"What'd he say?" Austin propped a hand on his hip, a pose that oddly mirrored Walt.

"He wants me and Lee at the —"

Austin's phone started playing a Johnny Cash song. His face reddened as he grabbed it from his pocket. "I'm with Lee and Marcus."

Walt's voice came slightly raised through his phone.

Austin pressed his lips together against a smile. He looked to Marcus. "He says you could've mentioned it, saved him a phone call."

Walt should have asked if he wanted to know. A growl pushed out of Marcus.

Austin ducked his head but failed to hide his grin. It faded before he looked up again.

16

"Right. . . . Lately? No . . . Of course they are."

Even Violet eyed him as the conversation lasted, as Austin scrubbed his hand through his blond hair and turned half toward the wall, focused on Walt's voice. Austin knew something. If Marcus didn't know better, he'd think the kid was . . .

Was he? Working for Walt?

"Crap," Austin said, and Walt spoke for only a moment before he cut him off. "You don't have to, I can guess. Okay. I'm on my way."

Something else from Walt, and Austin hung up. He pivoted to face them.

"Austin," Marcus said.

"You'll get answers at the office."

Marcus planted his feet. "Tell me what that was."

"Really, Marcus, we need to get you —"

"No."

"Guys, seriously." Violet stepped between them, and if she told Marcus to let it go, he'd do some more growling, but she turned to Austin. "Short version?"

Austin pocketed his phone and scrubbed at his hair again. He glanced at each of them, ending on Marcus. "Walt's my boss."

The information washed through Marcus, and a low simmer began inside. Austin and

Walt had both kept it from him, whatever they were working on. He should have been working with them.

"Can we go?"

"How long?" Marcus said.

A long sigh poured from Austin. "December."

Five months. Yet Walt still hadn't offered that kind of trust to Marcus, never mind that he'd been living in Walt's guest room since October. He gritted his teeth. Took out his keys. Marched to the door, shepherded everybody outside.

"Violet," he said when they all stood on the driveway, Lee already heading for her car. "One of us could take you home first."

Her hands popped to her hips, and her eyes widened. "You're kidding, right?"

"Walt didn't say —"

"I'm coming. Obviously." She cocked her head at Austin. "Ride with you?"

"Of course."

If she wouldn't be safe knowing, Austin would say so. Marcus watched them back down the driveway and pull away before heading for his truck, but Austin stopped at the end of the street. Waiting for him.

A chill ran down Marcus's back. He'd gotten the first call. This might be about him.

He didn't want it to end, this new start

God had given him. But he'd rather lose all of it than see these people hurt.

2

Something like this was always going to happen. Lee hadn't been the only one to know it. When the phone calls came, none of them was surprised. Austin apparently had an inside perspective of the goings-on between the new country of Texas and the American Constabulary. But even Violet's expression had held more *déjà vu* than panic.

Time to run for our lives? Just say the word.

Not even the enemy was new. Only the Constabulary could worry Walton Cantrell. If he was calling them to a meeting this late, he was worried.

Dusk was creeping in by the time their three vehicles parked at the Decatur office of the Texas Rangers. It was an old redbrick building with two sets of steps, separated by a cement landing, leading up to the main doors. The Lone Star flag hung from the flagpole on the right, barely moving in a breeze that fanned the drying sweat on Lee's neck. To the left of the building, an empty circle of concrete gave away the previous location of another flagpole. The American flag no longer flew here, and the authorities had chosen the symbolism of removal rather than replacing it with another Texas flag.

At this hour the office was closed to the public, but they were granted entrance. Walt must have told the night guard to expect them. He motioned them down a well-lit corridor, paneled wall on one side and wide windows on the other. Interview rooms. Each one they passed was empty and dark. They walked two by two, Marcus at her side. He smelled like soap, crisp and clean.

After a ten-hour shift at the hospital and nearly an hour's drive, Lee's steps should be dragging, but adrenaline quickened them. She'd never ventured so far into this building before, only to the visitor's desk to speak with Walt on occasion. He always came out to her.

At the end of the corridor, he stood with his arms folded, wearing his signature gray lapel jacket and Western hat. He strode forward to meet them.

"Thanks for coming, y'all. This way. I have a conference room for us."

Marcus struck out in front of her as if, whatever this was, he needed to face it first. Walt motioned them into the room then shut the door behind them and motioned again, inviting them to sit.

A long oak table surrounded by office chairs occupied the center of the room. An accordion folder lay in the center of the table. Austin took a chair at the far end, and Marcus sat to his right, facing the door. Lee sat next to him, her chair a few inches nearer the table than his. Maybe he'd left room to spring up and pace if needed. The tension in his shoulders looked ready to break.

Violet sat at Lee's other side, focused on Austin. His bland expression, the posture that tilted back in his chair — he'd withdrawn from them. Perhaps this was Austin at work.

Walt took a seat across from Lee and Marcus and Violet and pulled the accordion to him. He drew out several manila folders and set aside all but one.

"You fill them in?" Walt looked to Austin.

"Mostly."

"Austin's my researcher and quasi-CI. Less confidential now, obviously." He locked eyes with Marcus. "And let's get this one thing out of the way. No, I'm not bringing you into it."

Challenge leaped into Marcus's face. "I can —"

"You have no law enforcement training, Marcus. It's not your place. And it's not going to happen."

The fire in his eyes banked low as his shoulders relaxed. "Yeah. Okay."

"Now, to business." Walt looked to Austin. "Recently, Austin got wind of some rumors in the US. Rumors that we're planning to rejoin them. He believed these rumors."

"Self-preservation," Austin said to them, hackles rising in his voice. "If the trade embargos push gas prices to a week's minimum wage —"

"Won't happen. They need our oil, not the other way around."

"Fine. There are food embargos too. And if organizations like schools and social services can't continue operating without federal funds? People aren't going to want to live in a country that can't prosper. Freedom's not worth that much."

"To us, it is," Walt said.

Austin shook his head. "I don't believe that."

"We're not the first country to have a rough start. We'll make it through."

Silence veiled the room.

Walt took off his hat and threw it onto the table. "I'm not rehashing this conversation again, Austin. I looked into it. Nothing I've dug up suggests that we would ever consider rejoining them."

"So far," Austin said.

Walt blew out a breath and opened the folder. Before he could speak again, Austin leaned forward in his chair, reserve evaporating.

"Sir, if it's propaganda, what does the US have to gain when it doesn't happen? Why would they make this up?"

"They can claim we broke our word, point this out as another example of our unreliability. Or it's a red herring for the issue we should be talking about."

Austin sat back, but the mask from minutes before didn't return to his face. A furrow dug between his eyes. "Go on. I apologize."

His points seemed valid. And vital. But Walt was more than just another government official. He had described his level of security clearance as "the promotion in sci-fi movies where you step off the elevator onto a floor you didn't know about, and this is where they keep the aliens." How a Texas Ranger ranked that high, he wouldn't tell them, which probably meant he had worked for other agencies as well. Surely he would know of negotiations to end his country's existence.

He picked up his hat and stuffed it back onto his head. "Point is, we're not sitting by and letting our economy flounder. There've been discussions . . . negotiations. Trying to get food embargos lifted. The US agency that audits and monitors the Constabulary — they've been brought into the talks."

Lee's chest felt weighted. "Why?"

"Well, they're ticked off at us, being the public face of secession. Precedent for unrest, what have you. If they can get us to concede some things . . ."

Walt planted his elbows on the table and steepled his fingers. He glanced at each of them, sighed, and opened the folder.

"Governor Catalano negotiated an end to all grain and produce embargos. In exchange, our law enforcement will not interfere with the capture of any person on the Constabulary's Most Wanted list. We're not obligated to help find these people, but if we come across a Constabulary agent with one of them in custody, we don't have the authority to prevent the arrest. My men have to walk on eggshells with these hunter agents, because if they can prove they're here for someone on the list, well . . ."

The room's temperature hadn't changed, but Lee's fingers chilled, then her arms. She folded them and tried to rub the warmth back in. If Texas would yield in this instance, they'd do it in other instances as well.

"How many people are on it?" Austin said.

"Fifteen."

He slammed his fist on the table. "Can't you offer sanctuary or something?"

"We're forbidden to do that in the case of these fifteen people."

"There's no way this is legal. There's no way they —"

"Show us the list." Marcus's voice was steel.

With a huff that pushed one side of the folder, Walt picked up a sheet of paper. It wasn't only a list of names. With each name was a face, a paragraph of biographical details. Walt turned it, right side up for everyone but him, and pushed it across the table.

Lee didn't even see the other fourteen faces. Her vision funneled to the fourth one down, and time funneled to this moment. The fourth name, the fourth face, crushed the air from the room.

Marcus William Brenner, DOB June 7 . . . The picture was from his driver's license.

At both temples, his hair was brown.

The small cry to her right signaled when Violet's eyes found him on the page.

Austin stood and walked around the table to stare down at the list, as if his recognition could have been wrong. "It's not alphabetical. Is it ranked? I mean, by priority?"

"It is," Walt said.

"Crap."

No, God. Lee shoved away the shouting in her head and looked up from the name to the man.

Marcus hunched in his chair, eyes on the sheet of paper, unblinking. Lee had become accustomed to the changes in his appearance, but a past image brought them to notice again. His face was gaunter than the face in the picture. Silver threaded the hair at his right temple.

"Marcus," Walt said, "I'm going to fight this any way I can, and I think we should —"

"Marcus." Lee set a hand on his arm.

He didn't move. Of course, this blow had knocked the words from him, every last one of them. With one foot, she tugged her chair close to his. Their knees nearly touched.

"We're going to fight this," she said. Marcus didn't acknowledge her, but he was here, safe and well. Lee almost thanked God for that before slamming up against the fact that He shouldn't have allowed Marcus's name on the list to begin with. Perhaps later she could pray about it.

"You won't be taken back to Michigan."

His hand turned over to grip hers.

She gripped in return. "We'll talk this out, all of us. We'll solve it."

He met their eyes around the table. His nod seemed to draw him back from the wordless place. He was with them. She massaged his palm with her thumb, and he closed his fingers around hers.

Lee nudged the list toward Walt. "You started to make a recommendation on what we should do."

Walt cleared his throat and slid the paper back into the folder. "It's time for the church to know. In my opinion, the whole town needs to know."

Marcus stiffened, straightened in his chair.

"I've respected your privacy for six months, Marcus, and I'm not going to change that now. But in turn, you need to listen to what I'm saying. If one of these people unknowingly tips off an agent, what will we do?"

He shook his head.

"At least tell the church."

28

Another head shake.

"Would someone benefit by turning him in?" Austin rounded the table to take his seat. "Is there any sort of bounty?"

"They wanted us to offer one. The governor refused."

Austin looked to Lee. "What do you think?"

She tried to sort the options, but her mind felt like a sieve with holes wider than thoughts. She counted the collection of Marcus's clients against the complete strangers in town. There weren't many strangers in Kearby.

"Friends and acquaintances should know," she said.

Marcus drew in a long breath.

"For their safety as well as yours."

"What?" The glare he flicked toward her wasn't supposed to be encouraging, but it proved he hadn't shut down.

"They can't keep out of this situation if they don't know it exists."

"You think . . ." His jaw tensed with a hard swallow. "I'd be putting the church in danger."

"Keeping it from them? Possibly, yes."

"Jason will use them. If it's Jason."

That wasn't a question. She stayed quiet, as did the others, allowing Marcus to process connections only he knew of. He stared at the tabletop. When he looked up, his face had blanked.

"They have to be safe."

Walt sighed. "I'll put a meeting together, and you can —"

"No. Tell them about the list. Give them Jason's description."

"Marcus."

"That'll keep them safe."

"And you?"

Marcus held his eyes.

After a moment, Walt leaned back in his chair. "I still say you're safer if they know it's you."

Everyone in the room knew Marcus would never agree with that. Violet squirmed in her chair. Conflict between two people she respected must be like sandpaper under her skin.

"What else?" Austin said to Walt.

"I'm hoping and praying this is as far as it goes, but if I'm wrong . . ." He pulled a second manila folder from the accordion and opened it. He separated two forms from the paperwork inside and pushed one toward Lee, one toward Austin.

Immigration forms. Lee's mouth dried.

"There may come a day when undocumented immigrants are considered illegal.

You two need to become legal citizens of Texas, and you need to do it now. This list was agreed to because no one on it is a citizen. A few —" He gave a quick glance at Marcus "— had applied, but in the end that wasn't enough."

Violet's voice tiptoed, the pitch more girlish than usual. A giveaway that she was trying not to cry. "But Marcus applied for citizenship before I did. If his papers come through fast, he'll be safe. Right?"

Yes. Of course he would be. Lee inched her fingers toward the packet in front of her.

"I asked that question, too." Walt gave a long sigh. "In the interest of cooperation and negotiation . . . no."

The room tasted stale, compressed. Marcus reached for the paperwork and set it on her knees.

"You have to." His voice was quiet but hard.

"Absolutely not."

"They won't let you practice nursing with a Michigan license forever."

"Then I won't practice nursing."

A muscle jumped in his jaw. "This." He jerked a hand toward the forms. "Is the safest thing for you."

Lee pressed her spine against the metal chair back. "You cannot possibly expect me to become a citizen of a country that's betraying you."

"That's not what they're doing."

Heat rose in her face, coursed down her arms. She grabbed a form and smacked it onto the table. "You have a more accurate description?"

"Texas is protecting its people," Marcus said.

"And betraying you to do it."

"They don't know me." His voice dropped but didn't soften. "They don't know what I did or didn't do. Betraying is knowing the person. And knowing what you're going to do to him while you shake his hand."

He looked up and met their eyes, each in turn, and Austin nodded, acknowledging something Marcus hadn't said. He scowled but picked up his stack of papers and folded them.

Marcus turned to Lee. "You have to be safe. No matter what happens to me."

She ran her thumb over the pages in front of her. "Austin and I should not be the focus of this conversation."

Walt huffed. "All y'all are the focus of this conversation. Prevention."

"It's past that for Marcus. Focus on him."

Walt gave her his barely patient look that said he'd wanted to address this topic the whole time. "There is one thing in our favor. His name's not on the deed to that house."

Austin's eyebrows shot up. "Really? That'll help, at least."

Marcus had told Lee almost as a confession. *"I don't have credit here, so Walt offered to get the loan. If I turn him down, I might have to live in an RV park for years."* Later, when she could pray, she would thank God for this detail they hadn't known would matter.

She still wanted to curse the governor to his face.

"But his city of residence is on the citizenship application." Walt's voice punctured her ire. "We have to pray the Constabulary doesn't get their hands on that. Right now, they're not aware there *is* an application."

"We can't count on that forever," Austin said.

"I know."

"Is there any chance of reversing the negotiation?" Lee said.

Walt sighed. "I don't think it's impossible. The governor's sure not thrilled about it, and if public opinion somehow fell on our side, maybe he'd listen."

How could they manage that? Some Texans already wanted the borders closed, and all of them faced increasing grocery and gas prices. Trading economic health for the freedom of fifteen people didn't make sense.

"So what, we get somebody to blog about it?" Austin fisted his hands on the table. "Come on, Walt."

"I agree, it's a long shot at this point," Walt said.

"Then what do you suggest?" Lee said.

The five of them — though Violet was mostly quiet — strategized for hours, talked about Marcus's visibility and how to manage it, until fatigue dragged Lee's thoughts away from her. Sometime after midnight, Violet hid a yawn behind her hand. It was like a signal. Walt stood up from the table and announced that if the youngest in the room was tired, then all of them needed to go home and sleep.

When they split up to go to their separate vehicles, Violet followed not Lee but Austin. The pair stopped to talk at his car while Marcus walked Lee to hers. After she slid inside, he stood at her door, one hand braced on the car frame. The floodlight at his back threw shadows across his face.

"Well." His hand shifted on the car but didn't let go.

"How are you?"

He looked away from her, across the blacktop to the passing traffic. The shadows on his face slid to his profile without masking the wrinkle between his eyes. "I'm . . ."

He didn't say *okay.*

"Come over," she said.

"Thanks."

He went to his truck. Both of them sat idling until Violet said good night to Austin and jogged to Lee's car. Austin pulled out while Violet was still buckling in.

"You're quiet." Lee pulled out onto the road, and Marcus's headlights joined them in the rearview mirror.

"Just praying a lot. Since I can't contribute anything else."

"Neither can I."

"You had good ideas tonight. I can't think like that, even after everything." Violet turned her head to watch the truck's headlights. "Lee, is he okay?"

"Likely more shaken than he's letting on."

"I'd be scared. If it was me."

As would Lee, but voicing it was too much to admit. The rest of their drive was quiet. The truck's headlights in her rearview helped to keep her awake. He parked beside her in the apartment lot, ignoring the spots designated for visitors.

"Did you invite him?" Violet whispered as they got out of the car, though he wasn't near enough to overhear.

"I did."

"Oh, good." She jogged ahead of them into the building.

Exhaustion seized Lee halfway across the lobby. Marcus gripped the stairway rail as he followed her up, and through the fog she couldn't determine if he was favoring his knee or simply as depleted as she was. At her door, she shuffled through her keys. The jingle sounded too loud in the corridor.

"Lee."

She turned. He stood close.

"Violet would leave it unlocked for us," he said.

Of course. She tried the knob, and it turned. The living room was dark, but Violet's bedroom light was on.

Perhaps she should warm up soup for him. He seemed to shiver as he stood there, despite the eighty-degree night and Lee's aversion to air-conditioning. "Are you hungry? Thirsty?"

His eyes veiled. He leaned against the door and closed his eyes, then opened them. "I know what you meant."

"I meant both applications of the word."

"Well, the addict application is . . ." He swallowed so hard the cords pulled in his neck. "Is a *yes* right now."

He'd had more than one reason for driving to her house. "Coffee?"

"I can make it. Just go to bed, and I'll . . ."

Grapple alone. No. Their hands brushed as Lee moved to the kitchen, and the nerve endings danced all the way up her arm. Inappropriate timing.

His eyes bored into the back of her neck as she poured two scoops of coffee — hazelnut, his favorite — into the filter, filled the machine with water, and turned it on.

"No matter what I do." His words dropped to the counter and bounced up to her. "There'll be something. Somebody. It might be a year. Or a week. But they'll find me."

"Walt is on our side. Others are too." She sounded like an optimist. Perhaps she'd lost herself somewhere in the night.

"It doesn't matter."

No, it didn't. Nothing did, unless they reversed the decision.

Marcus bowed over the counter, so low his forehead rested on his clenched hands. The coffeepot gurgled, but he didn't look up. Reverence lined his weary posture. He was praying. Perhaps Lee should leave the room, respect the privacy of this act, but something drew her nearer. She stood at his side and watched him. He sighed.

"I know You're here."

She opened her mouth to confirm it, but

a shiver traced her shoulders. He wasn't speaking to her.

"Jesus, if this is what's next, if Your plan is . . ." He covered his face with open hands. "Don't leave me. Stay close. But I know You will."

Lee crept close enough to touch him. She reached out and rested her hand in the cleft between his shoulder blades.

Marcus jolted. She retreated several steps, but when he lifted his head, warmth filled his eyes.

"Lee."

"I thought you knew I was near. I apologize."

"I did know a minute ago. Just . . . things."

He breathed deep through his nose, the way he always did when coffee was brewing, a scent he no longer took for granted. Sometimes Lee wished he would take something for granted again. Anything.

He filled a mug, the white one adorned with the shape of Texas in blue, overlaid with a red star and the words *Welcome to Kearby.* She didn't know where he'd gotten it, but she was pretty sure leaving it behind one day had been a deliberate attempt at making himself a place here. As if he needed to.

They walked together into the living

room. Marcus sank onto the couch, held his mug between his hands and sipped. He hadn't bothered with creamer. He drank coffee black only when he'd been awake more than twenty-four hours or when his craving for whiskey was at its sharpest. All the things he'd lost, only some of which he'd regained — Lee had hoped the thirst would leave him alone forever.

He sipped from his mug, and she sat beside him. Across from them stood the bookcase he'd made for her thirty-first birthday. Five feet tall, four shelves. He'd left the wood natural so she could choose a stain color. Lee chose to keep it as it was, pale and smooth with a faint grain. It was simple work, no carving. All he'd had in him at the time, but she treasured it more because of that effort. She had collected almost thirty books since securing her job at the hospital. Keeping to her book budget was a challenge every month. While Marcus continued to sip his coffee, she crossed to her books and ran her fingers over their spines. Restoring her old library would take years, but she'd do it.

If they had to run again, she was taking her books. She'd haul them on her back if necessary.

After a few minutes, Marcus sighed behind her and set his mug on the table. Lee reclaimed her seat on the couch.

"Perhaps we could pray together?"

Creases formed around his eyes. "Yeah."

Lee tucked her chin, closed her eyes, waited for one of them to say something to God.

"Jesus," Marcus whispered. "Please. I know You're here, but I can't . . . words."

She had to speak. To pray. She tried not to see his wasted body, lying on a mattress in the corner of her clinic.

"Um, Jesus." The voice sounded close in front of them, soft but sure. Violet. A light hand settled onto Lee's shoulder. "We're here together to snuggle up in Your hands. And ask if You will please keep us safe here. I know everything happens in Your will for a reason, but I'm going to ask You, please — don't let anything else bad happen. Please give Texas the courage not to let the Constabulary come after anyone on that list, but because he's my brother, I'm asking You especially to take care of Marcus. Okay, that's all. Thanks for listening to us. Amen."

Marcus eased his grip on Lee's hands, but Violet's didn't move from her shoulder. Lee raised her head. Violet was kneeling next to them, her other hand on Marcus's shoulder. A triangle of prayer.

"Sorry if I barged in." Violet tugged at her pajama top, a shade brighter green than her eyes.

"Not at all," Lee said, and Marcus shook his head.

Violet studied them both, then leaned closer to Marcus and wrapped him in a hug. After a moment, he hugged her back.

"I'm going to bed. Which means, I'm going to give you guys some space. I'll keep praying."

She padded down the hall to her room. Marcus finished his coffee, and then he and Lee sat for a while, still, silent.

At last he got up, snagged his keys from the table, and limped to the door. Weariness always further impaired his gait. He stepped into the hall, then turned back to Lee and looked at her as if memorizing every feature.

She stood. "It's almost two in the morning."

"Yeah."

"You're all right?" To drive. To stay awake, yes, but more than that, to pass twenty-four-hour stores that carried liquor.

He paused a fraction of a second too long. Their eyes met and held.

"I can make it." And then he was pulling the door shut. "Good night."

"Marcus."

He went still.

"I think you should stay."

Caution smoothed his features, barricaded behind his eyes. "No."

"The couch is old but comfortable. Violet won't mind." After all, the three of them and Austin had once shared a single hotel room.

"This is your space, Lee. It wouldn't be right."

"I told you I'm fine with it."

"I'm not."

Because of their new relationship. Because of his promise — never to crowd her, never to push.

She went to the kitchen, which still smelled rich and bitter and of Marcus. She picked up her phone from the counter and dialed as she walked back to him. His buzzed from a pocket somewhere, and he pulled it out, brow furrowed even as his mouth tugged upward. He swiped the screen to answer it but didn't lift it to his ear.

Lee spoke into hers. "I'll get you home."

The nod tucked his chin, and he didn't look up as he stepped out the door and shut it behind him. From the phone and from the other side of the door, his voice was shredded. "Lee."

"I'm here."
"I know."

3

All the women in Lee's church group referred to this as the fireside room, and the
imitation flickers behind imitation logs in
the imitation fireplace did push some hominess into the mood. Then again, these seven
Christian women didn't need help with
hominess. They preferred couches to folding chairs and sat too close together, sometimes almost touching. They laughed and
patted each other's shoulders and offered
endless sympathy, whether their friend
reported an ailing cat or an ailing child. In
the beginning, Lee could hardly make
herself speak to them. Now, she tried to.
They were good women.

Tonight was Juana's turn to write down
prayer requests. Her handwriting looped
over a yellow sheet torn from a legal pad.

"Okay, last but not least." She turned her
smile on Lee. "Do you have anything tonight, Lee?"

Lee searched for the easiest thing. "I would like to ask for prayer that Violet will be guided to a new job. She's still saving for a car, and she wants her own apartment at some point. She needs something more substantial than retail to do that, but she's too young to have other experience."

Juana transcribed. "Is she watching the used-car thread on our email loop?"

"Religiously," Lee said, and a few laughs circled the room.

While Juana prayed for the requests on the paper, Lee silently added the ones she couldn't speak. For Austin, protection as he worked with Walt against the Constabulary. For Sam, safety and wellness as he paid for the crimes of everyone but himself.

For Marcus. Too many things.

Juana concluded by asking for safety for Becca Roddy, that she be found soon. A chill trickled into Lee's hands. The Constabulary might have nothing to do with Becca's vanishing, but experience said otherwise. Her name might have been farther down that list, farther than Lee's eyes had bothered to read.

When Bible study ended, no one left. Lee remained for ten minutes, smiled when she should, listened to their stories about the sale on baby formula, about a second baby's first tooth, about a kindergartner who came home from school with marker ink all over her face because she'd decided to be a rainbow that day.

Then Monique passed around her newest sonogram. Lee held it between her fingers and found the eye, then the nose and mouth and hand up near the face.

"Can you see him?" Monique said.

"Yes." Lee handed the glossy print back and hoped she was smiling.

"He looks so calm in there, you know? You'd never know how he rocks and rolls and keeps me up all night." She laughed and rubbed the curve of her belly.

"Activity is a healthy sign."

Monique blinked. "Well, sure, I know that. I wasn't complaining."

She shouldn't have said anything. "I didn't mean to imply that you were."

After a few more minutes, Lee scooped up her black rain jacket and her purse. She exited their classroom and stepped around a small crowd. A few people stopped her to say hello, ask how she was, how Marcus was, how work was going. She said *well* and *fine* and *it's a very fulfilling job,* which it was, but no one wanted to hear about ER cases, especially the ones that didn't end well. An elderly man whose name she couldn't recall asked if she would be preparing the church dinner tomorrow night and smiled when she said yes.

So many kind people. Accepting people. She wished she was more skilled in small talk.

She'd nearly reached the doors outside when Juana's voice rose above the drone behind her.

"Lee!"

She turned. Juana bustled up to her, tugging Damien by the hand.

"But, Mom, *all* the second graders are —"

"All the second graders didn't hide their homework under their mattress. Lee, I'm so glad I caught you. I wanted to give you a heads-up. Monique asked for your cell phone number. I gave it to her because I didn't think you'd mind, but from what the girls were saying, I'm the only person in our group that has your number. So if I shouldn't have given it out, well, I'm sorry."

The omission wasn't intentional. Lee had thought of offering her number once, months ago, when one of the women had said to another, *"I'll text you."*

"It's fine," she said.

"I have to take Damien home, but a few of the other girls were meeting up at Rosita's for fried ice cream. Monique's probably going to call you in a minute."

Oh. "All right."

"I'll see you Tuesday?"

"Four o'clock."

"My birthday party's on Tuesday," Damien said.

"Yes. That's why I'm coming." Lee smiled at him.

"Miss Lee is baking your cake," Juana said, "and helping me set up and clean up. The two biggest jobs."

Damien managed a polite nod, then tried to tug Juana toward the church doors.

"There's one thing," Juana said, pulling his hand back to her side. "Damien, stop. I'm talking to Miss Lee."

"Yes, ma'am. Sorry." He ducked his head.

Juana continued talking to Lee as if she'd never been interrupted. "Turns out Oscar has to work. Any chance you could stay for the party itself?"

One glance at Damien while he bounced in place next to his mother was enough to warn Lee off. Juana and Oscar's one-level home would teem with boys like a picnic basket left to ants. "Children aren't exactly my forte."

"Nothing to it. Cleaning up messes? Applying Band-Aids?" Juana tapped her index finger against each finger of her other hand.

"Preventing experiments like 'what if we put this action figure in the microwave?' Boys do take a little more corralling than girls, but their noise is a lower pitch even at this age."

Lee leaned back on her heels and considered. For Juana, she could do it. Her experience with children — a few older ones in the ER, not sorted to pediatrics yet, frightened and often in pain — should be enough to weather a birthday party. A memory flitted past, her black market clinic and Piper refusing to cry while Lee stitched the cut on her head.

"I'm available," Lee said.

"Great. Who knows, you might find your hidden calling as kid-whisperer."

"Not likely."

Juana laughed. "Call it practice for the future, then?"

A weight landed on Lee's chest. As she tried to find a response, too many moments passed.

Any other time, Juana would have noticed. Instead she waved, pulled her son through the doors, and disappeared into the parking lot throng. Lee should thank Damien for splitting his mother's focus.

Her phone chirped and lit up. Text from an unknown number. *Hi, Lee, this is Mo-*

*nique. Our group's going to Rosita's and we'd
love to have you join us.*

She ran her thumb over the face of her
phone. She should go. She should try harder
to integrate into their lives. Yet their conversations so often left a ball of ice in her
stomach. Husbands. Children. God. Sometimes even sex. Everything circled around
to one of those four topics.

She texted a decline and slid her phone
into her purse. Not tonight. She wasn't
prepared.

Next time. If she was invited again, she
would go.

She stopped halfway to her car, Mace
dispenser and keys dangling from her hand
with a soft jingle. Walt's car, beige like his
cowboy hat, pulled into a spot close to the
doors. He hopped out and crossed to open
the passenger door for . . . Becca.

Lee jogged up to them as if this situation
were somehow her business. Walt's mouth
tilted when he saw her, however, and the
welcome in Becca's eyes kept Lee's feet
moving.

"Hello," she said. "I'm sorry, I don't mean
to intrude, but it's good to see you."

Becca shut Walt's door and started walking toward the church. Her blue button-
down shirt was wrinkled, and what ap-

50

peared to be tearstains spotted the collar, but she smiled as she walked. "It's good to see you, too."

"You're all right?"

"Walt wanted me to go home and decompress after the Rangers talked to me, but I told him there's no better stress relief than seeing my small-group girls. I bet they won't mind my being late."

The Rangers. Lee glanced at Walt, and he shrugged. *Ask away.* "Then you were missing because . . ."

"An agent from Ohio. Parked his car next to mine and waited for me to leave for work this morning. I went with him at gunpoint. Agent Connelly."

"You knew him?"

"Knew of him, sure."

They reached the doors, and Becca reached for a handle, then went still. Her dark eyes rested on Lee's and held, and something flickered behind them, something less brave, less matter-of-fact, than her voice.

"You're all right?" Lee said.

The flicker grew. "I'd be over the border. Going to prison, at best. If it weren't for the Rangers."

Lee should feel relief, gratitude, even joy at Becca's rescue — and she did — but something else burrowed in, too. Something that made her fingers want to clench.

"I'm glad you're well," she said. "And safe."

"Thank you. I'm glad, too." Becca turned from the doors and threw her arms around Walt. White eyebrows shot up to his thinning hair, but he hugged her back. "Thank you, Walt. And thank the Rangers again for me."

"Sure will." They stepped apart, and Walt propped a hand on his hip. "Agent Connelly's being detained for questioning, but we need to keep a guard on you for the next few days. A Ranger's going to be waiting when you leave church, to shadow you home."

Detained for questioning. Then Becca wasn't on the list. Not if Texas was legally protecting her.

"I appreciate it," Becca said.

She entered the church, and the door had barely swished closed behind her when Walt gave a long sigh.

"Now, Lee."

"If Marcus disappears, will law enforcement even look for him?"

"Of course."

"Can you explain to me how you're allowed to detain one Constabulary agent for questioning but have to stand aside for others? And don't tell me it's politics, Walt. It's inconsistent. It makes no sense."

"Politics is often both those things. You'll get no argument from me."

Breathing was becoming a chore. "She knew the agent."

"Means nothing. The other targets we've recovered had never seen their hunters before."

"So you're calling this a coincidence."

Walt sidestepped as a family of four exited the church, then beckoned Lee to one side. They stood beside a cement planter, knee high to both of them. Lee dropped her gaze to the pansies and snapdragons, the purple and yellow a soothing combination.

She lowered her voice. "Have you questioned him about other hunters?"

"There's one thing consistent with every agent we've captured so far. They know there are others, but they don't know who. They don't even know how many. This guy has never met Mayweather, has never seen his face or heard his name. Trust me, Lee, I'm working every angle of this thing, including Jason Mayweather."

"He won't take Marcus back alive. And if he did . . ."

"Lee."

She cocked an eyebrow. Surely Walt didn't intend to reassure her, to downplay the danger. He knew better. All the frank discussions held around his kitchen table — planning accommodations for Marcus when he was still too weak to live alone, revealing Walt's new role as a task force leader to deal with the Constabulary. Even the easy discussions, the card games — Marcus and Lee, Walt and Millie, other couples from church — Walt had always respected Lee, listened to her.

His hand settled on her shoulder. "Don't go assuming the worst scenario."

"I wasn't."

He cocked his head.

"I'm grateful Marcus confided in you about Jason Mayweather."

He smiled. "Finally."

"He has the right to be cautious." Though it went deeper than that, and Walt knew it.

"That wasn't a criticism, Lee. If he didn't have trust issues right now, there'd be something wrong with him." His steely eyes didn't waver. "And I'm not going to waste that trust, okay? I'm working. There's plenty I can't tell y'all, but things are going on."

"Things you'll tell Austin?"

He gave her a slanted look. "Some of them."

"That wasn't a criticism." She smiled to prove it, and Walt nodded acceptance. "I simply wish to have as much information as possible."

"I wanted the kid to tell y'all back in December. He wouldn't."

Significant, if she could unravel why. "Thank you. For all you're doing."

"You mean my job?"

More than that. Texas had chosen to betray fifteen people — yes, *betray,* whether Marcus accepted that word or not — and Walt had chosen to defend them. She rubbed the petal of a pansy, satin soft, between her thumb and forefinger.

"I'm sorry to act as though you answer to me. I'll try to be more reasonable about this."

Walt chuckled.

"What?"

"In my experience, a woman in love isn't reasonable when her man's treated wrong. And if you try to deny it, I'm going to be disappointed in you." His smile deepened the age lines in his face.

"I . . ." Was she suddenly so transparent?

"Good." His eyes laughed at her but warmly. The way Sam's would have laughed if he'd been here, gotten to see the metamorphosis of the last few months.

Walt bade her good night, his eyes still twinkling, and walked back to his car. He pulled away, into the dusk-veiled street. She should leave too. But the urgency of this situation propelled her back inside the church, past trickles of people walking in the opposite direction.

At the other end of the hallway, Heath might be in his office. Whenever she volunteered in the church kitchen, he was down here studying, his door sometimes open and sometimes not.

The situation wasn't truly hers to share, but Marcus wouldn't object to her sharing. Not with Heath. She headed down the hall.

A rubber stopper propped the door half open . . . half shut.

She should go.

Heath glanced up from scribbling in a hardback journal with gilt-edged pages. "Lee. Come in."

"I'm interrupting."

"Yes, thank you. My eyes are starting to cross." He smiled. "How are you?"

She stepped inside and sat in the chair across from Heath's cherry wood desk, strewn with its usual notebook pages and books and pens and highlighters. The laptop was shut, blinking a white light. Heath loved to study his thick hardcover tomes. Lee once said she expected him to be reading by kerosene lamp in here after dark, and he'd laughed.

Clutter notwithstanding, the man knew how to design a calming space. Most of three walls held cherry bookshelves filled with texts in English, Greek, and Hebrew. On one corner of his desk, a fishbowl held a blue betta with purple-tipped fins. It swam among the roots of the plant that topped its home, and its fins undulated in the light from the desk lamp.

"What brings you to my rescue?" Heath shut the journal with a soft *thump.*

"I won't take much of your time. And I'd never break Marcus's confidence, especially in something like this, but he won't mind my telling you."

Heath stilled. "Something's wrong? His health?"

"No, he's well."

His posture eased.

"But he isn't safe."

He pushed the journal aside to lean forward and fold his arms on the desk.

She looked toward the corner of the office to the books, serene and soothing. She skimmed the titles as she spoke, noted the key words. *Grace. Holiness. Sanctification.*

"There is reason to believe that if a

57

Constabulary agent comes after him, he will not be protected by the Texas government."

Spiritual warfare. Discipleship.

"What do you mean?" Heath's voice gained a rare edge.

"The Constabulary have a list of most-wanted fugitives. I met Walt and Becca Roddy in the church parking lot and —"

"They found her?" Heath came half out of his chair. "Praise God."

"She'd been taken by an agent, Heath. And I'm not certain to what degree, but she knew that agent."

A soft intake of breath. A rustle as Heath settled back into the chair. Lee's eyes snagged on the final title at the end of the row, one word in the title bold and red. *Martyr.*

"You think Agent Mayweather is coming here for Marcus. With the permission of Texas."

She forced her gaze from the books. Heath's hazel eyes bored into her, not alarmed but somber. Somehow his knowledge lightened hers. The knot that had cinched tight in her chest yesterday began to loosen for the first time.

"Walt won't confirm it, but if state Constabularies are deliberately sending agents with knowledge of their targets, personal knowledge . . ."

"Does Marcus know?"

"Not about Becca yet."

"What can I do?"

She and Heath were both powerless. The Constabulary would come, Jason Mayweather would come. Or he wouldn't. There was one thing, however. The real reason she'd interrupted him.

"I wanted to ask . . ." The request tasted metallic and sharp. She couldn't voice it to Heath any more than to the women in her Bible study group. But she had to. "I wanted to ask if you'd be willing to pray."

His sandy eyebrows arched. "Of course I am."

"I'm not referring to a pastor's prayer for his church. I'm asking if you will pray for Marcus."

"I pray for Marcus daily."

His quiet words pierced. Lee breathed around the arrow of them, lodged in her chest. Specific, daily prayer for a single member of his congregation? Maybe this was typical of all pastors, but no. Heath had personally sought out handyman jobs throughout December, when Marcus was ready to begin light work. Perhaps he considered Marcus a friend.

When Heath bowed his head, she didn't

shut her eyes. The man prayed with folded hands, knuckles of his thumbs pressed to his forehead.

"Lord God, thank You for bringing our Michigan family to join us here, and thank You for the friendship You've gifted me in Lee and Marcus."

Her too? The arrow twisted.

"I ask that You grant continued healing in Marcus's body and in his mind. I ask that You grant him protection. If there's an agent here for Marcus, whoever he is, I ask that You thwart those efforts. You brought Marcus out of captivity and mistreatment, and You restored him from illness. I trust You will keep him in the palm of Your hand. Amen."

Closing her eyes now would be a lie. Heath lifted his head and smiled.

"You pray for him too, I hope," he said.

"I do."

"Good."

But not the way Heath could pray. Not with that simple assurance, and Marcus needed confident prayer. Experienced prayer. She stood, backed toward the door. He had work to finish.

"Are you sure there's not something else?" Heath said.

Her eyes roamed the room. Somehow,

whenever she met his, he saw straight into her. Heath watched her as she stepped closer to his desk and brushed her palm over the blades of green that grew at the mouth of the betta's bowl. She should go, but . . .

"Will God protect him?" The words came out nearly voiceless.

"I believe He will," Heath said.

"But you can't know."

"Lee, have you brought this to Him? Your fear?"

"It isn't fear." Her fingers curled into the fishbowl plant.

"You're not afraid for Marcus?"

Until yesterday, not really, not anymore. The ingraining new normalcy of Texas life had lulled her fears to dozing. Marcus's strength returned, slow but steady, and Lee's fear ebbed at the same rate. Until yesterday.

She faced Heath. "He can't be taken again. God can't allow it."

"You know God hasn't promised that."

Somehow, illogically, she'd hoped otherwise. She linked her fingers behind her back and stepped toward the door.

"Take this to God, all of it. The petitions for safety, the fear, the anger. Don't stop talking to Him about it."

"Is it comforting to you?" Her fingers wove tighter as she met his eyes over her shoulder. "Knowing He heard a request, even when He ignores it?"

"We're never ignored, Lee."

But God could deny any request He chose to. "I appreciate your time, Heath."

"I appreciate yours."

4

To Marcus, the most calming thing in Peter Gentry's office was the desk. The workmanship looked solid. Sturdy, simple, made of dark walnut. So polished, specks of dust must know better than to land on it. It held a laptop and several stacks of books but no paper. Pete didn't do clutter.

The other side of the office was more relaxed. Two stuffed chairs faced each other, and on the wall behind one hung a painting of a bridge, its sepia color scheme blending with the warm caramel walls. Marcus had asked Pete if it was by a famous painter, and he told him she was a local artist who'd be thrilled to know somebody had asked that question.

Against the far wall sat a tan microfiber couch with cushions more like pillows. The first time he'd come here, Marcus had wondered if Pete would try to make him lie on the couch and close his eyes. Instead

Pete let him sit or stand or pace, whatever was easiest for him. Three months of appointments, Thursday afternoons, three-thirty — he hadn't missed one yet.

Usually, these days, Marcus could relax enough to sit in one of the chairs while Pete sat in the other. But an itch crawled under his skin, up his spine and down his arms. No. He couldn't sit.

He paced.

Pete sat across from him wearing jeans, dress shirt, and tie. He offered his trademark half-smile, a literal one due to the mini-stroke that still affected the left side of Pete's mouth. Strange, Pete knowing so much of Marcus when he'd only last week found out about Pete's stroke.

"Good to see you," Pete said.

"You, too."

"So today's a pacing day."

He stilled. He cleared his throat. The words remained stuck.

Pete waited. Sometimes the way he read Marcus still made him fidget, even as he thanked God for Pete's help. He would wait until Marcus found the words, and knowing that made them easier to grasp.

"I . . . I'm." *I'm not going to be your client much longer.*

Pete leaned his elbows on his knees. "You

don't have an end to that sentence?"

"I . . ." He was being ridiculous. "If we could just talk first."

"Of course. Q and A?"

Easier than trying to make his own sentences from scratch. He nodded.

"Let's start with the basics. Sleep quality?"

"Um . . . awake most of last night. But the rest of the week was pretty good."

"Triggers? Anything new, or any you want to talk about?"

Marcus paced the stretch of carpet in front of the desk, then pressed his fist against it. The wood was sturdy, reassuring as it held up his weight. But his jaw stayed welded shut.

"Words seem to be hard today." Kindness steeped Pete's voice.

He nodded.

"If you can talk about what happened, we can work toward a solution."

"It's not that kind of thing."

"What kind of thing is it?"

He opened his hand and braced it on the desk. The breath shuddered out of him.

"Do we need to break for a minute?"

They hadn't even started yet. Marcus straightened and paced another few steps. Not helping. Try something else. He crossed to the empty chair and dropped into it.

"Okay," he said. "Walt talked to me Tuesday. Me and Lee. Austin and Violet were there, too."

Pete's expression didn't flicker as he waited.

"I can't become a citizen. Of Texas." As if Pete didn't know where he meant. His voice turned to sandpaper. "There's a most-wanted list. The US says Texas can't interfere. When they send agents in."

Pete gave a slow blink. "Constabulary agents?"

"Yeah."

"You're on the list."

"Yeah."

"And my country agreed to this?"

He planted his fists on the arms of the chair. "You know what I did."

"You protected people who would have gone to prison for their faith. If Texas knew your history, you'd be a public hero."

He didn't want to be a public hero. He just wanted a home.

No. He couldn't even want that now. He wanted to keep living in the sunlight. That was all. He ducked his head as his chest tightened, as his throat closed up and his eyes burned. He tucked his chin but couldn't get small enough. His shoulders

66

hunched forward, and his hands drew up to his chest. His heart started pounding.

"Marcus."

The tide was washing him away from himself. Smaller. Smaller target.

Something cold and pliable was pressed into his hand. "Come on, Marcus. Stay with me."

The hand putty. A boundary for his body. Stay here, with his body. Don't have to be smaller. He curled his fingers. One squeeze for *yes.*

"Good. Tell me where we are."

"Your office."

"Tell me one thing you can see."

He opened his eyes. "My hand."

"What color is the putty in your hand?"

"Green." Neon. Would probably glow in the dark. Pete had blue and orange, too.

"Good. Now find something else."

He lifted his head, straightened his shoulders. Breathed. "Your desk. Your books. The flowers in the painting."

"Good, good, and good. Flex your hands for me."

He obeyed.

"Tingling at all?"

"Not now."

He turned his head. Pete had pulled his own chair around so they were seated side by side, at eye level. He'd learned how to approach when Marcus came out of . . . whatever these things were. Not really a flashback, unless he came to with Pete standing over him and his brain decided the man was about to kick him in the ribs.

A few minutes went by. Quiet seeped into Marcus's skin and soothed him from the inside out. He set the putty on his good knee and squished his thumb into it, rolled it under his palm. Finally he looked back at Pete. *Okay.*

"Okay," Pete said. "Let's see if we can talk about what happened here."

Obvious. Marcus was a shameful mess. All God had given him, and this was how he thanked Him — by letting himself be swamped with every feeling *but* thankfulness. His heart still beat so hard he couldn't draw a deep breath.

"I'm not better," he whispered.

Pete's mouth pulled on one side, his version of a frown. "Because of what just happened?"

"Look at me. This. Still happening. For no reason."

"Are you sure? You've provided a very good reason why you might be overwhelmed right now."

"It shouldn't still happen."

"We've talked about emotional injuries. How they work, what to expect. And we've talked about a recommended timeline for you, for working on things."

"It's been three months."

"How long did I recommend you come see me before we reevaluate?"

Six. "I'm not saying I shouldn't have to come anymore."

"Okay."

"But it should be working."

"Three months ago, you would've taken ten minutes or more to come back. This episode lasted less than two."

Not the point. Well. Maybe part of the point.

"It might help to look at this another way."

Sometimes that did help. Like his first appointment, when he'd staggered in after two months of almost no sleep. Pete had suggested a night light, and Marcus had almost walked out of his office — until he explained the purpose was to make Marcus's bedroom at Walt's the opposite of the room where Jason had held him. The night light wasn't comfort for childish weakness. It was something to remind his brain where he was.

"In the last six months, you've recovered a lot. Weight training, nutrition, physical therapy. You can work at a job that's physically demanding."

Still couldn't run. But he nodded.

"But a few weeks ago, after all day up and down that ladder . . ." The level gaze invited Marcus to the conclusion.

Words — Pete stressed them too much. They both knew he got it. He didn't need to voice it. He cleared his throat. "Had to ice my knee. And couldn't work for a day."

"Emotional injuries sometimes do the same thing. We aggravate them, and they flare up. And it's safe to say the news you got yesterday had an emotional effect on you."

It shouldn't have. No place for the shock, the loss. The sense that Texas had rejected him personally.

"I thought about leaving last night."

Pete went quiet. Waiting. Watching him.

The words finally came. "About driving to Mexico. Or flying . . . somewhere. Overseas. England or somewhere. Or Canada. At least they wouldn't know me there."

He couldn't imagine any of those places becoming home the way Texas had. But *home* was an impossible word now anyway.

"Lee would come. I wouldn't have asked Violet or Austin. She belongs here, and he'd stay with her. But that's when I — thinking about Violet, and . . . I couldn't do it."

"Why not?"

For once, Pete asked a question Marcus already knew how to answer. "The church. They fed me. Housed me. Helped me find doctors, my house, the truck. I can't — I don't want to leave them."

Pete's frown pulled harder at one side of his mouth. "You shouldn't have to."

"Walt wants me to tell them everything."

"But you don't agree?"

"No."

"You don't want to leave them, but you don't trust them?"

Trust had nothing to do with it. It was simple fact, probability. Seven people in his church in Michigan. One traitor. Almost four hundred people in Grace Bible Church. That could mean at least fifty traitors.

"Marcus." Pete's voice quieted the way it did right before he sucker-punched you with truth. He leaned forward in his chair. "Every Christian you meet is not Clay Hansen."

"I know."

"You do know. And you don't. Like we've talked about before."

He held Pete's eyes. Maybe the man could see his jaw was welded shut. Maybe he'd give in, move on.

Pete didn't lean back, so he wasn't done

71

with him. "These people who you call your family. They *are* your family. The Bible confirms that for us."

Marcus forced himself to nod. Everything inside was tightening, hardening, trying to keep Pete's words out.

"You made some relevant points, you know. They took you in this past winter, and they'd want you to stay. And they'll be safer if they understand what you're dealing with."

"Walt's going to tell them everything. Except who I am."

"Then how can they help you?"

What Walt said. But forget the statistics, the fifty possible traitors. "One person, Pete. One."

"It's a risk."

"But you think I should tell them."

"I do."

He pushed to his feet. The pacing calmed his pulse. He tried to find a response, but what could he say? He pivoted to pace the other direction, and his knee wobbled. The tightness in his chest burst open, and he hit the desk with his open palm, welcoming the sting if it would keep the flood back. His hand clenched and he turned away. No punching allowed. Past that now.

Everything God had given him, saved him

from. The light he lived in now, the freedom, the blessings. Even if it all ended, Marcus had no right to feel like this. He pawed at his face. Dry cheeks, still. Good. He cleared his throat, and a choking sound escaped.

"Marcus." The kindness in Pete's voice was like a hand on his shoulder.

He stopped in the corner of Pete's office. He stared at the painting of the bridge, of the flowers blooming at the edge of the water. They looked real enough to touch. His throat closed around a hard lump as the flood inside faded.

"Of course, trust isn't as easy as one decision. And at the same time, it is. One choice at a time."

Except if he was wrong about this choice, he'd never get to make another one. No, stop. Focus on the right things. He backed away from the shelves until his calf bumped Pete's desk. He had to give God glory. He swallowed hard and listed the ways. Thankfulness. Obedience. Faith.

"I'm sorry," he said.

"No apologies in this room." One of Pete's mottos. He couldn't know Marcus hadn't been talking to him.

Marcus breathed deep, shut his eyes, opened them. *Get a grip. Be okay.* Yeah. Okay.

"What just happened?"

Heck, he hated that question. "Nothing."

"Where were you, in your head, a few seconds ago?"

"Listing. How to give God glory."

"And before that?"

"I . . ." His face warmed. "Finding the right things. To feel."

"Meaning . . . ?"

"Thankfulness. Sometimes other things — try to — but I don't let them."

"What other things?"

Things he didn't have words for. He shrugged one shoulder.

"Name me one thing you don't allow."

He buried a growl. "Things that aren't thankful."

Pete tilted his head, then sat forward in his chair. "I think you're saying that for the last . . . however many months . . . you've tried to control your emotional responses based on *should* and *should not.*"

He nodded. Why was Pete looking at him that way? No, they'd never talked about this, but he figured Pete would know. Marcus couldn't be the only client who ever . . . Or maybe Christians who'd belonged to Jesus longer, read and understood the Bible better . . . His face heated again.

Pete took a deep breath and seemed to be

formulating his next words. He did that sometimes, though not as often as Marcus did. But seconds ticked by, and he stayed silent.

"What?" Marcus said. "Do Christians not have to do that?"

"No, Christians do not have to suppress their feelings. No, Marcus."

But Pete didn't mean what he'd meant. The inflection was different. By *don't have to,* Pete meant *aren't required to.* That couldn't be right.

"Okay, this is important. None of your feelings are wrong."

If he only knew. "They get mixed up. All the time."

Pete motioned to the empty chair, question as well as invitation in the lifted corner of his mouth. Marcus took stock. Breathing easy, heartbeat normal, and the drive to pace had faded. He sat.

"Give me an example of when your feelings were mixed up."

He shifted in his seat. Most of them still lingered inside him. If he talked about them . . . but Pete said he wasn't supposed to bury them. Not even for God? In thankfulness?

"Let's start with one," Pete said.

One, okay. Something safe, something he

could detach from. "There was a movie on Walt's TV, and nobody in the room. I recognized it. Charlie Chaplin. I used to have a few of his movies, before."

"And you watched it?"

"I . . . I knew it was funny. I knew I was supposed to be laughing. Like I would have before. But it didn't feel funny."

"How did it feel?"

"Like nothing. Flat. Wrong."

"Okay. One more example."

Deep breath. "With Lee and Austin and Violet on Tuesday. Getting to show Austin and Violet the house. And Lee showing it to them. Like it was hers, too." This was going to sound stupid. "I was glad, but . . . but only for a second and then . . . then it was . . ."

Pete settled both hands on the arms of his chair. Showing he'd wait as long as Marcus needed.

He cleared his throat. "The gladness changed. That's all."

"Changed to what?"

"Something. I don't know. Heavy. Maybe, um . . . sad?"

"When you felt the new feeling, did you stay with it?"

"It was mixed up."

"So you told yourself to stop feeling the

76

sadness."

"Yeah." Of course.

"Okay." Pete flattened his hands on the chair arms. "You need to understand, first of all, that what you're describing to me isn't wrong. It doesn't mean you aren't recovering, and I promise you — I promise, Marcus — it isn't offensive to God."

He sounded so sure. "Is that in the Bible?"

"Homework, part one. Read some of David's psalms. You know David?"

His mouth tugged down as he tried to remember. David . . . "I think he was a king."

"He was. He's also the David who killed Goliath. You know that David?"

Marcus shook his head.

"Well, even before he was a king, he fought for God's honor. He was a warrior king later in his life. But here's the thing — he was also a songwriter, and Psalms is written largely by him, songs and prayers. Have you read any of them?"

"A few. I . . . some friends — Jim and Karlyn — they'd use the psalms to pray." Maybe they still did. From memory. Without each other.

Pete was studying him. "Were they part of your church, your lost church?"

He nodded and pushed away the pinching . . . sadness, yeah, that's what it was. Good to have a word for it, maybe.

"I'm sorry," Pete said. When Marcus didn't answer, he shifted forward in his chair. "Go and read the prayers David brought to God. The feelings he brought to God. Okay?"

"Okay."

"You know, a lot of my clients work to get to a place where their feelings don't determine their choices. Where their feelings no longer drown out their identity in Christ. And here you are, having to work toward the opposite."

He wasn't sure he followed that, but tiredness was starting to weigh on him. "It doesn't mean I'm not getting better. The — the feelings."

"That's right."

"So what does it mean?"

Pete measured him a long moment. "We've talked about trauma. We've agreed that you were traumatized."

The word made him feel like shrinking into the crevice between the chair cushions. Another word for broken, for the glitch in his brain, for the overreaction to triggers. So many words for the same stupid thing. He nodded.

"And it takes time to sort through trauma.

It shows up in the things we've been working on — difficulty sleeping, nightmares, flashbacks, edginess. Agreed?"

Another nod. He might've denied some of that before he came here, but these days, he'd learned to own all of it.

"Okay. Another way it can show up is in unpredictable feelings. Trauma is a kind of loss. And what do people have to do when they experience loss?"

"Move on."

"And before that?"

There was something else? He shrugged.

"They have to acknowledge the loss. Whether it's big or small, part of moving forward is saying to yourself, yes, this thing or person or ability that I valued — it's gone."

Ability. The word pierced straight through his center. He could feel in his chest exactly what Pete meant. Lost. Gone. Weak. He heaved in a breath.

"Make sense?"

"Yeah."

"None of this means you aren't thankful for the gifts God is giving you now. Only that you're processing loss. So you can move forward."

His knuckles massaged his chest. He lowered his hand to his side. "I, um . . . I don't know how to do that."

The tugging half-smile. "I'm starting to put that together."

Well, Marcus had made it pretty obvious.

"Now, homework part two. The next time you're hit with sadness or loss, try sitting with it for a minute. You can end with thankfulness, but try to pass *through* the sadness to get there. Like it's a river, and on the other side, there's thankfulness. How does that sound?"

You could drown in a river. He shook his head.

"See how you do with it once. And we'll talk about how it goes."

They ended the session the same way they always did. Talked through the gospel. Marcus took Pete's Bible from the desk and found that verse in Galatians, reminded himself it wasn't he who lived this life, but Jesus Who lived through Marcus. He knew that. He could do that part.

But he couldn't go into a river he might not come out of.

5

Children in toy stores had nothing on Marcus Brenner in a home-improvement store — today, at least. Lee paid almost no attention to the contents of the cart. She watched his face. So far, he hadn't seemed to notice.

This wasn't a trip to stock up on work materials. Everything in his shopping cart would be used to restore his own place. He'd walked up and down the kitchen flooring aisle for all of two minutes, studying the options, before choosing a laminate that resembled pine flooring. He spent less time picking out a faucet to replace the tarnished one in the bathroom. Yet the quick, matter-of-fact decisions didn't mask his pleasure in making them. His eyes had crinkled as he pulled the boxes of flooring from a shelf.

Maybe this was what people meant by practical faith. Marcus buying flooring for a house he might never live in if the Constabulary came to Kearby.

If he could choose to embrace real hope, real trust that God held their future, she had to do the same. She reached for lightness, and perhaps God helped her find it. Hard to explain her ability to browse for paint colors otherwise.

Lee held up two swatches in dark green. Respectable green. He had no right to frown at this color.

"Brown," he said.

"Marcus, the house is yellow."

He might have winced. "Barely."

"A brown door will not compliment that color."

He ambled to the display to pull out a dark chocolate swatch. "This."

"Why don't you want a green door?"

"Because."

Her mouth twitched. She ducked her head to hide it and pretended to ponder the two shades of green. "This one, Old Pine. It's an appropriate color for the outside of a house, an elegant color."

"Well, I'm not elegant."

"Are you going to repaint everything inside ivory, then?"

"What? No. Inside's different. Here. Espresso Bean. Elegant enough?"

Forget dissembling. Lee lifted her head and let the smile show, and she should have done that in the first place. Marcus chuckled. Something quivered in her stomach, possibly what was meant by the term *butterflies.*

You're becoming a schoolgirl. Stop it.

The crinkles deepened around his eyes. "My door. Espresso Bean. Put back that green stuff."

She did so. "How many rooms did you budget for?"

"Two. Rest'll have to wait. We've got a lot of wall scrubbing to do."

"Not a problem."

"What should we paint first?" he said. "You mentioned the kitchen before."

That launched them into a new debate, after which Marcus picked a cool beige called Rye Harvest. He was right that the pine tiles were a few shades lighter, and the two colors together would enlarge the room and blend well. But neither color was . . . a color.

He let her choose for the den. Stood back from the display and gave a sweeping motion, *whatever you want.* Lee paused as if in contemplation, then tugged from the display a swatch of dark strawberry. She held it up.

He knew she'd never paint a room pink, but this color wasn't exactly pink. His brow furrowed. "Lee."

"Are you going back on your word?"

"What's that even called?"

She checked, and the smile broke out. "Strawberry Sprinkles."

"Sprinkles? Come on." Marcus grabbed the swatch from her and grinned at the name. "Well, that's out, then."

"I was actually thinking red."

"Red? For a room?"

"Not all four walls. Do three in something neutral, like your Rye Harvest but warmer, and one wall in . . . this." She found a weathered shade that would remind Marcus of an old barn. He'd say yes.

He did.

By the time they left the store, both of them were ready for an early dinner. Marcus drove them to Lee's favorite restaurant in Decatur, Taste of India.

The restaurant stood across the street from Decatur's movie theater. A film was playing that Marcus said they'd both enjoy, and she had agreed to see it after checking out the trailers. It looked intriguing, as long as the "explosive climax" didn't get in the way of the character development.

She sidestepped a pothole in the parking lot, and in her peripheral vision, Marcus did the same. At the door, he stopped and looked far into the west.

"It's going to rain. A lot. See?"

The clouds were closer, darker than they had been this morning when she and Marcus had left Kearby. Good thing his new supplies were under the truck's cap. No gauzy veil trailed from the clouds' bottom edge, so wherever they were, they hadn't unleashed their rain yet.

Over dinner, the easiness of the day gave way to serious discussion. Lee told him about Becca's knowing the agent that had captured her, about Walt's response. Marcus said it didn't matter if Jason was here or not. He didn't lie to her, so he was lying to himself. They didn't revisit the topic of revealing his identity to the church, but she hoped he'd choose to trust the people who had more than proved themselves in the last few months. No room in him for that conversation as long as he sat here clenching his jaw, gripping his knife and fork too hard. Behind the glare, the distance in his eyes betrayed fear as well as anger. If she could only break through that. Help him break through it.

Lord Christ, please help me help him. And please help me be ready to be with him.

Something warmed the icy knot in her chest and let her breathe easier. *Be with me. Please don't forsake me.* God would never forsake Marcus, but she had so much yet to learn, do, become. Violet and Marcus and Juana — all of them would deny it, yet some days Lee felt it anyway, a cold fist in her stomach that she knew was the tenuousness of her relationship with God. But sitting in Taste of India with Marcus, watching his focused consumption of the buttered lamb and rice — times like this, Lee could trust more.

He had changed in ways that mattered less than the ways he'd stayed the same.

He glanced up, and the knife and fork stalled in his hands. She shook her head, and he resumed eating, accustomed to her scrutiny.

They walked outside after dinner and halted under the restaurant's awning. Rain cascaded from the sky. The clouds had arrived more quickly than Lee expected. Overhead, they churned the colors of bruises, some nearly black. Kearby lay directly east, where the horizon hadn't yet darkened.

"Here." Marcus handed her the keys.

"What are you doing?"

"No reason for you to get more wet."

She accepted the keys. "Ready?"

"Just run."

She plowed through the downpour without looking back, skipping around puddles. She unlocked the truck, too old for remote entry, and hopped inside and hit the door's unlock button. Rain streamed down the windshield. Marcus was a watery blur of white face, red T-shirt, dark jeans as he approached, his pace barely a jog. He wrenched open the driver's door and lurched inside. Water poured from his hair down his neck and face. The shoulders of his shirt were soaked through, and rain spattered his thighs.

Lee pulled the emergency blanket from behind the seat, and he took it and mopped his face and hair.

"No wind," he said. "Did you notice?"

"I was simply running."

"Could keep pouring for a while without moving on."

Inside the theater, they split up after buying tickets so Marcus could get his popcorn and Lee could use the restroom. She passed the concessions counter on her way to their theater. A group of people clustered to one side of the counter. They didn't seem to be together, and as they talked, they gestured to the main doors outside.

"I guess I'll be seeing a movie. Y'all have any recommendations?"

A few people laughed, and then one of

the women spoke. "I saw two cars off the road. More folks are going to be stopping here, I bet."

"It'll let up soon."

"Doesn't look like it."

Lee glanced to the doors. The rain did look to be pouring harder than it had been ten minutes ago. She walked away from concessions, down the corridor to Theater Five, and entered the darkness. The previews had started.

She didn't have to look for Marcus. He would only sit in the top row, the wall at his back. He leaned toward her as she sat down, and his breath smelled faintly of Coke and buttered popcorn.

"Everything okay?"

"People are talking about hazardous road conditions, due to the rain."

"Well, we have the perfect place to wait it out."

"True."

The movie wasn't excellent or awful. Marcus seemed to enjoy it more than she did, especially the extended car chase scene at the end. As the credits rolled, Marcus stood.

"Ready?"

Lee glanced around. About half the theater was getting up to leave. "It's customary to stay through the credits."

"Maybe." He shrugged. "Do you want to read them?"

"No."

"Well, then."

They emerged into the light side by side, their hands inches apart. It was also customary to hold the hand of one's date. Her fingers curled. She wished Marcus would reach for her hand, so she didn't have to reach for his. But he wouldn't.

"Do you think the rain's stopped?"

"Let's find out," he said.

At the doors, they watched rain stream down the glass, watched people walk inside with umbrellas and dash outside without them. Marcus waited a few minutes to ask an arriving man if the roads were drivable.

"Be smart, take it slow."

Marcus thanked him and turned to Lee. "Ready?"

She hoped so.

6

As long as Marcus kept the windshield wipers on high, visibility wasn't bad. Rain beat on the truck roof with less force than he'd expected. The car in front of him refused to drive faster than thirty-five, but he'd follow its example. After all, a Texan would have no idea how to drive in a Michigan winter. Maybe Marcus was underestimating the storm.

"They're slowing down ahead," Lee said.

"Yeah." Marcus braked.

Halfway across an overpass, the car in front of him stopped. Marcus's pulse shot up. He was too far across the bridge to back off it. Visibility wasn't good enough to pass, and the other driver knew that.

The car's emergency flashers began to blink. Marcus put the truck in reverse and got ready. If the car backed into him, if . . .

"Marcus."

The car didn't move.

"What are you doing?" Lee was staring at his hand on the gearshift.

"It's a trap." His voice grated.

"It's more likely a warning not to drive farther or that his car is stalled."

If Jason was driving that car, if any Constabulary agent was driving that car —

"Marcus. You need to relax."

Trust her. Her judgment wasn't jacked by adrenaline. He breathed in, out. "Okay."

An arm thrust out of the driver's window ahead of him. *Gun* — no. A hand. Beckoning.

"Stay here," Marcus said and got out of the truck. *God, whatever's happening, please protect Lee.*

He listened for her to open her door and follow him, but she didn't. He'd thank her later. His heart pounded as he approached the car. Water filled his shoes.

He stayed behind the driver's door and called out above the rain and a faint rushing noise. "Are you okay?"

"Look, look below us, those people . . ." The man gestured again with a wrinkled, trembling hand. "Do you see them?"

Marcus looked past the guardrail. The highway was . . . a river. Flowing northward, carrying branches and roots and saplings. A white minivan was stopped only feet from the underpass, windows rolled down. A thirty-something woman stood on top of it, waving one arm while her other clamped around the shoulders of a girl. The water reached almost high enough to flood the van. Downstream a few feet, closer to the highway shoulder, a man climbed out the window of a red pickup truck.

The vehicles had to be lodged on something below the water line or they would be swept away. Marcus dashed back to his truck and threw open the door.

"Flash flood. There's feet of water on the highway. People stranded."

Lee jumped out and ran to the edge of the bridge. The woman must have seen her, because shouts joined the rain, which had begun to fall harder.

The water was about chest level. The current looked manageable, but Marcus couldn't know that. *Be smart. Drowning won't help them.* He dug behind the truck's seat and found the rope he used to secure furniture deliveries. Sometimes he doubled it, sometimes tied multiple pieces of furniture together. It had to be twenty feet long.

"Lee." He waved her back. She slid into the truck, shut her door, and saw the rope. "Ready?"

"Ready."

Marcus prayed no one was coming from the other direction and gunned the truck into a U-turn. He left the road, skidding the truck over the grass that sloped down to the highway.

"Marcus, if it keeps rising —"

"I know. We've got to hurry."

Three people, two vehicles. *God, give me time to get them all.*

He parked the truck against a thick tree, wedging the front bumper as best he could. He got out and looped the rope around the tree trunk. At least it had roots. His truck would be taken before the tree. Maybe. The girl had started screaming when she saw him, and her mother didn't hush her.

"Help, help, help us!"

Lee appeared at his side. She swiped an arm across her forehead, but the rain kept pouring down her face, plastering her hair to her head and her shirt to her body.

"Please," she said.

"I'll be careful." She knew he would, but she seemed to breathe easier when he said it.

The rope was old, heavy, made of gritty hemp. It wouldn't float, and he had no way of directing it to the van, anyway. He had to get to the people and bring them back himself. He tied the rope around his waist, knotted the end, and tugged as hard as he could. It held.

"Wait," Lee said. "Lean back with all your body weight."

They didn't have time for this, but he did it. Then he walked into the water.

His first step onto pavement brought the water level to his knees. A few more steps and it sloshed against his hips. The current seemed to tug harder at his bad knee. He was closer to the truck than the van, and he angled toward it, but the man waved him off.

"Get the kid first."

Marcus slogged toward the van.

"Help, help, help." The girl shouted non-stop. Her mother tried to calm her now, but tears of panic strained both their voices.

Almost there. Still slack in the rope. Another foot or two. Water to his stomach, to his chest, so cold, and the current pushed and pulled, but he could withstand it. He grabbed hold of the van's window frame to steady himself. Water sloshed inside. Had it risen since he'd set out minutes ago?

The woman sobbed thank-yous down at him. She pushed the girl into his arms.

"You're taller, you can keep her head above —"

"No, take my mom, I can swim." The girl

shoved away from Marcus, and he tightened his grip on the window frame to keep his balance.

"Kayla. Let the man —"

"You're both coming." He lifted the girl over his head and set her on his shoulders. Her feet dangled to his waist, and his equilibrium wavered for a moment, but this way was the fastest.

The woman hadn't moved.

"Come on," he said. "You'll walk in front of me, holding the rope."

"I'll fall."

"I won't let you fall. Come on."

She wouldn't climb down until he raised his arms to help her. She was shaking hard, and she stared at him, eyes too wide. She let him take part of her weight and eased into the water. As she reached underwater for the rope, she tugged him halfway around, and his knee threatened to give out at the unexpected change of direction.

If he went down, they could die. He locked his knees the best he could and guided the woman in front of him. The water rose nearly to her neck, and she gave a garbled cry. She was going to latch onto him and kill all three of them.

"Hey," he said. "You don't have to swim. Hold the rope and walk."

"Walk." Her voice flattened. "Walk walk walk."

"Right. Count steps if you want."

She did. All the way back to the shoulder of the road, though by then the water was barely above her knees. Marcus crouched, and Kayla slid off his back, and willpower straightened both knees again. Lee stood ready at the edge of the water. She shepherded Kayla and her mother up the slope with a look back at Marcus, a question.

He nodded and stepped off the highway shoulder. The water reached his chest sooner now. Definitely rising. It almost hit his shoulders by the time he neared the truck.

The guy was young, barely twenty, cursing himself. "Went around the barricade. My own fault."

He slid off the roof of the truck into the water, gripped the side mirror until he could catch hold of the rope, then slipped into the water with a scissors kick and used the rope to pull himself through the water ahead of Marcus. They began the trudge back.

"Thanks."

"Sure."

"I'm Rob Stokes."

"Marcus. You said there's a barricade?"

"Not a mile up the highway. Shouldn't be

any more cars stuck here unless they get swept down from higher roads."

This trek was longest. The water was still deepening, rushing faster, and once a tree limb caught on the rope and nearly took their feet from under them. Rob held on while Marcus freed the branch.

Then the water was down to their waists, their knees, their ankles, squishing in their shoes as they struggled up the hill to Marcus's truck. Kayla and her mother sat in the cab, huddled together, wrapped in the fleece blanket he'd used to dry his face only hours ago. Lee stood at the front bumper, hands clenched together in front of her mouth. She didn't look as wet as he felt.

The rain had stopped.

"Hello," Lee said to Rob. "You're all right?"

"Right as rain." He grinned, but it faded as he shook Marcus's hand. "Y'all saved my life."

"Water's still rising," Marcus said. "Get in the truck."

Rob hopped over the tailgate into the bed, and Lee followed him. Marcus unknotted the rope from the tree, looped it over his shoulder a few times, and climbed into the cab. The knot at his waist could wait.

Kayla's mother sniffed back tears, but she

97

seemed calmer. "Thank you."

"Sure." He started the truck and gunned it in reverse, and it skidded along the grass and mud.

"Oh, no," Kayla said.

"Hush, honey."

God, I know You're holding us. I know we're going to make it. He floored the truck again. Once more. It rocketed up the slope, leaving deep ruts at the base of the tree. Only when the tires hit pavement did Marcus put the car in drive and head back to the bridge.

They had an audience.

Several cars were idling, including the old man's who'd stopped in front of them. On both sides of the road . . . traffic. Gawkers.

As he stopped the truck, Rob and Lee climbed out of the bed, and Kayla and her mother got out, too. Lee walked over to the old man, who stood at the bridge guardrail, and spoke to him. Marcus sat in his truck and gazed upward. He needed a minute. Sunshine poked through the fleece of gray that was stretching out, forming holes of blue. *Thank You.*

Lee got into the truck. "Let's go."

"They're car-less. We can't leave them here."

"Several people called fire and rescue."

"Maybe we should stay till they —"

"There will be police."

Six months in this country. Six months of freedom and trustworthy cops. Six months that meant nothing if they'd report fifteen people to the Constabulary.

"Didn't think of that." His voice shook.

"To barricade the area, for safety. Nothing criminal. But they may want to talk to you. You saved three lives."

He shook his head. God saved them. "I was here. That's all."

"It's all right for us to leave."

Halfway to the other side of the bridge, his side mirror caught the lights before his rearview did. Blue and red. Not green.

"Keep going," Lee said quietly.

Another squad car pulled onto the bridge, coming at them from the opposite direction. No siren, no lights. Marcus kept driving. The cop passed them with nothing more than a long look. Marcus nodded to him, and he returned it.

In a few miles, Lee said, "Pull over."

"Why?"

"You're shaking."

She was right, he was. This was a country highway, bare fields on either side, the last speed limit sign before Kearby passed a mile ago. Safe to stop. He parked the truck on the wide gravel shoulder but left it running.

Lee's hand rested on his arm. "We need to get you warm. Remove your shirt."

He stripped it off and threw it on the seat between them. Lee opened her door to wring the shirt out onto the ground and handed it back to him. He mopped off his dripping body while she towel-dried her hair with the blanket. Then she cranked the heat on high, although the temperature outside had never fallen below eighty.

"Lee, come on."

"Hypothermia means hospital." She turned to hand him the blanket.

He burrowed into the folds, damp but warmer than he was. The shivers wouldn't stop, so he let them come.

"I need to say something." She didn't meet his eyes.

"Okay."

"When you were out in the water, I . . ."

"It's okay."

"I railed at God. I wanted to rail at you. I saw everything possible. The knots slipping. The vehicles dislodging and sweeping those people away and you — you grabbing onto a door handle, something, trying to save them and . . . Or a tree hitting you, knocking you unconscious, so you drowned before I could get you out."

"Lee."

The line of her shoulders trembled.

He clenched his hands at his sides to keep from holding her. "Lee."

She looked up at him. Her mouth tightened.

"I'm right here," he said.

"It's so easy for me to . . ." She stared out the window, her back half to him.

"Say it."

"I blame Him before He even . . . fails me."

"He didn't fail us. Or those people in the water."

"Do you think no one died today in the flood?"

"I don't know. But it isn't failure on God's part."

"It's brokenness in the world. Because of sin."

"Right."

She faced forward. Breathed deep. "When you left the water for the last time, I wanted to check you for injuries. I was convinced you couldn't be all right."

"Well. I am."

"I know. I simply needed to verbalize this. If we're going to . . . to try this . . ."

Every time she brought it up, however she phrased it, a small bird of hope sang in his chest. He let her see the smile.

101

She gave a small smile back, but it flattened. "You need to know."

"You know what I'm going to say."

"Keep giving it to Him. No matter how many times I relapse."

"Right." Only Lee would use a medical term.

She laced her fingers in her lap, and he almost reached for her hand.

7

An hour after Lee left Marcus at Walton and Millie's, she was driving back to him. He'd invited her to return for dinner after she changed into dry clothes, and Millie had chimed in from the kitchen that there was plenty of food.

Lee had said she'd see them all in church tomorrow.

She ate a dinner of chicken tacos at Rosita's and thought she was going home to process. Alone. Violet was out with her church group tonight, so Lee wouldn't even have to greet her. The unsettled fatigue mirrored the way she felt after a session with Hannah, her counselor. Hannah was a gardener, turning the soil inside a person, dry and fallow and fenced off for valid reasons. Talking to her left Lee depleted and needing a day away from people, to process the overturned earth in herself and regenerate energy. But today Lee could attribute her upheaval only to her own heart.

She had stood on that highway slope, grass slick with rain, and silently screamed at God.

After dinner, solitude hadn't calmed her. She was no longer picturing him in a body bag, so . . . progress, at least. On the whole, she was all right. She simply wanted to spend more time with him before this day ended.

It was after eight when she rang Walt's doorbell. Three hours ago, they'd been leaving the movie theater.

The door opened to Millie. "I didn't save a plate. Didn't know you were coming back."

"Neither did I."

"I can heat up —"

"I ate. I came to . . . see . . ."

Millie smiled. "Glad you did. He's in the den."

"Thank you." Lee stepped inside and headed toward him.

"Can I get you anything? Sweet tea?"

"No, thank you." Anything but sweet tea.

"All right, dear. Well, you know your way around my house by now." Millie gestured down a dark hallway with a dim flicker at its end.

"I do. Thank you." Lee padded down the

plush green runner to the den. One of its French doors was shut, the other open wide.

She knocked and waited a few seconds before entering. He was watching a movie . . . oh. *Jaws.* Lee suppressed a sigh.

"Hi." His gaze flicked to her, then returned to the movie. "Thought you weren't coming back."

"I might not have, if I'd known sharks were the plan."

"One shark. The greatest shark. Ever."

"There's that other one they catch."

"Wasn't eating people. Doesn't count."

She sighed.

The leather ottoman and a pillow propped up his right leg. He was nestled at the center of the couch in two blankets, one blue and one red. Maybe lingering shivers from earlier, maybe not. Cold grabbed him too easily since the pneumonia.

His attention turned from the movie to her. "Nurse questions, go ahead."

"I didn't say —"

He gestured to his own face. "Written here."

Very well, then. She lifted her chin in the direction of his knee. "You're icing under the blankets?"

"Heat."

"Have you taken anything?"

"I didn't do anything to it. It's just aching a little."

"You didn't say anything."

"You know I would. If it was bad."

He didn't realize how skewed his own concept of pain had become in the last year. "Should you see Dr. Platt?"

"No. Anything else?"

Not really. She sat on the couch beside him.

"Okay."

He focused on the movie again. She pretended not to watch him. When she drew her legs up and settled in, he looked over at her and smiled. In another few minutes, Brody and Hooper and Quint headed into the open sea, and Lee wondered how many times she'd endured this movie for this man.

"Why does *Jaws* fascinate you to this degree?"

"It's a good movie."

She couldn't argue with that, from a cinematic standpoint. "I assume Brody is your favorite character."

"Sure."

"Because he kills the shark."

Brody uttered one of the most overly quoted lines in film history, and Marcus smiled.

"Men are predictable," Lee said.

"No."

"I was able to guess your favorite character with very little thought."

"But not why. It's not because he blows up the shark."

The den was overly air-conditioned, chilly even by non-Marcus standards. He wasn't icing, so this had to be the reason for the two blankets. Lee snagged a blue chenille throw, the only cover left, from the La-Z-Boy in one corner. She curled up on her cushion next to him and draped the throw over her shoulders.

Marcus clearly didn't plan to elaborate on Brody's attributes, or he'd forgotten to in the thrill of the shark chase.

"What is it, then?" she said.

He shifted his leg. "He's afraid of water."

Brody was? Lee thought over the scenes. "I had nearly forgotten that."

"It's not mentioned very much."

"I don't understand, Marcus."

"Really?"

She shook her head. If anything, he should scoff at Brody, not admire him, and Marcus's favorite character in a movie was always the one he admired.

He shrugged, and the motion brought his arm nearer to hers. "He's the most brave. Because his bravery costs the most."

Ah.

He shot her a crinkle-eyed smile. "Predictable?"

Her chest felt as if a bird pinged from wall to wall, fluttered to get out. She drew her knees to her chest, drew the throw closer around her, and tried to focus on the plight of a sheriff who ventured into the sea, despite his fear, to protect his town.

Near the end, Marcus shivered once, then again a few minutes later. She should move closer. Until her upper arm touched his, lending heat, a simple gesture that didn't have to be intimate.

But it would be.

She'd do this without pause in a survival situation, warding off hypothermia. She'd crawl into a sleeping bag with him if it would keep him alive. Yet she couldn't touch his arm, sitting beside him on Walt's couch with nothing at stake.

She swallowed hard. Breathed deep. *Speak louder than words.* His languages — action and touch. She inched nearer, and though his head didn't turn toward her, he knew. His awareness of her was inerrant, wherever they were, whatever the situation. Another few inches, and their arms would touch.

She froze.

Half an hour remained of the movie. This

wouldn't do. But she couldn't move, and Marcus didn't either, kept his eyes on the TV screen. Minutes crawled past, and she could hardly process the scenes, one after another. She reached for the remote and turned off the TV.

Questions creased Marcus's brow.

"I . . ." Lee folded her arms, and the throw fell off her shoulders. "It's happening to me right now."

He went still. As if a single breath from him would shatter them both.

"You asked me to tell you . . . anytime."

Marcus shifted to face her, repositioning his leg on the ottoman. "What do you need?"

She shut her eyes, but the only prayerful words she could find were those of a hymn. Perhaps borrowing them would be all right. *O Lord, be Thou near to me.* She opened her eyes and didn't look away from Marcus. Wouldn't look away.

Marcus. Her stone wall, her shield, her anchor.

"If you would listen? I believe Hannah would counsel me to talk through it."

"Okay."

"I might need to repeat things you already know about me."

"Okay."

Acid coated her tongue. She swallowed against a sudden gag reflex. "I want to be capable of . . . touching. But something about this setting. It's . . . I don't know. Comfortable and safe. But touch isn't — isn't — comfortable or safe."

He buried his hands in the blanket folds.

"It's not that I think you're going to pull a hood over my face and . . ." And punch her face, punch her breasts, throw her down on the blacktop, rape her and run away. Marcus looked into her eyes as if he could see each detail she'd told him. Perhaps he could.

The room had become an icebox, and her stomach roiled. Every fiber of her body wanted to stop the words in her mouth. Her arms drew in, crossing her wrists, pressing them to her breastbone. All her skin felt scorched.

"Just now, I wanted to sit closer to you, and then I felt . . . cold and . . . small. I think I wanted to hide from you."

Marcus opened his hands and pressed them against his thighs. "Can I do anything?"

"Sit with me, please. Until I'm all right."

She leaned her head back and counted to one hundred. A few minutes more and her stomach settled, and the cold in her chest trickled away. She sat forward again.

"Thank you for hearing me. For your patience."

"Lee."

"I want us to work, Marcus."

"I know." Light returned to his eyes.

"But there's still a core in me that uses . . . past experience . . . to define intimacy."

"I know."

"May I . . . attempt something . . . a test?" She could barely hear her own words.

Marcus nodded. When her hand curved over his, he swallowed hard, and a muscle jumped in his neck.

She held his left hand in both of hers and tugged it into her lap. Marcus didn't return her grip or even move his fingers. Lee traced her thumb over his knobby, callused knuckles. Rubbed each scar, lingering over the one he'd split open so many years ago when she'd told him the basic pieces of her story. The one he'd tried to hide from her, afraid of her fear, not wanting her to think he could attack her the way he attacked that porch beam.

She ran her fingers down the back of his hand, stopping at his wrist. She turned his hand over and placed her palm against his, her slender fingers looking dainty against his broad ones. She found calluses here, too, and scars. Her thumb drew a circle on his palm, and she turned his hand over again and looked up at him. His eyes were bright in the lamplight.

"I passed the test?" he said.

"I did." A smile found her lips.

"Then could I . . . ?"

Her stomach tightened, but she nodded. If they could ever be possible, then all of her, even the instincts and memories, had to learn that he would die before he would hurt her.

He imitated her tracing of thumb over knuckles and brought her hand up to his face. Her fingers brushed the rough shadow on his chin as he kissed the back of her hand. He turned it over with a slow gentleness that sent a shiver up her arm. He lowered his face into the cup of her hand and kissed her palm.

When he released her hand, Lee inched over the boundary of the cushion and leaned her arm into his. This smile crinkled his whole face.

"Another test?" he said.

"Body heat. You keep shivering."

He frowned at that, the way he always did when she called attention to a physical need he considered trivial.

"Marcus . . . If it never works. If I . . . can't."

"It's going to work."

"Hannah says I need time to — to redefine."

"There's time."

"I . . . I am . . ."

Marcus slowly lifted his left arm and draped it over her shoulders. She waited for the nausea, the panic, but there was only the warmth of his arm, the muscular weight, not a danger to her but protection. Always.

"Is this okay?" he said quietly.

Lee allowed herself a final move forward, something she'd sometimes wished to do. She rested her head on his shoulder. His arm tightened around her, not restraining but . . . holding. This was how it felt to be held. By Marcus. His hand cupped her shoulder, warm and careful.

Lee angled a glance at the dormant TV. "We probably missed that scene you like."

"Hmm." The sound rumbled, deeper with her ear so close. "I like all the scenes."

"The scars contest."

"Do you really want to watch what's left? The fake blood and fake screaming and shark meat rain?"

She smiled into his shoulder. Nothing like having her words lobbed back at her. "I'm not inclined to leave yet."

His chest caved with a sigh, and Lee relaxed against him and closed her eyes. He didn't move for the remote.

"You can turn it back on," she said.

"I've seen it a lot."

"This is true."

"Lee?"

She opened her eyes and angled her gaze. He was so near. He tilted his head to look at her. His breath, smelling of coffee, grazed her cheek.

"When did things change?" His voice remained hushed, content. "For you."

For her, of course, because he'd been steadfast. "I believe shortly after we made it here. Or . . ."

Memories surged. She blinked against them but then gave in to everything she'd felt on the frantic flight to Texas, everything she'd done to keep him alive.

"Or shortly before," she said.

Marcus tilted his head back against the couch. "Yeah."

"You suspected? Before I told you?"

"Yeah."

This should mortify her, but there wasn't room for that, not between them, not for years. "I never would have known."

His arm tightened around her again. "It had to be from you."

8

The congregation stood for the final song, and in that moment before the piano's first chords, Lee allowed herself a breath of anticipation — what would they sing, and would she know it? If she did, she could sing along. If she didn't, she would get to learn something new.

This melody wasn't familiar, block chords that sounded ancient. She followed the slides as those around her took up the song with varying success at the tune.

"O worship the King, all glorious above, and gratefully sing His power and His love. Our Shield and Defender, the Ancient of Days, pavilioned in splendor and girded with praise."

Lee closed her eyes. The first two lines were straightforward enough. *I do worship You.* She tried, at least. Depending on the definition of worship. Obviously, she knew the dictionary definition, but Christianity sometimes added layers to concepts. Perhaps she should ask Juana or Heath about it.

Our Shield and Defender. Yes, Lord Christ, we need this. She tried to praise Him, but the hollowness in her chest was far from exultant. She bowed her head. By the time the song ended, a cavity throbbed inside her. If she never achieved this — worship, praise, joy — how disappointing she would be to Him. She followed Marcus from the sanctuary. His gait was firm, the limp no more pronounced than normal. Heat must have helped.

They paused to greet and be greeted, even by some people they'd seen less than two hours ago in Sunday school. Violet bounced up to Lee and motioned her aside.

"I'm going shopping with Alexis and Tiff, and we'll probably see a movie."

"Can one of them bring you home?"

"Yeah. No worries. And I'm not buying anything but a movie ticket."

"That's your business, Violet." The smile stayed inside her, but Violet could be amusing, the way she wavered between independent one day and seeking approval the next.

"I have no business splurging on shoes when I could put that money toward the car fund. And the fish fund."

Ah, the fish fund. One of her friends had been giving away a complete aquarium setup — heater, filter, other items Lee hadn't known an aquarium needed. It bubbled now, empty, in the corner of Violet's room. She said the water had "cycled" long enough to add fish, as soon as she'd saved up for them.

"Sensible," Lee said, which seemed to be what Violet wanted to hear. She grinned and bounded off.

Lee was at last walking with Marcus toward the doors when Benjamin Schneider jogged up to them, the sleeves of his Hawaiian shirt flapping. He was the only person Lee had seen wear shorts to church, though many wore jeans. His grin enveloped both her and Marcus.

"Lunch, folks? There's a bunch of us going over to Charlie's."

Marcus inclined his head to her, and she barely dipped hers. Tex-Mex would be her choice, but Cajun sounded good, too. She'd have pistolettes.

Marcus smiled and turned back to Benjamin. "Sure."

"Great." That grin again, and Benjamin jogged away. How he maintained his husky build was a mystery.

It was still strange, this functioning as a

couple. Their actions hadn't changed; Marcus's head tilt wasn't a sign of dependence or control. Yet it held more significance now than it had before their dates, or perhaps that was only in Lee's head. He hadn't seemed to notice.

Heath caught them a few feet from the doors, followed by a man and woman in their fifties. The woman's dress and the man's shirt and khakis still bore manufacturer's creases. Refugees.

"Marcus, you have a minute?" Heath gestured to the strangers.

"Sure."

"Folks, this is our resident contractor, Marcus Brenner. Marcus, meet Al and Gwyneth Dunham, here from Oregon. They've been talking to Tim about a house he's got listed."

Al thrust out a hand, and Marcus shook it.

"It's the house on Tabitha," Gwyneth said. Her words slid together, more nervous than eager. "He says we could close on it within a week, but it won't pass all the inspections, and we should talk to you, and he had to leave so Pastor Heath offered to introduce us."

"Have you been inside?" Marcus rubbed his neck.

"Twice," Al said.

Gwyneth seemed to come up onto her tiptoes, which only raised her to about five-foot-two. "I don't mind a little slant to the floor. I really don't see what the issue is."

"It's slanted because half the weight-bearing beams in the basement are cracked. You need an I-beam and a support jack."

"The house is falling down?" Gwyneth's voice pitched higher.

"Not if I fix it," Marcus said.

Lee's mouth tugged. Yes, he would fix it. And he'd accept whatever payment they could afford, even if he took a loss. She wandered away from the conversation as a sudden warmth clogged her chest.

She pushed the door open and stepped into the humid heat. Texas's May was Michigan's July. At the end of the sidewalk, half a dozen people stood back to back, some sort of phalanx, signs in their hands instead of shields. The closest one, a woman no older than herself, saw her and glared. Lee's heartbeat skipped. She knew none of those people. The woman angled her sign for easy reading. *Stop Enabling Vagrants.*

Lee stepped forward without making eye contact again. She would go to her car and meet the others at Charlie's. Perhaps she should alert security, but going back into the church would look like retreat. Like fear. She relaxed her hands at her sides and was almost past the group when one of the men stepped out to stand in front of her.

"Hi." He was no taller than she was, but his white T-shirt rippled over muscle as he planted his hands on his hips.

Lee sidestepped.

"We'd like to talk to a staff person. Are you a staff person?"

"No."

"You one of the folks that sleep here? That mooch off the gullible folks who keep giving money to feed you?"

She squared her shoulders. *I have a job. I provide for myself.* But this man didn't deserve any information about her. Let him think what he wished.

She stepped around him, and he blocked her again, and in their shuffle, his breath warmed her collarbone. Saliva flooded her mouth. She was going to be sick.

"Leave her alone, Steve, that's not why we're here," another man said from behind her.

"I say it's exactly why we're —"

"Lee!"

The burning fury in Marcus's voice lifted the weight from her chest. Dispelled the nausea. She blinked, and it was gone, whatever hovering specter the stranger's accidental proximity had conjured. She half pivoted. Heath and Gloria approached along with Marcus, whose glare promised he'd smash the stranger's teeth in. He must have seen the whole encounter, and from a distance, it would appear more invasive than it had been.

He took her arm in a careful grip and tugged her behind him. As Steve stepped back, Heath stepped forward.

"What's going on out here?" Heath said.

"Do you work for the church?" Steve crossed his arms.

"I do." Heath frowned down at him.

"And you?"

"No," Marcus said.

Another of the men in the group stepped up, taller than the first but still inches shorter than Heath. He wore a suit and tie despite the weather, and his sign was written in smaller letters. *Texas Won't Survive If We Don't Make Hard Decisions Now.*

"We're here on behalf of all Texas taxpayers to demand this church stop housing non-citizens."

"That's right." Steve's arms tightened across his chest. "Everyone in the next two counties knows what goes on in this church."

"Good," Heath said.

"Well, you'd better quit it, or we're going to report you."

"To whom?"

"The immigration department. The governor. Whoever we have to go to."

"So the American border is closed now?"

"No, but —"

"Is applying for citizenship a legal requirement for Americans to stay here?"

"They should be applying if they're going to stay. Do you know how many of them are undocumented? It's going to create problems. It already is."

He wasn't wrong. Marcus and Violet had been right to apply for citizenship. An old argument with Marcus washed over Lee.

I don't think it's wise to put down roots prematurely.

"There's nowhere else to go."

Marcus's application hadn't mattered. Whatever had held Lee back from taking that step, perhaps they'd both been partially right.

Heath hung his hands on his hips, but the gesture wasn't challenging. His gaze took in the group. "Well, I'm sure folks who've been threatened and harassed and worse in their old homes are more likely to volunteer their information to our government after you've

123

welcomed them so warmly."

He nodded behind him, where a small cluster of people had gathered as they exited the church and spotted the commotion. Lee had met many of them on nights when she served them dinner. Al and Gwyneth from Oregon stood at the edge of the crowd.

"Let's go," said one of the women protesters. She'd turned her sign against her body, but the ink bled through to the back. *Close American Border NOW.*

"We've got legitimate reasons to protest here." The man in the suit glared at Heath.

"Unless this church starts using taxpayer dollars, no, you really don't. Not to mention this is private property."

Seconds wore on as no one moved or spoke. In front of Lee, Marcus all but quivered with tension. She didn't have to see his jaw to know he was clenching it. Heath eyed each of the protesters in turn, and now that Lee had calmed, she counted them. Only seven people. They'd seemed to be more a minute ago. They turned to go, loosely together except for Steve, who stood still an extra minute as if this made a point. Then he left too.

At the door of the church, everyone seemed frozen. Heath turned with a sigh.

"We might be dealing with more of this soon."

At this rate, Marcus would never feel safe enough to talk to the church. She met Heath's eyes, and his nod acknowledged her thought.

"Thank you for speaking to them," she said.

"Let's be glad they were easily deterred." He smiled.

Marcus hadn't moved. He watched the protesters disperse to their cars but shifted his focus when Lee moved to face him. "Are you okay?"

"I'm fine."

A few churchgoers Lee didn't know trickled toward them.

"Pastor Heath? Is protesting here legal, could they come back?"

"Why blame our church? We can vote to use offerings however we want."

Gloria stepped over to Marcus and Lee, clad in her usual Western shirt (purple and white plaid today) and a long white skirt. "Y'all okay?"

"They only talked," Lee said.

"Okay, good. Just checking."

She returned to her husband's side and more people clustered around, asking questions, voicing opinions.

Marcus tipped his head toward the parking lot. "Come on."

Lee followed him toward his truck, though her own car was parked across the lot. Sunlight glittered on the puddles that would disappear by tomorrow. Nothing about their little town suggested flash flooding had occurred a mere ten miles away yesterday.

Charlie's Cajun Kitchen was between the church and home, so Lee would drive her car to lunch, but Marcus didn't say "See you there." He continued walking, and something in the lines of his face kept her at his side. They reached his truck, and he turned to her.

"It looked like he was threatening you."

"He wasn't." But of everything those people had said, of course he had to fixate on the fact that a man had blocked Lee's path. "I'm perfectly fine."

"I know." He turned to open the truck door, grasped the handle, and stood there.

"Marcus?"

"If they knew. About the list. People like that would turn me in."

"Possibly."

"And Becca and that agent. I know I said it doesn't matter, if Jason's here or not. I'm trying not to let it matter, but I . . . What if being near me, what if you, and every-

126

body . . ." He gripped the back of his neck.

"It isn't on you."

He turned to face her, shoulders bowed, and something squeezed in her chest. She'd guessed right, though it wouldn't be a guess to anyone who knew him.

"You can't carry this, Marcus. No one person can carry this."

"Pete told me that once. When I first started seeing him. Not about this, but — other things."

"Please listen to both of us."

"I'm trying." The sigh seemed to empty him out. "Aubrey said it too."

There wasn't a response for that, not when he still carried more guilt for Aubrey's death than he deserved to. Lee tried to reach for his arm, but the safety of last night had deserted her. Her fingers curled into her palm.

"Let's go to lunch," she said. "Go and be with our friends."

He didn't move.

"They're our family." He couldn't deny that. If he ever did, he'd no longer be Marcus.

He straightened his shoulders. "Yeah. Okay. Lunch. And family."

9

On the satisfaction scale, cleaning walls couldn't compare with painting them, but in this house, both yielded visible results. Marcus had scrubbed colored stains and an oily film from the kitchen walls, and now they glistened with a coat of Rye Harvest. No longer ivory, the room was warmer, even with half the wall space occupied by pine cabinets. He'd do another coat tomorrow. He turned a slow circle in the center of the room, and a smile tugged his mouth. Good work.

He could start on the den, but it was after seven. He'd missed dinner. Even after eight hours of work for customers, the idea of stopping, of being idle, made his hands clench. Too much churning around in his head. The trust Walt and Pete were asking him to give his family. The protesters outside church yesterday. And of course the list, always the list.

Marcus had driven from the other side of town and worked three more hours. The weariness in his limbs was a good, healthy sort, but it was time to quit. He took his roller brush and drip pan to the sink in the mudroom and ran water over both. His stomach rumbled. Over the last ten minutes, as awareness of his hunger grew, tension had latched onto his neck.

Stupid triggers.

He left the still sealed paint cans in the den — that neutral color and the weathered red Lee had picked out. He pictured Lee painting this room with him tomorrow and had to smile again. She'd be here now if not for her shift at the hospital.

He left the way he'd come in, through the garage. No more entering and exiting through the front door; the house was his now. He'd sleep here soon.

He locked the side door to the garage, turned, and froze.

A dog stood next to his truck on the driveway. Looked like a boxer mixed with something stockier, fawn coloring with a white chest and dark shading on its muzzle. No collar, docked tail, floppy ears. It wagged its stub but didn't approach him.

"Hi," Marcus said.

The hindquarters wiggled too.

"You lost?"

The dog ducked its head as it slinked closer, but the stub tail kept wagging. Marcus took a step forward, and the dog rushed him with a growl. His heartbeat doubled, but he stood still. The growl melted into a whine and didn't end, a canine song of happiness. Its whole body wagged, all seventy-something pounds.

Or less. Bones protruded — ribs, shoulder blades, hips. Marcus reached out an open hand, and the dog sniffed, then licked it. Drool dripped to the concrete.

"Good dog," he said.

He slowly lifted his hand and ran it over the dog's dirty head. The whining grew louder. The dog pressed its head to his leg.

"Where'd you come from?" Marcus looked down the street, but his house was one of only three on this little court. The dog belonged to neither of his neighbors.

"I don't have any food here," he said.

The dog sat at his feet.

"Somebody trained you. Where are they?"

A dog didn't lose this much weight in a few days or even a week. Marcus walked to the porch and sat on the step. The dog followed. He checked it over for injuries and determined it was a neutered male. It seemed healthy, and the fur around its neck was worn a little thin. It had worn a collar but not for a while.

"Okay," he said, and the dog set its head on his good knee. "No, get up. We're going into town. We need to eat."

The moment Marcus opened the door of his truck, the dog gave a short bark and jumped up onto the seat. He rolled down the windows as he drove, and the dog thrust its nose out into the wind. Not timid. Not abused, but abandoned? Or lost, maybe. Some family might be searching.

His house was only a few miles outside downtown. In minutes, he pulled into the Kearby Family Diner on East Third and parked, leaving the windows open. The dog whined as Marcus got out of the truck.

"Stay," he said and shut the door. It growled, complaint rather than threat.

The diner looked straight out of a sixties film: white-and-black-tiled floor, red vinyl barstools with chrome legs, low-backed booths over which you could see the heads of the people to either side of you. The first time he'd been in here, Marcus almost expected a hostess to come at him wearing roller skates.

Today the Schneider family occupied a corner booth, and a woman Marcus didn't know sat at the far end of the counter, sip-ping a chocolate milkshake from a tall glass. He walked up to order, and Violet's friend Alexis grinned at him from behind the register.

"Hi," he said.

"Hey, Marcus, what can I get you?"

The woman with the milkshake lifted her head and looked at him. His skin prickled — scalp, neck, across his shoulders. *Hypervigilance. Get a grip.*

"Burger with everything," he said. "And can I get an extra burger on a plate? No bun or anything?"

Alexis tilted her head, and her auburn ponytail swayed. "To eat later?"

"I found a dog."

She leaned over the counter to look at the floor near his feet.

"Left him in my truck. Do you know anybody who's lost one, a boxer mix?"

A thing he'd learned fast about Kearby — the family-owned restaurants heard news first. Rosita and Charlie knew the latest on everyone, and the diner employees were almost as informed.

Alexis shook her head. "Haven't heard anything, and nobody's put up a notice on our board in a while."

"Okay, thanks."

"Fries and Coke with that?"

132

"Yeah."

He took a seat on a bar stool and waited for his order. Alexis served it across the counter to him on a red tray. The smell of the food made his mouth water, and he took a bite of the burger to calm the corner of his brain that refused to believe he'd ever eat again. He sipped his Coke, took a deep breath. Better already.

The dog should eat first, probably hadn't in days. But if it was that hungry, it might throw up in his truck. After finishing his own food, he filled one of the large paper cups with water from the pop machine.

He paid Alexis, and she smiled as she handed him the receipt. "If anybody comes in here looking for a boxer, I'll let them know he's with you."

Marcus dug in his wallet for a business card and handed it to her.

"Perfect. Awesome. Does he have tags?"

"No."

"So we don't know his name."

"No."

She ducked behind the counter for a sheet of paper and a length of tape. "Here."

She grabbed a purple highlighter from a basket of pens and wrote across the top and bottom of the paper: *FOUND: MALE BOXER DOG. NO TAGS.* Then she started to tape his business card to the page.

His pulse tripped. "No."

"Huh?" She stood with tape stuck to her fingers, holding his card.

Marcus cleared his throat. "You can give my number to somebody if they say they lost a dog. But keep the card behind the counter."

Her pinched frown said he was strange, but she tucked the card into a cubbyhole. Marcus thanked her and headed outside. The bell above the door jingled as he left.

The dog had stayed in his truck, its head thrust out the passenger window to watch the sparse traffic. Marcus opened the door, and it jumped down to stand beside him. He set the plate on the ground.

"Here."

The dog whined, and a drop of drool hit the gravel. Marcus stroked its back as it devoured the burger. He squatted to offer the cup of water, but the dog ignored it to lick his face, knocking him off balance. His hand shot out to catch himself against the door of the truck. The dog licked his chin again.

"Okay. Don't." A chuckle rose in his chest.

He shoved its muzzle away. It shoved its face into the cup, slobbered water and drool onto his hands.

The diner door opened, and out walked the milkshake woman with a paper cup of her own. She'd taken her shake to go. Wanting to catch him?

She watched the dog finish drinking and shake its head, muzzle flinging water. "That's one sorry-looking mutt."

"Yeah." He'd have to hose the dog off before bringing him into Walt and Millie's house.

"And if you're curious, I'd bet anything there's Rottweiler in him somewhere. He's all skin and bones right now, but he's got a thick chest like a Rottie, and something about that face."

"Thanks." Though it didn't matter. Not his dog. He rubbed behind its ear, and it pushed its head into his hand.

"Anyway, you're Marcus."

He nodded. Alexis had said his name, and he was becoming the go-to handyman and carpenter of Kearby. He opened the passenger door, and the dog barked, then jumped into the truck.

"I was driving through town. I barely hoped to find you. That is, I hope you're the right Marcus. Good thing your name isn't John or Jim." She held out her hand. "Nicole Stopczy from the *Decatur Clarion*."

Every muscle in his body froze.

135

Nicole glanced from her outstretched hand to his face.

Marcus tried to swallow, to say something. A reporter. Here for him. Why?

She lowered her hand and tilted her head. "I'm not here to harass you. I write human interest for the *Clarion,* and you could give me a great story. Everyday heroism and all that. My readers will inhale it."

Heroism. Human interest. Reporters didn't go away because you told them to. It was their job to keep poking. Kearby was too small to get lost in, and this woman knew he lived here.

Okay, think. She couldn't know everything. "You've got the wrong Marcus."

"You match the description perfectly."

He pulled in a breath. Police description? What was she talking about?

"You know, most fifteen-minute heroes are happy to stretch their minutes out as long as possible."

"What?"

"I can't keep you famous forever, of course." She tried to smile and failed.

"No."

"I'm sorry?"

"Just go."

"Have I offended you somehow? I assure you that wasn't my intent, and I drove a long way to hunt you down, and . . ." The wrinkles of confusion smoothed from her forehead. "Oh."

If she wouldn't leave, he would. He walked around the front of his truck and yanked open the driver's door.

"Mr. Brenner, please wait a minute."

Brenner. This woman had asked about him, and Alexis would have no reason not to give his last name. He got into the truck, slammed the door, and turned the key.

Nicole set a manicured hand on the window frame. Marcus didn't let himself roll the window up on her fingers. He glared at her, and she jerked her hand back.

"I'm talking about what you did on Saturday, during the flood."

Wait . . . that?

"One of the folks you rescued is my brother-in-law Rob. I wanted to tell the story of your bravery, find out what you were thinking, what made you do that for strangers."

Relief weakened his limbs. She didn't know anything. He shook his head.

"That's obviously not the story you thought I wanted."

He gripped the steering wheel the way he'd gripped that rope in the middle of the floodwaters.

"And between your reaction and your accent, odds are you came here to get away from the Constabulary."

"I won't talk to you," he said.

"Mr. Brenner, if you only knew how important this could be, for —"

"No. It isn't. I'm not."

"I won't ask questions, if you prefer that. An interview conducted entirely on your terms, saying whatever —"

"Step back."

She did.

Marcus rolled both windows up, and the dog whined. As the windows sealed, Nicole raised her voice.

"Please hear me out. I've been trying for months to find —"

He gunned the truck out onto the street and left the reporter calling into his dust. In another mile, he parked at the safest place he knew. Grace Bible Church.

He bowed his head. The dog nudged under his arm and whined. A reporter knew his name. His home. His history, enough of it.

"God," he said. "This could be bad."

One reporter was all it took. *If Jason's here . . .*

He opened the door and drew in a long breath. He gripped the door frame and pushed to his feet. Less than fifty feet away were the cement steps into the church, where he and Lee had sat on their first day in Texas, with the sun's warmth on their shoulders and its light in their eyes. He sank down on the steps.

He spent a little while whispering the words to Psalms he could recall and resolving to memorize more of them. Then he stood and walked back to the truck.

The dog had stretched out on the seat where he'd been, its head half drooping out of the open driver's side. It had been watching him. Marcus dropped his hand to its head.

"Good dog. Let's walk."

He stepped back from the truck and snapped his fingers, and the dog's ears pricked. Once more, and the dog jumped down and trotted around to stand at heel.

He led the dog across the back parking lot, where Heath's army-green Jeep gave away that he was working late tonight. Marcus walked around to the side of the church. The grass swished against the dog's flanks. This side of the church faced a vacant field, so it was always cut last. The length of the weeds was getting ridiculous. If the mower was gassed up, Marcus should cut it. Might as well, since he was here. Some of the trees had been cut down through the years, likely when they got too tall for the power line, and the stumps were never dug up. Made mowing a challenge.

The dog shadowed him the rest of the way around the building, across the main parking lot. As they reached a side exit, the door opened, and Heath stepped out.

He wore his customary khakis and a short-sleeved button-down, brown and white plaid. No doubt Gloria had bought him that shirt. He locked the side door and shuffled a Bible and two other books from one hand to the other, looked up, and smiled.

"Whose dog?"

"I don't know." Marcus followed him toward the Jeep.

"Looks like your dog to me."

"No."

"There's a spigot back here, and a hose in one of the closets inside. Unless you already let him in your truck like that."

"I'll deal with it later."

Heath gave him a long, searching look. The next minute held the sounds of cicadas and distant traffic and the dog's panting. They reached the Jeep, and Heath stowed his books on the passenger seat and shut the door. He turned to Marcus.

"So where'd you find him?"

"My place. I was doing some work. He showed up."

Heath held an open hand out to the dog. It nosed his palm then stepped back next to Marcus.

"Like I said, he appears to be yours."

"I fed him, that's all. He was . . ." Something twisted in Marcus's gut. He lifted a hand to his neck. "Alone. Hungry."

"I can see that."

"Well. I'll talk to you later."

"Marcus, why are you here?"

He shrugged. "Passing by."

Heath leveled him with a look.

"Just needed a minute."

"Ah. Church can be a good place for that. Even the parking lot." He smiled.

Marcus could say good night if he wanted to, could walk away. "I . . . The last few days have been . . . harder."

"Lee told me about the list."

"She thought I couldn't tell you?" Thought he needed coddling, a spokesperson? His face burned.

Heath's gaze was equally patient and unyielding. "I'm not going to bother answering that."

Right. He sighed, rubbed his neck. The bristling in him settled back down as quickly as it had stood up. Lee talking to Heath didn't make Marcus weak. Didn't mean Lee or Heath saw him as weak. Heck. One day he'd be past this touchiness, or so Pete said.

"So this dog," Heath said. "You're taking him back to Walt's place?"

"Sure."

"Wait here."

Heath jogged around to the side door, unlocked it, and disappeared inside. He reemerged with a bottle of cheap shampoo and a coil of hose.

"No guarantee this thing doesn't leak, but let's try it."

It did leak, in two places the size of pinholes. Fine sprays of water misted in the floodlight as soon as Heath turned on the spigot. Marcus lathered shampoo all over the dog, careful of its eyes. Heath rinsed its coat, and soap foamed on the grass at its feet. With a bark, it bounded off to shake and roll.

It hadn't been a two-man job. The dog had stood still, hadn't even complained with that half growl. Still, Heath didn't say good night or head for his Jeep. Marcus took the hose and rinsed his hands and arms. A few blotches of lather had landed on his T-shirt. He swept them off and rinsed his hands again.

"Thanks," he said.

"Millie would die if that beast came into her house tracking dirt."

Not what he meant, but he should let it go. He shut off the water and unscrewed the hose nozzle. He handed the hose to Heath.

"I thought you'd ask if I'm trusting God with . . . things."

"Are you?"

"I . . ." He gazed out over the grassy stretch between them and the parking lot. The dog still shook water from its coat. "He's always with me. I know that. And I feel it."

"But?"

But he still barked at people over nothing. Among other things. He raised his voice. "Dog."

The mutt loped in a wide circle, stopping every few seconds to shake itself.

He snapped his fingers and slapped his palm to his thigh. "Dog."

It turned toward him, then galloped over and stood at his feet.

"A name could be helpful." Heath smiled.

"Not mine." But the dog nudged Marcus's hand up to its head, and he had to smile, too.

On the way home, he stopped for dog food and two stainless steel bowls. The dog again waited in the car with the windows down and didn't hesitate to bound into Walt and Millie's house.

"I've got a notice up at the diner for him," Marcus told Millie.

"In the meantime, he's welcome." She smiled, and Marcus almost expected her to offer the dog a slice of pie.

"Where's Walt?"

"Ranger business, I think."

Marcus was tired enough for bed, though it was only nine o'clock. He'd learned to sleep when he could. He told Millie good night, and the dog followed him down the hall into the guestroom.

He set his keys and his phone on the dresser, showered, and put on a T-shirt and sleep pants. He'd be willing to bet Millie still checked on him at night, though he hadn't been awake to catch her at it in almost a month. Well, he couldn't blame her. In the first weeks he'd stayed with them, his dreams had woken them, often multiple times a night. Then the insomnia hit, and he still woke them up — limping around their house like a wounded dog, slamming into a panic attack every time a doorknob rattled.

It had been a long winter for all of them. But spring had come.

He sat on the side of the bed and took his Bible from the little pinewood nightstand. A psalm a night. Pete was right about King David. This was a man with a lot of feelings inside, feelings that brimmed over in his prayers. Marcus opened the Bible to a random place too far ahead — Romans — and a smile tugged his mouth. Most of the page was highlighted in pink. Violet hadn't understood why he wanted to keep this Bible rather than let her buy him a new one, unmarked by her enthusiasm. He couldn't explain, but this book was part of him. Even the ink from Violet's highlighter. He flipped back to Psalms and rested an open hand in the center of the pages, then began to read.

When he'd finished reading, he crawled under the covers, and the dog circled the room a few times before lying down on the carpet. After a few minutes, it stretched out on its side and shut its eyes.

"Night," Marcus said, and the dog sighed.

10

When he thought about it, the headache had about ten possible causes. Better not to think about them.

Easier said than done.

Marcus rubbed his neck with one hand while the other steered his truck toward home, leaving behind Decatur and his last job of the day. The throb was spreading, down into his shoulders. Maybe he could find a thought trail to distract him, relax him.

Except there was only one distraction his brain pulled toward. And it was dangerous.

For five weeks, he'd been careful. Strong. Of course, he thought about touching Lee every day. Every hour of every day. God was giving him patience — he knew it was God, because it sure as heck wasn't him.

That she was willing to try at all made Marcus want to kiss her breathless. Well, okay, he'd want that regardless. But he had to let her explore closeness with him on her terms. He'd known that when they started dating. Shouldn't knowing what Lee needed make him infinitely strong against his own wants? His jaw clenched. He measured a breath long enough to push the images away. He lowered his window all the way. The wind ruffled his hair.

Kissing the palm of her hand Saturday night. His lips on her skin. Her softness. Her head on his shoulder. Her hair near his face, the scent of her shampoo, flowers mixed with lemons. And her body tucked close to his, so slender and perfect, nestling into his arm —

Marcus growled.

If he could just kiss her for real.

He needed a distraction from distraction.

His phone buzzed in the cup holder. *Thanks, God, that works.* He grabbed it and took the call from Tim. "Hey."

"What are the odds you're working in Decatur today?"

Marcus glanced in his rearview. "Yeah, I am. Was."

"Long gone?"

"No." He'd only been on the highway five minutes.

"Great. You know the Dunhams, they're

new, probably buying the house on Tabitha?"

"Heath introduced us."

"Right, well, when their family ran, they had to split up. I guess one of their daughters showed up at the church shelter in Decatur and found them through that online refugee board. She's got no car, and they're ready to drive to get her, but I thought maybe you could save them the trip?"

"Sure." Marcus signaled for the next exit that would route him back the way he came.

"They'll appreciate it. Al said Gwyneth was down with a migraine earlier. They're staying at the hotel tonight to give her some quiet."

That was a lot of detail, but Tim tended to get details out of people without trying. "What's the daughter's name?"

"Alicia. She's twenty-three, red hair."

"Got it."

"Thanks, Marcus."

"Sure."

He hung up and drove back into Decatur. Every day he worked with refugees, God's goodness shone in the way things worked out for them. There was a verse about that. Romans, somewhere. The same place it talked about hardship. *"For Your sake we are killed all day long."*

God, I wish they could have all made it here. But You know that. And You know why they didn't.

Ten minutes later, he left the main road and pulled into the parking lot behind New Mercies Christian Church. They were small compared to Grace Bible Church, only two hundred people or so, and their building was too small to be a real shelter, but they kept people when they could. Last month, the members had run a food drive in Decatur and donated everything to Grace, to help with the many people who came and stayed for nights on end. Marcus had used his truck to transport boxes upon boxes of food.

He headed to the front doors. Tuesday evening meant no Bible classes, but there should still be somebody around to direct him. He went inside and paused in the foyer, carpeted in busy yellow spirals on a dark blue background. The visitors' counter, stacked with tracts and other handouts, was unoccupied.

He'd have to find someone and ask about Alicia Dunham. A low drone of voices came from both hallways, one on each end of the foyer. Laughter drifted from his right. He headed that way. At the far end of the hall, before it forked, a door opened. Two men stepped out, talking too low for Marcus to hear, shaking hands, turning to face him. The one on the left was an elder Marcus had talked to before, and the one on the right was . . .

Jason.

Marcus was standing in another hall, another door opening, Jason stepping out, *"She called for a ride?"*

Marcus was shoving to his feet, back to a dingy wall, another door opening, Jason stepping in, *"So. It really is you."*

Marcus was curling on the cold floor and trying to shield his broken ribs from Jason's booted kicks, *"I'm sick of coming here. I'm sick of you being alive every time I come here."*

At the end of this hallway, right now — those things were past, but this was now — blue eyes narrowed at him, and then feet pounded toward him. Marcus tried to move. Gritted his teeth. Turned. Ran. Into the foyer. Hit the door as Jason emerged from the hallway.

Through the door. Into the front lot. Around the building. His truck. His only chance. Make the back street before Jason saw him leave. He threw himself at the door, wrenched it open, fell inside, turned the key, gunned the engine, didn't squeal the tires, would have been a giveaway, drove too fast, blew through a stop sign and then another one. Car horn. Don't stop. *You're dead if you stop.*

Main road. Traffic light. Yellow. Don't stop. Car horn again. Drive.

His breathing filled the truck cab. Fractured, shallow. The tingling in his hands spread halfway up his arms. He checked the rearview mirror for a gray car, green lights, but no, Jason could be driving anything. Jason could do anything. Texas would do nothing —

The truck swerved, almost hopping the curb. The world through the windshield was fuzzy, half lost in a gray starburst. Ahead, on the right, entrance ramp for the freeway. Faster. Safer. He crossed two lanes and more horns blared. He hit the curving ramp too fast. Tires squealed. Keep going. Merge. Drive. No cars in the rearview that hadn't been there thirty seconds ago.

Not enough air. The tingling had spread up his arms to his shoulders. Go. Get away. But Jason was here. Jason already had him.

He was going to kill somebody.

The thought sifted through like one grain of gold in handfuls of sand. He could hardly see, hardly breathe, hardly hold onto the wheel. Somebody would die because of him.

But he couldn't stop.

"God. Don't let me hurt anybody."

He drove. No thinking. Just driving.

At some point, the streets had narrowed. He clenched his prickling hands on the wheel and leaned forward over it as if that would help him see. Something about this street . . . there, the green sign on the right, that would tell him where . . . Kearby.

He'd gone home.

No, what's wrong with you, Jason's coming to —

He braked. The downtown speed limit was thirty. He had to get out of here. He had to drive in the opposite direction for the rest of his life. He wouldn't bring Jason here. These treasured people.

Lee.

The weight on his chest grew heavier. Gray screened his vision. He slowed the truck to a crawl. Turned down a wide gravel path to the park. His park. Safe place.

He stopped the truck.

Not safe.

Didn't matter. He had to stop until he could breathe. He put the truck in park and groped for the door handle and pulled. Leaned his weight into it. Grabbed the steering wheel with his other hand to keep from falling out of the truck. Door open.

Air. He drew it in.

A spike drove through the center of his chest.

"God. Jesus." Psalms might help. "God and Savior. My help and portion. Strong tower."

Marcus gripped the door frame and pushed to his feet. Less than fifty feet away spread the wood chip path, a good place to talk to God, if he could get that far. He stumbled to his knees twice, and from the back of his mind came a warning. *Pain.* He couldn't focus on it, on anything, until he made it to his path. Then he sat with his back against a rotting log and sifted wood chips through his hands. The contact made the needles in his fingers prickle stronger, but then they seemed to fade.

Minutes crept on. The pounding of his heart didn't soften, didn't slow. He held his hand up, and he couldn't count his fingers.

He was shaking. "Praise the Lord . . . from the heavens . . . and . . . and the . . ."

His brain was in no better shape than his muscles. He let his hands droop beside him in the dirt. He had to keep breathing. He had to be okay. Because he had to drive away from here. Had to draw Jason away.

A booted foot bashed into his ribs, and he forgot all the psalms.

No. Jason's not here.

But he would be. Soon. Any minute.

Marcus groped for the phone in his pocket. His shaking hand dropped it into a fern. He dug it out.

Not safe. Lee would try to find him.

You're not thinking clearly.

Probably not.

So call Lee.

Not this time. He dropped the phone. Clutched his chest as the pain increased. Lowered his forehead to his knees. "Jesus, please help."

This was the last time Lee would volunteer at a child's birthday party. The noise level alone made her want to retreat. Juana had shot her grateful glances all afternoon as the two of them served homemade pizza and birthday cake, cleaned up the aftermath of one boy trying to start a food fight (the others, including Damien, were smart enough not to join in), and in general corralled the chaos of half a dozen seven- and eight-year-olds. *Corral* was in fact the perfect word. Boys this age couldn't be managed, couldn't be subdued. After four hours, Lee was ready for parents to show up and reclaim their sons. She slipped into Juana's library, caved onto the stuffed chair, and leaned back to close her eyes. From here, the boys were a distant scuffle, a shout or two, as they took turns at a video game, players and spectators equally engaged.

Lee opened her eyes to appreciate the

room. Juana and Oscar's house was a lovely one, especially this small study tucked at the north end, two windows on one wall and, built into the opposite wall, long oak bookshelves. Lee scanned the shelf that still intrigued her the most — Juana's collection of romance novels. Almost every title included the word *love*. Perhaps Lee could learn from them; after all, she'd gleaned substantial knowledge of humanity from the classic fiction she'd read over her lifetime. She stood and crossed the room to pull a book out at random. The back cover copy didn't sound educational. She put it back and slid out a few more.

At her fourth try, she froze. The cover showed a shirtless man holding a woman by the arms, bending her backward to press his body against hers. She wore a red dress, and her hand on his chest seemed to be trying to push him away. Trying and failing. Lee shoved the book back into its place.

Juana said they're romantic. If this was romance, Lee had too much to learn.

She couldn't learn to tolerate that.

She didn't have to. Marcus would never behave like the man on the book cover. Lee laced her fingers, turned the link of them inside out to stretch her arms. She was being absurd. The man on the book cover didn't exist. Marcus did. She folded her arms and stood still for a moment, collecting herself.

All right, then. No romance novels.

Juana might need assistance with the herd of boys. Lee headed for the kitchen.

"There you are." Juana looked up from rinsing red and blue frosting from six plates and placing them into the dishwasher. She grinned.

"I apologize for deserting."

"It is kind of a battlefield, isn't it?" Another grin clarified she didn't mind. "I figured you needed a few minutes away from the hollering."

Punctuating her words, a chorus of cheers rose from the living room. No discernible words. In the throes of video gaming, grunts and shouts and groans were all the communication required.

"What else needs to be done?" Lee said.

"At this point, we let them play until their parents show up. Which should be soon. Normally we wouldn't be doing this on a weekday, but Patrick's family is moving, and this was literally the only day he could come."

She finished with the plates and moved on to the frosting-crusted silverware. Lee stripped the plastic tablecloth from the kitchen table, a precaution she'd never have thought of that appeared to be vital. Parenting seemed to entail an endless list of precautions.

"Do you want to reuse this?" *Say no.*

Juana laughed. "Roll that thing up and throw it away. Immediately."

When the cleanup was done and several boys had gone home, Juana made a chai tea for Lee and a cappuccino for herself, and they sat at the table across from each other.

"So how do you feel about your first childcare experience?"

"It was fine." Not the friendliest word, though Juana seemed to accept it. "I'm glad I was here."

"Oh, good. I'm glad too. Monitoring this many boys on my own would have been slightly terrifying." A smile found her mouth and her eyes. "But pay no attention to the wiped-out woman behind the curtain. Wait until tomorrow when I'm back to being a tireless advocate for motherhood."

A familiar weight fell on Lee. She sipped her tea and searched for a neutral response.

Juana's dark brown eyes studied her. "What?"

"Nothing."

"Obviously, that struck a nerve."

Obviously? Because her silence lasted an

extra second? "No. It didn't."

"Come on, Lee." Juana nudged her mug to one side. Nothing buffered the space across the table. "Do you have any idea how often you do this to me?"

"Do what?" A calm breath, a sip of tea. *See? Unruffled.*

"Make me ask. Guess. Whatever. I don't know if you realize this, but you never actually told me when you and Marcus started dating. I put two and two together."

Of course she realized it, but *dating* had felt like a juvenile word in the beginning. A casual word. And verbally defining herself and Marcus had never been necessary before.

Juana sighed and shook her head. "Look, I have my push-button topics too. You already know a few."

Society's portrayal of the perfect size-zero woman — Juana was a twelve and proud of it. Suicide — Juana had lost an uncle to deliberate overdose when she was in high school. One flippantly portrayed suicide on a TV show, and she'd quit watching after years as a faithful fan.

Details. Intimate pieces of Juana.

Female friends expected a fair trade. Juana had been asking more questions lately, deeper questions. The woman knocked on

Lee's boundaries as if they were doors to open.

"I think I get it," Juana said, leaning back in her chair. "But you're not even thirty-two yet. And a lot of people have kids in their thirties."

Lee couldn't blink, couldn't look away from the compassion in Juana's face. The smile. The confidence. She fought the desire to say good-bye and go home.

"Okay, time out." Juana's voice softened. "I don't get it at all, do I."

Push back too hard, and Juana would walk away. Crack open her soul, and Juana would run.

And what, you'd miss her? Please.

But yes. She would. A hole would be ripped in her week. Juana's texts, phone calls, coffee dates.

Lee might as well test whether or not this bridge between them would burn, and if it did, well, better it happen before she'd stepped too far across. Besides, no friendship was worth being subjected to this topic time and again.

"I can't have children." Maybe she wouldn't have to say more.

"Oh . . . but . . . how do you know? I mean . . ." Juana ducked her head, then met Lee's eyes again. "I mean, is that what a doctor told you?"

"As a medical professional, I'm telling you it isn't physically possible for me to have a child."

She reached across the table and put her hand on Lee's. "Okay."

She means well. Don't pull away. Juana withdrew her hand after a moment, and her fingers flattened against the faux grain of the table. Her mug sat forgotten near her other hand.

"You really don't want to talk about it, do you."

"I don't."

"If you change your mind, let me know. Sometimes talking things out makes them less . . . I don't know . . . heavy."

"Thank you."

Juana tugged her cappuccino closer. As she looked up, Lee's phone buzzed from the far end of the counter, out of children's reach.

"Oh," Juana said. "I'm sorry. I think it buzzed once before, maybe half an hour ago? I forgot to tell you."

"Not a problem." Lee stood up and retrieved the phone. Voice mail from an unknown number.

"Hi, this message is for Lee Vaughn." A high male voice. "It's Tim Burke. We've met at church briefly. I work real estate, got the house for Marcus. Your number was in the church directory . . . I'm sorry to call you, and this sounds awkward now that I'm saying it. I was wondering if you could have Marcus call me? If he's with you or if you see him soon. There must be something wrong with his phone, but I don't think the battery's dead, because it's ringing. I've been trying for a while, and he won't pick up. He was supposed to do something tonight, for a couple of refugees, long story but he never showed up or called. Right, okay, I'll stop rambling. Thanks, Lee."

Lee called Marcus. His phone rang . . . and rang. "Hi, you've reached Marcus Brenner, leave a message."

"Lee?" Juana said.

Lee snapped an open hand up and ducked away from eye contact and redialed Marcus. Voice mail again. She didn't leave a message. They never left messages. He would see that she'd called twice in one minute and call her back. Now.

Another minute ticked by while she stared at her phone.

"Lee, you look like you're going to be sick."

She couldn't explain without sounding paranoid — not unless she told everything.

162

And she couldn't say aloud that Marcus could be handcuffed in the trunk of a car, helpless in the dark, being transported like contraband over the border into the States . . .

Lee called Walt.

"Talk to me," he said. She had never called him before.

"Is Marcus home?"

"No, haven't seen him since he left this morning."

A draft seemed to enter the room. Lee shuddered. "He isn't answering his phone."

"You do realize there could be plenty of normal, stress-free reasons for that?"

"Someone else called me, trying to get hold of him. He didn't show up somewhere he said he would."

Walt was silent.

"He isn't one to break a commitment, especially without a word."

"You've got a point. I'll find him."

"He worked in Decatur today. I don't know of any other stops he was making, but Tim Burke is the one who called me, if you need more information from him."

"I'm on it, Lee. Not far from Decatur myself. Keep trying, and let me know the minute you get hold of him."

She shut her eyes. *And if I don't?*

"You hear what I said?"

"Yes."

"Good." He hung up.

Juana's hand settled on her shoulder and steered her to the kitchen table. She pushed down gently until Lee surrendered enough to sit in one of the white wooden chairs. She hid her hands under her thighs and stared at her phone on the table. *Call me, Marcus.*

"Can you tell me what this is about?" Juana said quietly.

With her question, the room refocused. The boisterousness of the boys drifted from the next room. The scent of birthday cake still coated the kitchen. Lee faced Juana across the table.

"Marcus might be in danger."

Juana's hand went to her heart, a genuine gesture, not an attempt at drama. "From the Constabulary? Like Becca was?"

Not exactly. "Yes."

"And Walt Cantrell, he can help?"

"He's trying."

"Oh, Lee."

Lee shook her head. "Please — don't."

Juana studied her a moment before bowing her head. She didn't speak, simply sat with her hands folded on the table. Lee cupped her phone in her hand and closed her eyes. *Please.*

She redialed. The phone rang . . . rang . . . one more, and his voice mail would —

The line picked up. No one spoke, but rough breathing broke over the distance.

"Marcus?"

The breathing faltered.

Lee's heart pounded. She pushed to her feet. "Marcus, is that you?"

"Lee."

"Where are you?"

No answer beyond the struggle for air she'd heard countless times. If it were a flashback, he wouldn't have picked up the phone. He should know where he was.

"Are you in Decatur?"

"No." The word barely surfaced enough for her to hear.

She closed her eyes. "All right. You need to tell me where you are."

Again, no words.

"Marcus, please."

"I wanted . . . to stay. Here. With you."

Here meaning Kearby? "Marcus —"

He hung up.

Lee grabbed her purse from where it hung on the back of a chair. Shoved her phone inside. "I have to go."

Juana stood, too. "Please let me know when you find him."

"Of course."

She didn't remember until she was backing her car out of Juana's driveway that she should call Walt.

"I believe he's in Kearby," she said before Walt could speak, "but he wouldn't tell me."

"And he didn't explain why?"

"He was having an attack, Walt. He hung up on me."

"Okay. Call his counselor."

"I . . . I don't have the number." She had her own counselor. She never expected to call Pete Gentry. "Do you?"

He huffed. "Go online and find it when you hang up with me."

Of course. She had to stop panicking and think.

"Listen, we need to find him. I'm heading back, but I'm a ways out. If we need a search party, there's plenty of church folks that —"

"No."

"Lee, this can't be about his privacy if he's in danger."

He was right, but she couldn't allow them to see Marcus caught in a panic attack. Couldn't let them discover everything about him he didn't want them to know. She closed her eyes and tried to find another option.

"I'm leaving Juana Mercado's. She's not far from Heath and Gloria."

No one was far from anyone in Kearby. Lee could picture Walt nodding his head, the cowboy hat dipping over his eyes. "They know enough?"

"They know everything you know."

"Then go find him and call me." Again, Walt hung up without closing pleasantries.

Lee got a receptionist at Pete's office who said he was in an appointment but would return her call as soon as possible. She drove another few miles, navigated the ribbon of gravel that was Heath and Gloria's driveway, and parked on the concrete slab beside the house. Theirs was what Texans described as Acadian, a stucco-and-brick combination with a long sloping roof and covered porch. Lee walked to the front door.

She should have called ahead.

She rang the bell, and in a minute, Heath opened the door. His face lit when he saw her, then darkened.

"Come in. What is it?"

"I — do you have a minute, please?"

Something rocked Heath back on his heels, probably the stilted courtesy that came out of Lee's mouth, but she had to hold onto something, and courtesy was as good as anything else.

Heath pulled the door all the way open. "Come in, Lee."

He led her down the hallway to the den, where sunlight through the tall windows brightened the chocolate walls. Gloria sat cross-stitching. She lurched to the edge of her chair when Lee entered the room.

"Lee, what a pleasant . . ." Her eyes widened, and her lips pressed flat. "Sit. Let me get you some sweet tea."

"No, thank you." She pulled out her phone. "I apologize for intruding on your afternoon, but Marcus needs help. He's somewhere in town, and we need to find him."

"Danger?"

"I'm not sure. He sounded panicked, and now he won't answer his phone." As she spoke, she tried calling him again. Voice mail. She shoved the phone back into her purse. "We have to find him. Immediately."

"And you think he's in Kearby," Heath said.

"Somewhere he would consider safe. The church or the park."

Heath stood and towered over the room, both with his height and with his mood. "Then let's go find him."

12

He had to get up. Had to move, lead Jason away from here for good. But he'd tried three times to stand up. Running had done something to his knee, and all his limbs felt like jelly. No flashback had ever drained him like this. He let the rotting bark press into his back and drew the good knee to his chest. He could breathe now, chest pain faded to a hard ache. He tried to pray for strength to get up — for anything, really — but words spiraled away from him.

The sun had been down for about an hour, and night insects buzzed around him. The earth was cooling a little. A floodlight shone through the trees at the edge of the walking path. The branches shifted, letting more light through them, and then . . . crunching footsteps.

Marcus worked to push himself up. On his feet, weight off the knee. He had to run again. He'd blunder through the trees, and

Jason would catch him in seconds. But he couldn't stand frozen like this. *Go. Run.* The footsteps drew closer, and he tried to mute his breathing. He wasn't hidden from the path now that he was standing.

Heavy steps, not a woman's or a child's. Strong, even, sure. Marcus backed farther into the trees, and his right leg buckled. He grabbed for a branch, nearly missed, and a twig ripped his palm. The man crossed in front of him, looking first to the other side of the path and then straight at Marcus, and details finally sank in. Hazel eyes. Six-foot-five. Rounded shoulders.

"You're here," Heath said. "I wasn't sure I'd find you."

He wasn't Jason. Marcus fought to believe it.

"Marcus, what happened?"

He used the tree trunks around him as crutches. Ten steps to the path of wood chips. He tried to think, but everything in his head washed out with one piece of knowledge. Heath had his back. Heath would fight alongside him if Jason came. Marcus wasn't alone.

It wasn't right. Marcus held onto the last of his crutch trees and found the word he needed.

"Go."

"Good plan. Can you walk?"

"No . . . you go."

Heath cocked his head and studied Marcus for a long moment, then shook his head. "I'll be insulted later. You left your truck door open and the lights on, so the battery's dead. I'll jump it in the morning. For now, come back to my place."

"I can't."

"Why not?"

No more risk. Not for Heath and Gloria.

"If you aren't coming back with me, I need to know why."

"It's not safe."

"For me?"

Nod.

"Because of the list? Did something happen?"

"It's not safe."

Heath stood studying him for a long moment that chafed Marcus to his bones. He had to find more words, convince Heath — this wasn't about his screwed-up brain overreacting to perceived threats. This was fact. Jason was looking for him.

"Can you tell me what this is about?" Heath said.

"You need to go." That's what it was about.

"If I tell you you're not thinking straight,

will you trust me?"

He'd told himself that, hadn't he? Not long ago. He matched Heath's gaze, but his hands trembled. He clenched them.

"Marcus, I know something happened."

"Jason's here." The words barely hit a whisper, but they brought everything back. His heart skipped.

"Jason Mayweather. You saw him."

"He saw me."

"Here?"

"Church. New Mercies."

For a moment, Heath's gaze drifted over Marcus's shoulder, calculating. Then he refocused. "Does this man know who I am, have any way to connect me to you?"

Did he? Jason could know anything. No, not anything. Think. He was acting on his own here. He didn't have surveillance teams or technology on his side. He'd been in that church because it was a church, and Marcus would of course have joined — oh no, those people, if Jason thought they knew Marcus . . .

"Think about it," Heath said. "Jason Mayweather doesn't know anything about me."

"No."

"He's got no way to track you to my place. No reason to threaten me. That's right, isn't it?"

"Yeah."

Heath motioned Marcus to the path. "Come on then."

Marcus followed. Shielded by the darkness, he favored his knee as much as possible. The gravel parking lot seemed to be trying to trip him. The leg of his jeans was too tight against the swelling. He made it to the Jeep one step at a time.

He hoisted himself into the passenger seat, grabbed his leg in both hands, and pulled it inside. When the knee bent, he bit down on a cry.

Heath leaned in from the driver's side. "You're hurt?"

"Knee." Marcus exhaled long through clenched teeth.

"You need a doctor?"

If nobody ever asked him that again, it would be good. "No."

While Heath drove, he called Lee. Her voice on the other side of the phone was terse, but Marcus made out a low "thank you" before Heath hung up. He tried to figure out what he should think of this, Lee roping Heath into a search when they both knew the danger, but Marcus might still be huddled against that rotting log if Heath hadn't come. The relief and gratitude inside him had to be wrong, but he couldn't stop feeling it.

"Now call them." He had to force the words.

"Who?" Heath said.

"Church. Make sure they're okay."

"I'll do that when we're home."

"No. Now."

The call was brief, and then Heath dropped his phone into a cup holder between them. "They're all fine. And aware now."

"Thanks," Marcus whispered.

Easy silence filled the Jeep. Marcus tipped his head back and closed his eyes, then snapped them back open. Too vulnerable. His body would slam into a wall of panic.

But . . . no. His pulse didn't stutter. His lungs didn't squeeze. He glanced across the gearshift console, but Heath kept driving as if he hadn't noticed.

I'm not alone.

He drew in a shaky breath and let it out. "Thanks."

"Anytime."

Something was happening to him. As if he were seeing himself from above, a long camera shot in a movie — running from Jason when he should be standing his ground, driving with sweaty hands and gray-spotted vision when he should be pulling over, staggering along the park path unable to pray and then curling up there, scared. He lowered his head to his hands.

"Lord God," Heath said quietly. "Please come be with us."

Marcus couldn't lift his head.

"We need wisdom in how to deal with this. And we need safety. Please grant them in abundance. And, Father, I ask You put Your hand on Marcus right now. Give him strength and peace. Amen."

Amen. Not alone. A dry sob came from Marcus's gut. His shoulders shook.

"Close to home, brother," Heath said. "Hang on, Marcus."

Minutes passed. The Jeep slowed. Turned. Turned a few more times, and then stopped. Marcus forced his head up. Through the windshield shone a soft yellow porch light, and parked a few feet down the driveway was Lee's car. He opened his door and eased to the ground, biting the inside of his cheek to stay quiet. Heath loped over to him and tossed Marcus's arm over his shoulders, stooping to even their height.

They hobbled to the back door. Lee stood holding the screen open. She touched his shoulder as Heath passed through sideways and Marcus hopped over the threshold after him.

"Marcus?" Lee's voice was steady, but her lip quivered.

"I'm here." All he knew for sure.

She kept her hand on his back as Heath helped him to the living room and lowered him to the couch. Gloria appeared from the study at the other end of the room and watched them, one hand clutching a half-finished piece of stitched fabric.

He had to get his leg up. Pride couldn't matter, and anyway, Heath and Gloria had seen him rawer than this. Marcus reached for his leg, but Lee's hands grazed his.

"Let me." She lifted his leg onto the cushions, and the throbbing that kept time with his pulse faded a little.

Gloria perched on the low table in the center of the room, focusing on him. He swallowed. So much care in her eyes, in Heath's, but he might not be able to take that right now. His chest still felt bruised by booted kicks.

Lee kept her hand on his knee a second too long. Could probably feel the heat of it. Her eyes met his. "How bad?"

"Ice."

"All right." But she didn't move away from him. "I called Pete's office for . . . for assistance. He wasn't available at the time, but he called me back several minutes ago and said you can call him now if you need to."

The thought of hearing Pete's voice on the other side of the phone was enough to shake him up again. Maybe he should call, but he couldn't tonight.

"What happened?" Lee said.

Here with him, some of the dearest people he had. He could tell them everything. He brought a quaking hand to splay over his face.

"Marcus," Gloria said quietly.

They all thought Marcus was breaking. He had to prove he wasn't.

13

"It's okay." Gloria's voice was soft as a blanket.

Marcus's hand lowered to his side, and a crinkle formed between his eyes as he met hers. Color was seeping back into his face. Had his pallor persisted, Lee would have worried about shock. His movements were slow, heavy, as if staying upright required effort. Lee hadn't seen him so depleted since his days in physical therapy.

Gloria moved from her perch on the table to claim the chair nearest him. "Is there anything you need right now, anything you want?"

"A drink."

"I'm sorry?"

Lee's stomach clenched for him as he realized what he'd said. He shook his head while a shaky sigh poured out of him.

His gaze lifted to Heath and Gloria. "I've

been sober one year, five months, eleven days."

"Can we help you with that?" Gloria said.

"No. It's okay. I'm okay. You asked, and I said . . . my first thought." He latched a hand onto his neck.

"All right, then. Anything else you need?"

"Ice. Please."

Yes. Needed. Heat from the knee was radiating through his jeans. He might have sprained it. "Heath, do you have — ?"

"In the freezer door, there's an eye mask for headaches." Heath caught her eyes. "I'll show you."

He led her to the kitchen. Lee pulled open the freezer door. Gloria's voice continued from the other room, a balm for Lee's nerves. She found the gel eye mask, but it was too small to wrap around a knee. Instead, she grabbed a bag of peas. Heath stood in the corner of the counter between sink and oven, watching her.

"Thank you," she said.

"It was Jason Mayweather. Marcus saw him in Decatur and had to run. That's what triggered this."

Lee stopped breathing. "Did Mayweather identify him?"

"Marcus says he did."

"But didn't follow him?"

"I'm guessing we'd know by now if he had."

Her chilled hand contracted around the bag of peas. Mayweather. Here. Less than an hour's drive away.

They had to do something.

Such as?

"He tried to get me to leave him." Heath scrubbed at his hair.

"Not surprising."

"It was to me."

That wasn't a question. She didn't have to answer it. "I'd like to offer him ibuprofen as well, if you have it. He won't take Tylenol."

Heath's eyebrows drew together.

"He never took painkillers of any kind before . . ." In a blink, she was back in a metallic-smelling truck bed with Marcus, while he coughed and held his broken ribs. "Motrin was necessary for a while. He was terrified when he finally stopped taking it, that he'd go through withdrawal."

"Can people go through Motrin withdrawal?" But warmth entered Heath's eyes. Sympathy, not judgment.

"Not the way you're thinking. But I couldn't convince him of that."

He crossed the kitchen to a cabinet next to the sink, found a white plastic bottle, and shook two blue gel capsules into his hand. "It makes sense, in a way."

"It's utterly illogical."

"That, too. But sober eighteen months, that's still a tough road, even without all the rest of this."

"It was nine years before that."

Understanding entered Heath's eyes. He filled a glass with water and motioned her back to the living room. "I'm going to call New Mercies and find out whether Mayweather's been back there."

She couldn't hold in the shudder.

"Lee." He handed her the glass. "Why did he tell me to leave him?"

"For your protection, I'm sure."

"There was more to it than that."

She set the bag of peas on the counter. Perhaps ignoring the question wasn't fair to Heath or to Marcus.

"It's his distrust of the church. I'm part of the church."

"No. He's simply . . . He thrives among trustworthy people, yet isolation is his strongest defense mechanism." A concept Hannah had taught her.

She couldn't make Heath understand without a biographical summary, but it wasn't her place to tell Marcus's life story. That he'd clung to an old illustrated *Trea-*

sure Island all the way to adulthood because it was the only thing his mother ever bothered to give him. That he never knew his father, that he'd been an alcoholic by his senior year of high school. That since she'd known him, he had chosen isolation not only to protect himself and others, but also as penance for mistakes.

"Whatever he said, it wasn't personal against you."

"I'll trust that. Thank you."

Lee returned to the living room and sat again on the couch beside Marcus. He hissed as she lifted his leg and eased two pillows under his knee. When she tucked the frozen bag around it, he turned his face to the wall and blew out a long breath.

"All right?" she said quietly.

"Thanks," he said.

He took both pills, downed them, and drank the whole glass of water. He seemed steadier as he set the glass onto the table.

"Did Heath tell you?"

"You saw Mayweather."

"He was inside the church. Talking to people."

As if he'd heard the fear edging Marcus's voice, Heath ambled into the room and dropped a hand to Marcus's shoulder. His phone was held to his ear. "He'll probably be back. . . . Exactly. We're concerned for y'all. . . . I'd call them regardless of the results. But be aware of the possibilities here. . . . You, too." He closed the phone and spoke to Marcus. "If he comes back, they'll deny knowing you."

"He won't believe that."

"Do we run?" Lee said.

Heath and Gloria gaped at her as if she'd suggested something immoral, but this decision belonged only to Marcus. Some part of Lee screamed *run* while the rest of her demanded *where?* An aimless flight south. A nomad life. If they tore up their roots now, they might never replant. But she could live rootless with Marcus and never regret a moment.

Violet, however . . . she could not ask that of Violet.

Before Lee could catalog the people they would lose or determine what she'd choose if the choice belonged to her, Marcus was shaking his head. He held her gaze through a veil of fatigue.

He wasn't choosing isolation. He wasn't shutting everyone out. Lee took his hand. "You're certain this is what you want."

"No."

What?

"When I try to . . . in my head . . . to

leave . . . it's wrong." A crinkle formed between his brows, almost as if he were listening. "We're not supposed to."

"Good," Heath said.

The look Marcus shot at him was almost belligerent. "I don't know why."

"You don't have to right now, do you?"

"Would help."

Marcus raised his hand halfway to his neck, and a soft "oh" escaped Gloria. In his lap, the shaking had been less obvious. He clenched his fist and lowered it to his side.

"Adrenaline. I'm okay." His glance toward Lee acknowledged the definition he'd stretched with that statement.

Hannah had helped Lee establish a mental "safe place" for herself the first time they'd discussed the day she was raped. She'd chosen a garden that brimmed with flowers of every color and was always full of sunshine. She could lie on springy grass with blossoms near her face, smell them, watch them bob in a breeze. She hadn't needed the safe place until the second time. She'd been relating the story as clinically as possible when Hannah asked some gentle question — she still couldn't remember what it was — and in a heartbeat, Lee had been back to the place she visited only in nightmares, screaming through a black hood, pinned under warm weight, her skin bare below the waist and chafing against cold concrete. Hannah had worked hard to pull her back from that concrete to the warmth of her garden.

Pete might have helped Marcus create a safe place like that. Lee tried to imagine what his would be. A beach, maybe. Or a wide meadow, sky spreading in every direction, unobscured. If he could find that place, his body could rest sooner. But Lee didn't know how to help him find it.

She clenched her fists in her lap to keep from pounding the arm of the couch. He must have driven the expressway mid-attack. He could have been killed. But he wasn't.

And he'd somehow found his way to the park. It wasn't impossible for his panicked brain to latch onto a place he associated with both safety and calm. He'd been there enough times for the directions to come automatically.

No, I know this was You.

A blush was rising from Marcus's neck, pushing into his cheeks, and he shuddered as if buffeted by wind. He lifted his head. He glanced at Lee beside him. At Heath perched on the edge of the brick fireplace, knees poking up halfway to his chin. Then at Gloria.

"I'll be okay," he said.

Future tense. Full honesty. Lee squeezed his hand.

Gloria stood. "You're staying?"

"Yeah."

"We could play Pictionary."

The incongruity hung in the air a moment. A slow smile warmed Heath's eyes, and he wrapped an arm around his wife. Lee bit her lip against a welling in the back of her throat. These people never stopped giving.

Marcus let out a long breath. "Yeah. Okay. Pictionary."

Lee's phone vibrated in her pocket. She'd texted Violet and Austin when Heath called her, but neither had responded yet. She pulled out her phone — oh, Austin *had* texted her back. She had been too distracted to notice.

You have him yet?

She typed a response. *Yes. Mayweather was in Decatur.*

Inform Walt?

If you would please. He knows Marcus was found safely.

Calling him now.

The second text was Violet's, sent two minutes ago. *Still praying!*

Marcus is safe, Lee texted. *Details later.*

"Lee," Marcus said. "Who . . . ?"

"I asked Violet to pray. And if we hadn't found you soon, Walt and Austin would have joined the search."

His lips parted, and he shook his head.

"We're not going to lose you." The words came without being measured first, each with a fierceness that surprised her as much as the others in the room.

He reached for her hand and laced their fingers. Of course, he heard what she didn't say.

I'm not going to lose you. Again.

Gloria stood up. "I'll go get the game. Texas versus Michigan, or battle of the sexes?"

They chose the latter. In the next several hours, the tension in Marcus didn't release, and he was too quiet. But his hands stopped shaking in time for his first turn to draw. His breathing grew deeper, easier as the hours and the games wore on. He grinned at Gloria's attempt to draw a hair dryer. Heath shouted "Greenhouse!" after Marcus had sketched barely three lines, and they fist-bumped.

The word might as well scroll across his face. *Safe.*

Not long before midnight, Lee left him in the care of friends.

14

Soft voices. Marcus dragged his thoughts from the pit of sleep. It had to be late. Heck, he had to start sleeping at his own place. No more of this neediness. He'd lain awake on Heath and Gloria's couch for most of the night. Too much darkness, too much quiet, but mostly fear of moving in his sleep. The knee hurt. More than he could say to any of them, even Lee.

He stretched and bit back a moan. Yeah, he'd more than jacked it. This felt . . . well, a lot like the original injury, if he let himself touch those memories. He measured out a few breaths and tuned in to the hushed conversation that had pulled him awake.

"It'll come down to our safety," Gloria said. "For him, anyway."

"Which is why someone besides him has to be part of the strategy." Something creaked — Heath leaning back in one of the wooden chairs.

A beam of light from the kitchen cut a path across the carpet behind Marcus. The scent of coffee drifted through the house, along with something sweet and a little nutty. Pecan pie. What time was it?

Marcus pushed himself up and braced on his elbows. He lowered his foot to the floor. Heat pulsed through his leg. Long breath, in, out, then on his feet. The light from the kitchen — sunlight. It wasn't night, after all; the dark blue living room drapes were shut. He shuffled to the kitchen and blinked and squinted.

"Marcus." Gloria was on her feet before he could cross the threshold. "I've got biscuits and gravy."

"Thanks."

"And coffee, of course."

"Please."

Gloria beelined to the coffeepot and opened the cupboard for a mug.

The sound of the liquid pouring from the pot was enough to calm most of his lingering edginess. Marcus eased into an empty kitchen chair and swiveled toward the rooster clock on the wall above the stove. Six-thirty in the morning.

"Why are you up?" Neither of them were morning people, and if they didn't have to be anywhere . . .

Heath smiled, halfway through a slice of pecan pie. "Figured you'd want to get an early start. I won't be heading to church for another few hours."

"Sorry."

"Not at all. We're glad to have you."

He knew they meant it. Texans were some of the most hospitable people on the planet. But it wasn't only culture that made Heath and Gloria who they were. Gloria returned from the kitchen alcove to stand at his shoulder. She set the mug in front of him first, followed by a bottle of vanilla-flavored creamer and a plate of steaming biscuits, slathered in her spicy sausage gravy. His stomach rumbled. He added creamer to his mug, and the first sip soothed the tension in his neck.

"Eat up," Heath said, "and then we'll head to the park for your truck."

He dug into the biscuits and gravy. Gloria flitted off to the bathroom to finish her hair and makeup, and Heath got himself a second piece of pie. That wasn't his only breakfast, was it? In a few minutes, Gloria emerged looking, well, finished — black curls tamed to dip around her shoulders.

Heath used his fork to scrape up the last crumbs of pie from his plate. "We've been talking, Marcus. Kearby's not far from Decatur. Mayweather's likely to show up in town at some point."

Not a new thought, but the truth of it fed adrenaline into his system. He nodded.

"Walt's got the word out to most everyone about the list, and he gave Jason's description, but it's time for people to know your role in this."

Marcus clamped one hand onto his neck. Not this again.

"If the congregation knows, they'll be on guard on your behalf." When Marcus didn't answer, Heath nudged his plate away. "You still don't believe they'll do that."

The edge in Marcus pressed hard, a sensation almost as physical as a rib out of place. His right hand drew into his chest, feeling the phantom grip of a handshake he'd thought was a pledge of trust.

"So you've got a plan," he said. "Use them to guard me."

Heath's frown held more than disagreement. Offense was painted in it too. "Use them? They'll volunteer."

Yeah. Volunteer. Like Clay had volunteered Marcus's identity. "No."

"How do we prove it to you, brother? What do we have to do?"

We. But there was no proving it. Betrayal was a fact. As smart as Heath was, he was still naive. And Texas had been different, even before secession. Re-education had been respectful. Constabulary agents had targeted true threats whenever possible. Texans didn't really know the Constabulary. All the more reason Heath couldn't know how his church would respond.

"I've told you," Heath said, "a body doesn't amputate pieces of itself. Especially the body of Christ."

Marcus surged to his feet, fist hitting the table, chair teetering behind him. Forks jumped on plates. Coffee sloshed over the edge of his mug. Gloria stared at him. A sour taste filled his mouth.

"Sometimes it does," he said.

"Don't let —"

"I was a part, Heath. And I got amputated."

Heath winced, and then something full and heavy entered his eyes. Sadness, maybe.

The rush of heat left Marcus's face. He slumped into his chair. Grabbed a napkin from the holder on the table and soaked up the ring of coffee around his mug. Kept his head down. Something deep in him struggled to speak, if he could figure out what it wanted to say. To ask.

Heath's chair creaked. "There's something else, Marcus."

He lifted his head. "Okay."

"Agent Mayweather. Do you know him well enough to anticipate his plan?"

Yesterday's images struck him in the chest. Jason's blue eyes widening, the moment of stillness before he broke into a run. He curved his hands around his coffee mug.

He cleared his throat. "His plan is to find me and kill me."

They waited while he tried to decide what else they needed to know. "Go on," Gloria said.

"He doesn't have access to Constabulary resources. He's on his own. Tracking me the old-fashioned way. So he's frustrated. And now he's seen me, so he's more frustrated."

"So what'll he do?"

"Jason doesn't plan. He doesn't stop and think. He acts based on . . . his mood. How his day went. What he wants right then, not what he might want in an hour. You can't predict him."

"Okay," Heath said. "Are you concerned he'll threaten the church to get to you?"

"I walked into New Mercies. Like I belonged. He saw that. He won't leave them alone. But that doesn't mean he's planning against them. It's not that . . . organized, in his head."

Gloria shifted in her seat. "Why didn't he kill you before, Marcus?"

Cold metal barrel against his temple. It had happened so many times. He breathed in as if to remind himself Jason hadn't ever pulled the trigger.

"Marcus?"

"Sometimes I think he just never wanted to kill me more than he wanted . . ." *To break me.* "Sometimes it was like he couldn't kill me because he still hadn't figured out why he hadn't, before. But sometimes I think . . . This might not be in the Bible, but sometimes I think God didn't let him."

They sat quietly. After a minute, Marcus could eat again. He finished his biscuits and washed his dishes, ignoring Gloria's protest. Then he and Heath headed out to the Jeep. They didn't talk on the short drive to the park, and their conversation while jumping the truck consisted of "Okay, ready, give it a try."

Even when Marcus sat behind the wheel of his idling truck, nothing was said. Heath seemed to have a thought lurking behind his eyes, something he wanted to say, and maybe Marcus should have asked, but instead he thanked Heath again and left. He pulled out his cell as he headed to Walt and Millie's and called to cancel his three clients scheduled today. Nobody seemed upset, but the Dunhams again stated that they didn't want to close on their house until he'd looked it over. He had explained he wasn't an inspector, and Gwyneth said he was "better than nothing," then blushed at his smile. He could like them both, if they stayed. On the phone now, Al told him their daughter had been brought to them late last night by one of the New Mercies church members and didn't ask what had prevented Marcus.

When he reached Walt's place, the beige car sat in the drive. Great. He'd talked to Walt last night long enough to inform him. Not long enough to argue. Marcus went inside and fed the dog.

Yesterday's events had cemented at least one thing for him. Whenever Jason caught up with him, he couldn't be living in somebody else's home. If Jason decided to shoot at him from across a room, from outside a house, it had to be Marcus's house that was shot up, Marcus alone whose body could catch that bullet.

He packed his clothes and his Bible into a few plastic grocery bags he found in a stash under the kitchen sink. He filled another bag with the semi-quiet fan he used at night, the lavender candles he lit an hour before bed, suggestions from Pete to ground each of his senses while he slept. Lastly, from the plug in the corner, he grabbed his personal night light — a red-caped cartoon superhero. He'd been in the store trying to find a plain white cover, frustrated by all the Disney princesses and butterflies, when he found this one. Pete would have frowned at the choice, given its connection to Jason, but Marcus didn't *want* to forget Jason's kid. Ever. The night light, so similar to the one in J.R.'s bedroom, reminded Marcus to pray for him.

Nothing else in Walt and Millie's house belonged to him. Except, well, the dog.

Walt must be upstairs. Preoccupied. Leaving without a word chafed at Marcus. If they were going to have a confrontation, they might as well have one now.

He stood at the bottom of the stairs and called up. "Walt." He went back to the kitchen.

Walt lumbered in a minute later. "You're right, we need to talk."

"Go ahead." He had nothing to say.

Walt perched on a stool at the kitchen bar and planted his elbows on the counter. "Either you tell them, or I tell them."

Hot and cold flooded his body. He didn't

let himself shiver. "The church."

"I'm sorry, Marcus. But you're wrong about this, and I can't let you endanger yourself. It's my job to keep you out of Jason Mayweather's custody if I can. And I'm done letting you fight me on it."

"Walt —"

"Will you tell them?"

He braced his arm on the wall. His legs might not hold him up.

Walt's hands steepled. "It's necessary. You've got to know that, after all this."

" 'All this' proves they shouldn't know. He's close. He's going to come here. He's going to ask."

"I'm done trying to convince you. I'm telling you as a law enforcement officer tasked with your safety that I'm calling a church meeting, and those in attendance will be informed that you're a target of the Constabulary."

Marcus shuffled to the kitchen table, pulled out a chair, and sank into it. Cold dripped into his body. He folded his arms against the freeze in his chest.

"If you want me to do the talking, I will."

"No." That would be wrong.

"The meeting won't be announced at church, so we won't have any Constabulary stalkers. I won't give details in the email.

We don't want anything Mayweather could get his hands on later."

A nod. All he had in him.

"I'll get in touch with a few folks and let you know what day this week. Your choice to be there or not."

He nodded again. Tightened his arms against his body and shivered.

"I'm sorry. I hope you believe that."

Sorry didn't matter if he told them anyway. If Marcus got amputated from this body too.

"What's in all the grocery sacks here?"

He lifted his head. "My place is ready. I'm moving in."

"Ready? There's not a stick of furniture in there."

"I'll get some today."

Walt's mouth crimped. "That's not necessary, Marcus."

"It is."

"I guess a house in someone else's name is as safe as anywhere for you right now." He shook his head and clapped Marcus on the shoulder. "Going to miss you, though."

"I'll be back for dinner sometimes." But not before Jason's presence was resolved.

The seventeen-pound bag of dog food lay on the lowest shelf of Millie's pantry. Marcus stacked the stainless steel bowls on top and managed to lift it without bending his knee too far, but carrying it to the truck, the added weight on his leg, was a struggle. Good thing he hadn't bought a bigger bag. And good thing he hadn't tried to work today.

He started driving. The dog thrust its nose out the window and shut its eyes against the wind, and a smile stole onto Marcus's face.

"You need a name, dog."

At his place, he got the bag of dog food inside the back door and dropped it with a thud that made the dog's ears lower. Marcus petted its head and looked around his house. Sturdy, good . . . and empty.

Even if he didn't mind sleeping on the bare floor, the knee wouldn't tolerate that.

He needed a mattress and enough pillows to keep it elevated while he slept. A chair or two, a table, would be a bonus, but he could move in without that. He wasn't running the AC given how infrequently he was here, but he could turn it on anytime. The utilities were on in his name.

Could Jason get access to utility bills?

No. What would he do, call the electric company and ask for Marcus's address? They'd never give it to him.

Unless he claimed to be legitimate police. No, not even then. He'd have to prove it in writing. He couldn't call for something like that.

Marcus sighed and limped to the living room. He should try to get some kind of work done, if not for his clients then for himself. He wouldn't be able to stand long enough to paint the walls, but the baseboards could be painted while he sat on the floor. He'd already taped them off, last week when crouching had been doable.

Paint had a productive smell that had never bothered him, but he opened a window in case dogs were sensitive to it. Then he opened a small can of ivory semigloss and settled in. His shoulders relaxed as he worked. An hour wore away, and he made decent progress. Jason was never far from his mind, but he could focus on the task of his hands. When he couldn't, he prayed.

The dog lay down in the middle of the room as though trying to hide the worst of the carpet stains. Marcus had only laid a drop cloth here in the corner where he painted, dragging it along with him.

He'd left his phone on the kitchen counter and barely noticed when it began to buzz. He pushed to his feet, one hand bracing on the wall, hopping on one foot until he regained his balance. He hobbled to the kitchen. Lee was at work, and he'd called his clients, and random people didn't tend to call him at not quite ten in the morning.

He picked up his phone as it went to voice mail. Chuck Vitale.

Marcus's protocol was clear: *don't call me, I'll call you.* He'd changed his cell number the week he got to Texas, and a Texas number couldn't be a contact in Chuck's phone. Probably Marcus shouldn't call him either, but Belinda would never have stood for that, and anyway . . . Sometimes, Marcus wanted to hear their voices. Wanted to hear about their bird-watching trips and their grandkids he'd never meet.

Well, Chuck wasn't breaking the rules to tell him about bird watching. Marcus cupped his phone in his hand and stared at it. Was it safe to call them back?

He tapped the screen to redial. If he got voice mail, he wouldn't leave a message.

"There you are." The gruff voice pulled a smile onto Marcus's face. "Didn't think you'd call back so fast. Figured you were working."

"I took a day off." Marcus leaned against the counter.

"A sick day? You doing all right?"

"Just needed a day."

"Doesn't sound like you."

"I, um . . ." He'd avoided this kind of conversation for half a year. Easy to do from a distance. Maybe it was time for Chuck to know a little more. "I've got a bad knee. Did a number on it yesterday."

"A permanently bad knee?"

"Yeah."

The slight pause waited for Marcus to clarify this wasn't the doing of the Constabulary, and then Chuck sighed. "Tell you what, get some ice on it and you'll be back to work in no time. I remember our youngest messing up his shoulder in hockey when he was a kid, and ice made all the difference."

"Okay." Marcus leaned both elbows on the counter, all his weight on his left leg. "Chuck, why'd you call me?"

"It's kind of funny. Now we're talking, it's not an easy thing to find words for."

Marcus's neck tightened. "What's wrong?"

"Nothing, not a thing. Belinda's fine, I'm fine. It's about that Bible you gave me."

"No. Don't." Danger washed over Marcus.

"Nobody's listening in on an old man's phone conversations."

An old man whose house had been used as a haven for Christian fugitives. An old man who had traceable connections — minor, but still — to the former resistance leader. Chuck had no guarantee he wasn't being watched. The dog padded into the kitchen and stared up at Marcus while he shook his head as if Chuck could see him.

"You've been gone six months, son, and in that time I've done nothing against them. I promise you, they're not paying any attention to me."

"Okay." His voice rasped.

"I read that Bible."

He hopped to the corner of the counter, next to the sink, and leaned on his elbows. The square edge dug into his back. "All of it?"

"Started in Matthew, like you told me. Stopped for a while when . . . you know, when we lost you. Then started back up.

Read the whole New Testament. That book Acts of the Apostles, I liked that one a lot. They were something else, those guys."

"Yeah."

"Figured I should read the Old Testament, too. So I did."

"Well, then you've read more than me."

"Some of those prophets, now. That's grit right there. Don't know there's anyone left like them anymore."

"I haven't read all the prophets."

"Check out Hosea some time."

"Okay."

A pause, and then Chuck cleared his throat. "Anyway, when I finished Malachi, I told myself — well, old man, you did what Marcus asked. You read the Bible."

Marcus had asked him to read the Gospels, not the entire book, but he let Chuck tell the story in his own time. A prayer filled him, wordless, Chuck's name in his head, in his hands as he brought it to God's throne and left it there.

"Then I asked myself if I believed it when it claims to be the words of God Himself. Or if I thought it was just some historical document. And, son, I was nervous about believing it. I knew what God said, see. I knew what His Son said. If I believed it, I had to do something with it. And being

205

nervous like I was, I finally realized — I wouldn't be if I didn't know in my gut that it's all true."

Marcus bowed his head, chin to his chest, and closed his eyes. "It is."

"I know, Marcus. All this time, you were right." Chuck's voice caught. "I believe, son."

A noise choked out of Marcus. *Thank You, God.*

Chuck's quiet laugh choked a little, too. "Bet you never expected to hear those words from this stubborn old man."

"Prayed to."

"Oh, I bet you did. We're two stubborn peas in a pod."

Marcus huffed, and Chuck laughed. For a minute, they were quiet. He pushed away from the counter and gritted his teeth at each step back to the living room. The dog followed. Marcus slid down the wall, right leg extended, and the dog shook itself, then padded over to lie at his feet.

"You remember what you told me the night Aubrey Weston died?"

Marcus closed his eyes. "Probably not. Parts of that night are sharp for me . . ." *Too sharp.* "But parts are blurry."

"But you remember the girl, Payton?"

"Yeah."

"You said, 'God has to pay for it.' Not me."

Maybe he had said that. All his words that night were part of the blur.

"I know it wasn't a sin the way we think of them. Not willful, you know. But it's good to have the stain washed off."

Yeah, he got that. He couldn't find anything to add to Chuck's words, and quiet nestled around him again.

"So now," Chuck said, "we pray for our women."

"Lee's a Christian, Chuck."

"Since when?"

The hint of indignation pulled Marcus's face into a smile. "Since October. A few days after we got here."

"Well, how about that. I'll have to tell Belinda she's the last hold-out. See how she likes those apples."

"Is she reading the Bible?"

"I think she made it through Matthew. Then she stopped."

They talked awhile, longer than they'd talked since last summer. Chuck steered the rest of their conversation to the kind of small talk they had fallen into when Marcus used to work on projects at the Vitale house. Weather, of course. Chuck swore when Marcus told him about Kearby's week of

207

eighty degrees. Then the economy, the yard work Chuck had been tackling now that the snow had melted, and Marcus's new place, about which Chuck had endless questions.

"Send me pictures when you're finished with it," he said.

A senseless piece of Marcus wanted to tell Chuck about Jason. About the tremor in his limbs today every time he relived yesterday, every time he imagined the next time Jason found him. But he couldn't say any of it. Chuck hung up a few minutes later with no idea.

Marcus set his phone on the carpet beside him. Time to get back to work on the baseboards. Using both hands and his left leg, he pushed himself backward across the floor toward drop cloth, paint can, and brush.

The dog stood watching until Marcus had settled into place. Then it stretched out next to him and laid its head on his thigh, and for a second this dog could have been Indy. Marcus rested his hand on its head, and it licked its lips and gave a sigh.

"I hope they didn't have to shoot her," he said to the dog. "I hope she let them pen her and take her somewhere, and they put her to sleep. Sometimes I hope she got adopted. But she would have protected the house. Even though I was — was already —"

It wasn't a flashback this time, the dark room. It was a memory, pulling its claws through his brain. He stayed here, in the sunlight that shone through the windows of his Texas house, knowing the hunger in the dark wasn't now. The congestion in his lungs, the fever. The loneliness so sharp he could have bled from it. None of it was now.

He closed his eyes. "I miss that dog."

The back of his throat burned. His new dog lifted its head to lick his chin. He fought the surge inside and wondered if, for Indy, he'd lose the fight this time, but his eyes stayed dry.

He drew in a shaky breath and assessed the leg. No standing. No walking. Not yet. He had to stay here on the floor a little while longer, and then he'd get up and go buy pillows and a mattress and maybe a few other things to make this house ready for a man and a dog.

Violet was late.

Lee had already changed the Cidex and run the autoclave. True, she'd arrived early. The church clinic's official hours weren't until ten-thirty. But last night's sleep had been fitful. The minute she knew she could start setting up without triggering questions, she'd driven over here to work. She had looked forward to Violet's presence.

Pointlessly, it appeared.

She grabbed a roll of Scotch tape and the laminated signs from one of the kitchen-turned-clinic's cupboards and headed outside. The air-conditioning gusted out after her as she entered bright warmth, and she stood a moment with the sun warming the top of her head. Then she got to work — a sign for each church door, arrows directing them to the door nearest the old kitchen: *Walk-In Clinic This Way.*

By the time she returned inside, her phone

had received a text from Cora Hendershot. A work emergency. Possibly not showing up for a few hours. Lee and Violet would be fine, of course. Lee had worked her own clinic enough months that she could get by without an MD's guidance in many cases, though Cora had taught her a lot about what they referred to as "frontier" medicine. The first few times she'd worked as Cora's secondary had felt strange, but she had grown accustomed to her place. Violet was happy to observe most of the time, taking vitals when they were busy.

About half their patients came more than once. The others ghosted in, nervous and quiet, for conditions sometimes more serious than they knew or would admit. Lee had seen several cases of walking pneumonia, a baby with croup, a man with a broken toe. Her worst case had been a woman nine weeks pregnant, scared and bleeding. Lee sat with and cared for the woman as she lost her baby. That night had brought an old nightmare, and Lee awakened to Violet's voice praying. Violet didn't ask for details, but Lee nearly told her anyway, an overdue answer to the night she *had* asked. The night they met.

Lee taped the last sign to the main doors and returned inside. The door wasn't visible from inside the kitchen, but the short hallway connecting them carried the sound of the door opening. Lee attached a little bell to the inside handle and began to sanitize the room, white countertops and white walls and steel sinks, all of which were already clean. Her purse was in a locked cabinet, but her phone sat on the far counter, in the corner. It remained silent and dark.

About ten minutes to eleven, the bell tinkled against the door. Lee stepped into the hallway.

Violet hurried to her, tears drying on her cheeks. "I am so sorry, I know I'm twenty minutes late, and I know I don't do as much as I did when it was just us, but still, I said I'd be here."

"No one's shown up yet."

"Oh, good."

"Including Cora. You might be assisting me more than usual."

"You're by yourself?"

"Not entirely." Someone else must be somewhere in the building.

"Are you safe though, with that agent around? He knows you, too, not just Marcus."

She hadn't thought about herself, not as a target. But the man had met her. Had once

212

asserted dominance by touching her hair. She swallowed. "It's a valid point. I'll be more careful."

"Okay, good."

Most of Violet's tears had dried, but they shouldn't be ignored. "You weren't crying because you're late."

"N-no." She bit her lip.

"If you don't wish to talk about it —"

"I . . . actually . . . I guess I should tell somebody, and I'd rather tell you than anybody else."

A nettle of caution pricked between Lee's shoulders. "Are you all right?"

"Absolutely not."

Lee turned and marched back to the kitchen. Violet followed, and Lee shut the door while scenarios roared in her head. She motioned Violet to sit on the exam chair.

"I'm not hurt or anything." Violet perched on the edge of the chair. "It's . . . when Austin drove me over here . . ." She hid her face in her hands. "He kissed me. And . . . I . . . kissed him back. For a few whole seconds."

Lee sat on the wheeled office chair in the corner, drew her feet under her, and hooked the toe of one shoe on the wheeled chair base. Violet needed advice. She had none to offer.

"He's a ridiculously good kisser. I wish he wasn't."

What did that mean?

Violet jumped down from the exam chair and stood in front of Lee like a shamed student in the principal's office. Her thumb rubbed her wrist, a habit she'd nearly broken in the last month. "That sounds so shallow. Good grief. I'm pathetic."

"No," Lee said, because she knew at least that much. "You're conflicted."

"I can't be with him. The Bible says so. I tell myself eighteen's too young to know anyway. My mom would say it is. But it feels . . . being with him, it feels . . ."

"Safe?"

"Um, that's not the first word in my head for us."

Shouldn't it be?

"But sure, it's that too. If anybody ever tried to hurt me, Austin would hunt them down and shoot them. I really think he'd be mad enough to do it."

Not unlike Marcus, grabbing a gas station attendant and pinning him against a wall when he mistook the man for Lee's attacker. Such an old memory. But no, it had happened less than two years ago.

Violet wandered to the sink and started to wash her hands as she continued to speak. "It hurts him, being so far away from his sisters. Not being able to see they're safe. They talk on the phone at least once a week, but he says it isn't enough. I . . . I love that about him. I love how smart he is, the things he thinks about. I love his voice when he sings. And how we can ask each other anything. And, Lee, he really likes me. Not my body, me."

"You're surprised by that?"

"Not anymore, I guess." Red bloomed in her cheeks, and she dried her hands on a C-fold towel from the dispenser over the sink. "If we got married, my initials would stay the same. DuBay to Delvecchio. I think about that kind of crazy stuff all the time. I shouldn't."

"It seems natural to think about it." After all, she'd wondered if she would ever be Lee Brenner.

"Do I have to break us up? I mean, we're not dating anymore, but do I have to stop being his friend too?"

Lee tucked her hands under her thighs. "I'm sorry, Violet. I don't know."

"Oh."

The disappointment in her voice stung Lee like a slap. "I assume there's a passage in the Bible forbidding Christians and non-Christians to . . . marry."

"There is." New tears filled Violet's eyes. "And I get why. But I . . . but I'm making this sound like he needs to become a Christian so I can date him. That's not what I mean."

"I know."

"Okay." She grabbed another C-fold towel and dabbed it under her eyes. "Sorry. I've been trying not to talk about this with you."

Lee's face warmed. Of course, Violet knew Lee couldn't help with this. Of the two of them, Lee should be the one asking Violet for romantic advice. She stood and walked to the sink to hide her blush. Might as well wash her hands.

"Lee?"

"Yes?"

"I didn't mean I don't *want* to talk to you about Austin."

"It's fine. I'm hardly well-versed in the topic of male-female relationships."

Violet stepped closer to stand at her shoulder. "I thought it would annoy you. All my teen girl drama."

Oh. Lee shut off the faucet and faced her.

"Oh, Lee." Violet hugged her, hands flat against Lee's back. She'd have to rewash them. "I love you."

216

Violet said the words as easily as Lee said *no* and *yes.* Lee returned the hug.

When they stepped back, an idea came. "You could speak to Marcus about Austin."

Violet's eyebrows drew down. "Marcus is a guy."

"After his conversion, he remained my friend, despite the fact that he wanted more from our relationship."

"Oh, yeah." Violet started to wash her hands again. "Still, it seems weird, but maybe I'll —"

The bell on their door jingled, followed by a male voice. "Hello?"

Lee stepped into the hallway, face-to-face with a tall middle-aged man in jean shorts, sandals, and a button-down shirt. He held a bloody towel around his forearm, elbow bent to keep the wound above his heart. Intelligent patients always made Lee's job easier.

"Hello," she said, "please come in. How were you injured?"

"I live outside Decatur, where we had all the flooding." He followed her into the clinic and sat on the nearest exam chair. "Been cleaning out the basement now the water's gone down, ton of junk down there, including some old ductwork. Guess I wasn't careful enough."

"And you drove here?"

His hazel eyes were steady. "You know how it is, ma'am."

The only admission Lee needed. He was a displaced Christian without full-time work or health insurance. He probably wouldn't tell her his name; old habits lingered for many. She turned to Violet. "If you could draw up lidocaine and —"

"Iodine sponge and suture needle, I'm on it."

"Thank you."

They fell into a comfortable routine. While Violet gauzed away the seeping blood, Lee sutured the gaping inch-long wound. When she'd finished, the man fished several twenties out of his wallet.

"Will this at least cover your cost?"

"Of course," she said. "Thank you."

"Thanks for being here."

"Did you have a lot of damage to your house?" Violet wiped down the exam chair with an alcohol wipe and didn't look at him, reducing the gravity of the question.

"Some." He looked toward the door.

"In case you're not aware," Lee said before he could bolt, "a group from our church has been working in your area to help with cleanup. Feel free to contact us."

"I have a few neighbors who might need

the help. I'll see what they say."

Thinking of his neighbors, while he stood here with nine sutures in his arm. Lee motioned to the gauze pad she had taped over the wound. "Remember, it needs to stay dry."

"Thank you again." He gave a grim smile and walked out, and a moment later, the bell jingled.

Over the next several hours, the topic of Austin wasn't revisited, mainly due to a steady flow of patients. Lee provided free NSAIDs and cough drops, trimmed an elderly woman's toenails, and informed a man that she wouldn't be prescribing him Vicodin for any reason. He huffed and cajoled and complained until Lee added that their clinic didn't prescribe medications of any kind to anyone. At that point, he walked out.

"Bet we don't get any referrals from him." Violet rolled her eyes as she disinfected the counter and exam chairs and Lee packed instruments for the autoclave. Amazing the things a determined congregation could raise money for, all to help others.

Lee's phone chirped from its place in the corner. She finished the instrument pack in front of her, then checked it. Marcus. *Call me when clinic's done.*

When she had loaded the autoclave and all that remained was running it, she dialed him. He picked up after one ring.

"Hi." Tension laced his voice.

"Is everything all right?"

"Yeah, but I . . . if you're free, I could use a favor."

"Of course."

Violet stood near the doorway, ready to leave, eyes on Lee. She gave a slight nod: *nothing's wrong.* Violet nodded back.

"I can't stay at Walt and Millie's," Marcus said. "I'm moving into my place."

"Without furniture?"

"It's clean. All I need is a mattress."

"Marcus."

"Lee."

She poured a sigh into his ear. "All right. The mattress is the favor?"

"I'll reimburse you. Obviously."

That wasn't the only obvious fact. "Hauling a heavy object wouldn't be possible with your knee."

"Not today."

"Don't you need more than a mattress?" She would pick up groceries for him as well. Soap. The man had no concept of what was necessary to spend a night in a house.

"A few pillows would be good."

For his knee. He didn't sleep on pillows.

"And, um, that should be it."

He was absurd. "Not a problem."

"Okay. I'll see you in a couple hours?"

"Yes."

"Thanks."

He hung up, and Lee shoved her phone into her purse and motioned Violet to the door. "It appears I'm shopping for Marcus. If you'd like to come along, you could ask him your questions."

Violet rubbed her wrist and followed Lee to her car. She didn't speak until they were driving. "So we're buying a mattress?"

"He believes he doesn't need anything else to move into his house."

Violet laughed.

"Precisely."

"Guys. Seriously. Lee, how much money do we have?"

She darted a glance across the console. Violet's green eyes sparkled with plans. "We need to be frugal about this."

"Let's get him a painting to hang on the wall. Some old movie art or something. Or an artsy photo of a crumbling old farmhouse. He'd love that."

"Violet."

"Okay, but you're not going to buy him only a mattress, are you?"

"I had planned on food as well."

17

She purchased the mattress first. Sleeping on soft couches bothered his neck, so she chose semi-firm. At the nearest Walmart, she started in the grocery aisles, then meandered to home décor and had to say no to Violet at least once per aisle. Still, by the time they left, she'd spent double what she intended and regretted nothing. As they loaded bags into her car, Violet poked at one already tucked behind the front seat. Not Walmart.

"What's in that?"

Lee had nearly forgotten it was in her car. She deposited her bags on the other side of the car. "A casserole dish."

"Why don't you bring it in? We could use it."

"It isn't for me."

"Who, then?"

She didn't care to tell the whole story. "I broke something of Juana's, and I bought that as . . . a replacement."

They got into the car, and Lee headed back to the mattress store to pick up their first purchase. Violet waited a few minutes to make the obvious statement.

"Lee, you see Juana all the time. Did you just buy that yesterday or something?"

"No." She didn't allow herself to calculate how many months it had been in her car.

"Okay . . ."

She was a coward. That was the summary of the story. She didn't know how to bring up something that had happened last fall, something that had been her fault, something that she couldn't undo by offering a replacement off a store shelf. Not when the broken item had been an heirloom. She never should have bought it. She should take it back.

"Well, whenever you give it to her, I bet she'll like it," Violet said. The warmth in her smile held amusement too. She knew Lee well enough to guess any gift would be over-analyzed.

"Thank you." For not prying. Violet might be the only person Lee had ever genuinely wanted to hug.

They tied the mattress down to the roof of Lee's car, a more difficult feat than she expected. But their handiwork held, and a smile tugged her face as they neared Marcus's house. She parked in the garage, and her old car seemed to belong there beside his truck. She shuffled grocery bags to one arm and let herself and Violet in with her key.

A low growl came from the living room. Violet's wide eyes darted to hers.

Lee held up her hand. "Marcus?"

"Friends," came his voice, and the growl ended on a short bark. "Stop, dog."

"Is it safe?" Violet called.

"Violet? Hi. Yeah. Come in."

"So you have a . . ." Violet's voice trailed off as they entered the living room.

Marcus sat in the middle of the room. The dog, some kind of boxer mix, stood sentry, head lowered close to Marcus's chest, eyes on Violet and Lee, ears flat against its head. Marcus lifted a hand to its back.

"A dog, yeah," he said. "You didn't see his bowls in the mud room?"

"Our hands were full." Violet hefted her rustling grocery bags.

"Food?" Marcus's face brightened.

Lee plopped her armload down and set her hands on her hips. "A necessity of life."

"Right. Thanks. I was going to eat in town."

"So you brought dog food but no people

food?" Violet was clearly straining to hold back the smile; after a moment, half of her mouth tilted anyway.

"He showed up outside when I was leaving two nights ago. Nobody's claimed him yet. I put a notice on the board in the diner."

"Cool."

Violet ventured close and stroked the dog's head. It ignored her, focused on guarding Marcus, who still hadn't moved from the floor.

"Marcus," Lee said. "How bad is your knee?"

He turned his head and met her eyes, steady but worn to a fray. "I can't get up."

Her stomach clenched as she knelt beside him. "All right. We need to elevate the leg. I bought an ice pack, but it needs to go into the freezer first."

Relief filled his face, so intense it could have been a threat of tears if he were anyone else. "Thanks."

"We'll bring everything in. Don't try to get up."

"Okay." The dog sat next to him and nudged his shoulder.

She and Violet carried the mattress, tilting it to get it through the doorway, then tilting it again down the hallway to the master bedroom. They dropped it with a thud in the center of the room, and then they went out for the other large items. While Lee knelt in the living room and snapped tags off the accent pillows, Violet set the single kitchen chair in front of Marcus with a flourish. She sat in slow motion, crossing her leg and touching a pointer finger to the corner of her mouth in a model pose.

"This," she said, "is a chair."

"Okay."

"You sit in it."

"Sure."

"You're not allowed to live here without one."

"Well. Good you got one, then." Crinkles formed around Marcus's eyes.

Violet sprang out of the chair and pulled it to the open area connecting the kitchen and living room. She positioned it at the best angle to observe both rooms. "You can sit here and tell us where to put stuff."

Marcus's gaze traveled from Violet to Lee. "Stuff? You mean the food?"

"And some other stuff." Violet grinned.

He frowned. "Lee."

"Everything was clearance," Lee said. "Besides the mattress, we spent less than a hundred dollars." About thirty cents less, but Marcus's expression smoothed out.

"Wait until you see." Violet headed back

out to the car, still grinning.

Marcus looked across the room at the chair and gave a sigh. Lee helped him to his feet, and they teetered a moment, then steadied with her arm around his back and his arm over her shoulders. He didn't straighten his right knee, and his foot barely touched the floor.

"Ready?" she said.

"Yeah."

They hobbled fairly competently to the chair, and Marcus collapsed into it with a hard exhale.

"Will you see Dr. Platt?"

"I'll be okay in a day or two."

Before either of them could say more, Violet skipped into the room with more plastic bags looped over her arms.

"Stuff." She dropped everything at her feet and then stuck a hand into one of the bags. "Nothing but necessities."

She tossed a package of taupe queen-sized sheets to Marcus, and he caught them against his chest. She followed that reveal with the cheapest quilt (not patterned in flowers) that Lee had been able to find, a log cabin pattern in browns and greens.

"Totally manly bed," Violet said.

Marcus's shoulders shook in what might have been a chuckle.

"You desperately need a couch in here, but Lee convinced me you can live without one."

"Thanks," he said to Lee.

"Of course." She didn't try to hide her smile.

Violet's hands dove into another bag. "Kitchen stuff — first and foremost, a coffeemaker, of course. And we got paper plates. And plasticware. But that means you'll have stuff to throw away, which didn't occur to you, did it?"

"Um," Marcus said.

"So I present . . ." She ducked around the wall and produced the white plastic garbage can — lidless, basic, inexpensive. "We even have bags."

She waited until he nodded his approval, then showed him the can opener, the single blue bath towel, and the package of disposable razors, the last of which Lee had thought of while walking herself through his morning routine.

"These," Violet said, pulling out a bottle each of soap and shampoo, "are not for you, they're for everyone else."

He gave a twitch of a smile.

Violet's grin faded as she shifted from foot to foot. "One more thing."

Ah. The housewarming gift she'd insisted

on going to hunt for while Lee took everything else to the checkout line. Violet had gone through a separate line, paid for it herself, and hidden it inside the bag before Lee could see it.

She pulled said bag, small and folded over itself, from one of the regular grocery bags and opened it. Inside tissue paper nestled a small square of stained glass. A sun catcher? Interesting choice. As Violet held it up, light caught the design of a tree with green leaves surrounded by blue sky and yellow sun. The grass at the base of the square was lighter green, and the branches were a shade of brown that looked almost orange as the light played in it.

Violet set it in Marcus's hand. He cleared his throat, and she waited. When he said nothing, Violet rubbed at her wrist.

"Because you like the light," she said. "Sunlight, I mean, and you don't need a table to put this on, and you like to work with wood, which comes from trees, and everything else was butterflies and flowers."

Marcus's fingers curled around the square, dwarfing it.

"I wanted you to have something without any usefulness but being pretty."

He nodded.

"And . . ." Violet's voice fell. "I remember

when we first got to Texas how you watched everything outside, especially the trees. I wondered what it was about them that made you look at them so hard."

His thumb rubbed the stained-glass leaves. His other hand palmed at his cheeks, though his eyes were dry.

"Do . . . do you like it?"

He nodded.

"Okay." Violet stepped back, and her eyes found Lee's with a clear plea for help.

What could Lee say? She would never have chosen this gift for him. She knew everything about him Violet had said, yet the combination of them was uniquely Violet's.

"Would you hang it there?" He gestured to the living room window.

Violet fastened the suction cup and stepped back. Sunlight caught the colors, warming them and throwing them across the carpet in front of the window.

"Wow," she said. "Those fluorescent lights in the store didn't do it justice."

Marcus hunched silently in the chair, staring at the square of color.

"If it's not a good present, I could take it back."

"No," he said. "I didn't . . . expect it. But it's good. The house needs colors."

Violet smiled. "That's what I thought, too."

Lee supported him into the kitchen while Violet brought the chair. Most of the food required refrigeration, and they hadn't bought more than a week's worth. Lee left the two of them to the groceries and took the personal items into the master bathroom.

She put shampoo and soap and razors in his shower and was suddenly aware that he'd be using them, standing here with water streaming over his body. She hurried out of the bathroom and began to make the bed. The bed where he would sleep, clad in sleep pants and a T-shirt, stretched out on his stomach, arms splayed out from his sides. She tucked the quilt around the corners of the mattress and then sat on it, knees up, wrestling with herself over something she couldn't even name.

She didn't have to try to eavesdrop. The one-level house wasn't large enough. Violet's voice came clearly down the hall from the kitchen.

"I didn't come with Lee only to help out. I wanted to ask you something."

Silence. Marcus would never prod.

"In your opinion — I mean, your opinion based on the Bible — should I break up with Austin? I'm not dating him, but we're trying to be friends, and I don't think it's working, and I thought maybe . . ."

"Why ask me?"

"Well, Lee thought since you were . . . Good grief, forget it. Too awkward. I can't."

"Oh."

Somehow, when Lee had suggested it, the possibility of awkwardness hadn't entered her mind. But the quiet continued until Violet broke it.

"Soup in the pantry?"

"No," he said quickly. "That cupboard by the stove. Or any cupboard."

"Okay." A cupboard door opened with a *bang*. "Sorry, the hinge is kind of flimsy or something."

"Wait." A pause, and then his voice came more quietly. "The pantry's okay."

"Cool. Wow, nice shelves left in here."

"I can't tell you what to do about Austin," Marcus said.

"Oh," Violet said.

"I've read the verse about being unequally yoked. I've read the whole chapter. And I don't think God would want you to date him."

"What about friends?"

"Can Austin do that?"

"I . . ." Her voice fell to a whisper. "I don't

even know if I can do it."

"Well. Maybe somebody else can tell you more. I read that verse for the first time years ago. I knew what it was talking about. But if Lee . . ."

Warmth crept over Lee. She shouldn't want him to say what he was about to say. She hugged herself, hands crossing to opposite shoulders. His certainty had frightened her when they first met, had unnerved her no more than a year ago. Now it had become something to wrap around herself as a fortification when she wondered if she could ever be a wife.

"I would've been with her, Violet. If she'd ever said yes. Even knowing it was wrong."

Violet sighed. "You guys aren't any help at all."

"Sorry."

"It worked out for you, though. You're officially dating."

"I think Heath would call it redemption."

"Meaning, the choice was so messed up it needed redeeming? Like I said, no help." Her voice rose. "Lee, are you avoiding us?"

Lee stepped into the kitchen. The dog sat beside Marcus, both of them watching Violet as she shoved soup cans onto a shoulder-level shelf. Marcus rubbed behind one of the dog's ears, and it leaned against the chair and set its head on his lap.

"What should we name the dog?" he said.

Lee ran her hand over its head. A name to symbolize their new life in Texas? Too precarious. This dog needed a reminding sort of name — that they might need grit and courage soon. That they'd displayed both those things before and could again.

"Call him Brody," she said.

A slow smile touched his face. "The most brave. And it has a couple of Indy's letters."

Lee hadn't thought of Indy in too long. "Would you prefer not to use it?"

"No. I mean, it's a good name. Let's use it."

"Why is Brody a brave name?" Violet turned from the pantry as Marcus explained, then rolled her eyes. "That movie is gross. But you're right, it's a good name."

18

Not long after noon, Marcus had finished painting the shoe molding. He dredged for something, anything, he could do to fill his day. He texted Tim Burke. *Can look at the Tabitha house today. Need lockbox code.* A walk-through didn't count as work.

He used the wall to get to his feet and made it this time. He tested weight on his knee, then limped toward the back door, snatching up his keys from the kitchen counter as he passed. Brody followed with hesitant strides that refused to outpace Marcus.

His phone buzzed with Tim's response. *Gwyn wants to be there. Give them half an hour. Lockbox CAT.*

Ten minutes later, he'd let Brody outside and back in, filled his travel mug with coffee, and locked up the house. While he drove, he tried to put words together. Figure out what he would say to the church at the meeting Walt was sure to schedule in the next day or so. He'd gotten nowhere by the time he drove down Tabitha and parked at the street.

Al and Gwyneth showed at the house almost the same minute he did, Al in a T-shirt and jeans, Gwyneth wearing a flowered blouse and a green skirt that flowed around her ankles. They walked through together while Marcus sipped his coffee and Gwyneth peppered him with questions. He graded the severity of the problems he saw and told them which ones he could fix. The I-beam support needed in the basement would be a two-man job, and they asked him to find a second man and let them know as soon as he could begin the work.

They all stopped on the porch for Marcus to relock the place, and Gwyneth faced him with her hands shoved into her skirt's invisible pockets.

"So it passes inspection?" she said.

Marcus tilted his head. "This isn't an inspection. Just the opinion of a guy who's worked on a lot of houses. You're buying it as-is. Taking a chance I missed something."

"But what's your opinion?" Gwyneth spread her feet, as if Marcus's next words could knock her over.

"Get the support beams reinforced now.

Work on the rest as you can. I can do most of it cheap."

"But it's a good house."

It was. Marcus knew that the way he knew anything else in his work, professional inspector or not. He nodded, and Gwyneth's smile brightened her eyes. She looked ready to hug him.

"When can you start?" Al said.

Marcus estimated time for his current jobs, added a few days for the knee to improve. "Two weeks."

"Perfect."

He led them both down the steps toward their car. Al slid behind the wheel of their minivan and rolled down the window to finish his good-bye.

An odd vehicle choice for two people with a twenty-something daughter, but then, this house was larger than Marcus would expect too. He studied them anew: older than he was but not old, sandy blond hair on both of them, red glints in Al's beard. Not fifty yet, he'd guess, either one.

"Sorry I couldn't bring Alicia to you Tuesday night."

"It worked out fine." Al smiled as he started the van. "And we appreciate your inspection . . . opinion — whatever — on the house. We really do."

Is she your only kid? They might have to give an answer filled with grief. There might be holes in each of them, holes that ached at night.

"Oh, by the way," Al said as he put the van in drive but kept his foot on the brake. "That email from the church elders, the meeting on Saturday — you know what that's about?"

Marcus stood like a statue beside the van. His fingers curled into his palms. He hardly ever checked his email, but he should have. Walt would waste no time.

"Just wondering, since you're so involved at church. With the refugees and all. Thought you'd know."

"I'll be there. At the meeting."

Gwyneth looked ready to call him on the non-answer, but Al smiled. "Fair enough. Thank you again, Marcus."

They all said good-bye, and Marcus let the Dunhams leave first. Watched them disappear around the corner. Had he put them at risk, meeting them here in the open where Jason could spot him?

He might never work on this house.

He headed back into town, what remained of the day opening before him. He had energy to work, jobs to finish, hours in which to finish them, and one body part that wouldn't cooperate. There had to be something he could do. He'd stop by the church and see if the refugee volunteers needed a hand, even just a church member to be on the premises so others could go home. A smile found him. Yeah. He could do that.

No, he couldn't. Not with Jason searching churches for him. The safest thing for everybody might be for him to hide out in his house for a month.

He growled and rubbed his neck. Food first. Plan second.

Al's words nibbled at him while he drove into town. *"So involved at church."* He was. Four hundred or more people, and most of them knew his name. Knew his work. Knew he'd come from Michigan to live here in freedom, but that wasn't noteworthy among so many immigrants.

For a glimmer of a moment, Heath's frustration with him made sense. He saw himself laboring to help them, earning their trust, and never giving trust back.

Well, what was the alternative? Inviting the church to turn him in?

Heath thought so. Walt thought so. And Walt was making the call. By the time Marcus hit town, his jaw felt like a marble sculpture with cracks running in every direction.

Rosita's was never empty. A few people sat at the outside tables, including Heath. Marcus ambled over. Heath looked up, saw him, and smiled.

"Everybody comes to Rosita's," he said, eyes twinkling at his own reference.

Marcus grinned his appreciation.

"Stepped away from studying for some fried ice cream. You?"

"Looked over that house for the Dunhams."

"Excellent." Heath pushed the metal-backed chair away from the table, stretched his legs, and stood. "Now it's back to the books. One in particular."

The conversation was no different from any other, as if Marcus hadn't fallen apart in front of Heath last night and pounded his fist on the man's kitchen table this morning. He stepped into the restaurant letting Heath's acceptance soak into him. Sometimes their friendship felt uneven, Heath doing all the giving. He knew what Pete would say, that this was a season, that as he recovered, he would regain the ability to give back. In the meantime . . . *Thank You for the people who stick with me.*

The prayer poked at him, though. Al's

240

words, his perception of Marcus. The deliberate unevenness of his relationships at church, never letting them see him all the way. He shoved it aside and looked around the restaurant for Austin.

Alejandra, Rosita's daughter, glided around the room filling water glasses, pausing to take a new patron's order. She wore the uniform white dress shirt and black pants, but in her black tennis shoes she still moved like a dancer — or at least, the way Marcus assumed a dancer would move. Alejandra never seemed to touch the floor.

Austin was manning the takeout counter. Odd. Marcus walked over and cocked an eyebrow at the kid.

"Hi."

"Short-staffed today," Austin said. "I've been running between here and the kitchen for the last four hours, and nobody —"

Crack.

Marcus and Austin jumped in the same heartbeat.

Austin burst out from behind the counter toward the exit. Marcus followed at the fastest jog he could manage. It was a gunshot, it had to be, nothing else sounded like —

Austin hit the door hard enough to swing it open and then ducked to one side of it. Tires squealed from the parking lot. Marcus stood on the other side of the door, waiting for a cue from the kid — the cop. His heart thudded. Everyone in the restaurant stared at him and at Austin. Nobody spoke, making the Spanish guitar pouring from the overhead speakers sound louder. Austin held Marcus's eyes for a moment, bent down and drew a small pistol from a holster at his ankle, then surged through the doorway into the parking lot. Marcus followed and tried to see everything at once, see enough to cover Austin's back, to know what had happened in an instant.

Heath was gone. But his Jeep wasn't.

Austin held his gun in front of him, both hands steadying it, pivoting slowly to sweep the area. Marcus stepped past him into the lot.

"Marcus," Austin said.

On the concrete. Something wet. Catching the glare of the sunlight, only a dime-sized drop, but then another. Marcus stood over it, looked back at Austin, who pointed his gun skyward.

"Blood," Marcus said.

Austin shook his head. "What . . . ?"

"Come on." He hurried to his truck and started it up as Austin jumped in.

"If it's Jason, you should —"

"No." Marcus gunned the truck onto the

street, in the direction of rubber tracks that hadn't been there when he arrived.

"Okay," Austin said. "But let me be the cop. Will you do that?"

"You be the cop. I'll be the bait."

19

Less than a mile from Rosita's, sun glinted off the bumper of a small white car about half a mile ahead. Marcus kept pace, driving fifty miles an hour through Kearby's drowsy residential neighborhoods, blowing through multiple stop signs and not slowing when parked cars narrowed the streets. Whoever was driving that car had to know he had a tail, but nothing could be done about that.

Austin was quiet, resting the gun in hand on his thigh, watching the street ahead. Then he turned his head to watch Marcus.

"You think it's him."

"Heath was at one of the tables."

"What?"

Marcus hung a hard left without decelerating, and an oncoming car squealed its brakes. If he lost the white car, he wouldn't get there in time.

In time? To do what?

Show me, God.

"You think — no, that doesn't make sense, Marcus."

"The Jeep was there. He wasn't."

"But why?"

They'd find out. As soon as they caught up.

"This might not be Jason. And if it is . . ."

"Call Heath. If he picks up, we'll break off."

Austin picked up his phone from the console, browsed his contacts, dialed.

He lowered the phone and shook his head. "Voice mail."

Whether this was Jason or not, something had happened to Heath. Marcus squinted and made out a head in the passenger seat that cleared the headrest. Heath's height would do that.

"He's not going to the highway," Marcus said.

"Or he'd have taken Third Street west."

"Weaving around neighborhoods makes no sense unless . . ." A chill ran up Marcus's spine as heat flushed into his arms, down his legs. "He wants to lose us long enough to get rid of Heath."

"Marcus."

If Heath were dead, Jason would have left the body. Marcus mapped their trajectory through this neighborhood, the quickest way out, which Jason seemed to want. But if Marcus broke off following and he was wrong, he'd lose Jason altogether. They turned down Third Street. He'd driven it dozens of times. Slightly wider and older, it cut a main path through this subdivision that would fork in less than a mile with Morning Drive. Marcus swerved left down a new street, gunned the truck past houses and trees and sidewalks and a few people. He made a right down the next street without braking. Hit sixty miles an hour.

"Marcus."

"We've got to get ahead of him."

"Not at the risk of pedestrians, okay?"

He drove and watched everything around him and the next few minutes ticked by too fast. He couldn't let Jason get ahead of them again. One more right onto Morning, and then ahead of them the street forked with Third. Marcus swung the truck into the sharp curve, and Austin rolled down his window and held his gun up at his shoulder.

The white car hurtled toward them, skidding, braking. Marcus angled the front of his truck to take the impact on his side of the bumper, and then he mashed the brake pedal to the floor and the squealing tires were both his and Jason's as the white car swerved to a stop and crunched into the truck at the same time. Marcus's head snapped forward, but the impact wasn't as hard as he'd expected.

Austin was out of the truck. Gun leveled. Still in the car, Jason held a gun too. Aimed at his passenger's head.

Heath sat hunched forward. Head down. Not moving. Not belted in, but upright, so he had to be conscious.

"Put the gun down." Austin barely raised his voice. Jason's window was rolled down.

"Didn't expect to see you, kid."

Six months since Marcus had heard that voice. Sweat broke out on his forehead, on the back of his neck. He pulled air into his lungs, deeper, longer, until his right ribs grated. Then he let it out. His vision stayed clear.

"Put the gun down," Austin said.

Jason's aim didn't waver even as he watched Austin out the open window. "I'm thinking that would be counterproductive."

Distract him. Give Austin the chance he needed. Marcus opened his door. Jason's eyes darted to him as he climbed down. Widened. Turned frosty.

"Come to trade yourself, Brenner?"

"Yeah." He forced equal weight on both his legs, around to the front of the truck.

He stood at the point of impact between his bumper and Jason's, to one side, behind the front wheel. Jason couldn't run him over from this angle, but Marcus was now a bigger target through the windshield than Austin was.

"This guy knew me." Jason canted his head toward Heath. "So my guess is, he knows you."

"No."

"You're lying."

"He has nothing to do with this," Marcus said.

"Exactly what you said about Clay Hansen, if my guys reported the incident accurately."

Don't feel that. Stay on task. *Come on, Austin, take your shot.* But he couldn't, not while Jason's gun was trained on Heath's head.

Heath was smart enough to keep silent, chin tucked to his chest. With the glare on the windshield, Marcus couldn't see if he was bleeding.

"Jason," Austin said. "Put the gun down or you will be shot."

As if he hadn't spoken, Jason's focus remained on Marcus. "Brenner, I'll let this guy go after you get into my car."

No, he wouldn't. Marcus would have to

get into the back as long as Heath sat in the front. If he let Heath go, Jason would lose his leverage, and Austin would take him out, and everybody here knew that.

"Either you get in my car, or I shoot this man in the head."

Sweat ran down Marcus's back. He clenched his hands against the shaking. *God, please. Help.*

"Come on, Brenner. You know I do my job, whatever it takes."

Yeah. No choice. Marcus took a step toward Jason's car.

"Marcus!" Austin's voice snapped. "Do not move! Jason, put the gun down!"

One smooth motion. Jason's body twisting toward Austin, his arm sweeping around, taking aim not at Marcus but at Austin, Jason's face set like stone and Heath doubling forward. There was a *crack* and a crinkling shatter of the window past Heath. Jason slumped until his head hit the steering wheel and his arm fell to his side.

Marcus ran. Threw open the passenger door. Hauled Heath out of the car, dead weight in his arms. He dropped to his knees on the concrete, lowering Heath slowly. He looked up into the car from his place on the pavement, into the open door. Jason didn't move. The back of his head was gone. Blood dripped down the steering wheel into his lap.

Austin lowered the gun.

Marcus gripped Heath's shoulder. "Heath."

A long breath and a shudder. Heath tried to push himself up, fell back. Marcus caught him around the shoulders before he could hit his head on the concrete. Lowered him.

Austin's voice came from the other side of the car. "We need an ambulance at Third and Morning, and police. There's been a shooting."

Heath's shirt was dark brown, but this close the blood was easy to spot, a growing and glistening stain on his left side. Marcus pressed both hands to the wound, and Heath's eyes opened as a gasp filled his lungs. Warm blood seeped between Marcus's fingers. Heath's body arched against the pressure on the wound.

"Don't move," Marcus said.

Heath's glazing eyes found him, but he didn't speak.

Marcus tried to envision the vital organs, how near they were to the wound beneath his hands. Lee would know. Heath's face seemed to be paling by the second. His mouth, eyebrows, forehead all scrunched with pain.

"They're on their way." Austin's shadow fell over them.

Marcus pressed two fingers to Heath's neck, and they smeared blood under his jaw. A strong, fast pulse beat beneath them. He pressed both hands to the wound again, and Heath cried out.

"Marcus," Austin said. "Police will be here in a few minutes. I think you should go."

Marcus shook his head.

"This is going to require an investigation, and if you're a witness, your name will be on reports, official —"

"No," Marcus said. The flow of blood wasn't slowing. He wouldn't leave Heath here to die in the street. *God, please.*

Minutes wore on. Heath's breathing labored. Voices filtered around Marcus as sirens neared. Red and blue lights bathed the concrete, made Heath squint. Car doors opened. Marcus looked up.

Two squad cars, three officers, each approaching with a hand on his sidearm.

Austin had raised his hands. "I'm armed."

"Keep your hands up."

"Yes, sir."

The tallest of the officers was a gray-haired white guy with a birthmark on one eyelid that wasn't noticeable until he blinked. The other two were Hispanic, one stocky and one thinner with a face that would look twenty his whole life. As they came nearer, Marcus could read their names on their uniforms. Page. Guzman. Nunez.

Officer Guzman disarmed Austin and patted him down. Nunez went to Marcus and knelt beside Heath, pressed two fingers to his neck and waited about ten seconds, then nodded to himself.

"Can you keep pressure on it?"

"Yeah." Marcus tried to hear what the other two were saying to Austin.

"Ambulance should be here soon," Officer Nunez said. "Are you hurt?"

"No."

"Are you sure? No pain anywhere?"

"No."

Nunez angled his gaze, wanting clarification.

"I'm not hurt."

Something rattled and clicked. Marcus looked up from the blood still seeping between his fingers, warming them.

The cops were handcuffing Austin.

He had to catch his breath. "Are you arresting him?"

"Not right now," Officer Page said.

"Jason was going to shoot us."

Page stayed next to Austin while Guzman

bent to study Jason's body through the open car window. He straightened to face Marcus over the car hood.

"You know this man."

"Jason Mayweather," Marcus said.

"You're Marcus Brenner, aren't you."

Another second of breathlessness. The weight on his chest increased. Pete would tell him to take a step back, find his beach and breathe for a minute. But this wasn't a safe place.

"I know about the list," Marcus said. If they had to turn him over, they should tell him.

"Yeah," Nunez said. "The list."

"You're witness to a homicide right now," Guzman said. "That's all."

"Homicide?"

"Means death by human," Austin said. "Not murder necessarily."

A siren wailed toward them from a distance. The ambulance stopped, and three paramedics hustled toward Heath and Marcus. Heath coughed but didn't open his eyes. Latex-gloved hands pushed Marcus's aside. Another medic took Heath's pulse.

Marcus tried to stand and fell against Jason's car, one hand smearing blood over the hood. He pushed away from the car, away from the body with staring blue eyes and a jagged circle of red between them.

The paramedics had an oxygen mask over Heath's face, and two of them lifted him to a gurney while another kept pressure on his wound.

"Where —" Marcus's voice broke. "Where are you taking him?"

"Decatur," somebody said.

They loaded Heath into the first ambulance as a second arrived. This one's lights rotated over the scene — the white car, the concrete, Austin, and the cops and all the vehicles. The white car and the blue truck, crunched together, were being blocked off by still more cop cars. The second ambulance wasn't using its siren.

Marcus looked at his truck, damaged but drivable, but the cops would never let him leave in it. Evidence. Somebody was dead here. Somebody else might be dying.

"Sir?"

Another paramedic. How many people were here? Marcus looked past the man approaching him. Yellow tape. More cops. A lot of cops. He was standing in the center of a crime scene that buzzed with brisk voices and smelled like blood. Several uniformed technicians were combing through Jason's car. They hadn't moved the body. One cop seemed to be taking a picture every second with an endless *click click click* of his camera — pictures of Marcus's truck, Jason's car, the street, the blood, the body.

"Sir, do you know where you're hurt?"

He looked down. His shirt. Blood. "It's Heath's. The — the guy you already took."

"You're not bleeding?"

Marcus shook his head.

"Can I make sure of that?"

Leave me alone. "Okay."

The medic led him to the back of the second ambulance and had him sit on the bumper. Asked his name. Checked him over. Studied Marcus's face as if something was wrong with him.

"Can you tell me where the pain is, Marcus?"

How many times did he have to say he wasn't hurt? He took five minutes trying to convince the man before he remembered to explain about the knee, and then the paramedic wanted to take him to the hospital. Made him sign a sheet saying he was refusing medical treatment. Finally left him alone. Marcus got up and rounded the hulk of the ambulance that had been blocking his line of sight to everybody else.

They had Austin in a cop car.

"Marcus."

He turned slowly, letting his good leg take

most of the movement. It was the young cop, Nunez. His dark eyes were measuring Marcus.

"I need to ask you about what happened here."

Maybe Austin was right. Maybe he should have tried to disappear from the scene. But nothing mattered as long as Heath might die.

"Just basic questions for the moment, but you'll have to come in to give your statement."

"I've got to call his wife. Heath's wife."

"We'll inform her."

Nunez didn't understand. Gloria should hear it from Marcus. From the person Jason had been after when Heath somehow got in the way.

"Do you know what started the altercation?"

"Me." The word cracked. Marcus cleared his throat. "He said he'd kill Heath if I didn't go with him."

Nunez gazed a moment down the street, past the barricades. Then he looked back at Marcus.

"Mayweather talked to me a few days ago, asking if I knew anything about you. Showed your picture. My understanding is he asked a lot of my colleagues, too." The man's eyes were steady, devoid of pity or challenge, simply watching Marcus's reaction to his words.

"I know Texas isn't giving me sanctuary anymore."

"Yeah," Nunez said.

Quiet draped them. Marcus looked down at the concrete, at Heath's blood drying, smeared by a forensic swab.

"What's going to happen to Austin?"

"It'll depend on the evidence."

Nunez advised Marcus to get checked out at the hospital but let it go when Marcus said he'd already signed a waiver. Marcus followed him to a squad car. The one holding Austin had already left.

"There's somebody I need to call."

"Go ahead."

He dialed.

"Marcus," Walt said.

The weight was crushing his chest. "Jason's dead."

"Okay, talk to me."

Marcus told him as much as he could in a space of minutes. "They took Austin in handcuffs."

"That's procedure. It doesn't mean they're charging him."

"Can you do anything?"

"I'll be there when I can." He hung up.

Marcus lowered the phone. Nunez stood against the squad car and watched the evidence techs working the scene, but no doubt he'd listened to every word Marcus said. One more phone call. He wasn't under arrest; he could call anybody he wanted, and now that Walt knew, he could give in to the trembling core of him that wanted to hear . . .

"Marcus."

"Something happened."

One beat, less than a full breath, long enough to draw Lee's voice taut with concern. "Can you explain, please?"

"Jason." His voice shook. "Jason shot Heath and Austin shot Jason."

The smallest whimper came over the line. "Heath?"

"They took him to the hospital."

"And Jason?"

"Jason's dead."

"Are you safe? Were you injured?"

"The ambulance took Heath. It's in his side."

"Right or left side?"

"I don't know." He fought to sharpen the blur of the last twenty minutes. He lifted his hand to grip his neck, but every crease in his skin was lined with dry blood. The hand began to shake. "Lee, I can't remember. I was putting pressure on it and I can't remember."

"Marcus. Can you listen to me?"

"Yeah. Listening."

"Are you safe?"

"Yeah."

"Are you injured?"

"No."

He told her about going to the police station, leaving the truck, talking to Walt. He told her he'd be at the hospital as soon as he could. He didn't want to hang up, but Nunez cast a long glance at him.

"I have to go," Marcus said.

"All right. Be careful."

"You, too."

He hung up. Shoved the phone into his pocket. Nunez opened the door, and Marcus eased into the back, behind the cage. The door shut. *Let me out.* No. He was okay. These cops didn't wear gray, didn't drive cars topped with green lights. These cops took care of people. He let his body cave into the seat, tried to stretch his leg, but there was no room. He blew out a hard breath as a bump in the road jarred his knee.

He might get locked up again. Or the Constabulary might kill him. He huddled in the back of the cop car and prayed for Heath, for Austin. For Gloria and the church if Heath didn't — no, he had to make it. For Violet. For Lee, that God would take care of her, that she'd trust Him if she lost Marcus again.

For everybody.

Then he opened his eyes and looked out the window at the Texas highway rushing by. *And for me. Jesus, please stay close.*

Something touched him, deep in his chest, where the panic was hovering with its hand around his heart, waiting to squeeze. It didn't dissipate, but a texture of peace wrapped around it. He'd be okay. God's hands were on him. He could almost feel their warmth, one on his shoulder, one on the top of his head. He bent forward and pictured himself bowed before his Father God, but the image morphed in his mind — not a man bowing but a boy clinging, arms around the waist of his dad, and his dad's hands resting on him. One on his shoulder. One on the top of his head.

20

By the time Lee reached the hospital waiting room, Gloria was already there. Sitting
in a corner chair, arms around herself. She
looked up.

"Lee."

"What have they told you?"

"The police came. To our house. Someone
shot him, and he's in surgery, internal damage — the nurse said they wouldn't know
how bad until they looked inside." Gloria
rubbed her arms. "How did you know to
come? I — I should have called someone,
but all I could think about was getting here."

Lee sat in the chair next to her and linked
her fingers between her knees. "Marcus
called me."

"Marcus . . . what?"

"He's being questioned by the police. As
a witness."

"You know who did this?"

"Yes."

"Dear Jesus." Gloria covered her face and spoke through her fingers. "It was that agent who's after Marcus."

"Yes."

"Dear Jesus." She caved forward, elbows on her thighs, fingers digging into her hair. Lee waited, but Gloria didn't move.

They sat in the distant but incessant noise of the hospital — beeping machines, overhead pages, voices down corridors. Lee lived in this current of activity forty-eight hours a week, thrived in the efficiency, the dedication, the ebb and flow of life and death. But none of it applied to this moment, seated in a padded chair on the other side of the work, helpless to make Heath continue breathing.

Lee's phone began to ring. Juana. She answered it and paced away from Gloria.

"Hello."

"Lee, I just saw on the news. Are you okay? Is Marcus okay?"

"What did you see on the news?"

"Two people shot in Kearby, one dead. No names. I thought — I thought one of them might be Marcus. Lee, it happened on Third Street. That's three blocks from church."

"I know."

"Then you saw the story too."

"No. Marcus called me."

"What do you mean?"

The church shouldn't find out from media sources. Lee had to call someone as soon as she was off the phone with Juana. Someone who could spread the word. Bring the people together.

"There was a connection to Marcus, but he wasn't shot." She dropped her voice. "Juana, the person who survived the injuries was Heath."

"Wh— what?"

"I'm at the hospital with Gloria."

"Pastor Heath? Pastor Heath was shot? No, Lee, there's got to be some —"

"He's just coming out of surgery."

Silence over the phone, then quiet tears.

"Juana, I need to contact people. The church. But I don't have numbers."

"I — I can get them for you." Paper rustled, and in the background, Damien cheered in a way Lee could now interpret as a video game victory. Lee went to her purse sitting on her chair and found a pen and paper.

Juana provided two numbers, one for Benjamin Schneider and one for a woman named Brooke. She said these two were the heads of the email directory and would spread the word online.

Lee hung up, then looked down at the names in her handwriting. Looked at the numbers. Couldn't make sense of them.

Jason Mayweather was dead.

She leaned forward in the chair and allowed herself to absorb that knowledge. To hold it in front of her and study it. Not to feel it, though. This wasn't the time to feel anything.

She tried Benjamin first, and he picked up. She expected Benjamin to break out in prayer right there on the phone with her, but he was quiet, asking her to tell him everything, then saying he'd "take it from here." Lee finally set her phone on her knee and stared at the display until it darkened. When she lifted her head, Gloria was watching her.

"Thank you for doing that."

"Of course."

Gloria sat in her chair looking smaller than Lee had ever seen her, caved in at the shoulders, neck hunched. She was a petite woman, and Heath's stature had always dwarfed her further.

He had to stand beside Gloria again. He had to. Lee folded her hands and brought them up to support her head. Heath's pose. She closed her eyes. Within his body, anything could happen from this point forward.

He could be fine, no lasting effects at all. He could develop an infection. He could . . . She closed her eyes and willed Marcus to arrive soon. She'd heard nothing from him since the first phone call. Walt had let her know he was working with the detectives and police and had seen Marcus at the station, and she'd thanked him, but she yearned for Marcus's call. Better, his presence.

Two hours later, a white-coated older man appeared at the far side of the waiting room. Lee's heartbeat stuttered, and her fingernails dug into her palm. The doctor crossed to her and Gloria with a hint of smile behind his eyes.

"You're here for Heath Carter," the doctor said. "I'm Dr. Stamos."

Gloria stood. "I'm Heath's wife. Gloria. This is our friend Lee."

"Would you like to speak with me in private?"

"No, thank you."

"Well, Heath came through surgery very well. The bullet broke a rib, and a few bone fragments tore into his spleen. We'll be watching him carefully for onset of infection, but both the spleen and the bullet were removed without any difficulty."

"Without any . . . ?" Gloria looked from

the doctor to Lee. "He isn't dying."

Dr. Stamos shifted his weight from one foot to the other. "Not at all. Heath's doing well. You should be able to see him in an hour or two."

Gloria dropped into her chair and expelled a long, broken breath. "Thank You, Jesus."

"It was my understanding someone had spoken to you before."

Gloria shook her head, ducking his eyes.

"Nothing was sure at that point," Lee said.

The waiting now was a different sort. As Lee's concern for Heath receded, it rose for Marcus and Austin. She checked her phone. She had texted Marcus — *Heath is out of surgery. Doctor optimistic* — but she got no response. How long would the police hold them?

Another hour passed, and then a young nurse came for Gloria, eyes too blue behind blue-framed glasses, cheeks as rosy as if she'd just scrubbed them.

"He's sleeping," the girl whispered, as if she could awaken Heath from here. "But you can see him."

Gloria followed as Lee's phone vibrated in her purse. She dug it out. Marcus.

Coming.

She pressed the phone to her chest before realizing how absurd she looked. She tried to compose a response and settled on *All right.*

Minutes after the nurse and Gloria left, footsteps sounded from the direction of the elevator. Lee stirred in her chair. Marcus and Austin? Too soon. She stood.

A couple from church. She didn't know their names. The husband was crying, and the wife looked about to.

"What's the latest?" the man said.

They were the first of an influx. Within fifteen minutes, a dozen people stood and sat around the waiting room, calling themselves the "first shift" and drilling Lee with questions about Heath's condition. About the shooting. She was their only source of information, and she couldn't tell most of what she knew. She kept to medical information and said someone else would have to relay the details of the incident.

"Where's Gloria?" someone said.

"A nurse took her back to see him," Lee said.

But hospital protocol wouldn't allow her to be sitting with Heath all this time, not when he'd just been brought to recovery. Lee took out her phone and sent a text: *Where are you?*

Gloria took a minute to respond. *The chapel. Are you being inundated?*

Concerned for others, even now. Lee shook her head. *We're fine. Take as much time as you need.*

Thanks. I won't be much longer.

Five minutes later, Gloria approached from the far corridor. Dried tears stained her cheeks, and her eyes were swollen, but she smiled around the waiting room at the church members. A few of them pressed forward to hug her, and she held onto each of them for a long moment.

"I've spoken to the doctors," Gloria said, and the room hushed. "They're watching Heath very closely, but they believe he will pull through."

Praises and cheers chimed around their huddle.

"I'm guessing Lee filled you in on the medical side of this?"

Nods. A few smiles at Lee, though she hadn't done anything to merit them.

"Good," Gloria said. "We need to pray that God will keep infection away, and that Heath's rib and the damaged tissue inside him will heal. He'll have a period of recovery, probably a few months. But he's strong and he's stable."

No one wanted to move away from her. Lee had seen their love for Gloria in the time she'd spent at church, but this was something else. A claiming of her and Heath as their own. A circling of unity in purpose, and their purpose was to uplift Gloria. She spoke with different people, each in turn — first those that came to her, then those who stayed in their seats.

She came last to Lee.

"Thank you for passing on the information. I needed some time with the Lord. There was a lot to sort out. Still is."

"If I can help in any way . . ."

"You are. I know you care about my husband, and that helps me right here." Gloria put a hand to her heart. "I know you'll pray."

Lee allowed her eyes to make the promise. Now she had to pray. But prayer might not be appropriate when trust wasn't full.

Gloria half smiled, knowing. Before the pause could force Lee to say more, a woman Lee didn't know joined them and hugged Gloria, moving her away.

The elevator opened again, and recently born habit caused Lee to glance toward it, not really expecting . . .

Marcus and Austin. She sprang to her feet and barreled toward them and stopped.

Austin's expression was drained, his hair mussed, his burgundy and green Rosita's work polo hanging on his slumped shoulders. Marcus followed a few steps behind him, limping too badly to keep pace. He wore a black T-shirt printed with bold white words: *Hello, I'm Johnny Cash.* His jeans were dirty at the knees. He looked up and saw her, and his face crumpled.

She went to them. Austin gave her a nod as he passed to join the church group, but she turned to block him.

"Are you all right?"

His mouth twisted. "Relatively speaking."

"Heath?" Marcus said.

"Nothing new since I texted you."

Faint tremors gripped Marcus's body, a sure sign of an adrenaline attack that had lasted too long. A muscle jumped in Austin's jaw. They stood side by side, not touching yet seeming to brace each other.

"Do we know anything definite?" she said.

"I was admonished not to leave the country," Austin said. "But working for Walt is making a difference. He's got more pull than I thought."

"They have to know it was self-defense," she said.

"The evidence will back us up, of course, but they don't know anything right now. I shot someone, Lee."

No give in his voice when he said it, but he looked past her, toward the waiting room.

"Would you like to join the others?"

Marcus and Austin nodded, again seeming linked somehow.

Lee gestured to the shirt Marcus wore. "Not yours."

"Walt's. Mine was . . . was . . . Blood."

She squeezed his hand, held it until they stepped into the waiting room. The group enveloped Austin in welcome and curiosity — did they know him from somewhere, did he know their pastor, did he know anything about the attack?

Marcus went straight to Gloria.

She looked up and seemed to take him in, the shirt that didn't fit him, the tension in his every muscle as he stood in front of her with hands clenched. For the moment, no one else sat near enough to overhear them.

"Marcus." Gentleness overflowed from the word.

He came closer, his whole frame shaking. "I'm sorry. Gloria, I'm sorry."

"No," she said. "It isn't your fault."

"It was Jason. He shot Heath."

She flinched at Heath's name but shook her head. "I'm never going to blame you for this. Whatever happens, it isn't your fault."

Marcus shut his eyes a long moment, then opened them and eased into the chair at her side. Lee sat next to him.

"I want to know what happened," Gloria said quietly.

Marcus cleared his throat. Rubbed the back of his neck. "Austin."

Austin stood across the room, back to a corner, paging through a *Reader's Digest.* He looked up, found Marcus, and came to them. He set the magazine aside on a low table and claimed an empty chair, tugged it around to half face them.

"Gloria was asking," Marcus said.

Austin's movement to Gloria had caught attention. Several people approached to listen.

This was the end of Marcus's secret. They would all know after today, would infer it from his presence at the shooting of a Constabulary agent. Did he realize that?

"It started at Rosita's," Austin said. "Jason claimed Heath recognized him, which seems unlikely, but regardless, he was going to kill Heath or Marcus. Or me. So I shot him."

Reactions rippled through the group — sidelong glances, tiny gasps.

"And Jason is dead?" Gloria whispered.

"Yes. He is."

"Did you see . . . my husband . . . ?"

"No, ma'am. I was inside Rosita's with Marcus. I don't think anyone saw what happened. Heath will have to tell us."

She closed her eyes, and one tear fell.

Austin locked his gaze on Marcus. "He didn't believe me. He turned on me because he didn't believe I'd shoot him."

Something passed between them, knowledge of Jason that no one else in this room would ever share. Lee's stomach tightened.

"I saw it," Austin said. "In his face. He never believed I'd do it."

"You had to," Marcus said.

"I know that." He rocked forward, then straightened again. "I'm not sorry."

Lee thought Austin would leave, but he didn't. After a while, he walked away to call Violet. Marcus fidgeted but didn't stand to pace, keeping his leg stretched out in front of him.

Lee went to the closest nurse's station and asked for a bag of ice. She brought it to Marcus and tucked it around his knee, and his grip of gratitude nearly crushed her hand. Perhaps helping him could somehow transfer to Heath's nurses and doctors as they worked. She'd been a nurse too long to believe in luck or coincidence, but she'd never argue against the energy people gained and passed on when helping to heal others.

She'd promised Gloria she would pray. As

this crop of people drifted from the waiting room and a new group drifted in, Lee bowed her head and tried to keep her promise.

A hand rested high on her back. Too broad for Gloria's. Lee kept her head down, and Marcus's hand remained. She shuddered under the knowledge of everything that could go wrong. The weight of her own body, healthy and strong and whole, seemed too much. She leaned into Marcus's hand, and he put his arm around her shoulders.

When she looked up, Austin stood in front of her. "Violet's asking me to come get her from work."

"Her shift isn't over," Lee said.

"She wants to be here."

"You'll go get her?"

"Not a problem." He was already backing up. He disappeared around the corner toward the elevators.

She and Marcus were quiet after that. Gloria made periodic sweeps around the room, thanking each new person who showed up for Heath and saying good-bye to each person who left. How did she manage to spill herself out for them at a time like this?

Lee's imagination was creating multiple versions of the scene while she sat here. Jason and Heath, Marcus and Austin, two shot and two unscathed. It could have gone any other way. She leaned into Marcus's arm, likely cutting off his circulation, but he didn't shift away from her. Didn't move at all.

The elevator opened again, but with Marcus beside her and Austin out retrieving Violet, Lee didn't bother to look up until Marcus's breathing hitched. She followed his gaze to the newcomer.

Pete Gentry. Not out of place — he was a member of their church. A well-known member. But she hadn't expected to see him. He melded into a small group to one side, welcomed with handshakes and hugs.

Marcus glanced around the waiting room, seeming to measure what he wanted to tell her against the risk of being overheard. No one sat near enough, if they lowered their voices. She leaned closer.

"I . . ." He gripped the arm of the chair. "I need to talk to him, Lee."

"Now?"

"I . . . I . . ."

She covered his hand with hers. "It's all right."

He tucked his chin to his chest. His fingers tightened on the chair.

"You want to speak to him without attracting attention."

"I need to."

"Then we'll make that happen. Leave in the direction of the restroom and wait there a few minutes, and I'll ask him to go to you."

He drew a ragged breath.

"Thanks."

"Of course."

He lurched to his feet and limped from the room without a look back, shoulders straight, appearing fine. No one noticed.

Privacy had always felt safe, never empty, but for a moment, Lee wished she didn't have to hide this from the people she and Marcus claimed as theirs. Other than Gloria, no one here knew Marcus was in counseling. No one here knew any reason he would need it. Even if they discovered he was a Constabulary target, it didn't follow that he'd been a prisoner. That he'd been starved, beaten, locked in the dark.

She waited until Pete finished his conversation with someone she didn't know. Then she edged over to him, approached at ease, smiled.

"Hello," she said.

"How are you doing, Lee?"

"I'm fine." She hoped he caught the faint emphasis on the first word.

"Thought so." The man missed nothing.

"And if he asked to talk to me . . . That's important progress."

"He's waiting down the corridor."

"Thanks."

Pete left, and Lee returned to her chair. She pressed her back against it, closed her eyes, and kept her word. Silent, alone, she prayed for Heath.

Until someone moved to her left. She opened her eyes. Juana perched on the edge of the chair Marcus had occupied. "Hey, friend. Come on over." She gestured with her eyes to where two other women from Bible study sat on the other side of the room.

Lee arched an eyebrow.

"Yes, I'm sure." Juana smiled.

Not prepared. She'd wished minutes ago to belong to them without concealment, yet she held too much in her heart to share. Too much that might spew out if they expected her to converse with them. She shook her head.

"Lee. Come pray with us."

She had no choice. The Bible commanded Christians to fellowship and pray together. If she remained in her solitude, she would be falling short of what was required.

Her throat burned, and the points of her jaw ached. But she would do this thing God asked of her. She stood and followed Juana across the waiting room to the others.

21

When Pete came into view, Marcus had to grit his teeth against a sob. He should be stronger, but Pete halted in front of him, and the acceptance in his eyes cut Marcus's last thread of composure.

"I think . . . I . . ."

If Pete responded, Marcus couldn't make it out through the roaring in his head. So much adrenaline. Heartbeat out of control. Starting to scare him a little if he could think about it.

"Marcus."

Okay, he heard that. "Yeah."

"The chapel's private. Let's go there."

"It's not my day for an appointment."

"I'm good with it if you are."

He followed Pete to the elevators. Everything around him had started to blur. He didn't know what floor number Pete pushed, didn't hear the elevator chime as it stopped and the doors opened. Didn't know the color of these walls or this carpet as Pete led him into a softly lit room with pews and an altar at the front.

He did know they were alone in the room. Somehow the blur of everything else wasn't strong enough to drown out the screaming hypervigilance that had to assess the room for threats.

"First things first. You need to stay with me." Pete's voice, calm and firm, sharpened the room around him. "Tell me what's happening right now."

Now? Heath was shot. That was now. And Jason's eyes. Blue. Forever unblinking.

"Talk to me," Pete said.

Nausea welled up. "I need help."

"What I'm here for."

"Heath."

"Tell me about Heath."

"You know." Bile rose in his throat. He choked it down.

"Tell me anyway."

The shaking buckled his legs, and he went down in the aisle alongside the wall. He slouched, the wall bracing his back. A low lamp above him threw shadows from the pews. Pete's legs folded to sit facing Marcus.

"Okay. Let's take some time. If you can, answer me one thing — did the adrenaline just hit you, or have you been midattack for a while?"

"While."

"Since the shooting?"

"Yeah."

"Okay. Let's do what we can to bring you out."

Marcus pressed his back to the wall and tried to slow his heartbeat, but he'd been trying since the ride in the cop car.

"Breathe," Pete said. "In two three four five, out two three four five."

The hammer in his chest kept beating, harder and harder, until he could have cried. It hurt. It might beat itself to death inside him. He shut his eyes, but he could see Jason's, staring through him. He opened them again.

"Easy, Marcus," Pete said. "Take it easy."

He hadn't said anything. He might have whimpered, though.

"If you close your eyes, can you see your beach?"

Sand. Sky. Hear the waves. Feel them lapping his toes. Gulls crying overhead. Smell of the water and the sand and the sun. He tried to find it all, but Heath was shot.

"Blood."

"I know," Pete said. "But Heath's alive. He's safe now. He isn't bleeding."

"Safe." The word broke. Heath was safe, but Marcus wasn't.

Yeah, he was. Here in the hospital chapel. He had to explain what Pete couldn't guess was going on inside his head. *Get a grip and talk to him.* The trigger wasn't Heath.

"It was Jason's voice," he said. "When I heard his voice. I was . . . I was . . ."

Pete settled his hands on his knees and waited.

"It wasn't a flashback. I wasn't in the room again." He shut his eyes and tried to apply what he'd learned. "But I think my brain heard a threat and — and I can't shut it off."

"Sounds exactly right. That's why we came here, to get you through it."

"Thanks." The word came out on a gasp.

"You've been fighting this since you heard Jason's voice?"

Another nod. "Up and down."

"Okay. Look around this room and tell me everything you see."

He cataloged the items in the room, then the smells — lemon dusting polish, old books though he didn't see any nearby. When his breathing came easier and his chest no longer throbbed, only ached, Pete helped him recreate the moment he heard Jason's voice. Marcus could repeat word for word everything Jason had said.

"And then Austin shot him. And now he's dead."

"Yes. He's dead. You'll never hear his voice again."

"I know. But I think I . . . I don't believe it yet."

"That's normal too. All of this is normal."

"For somebody with PTSD." He hated that label, but he couldn't deny it.

Pete's mouth twisted, uneven, could be a frown or a smile. "You want to talk about that?"

"No."

"You're doing the work. Improving all the time. I told you, that's what's important."

He pulled his good knee into his chest.

"How are we doing?" Pete said.

He breathed in, assessed his surroundings, his body, his thoughts. The voice that screamed he wasn't safe seemed quiet for now. Quieter, anyway. "Okay."

"When did you eat last?"

"Um . . ." The detectives had offered him something, but his stomach had been too tense.

"Still feeling nauseous?"

"No."

"Then let's get you some food." Pete helped him to his feet. They headed for the elevator.

When they stepped into the cafeteria, the magnified echo of conversations hit Marcus like a slap, ending the ricochet of Jason's voice in his head. By the time they got to a table — Pete with a bowl of beef and barley soup, Marcus with a roast beef sandwich — even the ache in his chest had faded away. They didn't talk while they ate. Marcus dug into the sandwich, and another measure of safety trickled into him. In the midst of everything else, he hadn't noticed he was hungry.

22

By the time Marcus and Pete returned from the cafeteria, Austin had come back with Violet. He left not long after, and Violet's face crinkled as she watched him walk to the elevator. The afternoon ticked on, marked by arrivals and departures. Church members flocked in and out of the waiting room for hours, hugging Gloria and hugging each other. Marcus sat with the group when he could, got up and paced the corridor when the itch under his skin threatened to break him open in front of everybody. Nodded an *okay* to Lee each time he came back.

Adrenaline dogged him, hours longer than normal. Nothing to do now but ride it out. When Violet sat next to him, he smiled with effort.

"Hey," he said.

"I was hoping Austin would come back, but I don't think he's going to."

"Yeah."

"I keep praying, but he doesn't even want to be here with everybody."

"With everybody praying and hugging?"

Her mouth turned down. "You make it sound like we're creepy and mumbling and squashing each other."

A chuckle shook him. He squeezed her shoulder. "I would've felt squashed here. Before."

"Before you were a Christian."

"And even after, at first. It's hard sometimes to trust all this. That it's real."

"You mean, that the people are real? And honest?"

He nodded.

"You don't really trust that now, either," she whispered.

He flinched. But he couldn't deny it.

Violet stretched her feet out from the chair and sighed. "I keep telling him. Maybe I should chill out a little."

"Lee had to choose God on her own. For herself."

"Yeah." Violet's eyes filled. "I just want him to so bad."

A struggle Marcus had known for almost twelve years. "I know."

"I know you do. And you're right. I don't want to freak him out. Or squash him."

"Good." He tried to smile, must have succeeded. Violet returned it and in another minute hopped up to greet newcomers to their circle. She knew everybody.

As people came and went, rumors were spreading. No less than a dozen of them asked Marcus if he'd been at the scene, and when he confirmed it, they wanted to know who would have reason to harm Heath and whether Marcus had ever seen the shooter around town. He didn't lie to them, but he didn't tell the truth either. Every vague avoidance jabbed his conscience, but he couldn't push past the adrenaline to say what . . . what he should? Did God want him to tell them everything right here in the waiting room?

Real and honest. The next time somebody asked, he tried to give a whole answer, but the words wouldn't come out.

By five, Lee was flagging. Too many people, too much noise. Volume wore her out faster, but endless talk got to her too. She called it "droning." You wouldn't know, if you didn't know Lee, but her hands were folded in her lap, fingers laced, knuckles strained white. The message was as loud as words to Marcus: *I hate people now and I won't stop hating them until I get away from them.*

He set a hand on her shoulder. "We can go."

"Not until Heath wakes up."

That's what had held her here all this time? "You said that won't be until tomorrow."

"Yes." She pulled her woven fingers closer to her body.

"Lee, we can't spend the night here."

"I know."

She wasn't making sense. He waited.

"I . . ." Weariness and worry lined her face. "I'm attempting to be a proper member of the church."

Oh, Lee. "People came and went all day. Nobody's stayed longer than an hour or two."

Her spine stiffened. "I'm aware of that."

"Okay."

"I . . . I thought . . . At some point, Gloria will reach the point of exhaustion, and if everyone else has gone home, she'll need help. I don't wish her to face this night by herself, if he hasn't awakened by then. It is . . . difficult . . . being unable to speak to someone and reassure yourself that they're well."

The stilted selection of her words gave away what she wasn't saying. Marcus took both her hands and held her eyes with his.

288

He lowered his voice. "I'm okay, Lee."

Her bottom lip trembled. "I'm aware of that. And I'm aware this situation is different. She knows he's still breathing."

Marcus would never know how she'd felt, but when he tried to imagine four months of believing Lee was dead . . . "Go talk to Gloria. See if she has anyone to stay with her tonight. If she doesn't, we'll figure something out for her."

Lee and Gloria talked quietly in a corner, several minutes longer than necessary to fill somebody in on simple plans. Lee ducked her head once, and Gloria's smile replaced the tired creases in her face with affectionate ones. By the time Lee skirted a few people and a low table in the center of the room and came back to Marcus, his brain had finally gotten through to him with a message it had probably been sending for a while.

He was crashing.

"Gloria has a sister," Lee said. She hid her hands behind her back, but her shoulders had relaxed. "She lives in Illinois, so she isn't able to be here in person, but they've planned to speak on the phone tonight until Gloria is able to sleep. She says she'll be fine."

"Is that safe? For her sister?"

"Gloria says she's an atheist. In no danger from the Constabulary, even with a Texas pastor for a brother-in-law."

"Okay."

"And she encouraged us to go home. I suppose I'm ready to leave. If you are."

He pushed to his feet. All his limbs were loose, quivery. Lifting his arms over his head would take multiple tries. He funneled his focus to his legs and kept them following Lee back to Gloria to say good night, then over to Violet.

Violet hugged him so hard, he almost tipped backward onto the floor. She held on an extra few seconds before stepping back.

"Austin said he'll come get me and take me back to Lee's whenever I call him. Want me to text you guys when Pastor Heath wakes up?"

"Yeah."

"When's too late?"

"Any time is fine," Lee said.

"Okay." She hugged Marcus again. "Thanks for the advice. Pray for me?"

"Sure." He loosened his arms, started to step back, but she held on. It was what he needed, to help him say the rest. "Violet, if you'd pray for me too. Please."

"You bet."

They said good night, and Marcus forced his legs to follow Lee to the elevator, empty except for them. A long sigh poured out of him, along with his body's last reserves. He collapsed into the corner, kept upright by the wall.

"Lee . . ." *Aftermath. Crashing. Help.*

She stood in the corner with him, close, arms touching. "I know."

"Oh."

"As you knew I needed escape from the droning."

"Yeah."

The elevator dinged, the doors opened, and several men and women in scrubs waited for Marcus and Lee to exit before stepping inside. The doors closed. They crossed the lobby. Stepped outside into a humid evening filled with sweet flowers and insect songs and . . .

People. Half a dozen of them, wearing business casual and carrying their phones like weapons, at least three of them cradling cameras . . . Cameras.

Marcus broke eye contact with the man nearest them, glued his attention to Lee. "Reporters."

"Perhaps if we ignore them," she said.

"Here about the shooting?"

"Kearby doesn't have a hospital. It's logical they'd try the closest one."

"What if they — ?"

One of the reporters broke from the group and started toward him and Lee. No, toward him. He gritted his teeth. Nicole Stopczy. She stopped in front of them and shoved her phone into her pocket. She stood almost eye level with him. In heels? Yeah. She must have been wearing flats at the diner.

"Mr. Brenner."

"No." *Help, God, I can't do this right now.*

"How's that dog?"

He might have reared back a step, but the surprise was owed to his fuzzy mind. She was obvious, reminding him of the personal connection first. Her hands hung at her sides, non-threatening. Right.

Lee glared frost-tipped darts into the woman's face but said nothing.

Marcus took a step around the reporter. "I told you I'm not talking to you. About anything."

"Were you present at the shooting today?"

No more words. He turned his palm toward Lee, and she laced her fingers through his, and they left the sidewalk.

Nicole Stopczy trailed them by a few steps. Her heels tapped the pavement, and her voice pitched lower over Marcus's shoulder. "Fine. Don't talk to me. But don't talk to any of them either, all right?"

Them. The cluster of people was following Nicole. Following Marcus.

"But I want you to know, if the dead shooter was working for the Constabulary, this isn't going away. Especially if the other victim dies."

Marcus drew a long breath and let it out. She was trying to shock a response out of him. That was all.

Her voice was nearly inaudible, as if she wanted Marcus to lean in to hear her. "Or if you're on their list."

His stomach hollowed. "What?"

Nicole held his gaze with eyes like blue lasers.

"You're not human interest," he said, and Lee's hand squeezed his so hard she might crack bones. Maybe it was the fatigue that pushed him over the edge into a risk he couldn't take back.

"I'm not *only* human interest," Nicole said.

"Hey, Nic, you know these people?" A guy's voice from behind them, too smooth, condescending. Marcus tugged Lee's hand and increased their pace enough to look annoyed but not desperate. *See, not running away. No reason to.*

"Y'all hold up a minute," the man said.

He circled to stand in front of them, suit jacket open, no tie, dark hair mussed. Taller than Marcus, but reedy. Long fingers, white hands. The lack of adrenaline proved the guy was no threat, not even to Marcus's overreactive brain.

But Lee's hand tensed.

Yeah. The guy was in their space. Marcus dropped her hand and stepped forward, and the man tried for less than a second not to give ground, then backed up several feet. They stared at each other.

"If you have any knowledge of —"

"No," Marcus said.

"Does that mean — ?"

"No."

The man moved to one side and swept out his hand, his head slightly bowed, permission for them to pass. The gesture was as patronizing as his tone. Marcus should slug him.

Lee's cool hand slid into his again, and her thumb ran over his knuckles. The scarred ones. Yeah, okay. No hitting things. Or people.

They crossed the open lanes for standing cars, for dropping patients near the doors. Nobody followed them, not even Nicole Stopczy. Halfway to the lot itself, his knee gave out, and he had to check his balance.

He hadn't been allowing the limp since spotting the reporters, so to an onlooker he'd appear to have misplaced his footing, nothing more. Lee stepped closer and draped his arm over her shoulders.

"I can —"

"I know you can. Lean anyway."

"They're watching us." He tried to pull away, but he was too spent, and she knew it.

Before he could growl at her, Lee angled their bodies so that she appeared to be leaning into him as much as he was leaning into her. Her head tilted up to his, and her lips were so close, inches away, turning up a little.

"See?" she said. "A public display of affection."

He couldn't look at anything but her mouth.

"Marcus." Concern nested between her eyebrows, but her cheeks reddened — Lee, blushing. She blushed less than yearly.

Kiss me. "Okay."

He relaxed into her, not fully but enough to relieve his knee and the quivering muscles in his legs. His hands shook even more. She stood four inches shorter, her frame slim but strong, and they'd walked this way countless times during his physical therapy.

He'd been rigid then, fighting her, hating every step he couldn't make on his own. He tried not to be that way now. But it still didn't feel right, leaning like this. Needing like this.

He couldn't even drive himself home with his truck impounded by the cops. But that was a shallow worry after everything that had happened today.

"I was hoping we could get dinner," Lee said when they reached her car.

The cafeteria sandwich had been hours ago. "Let's do it."

Lee drove them to a Schlotzky's, where she ordered one of those salads with apple wedges in it and Marcus got the original sandwich. One bite made him close his eyes with pleasure and thankfulness and . . . *Thank You, God, that I'm alive today. That Heath and Austin are alive.*

The food shored him up. Lee knew it would, of course. She drove him home, and they both stared at the car in the driveway. A dark blue compact thing he'd recognize anywhere though he'd never seen it outside Walt's garage.

"Millie's old car," he said. He pulled out his phone to call Walt, but a text had come through an hour ago from Austin. *You've got transportation. Walt and I left a car at your place.*

He texted back. *Thanks.* "Walt and Austin," he said to Lee.

Austin's reply pinged back in less than a minute. *No problem.*

"That was kind of them."

"Yeah."

They got out and walked up to the orange front door.

Marcus unlocked the door and leaned on the frame. "Violet didn't text yet."

"It doesn't mean anything dire. He's going to be asleep more often than he's awake for at least a few days."

"Okay."

Lee turned toward her car, then back to him. "Marcus, I . . ."

She closed the distance between them. Reached a hand up and touched his face, thumb on the point of his cheekbone, fingers grazing the stubble of his jaw and drawing away at his chin.

She couldn't do this to him. It was too much. He was too raw. He'd hold her against him and hide his face in her hair. Hide with Lee from all of this. He should step back. He should go into the house. From the other side of the door, the dog whined. Probably had left a puddle some-

297

where by now.

Lee's hand inched up to the back of his head, and the tips of her fingers brushed his hair. His breath caught in his chest.

"Lee," he whispered. *Please. I can't.*

She combed her fingers deeper into his hair, and the gentleness in the touch brought a burning to his eyes. Once more, her hand combed through, this time on the top of his head. She ran her thumb over the cowlick at the base of his neck.

Then she touched his right temple, the hair that had gone silver this past winter. Her thumb stroked there, and her fingers cupped the back of his head and immersed in his hair. He shut his eyes against everything he wanted, but her hand didn't draw away. Lee, touching him, not like a nurse, not like a friend. She was close to him, breathing, being, trusting him as she discovered how near they could be.

Her fingers curled in his hair, barely gripping the back of his head. He turned his face into her hand and kissed it. She took his left hand and lifted it to her hair, and as his fingers threaded through, everything inside him ignited. He had to hold her. He had to. Did she know?

"Lee, I . . ."

"Marcus," she said.

He closed his eyes. Shook his head. Her hands drew away from him. He opened his eyes.

"I thought . . . You don't want to kiss me?"

"Yeah. I do."

Confusion tugged the corners of her mouth.

He slid his fingers through her hair to keep from touching her lips. "Not tonight."

She looked about to ask him why, but she shook her head and took his hand instead. Ran her thumb over the knuckles. He lifted her other hand to his lips and kissed it. Anything more would not fit with this day. Would not be right. He hoped she understood, because he couldn't explain what he knew.

23

Around eight at night, Violet slipped in the door of their apartment, and shortly thereafter she disappeared into her room. She wasn't the type to avoid company even in stressful situations, so Lee must have conveyed her desire for solitude somehow. During the next two hours of reading, Lee closed her book and stood three times, but each time she curled up in the big chair again.

She would have kissed Marcus. She'd told herself to be ready for this. To be a physical comfort. He'd been walking through the day with woundedness in his eyes. Kissing him had seemed like common sense. Had her hesitation ruined her effort to help?

She shut her book harder than necessary. She had to stop this pointless analysis. But recapturing her thoughts sufficiently for reading wasn't going to happen tonight.

Someone knocked on her door.

Lee's stomach knotted. She glanced down the hall to the bedrooms, but Violet didn't emerge. She must not have heard. Lee rose from her reading chair and went to the spy hole. Juana. She opened the door.

Juana wore purple yoga pants and a mint green graphic tee printed with a cluster of purple hearts. Her long black hair was pulled back in a ponytail, and she wasn't wearing her usual mascara and lip gloss. Lee let her in and locked the door behind her.

"Is something wrong?"

"I would've brought you a chai tea, but the café's closed, of course. Anyway, I guess it's too late for tea." She glanced around the room, then peeked down the hall toward Violet's room.

"Juana," Lee said. "What are you doing here?"

Juana tightened her ponytail. "I felt like I should come."

"Why?"

She sat on the couch and waited until Lee claimed the reading chair. Something wasn't right. Lee fought the impulse to pull her knees up.

"I should have called or texted you, but I knew if I did that, you'd say you were fine, because you actually think you are fine."

301

Lee's body tightened from her neck to her toes. "This isn't —"

"Lee, whatever happened in Michigan, I have eyes. I saw you two today in the hospital. And I thought, there's no way they'll be able to sleep tonight. So here I am."

Say something. Do something.

"We can talk about whatever. Or we can watch a movie or play Scrabble or something."

"I . . ." Put a stop to this now, or Juana would think it appropriate to invade Lee's space whenever she chose to. "Thank you, but this isn't necessary."

"I don't mind." Juana stretched her legs out on the couch.

"I'm saying I would prefer you to go."

"And I'm saying you need a friend right now, whether you want to admit it or not."

"No. I don't."

Juana blinked. The calm openness in her face fractured into uncertainty. "You really want me to . . . go?"

"I believe I said that."

Juana stood as if in slow motion, one foot at a time touching the floor, arms pushing herself up. "We . . . we all annoy you, don't we? I annoy you."

Cold crept over Lee, starting at her back

and folding forward like a cape over her shoulders, trickling into her chest. She planted her hands on the armrests of her chair.

"Lee, if you don't want to be part of the women's group, then why are you?"

The cold around Lee hardened. She stood. "I've tried to contribute whenever possible."

"Sure, you serve every week. You serve more than a lot of us do. I thought you wanted to. But today at the hospital, when I invited you to pray with us, you looked like I'd asked you to walk on hot coals."

Mortifying, the transparency. At least only Juana saw through her. Unless . . . "Do the others perceive me this way as well?"

"I doubt it. Ruby and Monique mentioned you aren't around much, but they think it's because of your work schedule."

Was she . . . faking? Did she truly not wish to be part of them? Perhaps she didn't understand herself anymore. She walked to the door and kept her face turned away from Juana.

"I don't see the benefit in discussing this further. Thank you for making me aware of . . ."

"Of what?"

"The inadequacy of my attempts."

303

Juana's voice came close behind her. "Are you trying to offend me until I walk out? Not happening. Especially today."

What?

Lee turned. "I don't understand what you want."

"Nothing. I want to be here for you. You don't have to do a thing."

"I'm speaking of the bigger picture."

Juana tightened her ponytail again and sighed. "I guess, eventually, I'd like honesty."

Honesty was the least of what she owed Juana. She owed friendship, too. But she might not be able to give it tonight. She laced her fingers behind her back and leaned into the wall. Honesty.

"The women's group does not annoy me. Interacting with them takes effort. That's all."

"Why?"

The word was a lance. Reasons festered in Lee like infected boils. She tried to maintain eye contact, to coerce Juana on to another subject with the strength of her glare, but Juana shook her head.

Lee had to pray about this. Pray for assistance, for the ability to preserve the friendship. She shuffled to the reading chair and curled up in it, though the fetal position would ruin her attempts to look composed. Something flickered in Juana's eyes when Lee wrapped her arms around her knees, but she waited for Lee to speak.

"I have nothing in common with other women — that is, with other women my age in a church setting. Most of them are married. Most of them are raising children, and many of them are pregnant, and their conversations tend to revolve around things I can't . . . things I have not experienced."

Juana sat on the couch across from her. "Because you can't have children."

"Precisely."

"Does it . . . hurt you? To be around all the moms?"

"I have nothing to contribute to their daily lives. I don't see us ever . . . bonding in friendship, when our lives are so different."

"You know, I've known two women who are mothers now — I mean, biologically — who the doctors said would never have a baby. One of them has three kids."

Lee's eyes burned.

"But that's a topic for another day. Tell me what else is going on with you."

"What else?" She'd said quite enough.

"You might as well spill everything in one night."

She shook her head.

"Lee, come on. We've made it this far."

How to say more without saying too much? Lee sorted through her thoughts and found no halfway road. Either she refused to reveal one more thing, or she revealed everything.

"I've been seeing a counselor since . . ." Effect seemed an easier place to begin than cause, yet already she was stumbling over the topic.

She'd been seeing Hannah since December, but that first month of sessions had nothing to do with Lee. She'd gone to Hannah and requested information on how to help Marcus. By January, they agreed he had to ask for help himself, that Lee couldn't heal him and had to give him space to realize what he needed. Lee had seen this as a parting of ways until Hannah asked if she'd like to continue coming. To work on herself. It had to be the work of God's Spirit that Lee said yes.

Two months later — outlasting Hannah's wildest estimation for how long he could keep functioning without sleep, without help — Marcus called Lee at three in the morning.

"I'm sorry . . . but please come."

He'd had enough presence of mind not to drive to her. They sat in Walt's guestroom together until an overcast dawn crept into the room. Sometime in those hours, Marcus had consented to see a counselor. Not hers — they agreed on the awkwardness of that. Hannah had given Lee one of Pete's business cards two months prior, and she'd kept it in her glove box. She dashed through a thunderstorm, to her car and back again. She offered it to him shiny and laminated against the rain. Marcus crushed it in his hand. But he called the number.

To tell Juana she'd begun counseling in January wasn't true. But to tell her she'd started in December implied she'd been working on herself that long.

"I'm seeing a counselor," she said.

Juana curled her legs to one side, elbow propped on the arm of the couch. She nodded Lee on.

"Once a month. I started with twice a month."

Another nod.

And now the cause. "When I was eighteen, I was assaulted and raped."

Juana remained quiet and motionless. Perhaps Lee could do this.

"I became pregnant."

"Oh, Lee."

"I knew my parents would not be pleased, so I kept it from them as long as possible.

Several months. Eventually, no amount of loose clothing could conceal the . . . the baby. I went to my mother and asked for help."

If she continued from this point, Juana might walk out and never come back.

"Lee? Are you okay?"

"Fine."

"What happened when you went to your parents?"

"My mother told my father, who took me for an abortion. I refused to sign the paperwork." She suppressed an instinct to press her hand to her abdomen, where she'd once felt movement. Life.

She looked up. Juana still watched her, listening, expression open to whatever Lee said next.

"My father was a city official, an elected position. He'd run on a homegrown-morality sort of campaign. Since there was no police report, he feared judgment from his constituents."

"No police report?"

"I drove home after the incident. My mother asked if I wanted to go to the police, and I said no." Lee drew in a long breath and held it, readied herself for the rest of the story. The part that might end this friendship. "After my act of rebellion, my father drove me home and told me I had two options. I could get an abortion, or I could move out. Support myself and the —"

Another breath. *The bastard,* he'd called it. Never *the baby* or *the child* or even *the fetus.* She hadn't expected anything as sentimental as *my grandchild,* but she hadn't expected *bastard* either, though he was linguistically correct.

"If I got an abortion, he told me we would act as if nothing had happened. He would pay for me to go to culinary school, as he'd always said he would. And I could live at home until I finished my degree."

Juana's eyes were filling, and one tear trailed down her cheek. "You were eighteen."

"I was a legal adult who knew her daughter was a person and had her killed anyway so I could go to school."

"And now you're a nurse."

"It was the worst penance I could dream for myself, at the time." She shivered. "Ironically, halfway through the degree, I discovered I didn't hate it. Helping others heal is — well, rewarding. Perhaps by now I'd have tired of culinary arts."

"I don't . . ." Juana wrapped her arms around herself and sat forward, eyes earnest. "I don't know what to say."

That didn't sound like good-bye. A weight lifted from Lee's shoulders that she hadn't known was there.

"Lee, there's nothing I can say except that I'm sorry. If I've said anything . . . callous, since we met. I mean, there's no *if*, I know I've said things."

"You have never offended me." Strained her patience, perhaps, but who didn't do that to Lee? And she surely tried Juana's; tonight was proof of that.

"Is your counselor Hannah Garcia, from church?"

Lee arched her eyebrows. "She is."

"Just a guess. But I'm glad it's her."

"Yes." Lee stretched her legs and rested her feet on the floor. She didn't feel sick, or panicked, or exposed. She didn't want to drag Juana out into the corridor and lock the door after her. In fact, it was almost comfortable, Juana's knowledge of these things. A relief.

"Does anyone else know?"

"Only Marcus. He forgave me."

He saw she wouldn't relent, after he protested he had nothing to forgive. Still, his forgiveness had sealed cracks in her. Until last year, he'd held an incorrect story in his head, one Sam had assumed and Marcus had accepted from him — that Lee had been physically coerced to have an abortion. She'd never wanted either of them to know about her signature on the consent form.

"Forgave you?" Juana's face crinkled.

"I developed a severe infection after the abortion. A hysterectomy was required."

Juana shook her head, still not understanding.

"Marcus would have wanted children. Would have been a good father." Her voice broke, and she blinked away the burning in her eyes. They might have saved her uterus if she'd sought treatment sooner. Instead, she'd moaned into her pillow, borne the pain as just recompense for the life destroyed, and taken days to realize something was wrong.

"I'm so sorry."

Lee shook her head.

"For how you were treated. For everything that happened to you."

"I have been . . . Hannah's showing me that I have been closed off. Within myself, and with God, and with others. That I didn't deal properly with . . . with any of it." She folded her hands and leaned her elbows on her knees, mirroring Juana's posture. "I'm learning how to do that, but it is . . . a slow process."

"Take your time."

"I don't seem to have a choice in that."

"Sorry if I was pushy. I can be, you know."

"Anything less might have been unsuccessful." Lee let a smile push at her mouth.

Juana grinned. "I know you say Marcus is the most stubborn person on the planet, but I think he's got competition."

"He would agree with you."

"I'm so happy you found each other. He's a good man."

Juana had only the shallowest concept of his goodness. So many secrets excised tonight, Lee nearly told her this one — everything Marcus had done in Michigan for the church family, everything it had cost him — but it wasn't hers to tell. And as long as a fraction of him suspected everyone capable of betrayal like Clay Hansen's, Marcus wouldn't tell it either. The thought ached anew.

"Thank you for trusting me," Juana said. "When you're ready, I think you should talk to the other girls, too. But not until you're ready."

"I'm not."

Juana stretched her legs out on the couch and stood. "I can go, if you want. This day's been long and rough."

"I could make you a chai tea."

How was she doing this, showing the hospitality of Belinda Vitale? Well, not exactly. Belinda would have served Juana three varieties of dessert by now. Lee waited while Juana studied her with a slow smile.

"So not too late then?"

"Never," Lee said.

Minutes later, two steaming mugs in hand, Lee passed her phone on the counter as it buzzed with a text message. Gloria's name lit her screen, and she set the mugs on the counter and retrieved the text with trembling fingers. Texts — two of them, three minutes apart.

Heath is awake.

Lee's heart quaked in gratitude. She pressed a hand to it, understanding that gesture of Juana's for the first time. She scrolled to the next message.

His second request was, "Can I see my wife?" His first request was, "Do y'all have any pecan pie?" Good thing he's easy to forgive.

The smile hurt her face as she took her phone and the tea mugs back to the living room, as thanksgiving filled her in a way she'd never felt before. And that's what this was. A feeling. A warmth toward her God she didn't know what to do with, swelling inside her as she imagined Heath and Gloria sharing a slice of pecan pie. She let it overflow into a silent hymn and lifted it toward Him and hoped it was as acceptable to Him as the songs she sang on Sunday morning. Something deep inside her whispered that it was.

24

He slept in snatches, half an hour, fifteen minutes, lying rigid on his mattress for hours in between. When he was awake, his head ached. When he thrashed in his sleep, the wrenching of his knee brought him out of the nightmares with pain that blinded him, knifing up and down his leg. Every time he drifted off, he watched Jason shoot Heath and Gloria, Violet and Austin, firing squad lines of people from church who stood crying, asking for help, as Jason walked down the row of them and put a bullet in each of their foreheads. The gunshots cracked. The blood spurted. Coated Marcus's hands. And then he watched while Jason shot Lee from so far away, Marcus couldn't get there in time to stand between her and the riddling bullets, but he was there beside her when she fell. He always caught her. She was always dead.

He woke for the tenth time around one in

the morning, shivering while the sweat dripped down his temples. His T-shirt was long saturated with it. He lay on his back, gulping air and squeezing his eyes shut while his leg . . . His right hand reached for it, a reflex, but he knew better than to touch it when the swelling was this bad. He gritted his teeth but let himself moan. Nobody to hear, and for some reason, releasing the pain like this made it easier to take than keeping silent.

A wet tongue lapped his face.

His body jerked at the shock of the contact, then relaxed. Dog breath was easy to recognize even at a time like this.

He lifted a shaking hand and set it on Brody's head. The dog whined and nosed Marcus's chest. Marcus expelled a long, broken breath, and Brody whined in chorus. His hand fell to the sudden stab in his side. He'd done something in his sleep to displace a rib.

God . . . this night. Not the worst night of his life. But Pete would say that didn't negate what he felt right now, this minute. He pressed his hand against the stabbing. *This night is long, Jesus. But I know You're close.*

His heart still pounded from the dream. He couldn't stop seeing them. The dead.

His mouth was cotton. He needed water. But that would require walking. He opened his eyes and locked gazes with his dog. Brody set a paw on Marcus's chest and let out a growling whine, the same sound he'd made when he showed up at Marcus's door.

"What?"

Brody nosed under his chin and then set his two front paws on the mattress at Marcus's shoulder. Marcus stroked his back.

"I'm okay." The rasp of his voice wouldn't fool even a dog.

Brody hopped up onto the mattress and stretched out next to him, burrowing against his left side, head under his arm. Warmth from the dog's body seeped into Marcus, and Brody's breathing was even, calm, not panting.

"Okay. Good dog."

Marcus pressed the heel of his hand to the rib, and on the third try it shifted to let him breathe easy again. He closed his eyes. He prayed for Heath as his thoughts fragmented into sleep.

With Brody's head on his chest, he slept long and hard. The dreams came a few times — he remembered flashes of them when he woke — but he didn't seem to have moved. The pain from the night had dulled, receded a little. Or maybe not. Everything felt worse in the dark. Even with a night light.

The sunrise striped the ivory carpet with a pink glow. Brody slept on as Marcus lay there, petting his head, fingering one of his ears. Yesterday he'd set the wooden chair in the corner of the bedroom and left his phone there, and now it buzzed and vibrated, sinking to the center of the chair's seat. Marcus rolled off the mattress and crawled to the chair, keeping his right knee off the floor.

A text from Austin. *Working today. Need to talk to you.*

He checked the time on his phone — after seven. Sleeping almost six hours straight was rare even on the best nights. Brody stretched and padded to his side, and he rubbed behind one of the dog's ears.

"Thanks, dog."

Marcus used the chair to get to his feet and headed for the shower. Looked like he'd be having an egg and sausage burrito for breakfast.

After confirming Austin was working the breakfast shift, Marcus drove over. Millie's car pulled to the left, and according to the chiming alert when he started the car, it needed an oil change. He'd have to do that before he returned it to Walt. His first stop when he hit town was to take down the found dog notice at the diner. Alexis would still let him know if somebody came looking — only right thing to do — but he hoped nobody came. Then he headed to Rosita's.

The restaurant's parking lot was mostly empty. Expected aftermath of a shooting. He shuddered as he limped to the patio dining area. Heath's blood had dripped here, dried or smudged away now. Marcus pulled open the door of Rosita's and blinked in the dim lighting.

Austin wasn't manning the takeout counter today. Probably in the kitchen, like usual. Marcus poked his head around a stucco column that half walled the kitchen from the dining area. Austin stood over a long counter, assembling burritos. For a minute, Marcus watched the kid work. The movements of his hands were sure, quick. Skilled. He could make a good carpenter, if he wanted to.

Austin glanced up as if sensing Marcus's gaze. "Hey. Five minutes?"

"Sure."

Rosita herself bustled in from the other side of the dining room. "*Hola*, Marcus."

"*Hola*, Rosita." He also knew *gracias*. And . . . that was about it.

Rosita spoke quickly to Austin, several

sentences, all in Spanish. He replied, and she beamed at him and headed back to her patrons. Marcus cocked his head at the kid.

Austin grinned. "Been working here six months — almost seven. Have to pick up a few phrases."

Right. Marcus could work here for six years, and his Spanish would never sound that effortless.

Austin finished preparing the entrees in front of him, tucking in the corners of flour tortillas as if he'd been doing it all his life. He plated the food and put it up on the cooling shelf for the servers, an order slip peeking from under each plate. Then he washed his hands and turned to Marcus.

"Okay. I've got a fifteen-minute break. I told Rosita I'm taking it now."

They went outside. Marcus squinted in the sun. He wondered sometimes if sunlight were brighter here, or if he felt it more now than he had before. Austin followed him to a table across the walkway from where Heath had sat yesterday. Marcus eased into the chair and folded his arms on the table. Austin copied him, leaning forward, blue eyes serious.

"Thanks for coming over here."

"Thanks again for the car."

"How's your pastor doing?"

"Woke up last night. He's stable, last I heard."

"Good. When it happened, I thought . . . Anyway. Have you seen the news this morning?"

Marcus's heartbeat tripped. "No."

"Jason's name was released."

He leaned back in the chair. Pulled for a deep breath, and the rib he'd adjusted last night gave a lingering stab.

"Mine's next," Austin said, thumb rubbing the knuckles of his other hand. A small shiver grabbed his shoulders, and he stiffened in the chair as if to hide it. "I talked to the detectives again last night, late. Walt showed up. They're saying they can protect me from Michigan — yeah, I shot an American, but he shot a Texan. They're not going to hand me over. But I don't know, Marcus. We've already seen that the Constabulary doesn't adhere to the law if it gets in their way."

Marcus's witness statement of self-defense wouldn't matter. Heath's medical report wouldn't matter. Nothing would except that Austin was an agent who'd shot an agent. For being one of them, the Constabulary would want his blood.

"We'll find a way."

Austin scrubbed a hand through his hair.

"You don't mean the church, I hope."

"I mean us. You and me. Lee and Violet."

"I . . ." Austin gave a long sigh and pushed his chair back from the table, its metal legs scraping the patio. "I don't think so."

He hadn't asked Marcus here to strategize with him. Didn't need help with a plan. He already had one. Certainty crystallized in Marcus from the inside out. He waited for Austin to tell him. The kid looked as frayed as Marcus felt, a thread away from snapping. Dusky circles sat under Austin's eyes.

"It's not forever, necessarily." Austin looked down at his hands.

Understanding panged Marcus, sharp as a trick rib. His feet itched to pace. His left heel pushed against the patio stone, keeping him in the chair.

"Don't," he said.

"I won't last long in the States, Walt said. He's talking about Canada. Not sure how long."

No flinch in the blue eyes, no hesitation. No possibility of being talked down. But Austin's mouth pressed too firm a line, and the hand he lifted toward his hair trembled before he lowered it. Eyes open, locked on Austin's, Marcus prayed. *Show me.*

"I was never going to stay in Texas, Marcus."

No, he wasn't. A protection detail. That's what this had been. Long over now. But . . . "Violet?"

"I won't be the guy who tried to come between her and God. And I wouldn't be her choice, believe me."

"Austin . . ."

"Am I in love with her?"

"Yeah."

Austin looked away. A muscle twitched in his jaw. "She's the purest, most beautiful woman I've ever met. And yes."

"Then stay. And let us find a way."

"That's exactly it. I need to find a way, myself. I need to . . ." He shook his head, and this time his hand made it all the way to his hair, raking up and down. "I can't trade one indoctrination for another, Marcus. I won't."

Marcus planted his elbows on the table and watched while Austin, the kid who could pick up Spanish without trying, sorted through the words in his head with a frown etched over his face. After a minute, he looked back at Marcus.

"All I know are the extremes. The Constabulary and the Christians. I need to walk a few miles of middle ground."

The simmer in Marcus wasn't anger, wasn't offense, but it burned too hot to ignore, a candle lit inside him that flared to flame. Was he supposed to speak, even after he'd convinced Violet to give Austin space?

Yes.

Marcus leaned over the table, hands flat on its surface. Austin didn't look away. Respect flickered in his eyes, a respect Marcus hoped he mirrored. This kid — no, this man — had saved his life more than once.

"There's no middle ground," Marcus said. "The world's at war."

Motionless, Austin considered the words. Then nodded. "I've seen that much."

"And there's no neutral."

"And we're not talking about the Constabulary anymore."

"No."

Austin sat back. "I've decided one thing in the last month. It matters. I told Violet once it would matter if you guys were right, and I meant it, but . . . not the way I mean it now. Philosophies aren't entertainment anymore. I mull them over until I'm thinking in circles."

"Get a Bible."

"Maybe. I've read some of it."

"At the Constabulary academy? Are you sure it was the Bible?"

"Fair point."

"You can't know what you think of Jesus

if you've never read His words."

"I guess that's logical."

A smile twitched Marcus's mouth. Austin sounded like Lee.

"But I can't stay here, man. If I'm going to sort this stuff out, I need space to do it. All this with Jason . . . . this . . ." A curtain dropped in front of his eyes, snuffing out the momentary spark of confusion, disquiet, maybe hurt. Of course. It had to hurt to kill a man, even a man like Jason. Austin cleared his throat. "I planned on leaving months ago. Should have. But Violet — she's . . . It's not easy, letting her go."

No, it wouldn't be. Marcus couldn't do it. He'd proved that for years. But if Austin needed to leave, Marcus wouldn't talk him out of it. Maybe he was right. If Walt could make it happen, Austin could watch from a safe distance. See how Texas dealt with US demands, see if freedom here was a passing thing or a permanent one. If it died, he never had to come back.

"Okay," Marcus said.

Austin grinned. "That was easier than I expected."

"It makes sense. For now."

They were quiet a few minutes, sitting at the table, cicadas loud in the bushes behind the restaurant. From inside came the mur-

mur of conversation and the clinking of dishes and silverware and Rosita's voice rising to call a server girl.

Marcus couldn't let Austin leave without one topic opened. And only he could open it. Yesterday, in the hospital waiting room, the shock had weighted them both like wet cement, too heavy to see through, move through, speak through. But if Austin didn't talk about it, the veil that had fallen over his expression would thicken with time. Pete had taught Marcus that much.

"Jason," Marcus said. Full sentences about yesterday still fought him.

Austin's eyes locked on his. "You mean the man I shot?"

Yeah, there it was. Hovering under everything Austin said, every blink, every movement of his hands. Whatever you called it — confusion or shock or whatever — Austin didn't try to hide it. Well, there'd be no point in hiding it from Marcus.

"He's dead." Austin shook his head, gripped his knees. "You want to know how I'm coping with it."

"Yeah."

"I was in my apartment last night, sitting on the couch, reading. I turned a page, dropped the book, ran to the bathroom, and threw up."

"Okay."

"Kind of a delayed reaction. Not sure what that says about my moral fortitude."

"He would have killed somebody." It didn't change Austin's feelings, but in the equation of justice, it mattered.

"He had kids. Did you know that? A wife and — and boys, I think. I can't remember, but he told me once."

The tide of memory swept Marcus's composure out from under him, a wave of images, voices, a superhero night light, a high little voice reciting his holiday wish list. A woman with burgundy curls, kneading bread dough and extolling the Constabulary's virtues. That same small boy's voice shouting, *"Mr. Brenner! You got your toolbox!"*

Marcus fisted his hand on the table, pushed back against the flood. "Three boys."

Austin quirked an eyebrow, and then realization opened his expression all the way as he forgot to filter it. "You knew his family?"

"Met them." Twice. "His wife's name is Pamela. His boy J.R. is . . ."

Calculating any time in the last year still muddled his brain. He hoped it wouldn't always. He grabbed onto the months he could hold and tried to keep clear of the black hole in the middle of them, the four-month hole. J.R. had been six years old in December — not this past one, the one before — so seven this past December, maybe. No older than eight.

"He's probably seven," Marcus said. "The oldest."

By now, Pamela had been informed. An officer at her door, and unlike Gloria, she wouldn't hear that her husband was still alive.

"I didn't know." Austin ran a finger along the edge of the table, watching Marcus. "How . . . personal . . . it all was."

They needed to get back to the important topic, but Marcus's words had dried up.

"I told you in the hospital, I'm not sorry."

There. He nodded Austin on.

"I'll be fine, but I won't be who I was before I killed him. And if that makes sense, it shouldn't, because I don't understand it yet myself. But I know it."

"Okay," Marcus said. He waited, but Austin was quiet, staring out across the parking lot, probably at memories. "When're you leaving?"

"Rosita deserves two weeks' notice, but it feels . . ."

Unsafe. Yeah. The Constabulary could add Austin to their list and lay siege to Kearby any time they chose.

"You'll say good-bye?"

"I have to clear it all with Walt and the detectives. They might not let me go."

Right.

Austin stood, and Marcus did the same. He held out his hand, and Austin shook it, his grip firm and steady.

"Come back," Marcus said.

"I'll try."

25

Maybe because Marcus had been Walt's houseguest, maybe because he was a wanted man, Walt always picked up the phone when he called. Time and place didn't matter. Marcus didn't want to abuse that status with him.

This seemed worth interrupting him for, though.

The phone rang four times. "What's going on?"

"Not an emergency," Marcus said, though it felt like one. "But if you can talk . . ."

"Phone?"

"In person. When you can."

"At the park in an hour?"

"Okay."

They met at one of the benches along the winding cement path. Neither of them had heard from Gloria since last night, but Walt insisted no news was good news. Still, Marcus would go see Heath for himself tonight.

With Lee. After she got off work, they were meeting at his place for dinner. Not likely to get any work done between then and heading to the hospital, but he had to feed and let Brody out, so they might as well eat there.

"No cookware," he'd said. *"You have a plan?"*

"I thought we could be spontaneous."

A silence fell between him and Walt, lightened by laughter from a group of people at one of the picnic tables. Marcus collected words for the thoughts he'd organized on his way here. A sparrow perched a few feet from him on one of the bench slats. He held still until it flew off. When he looked up, Walt was watching him.

"There's a reporter named Nicole Stopczy who works for the *Decatur Clarion.* She knows about the list."

"What?" Walt's eyes narrowed. "How?"

"I don't know."

"Is she running a story?"

"Isn't that what you want? Public opinion?"

"There's what I want and there's what the governor wants."

"Walt."

"You don't know all the factors, Marcus. There's a lot at stake."

"I know what's at stake." Tension ached down his neck, into his shoulders. "This woman knows I was a fugitive."

Walt crossed his arms. "You talk to her?"

"No. She — that flash flood last week, I pulled some people out. She wanted a story on that. Found me at the diner."

Walt crossed an ankle over his other knee with unfair ease.

Marcus shook the thought away. "She figured out why I didn't want a story. Then yesterday, leaving the hospital with Lee — a lot of reporters by the doors, waiting, and she saw me."

Walt squeezed his eyes shut and pinched between them. "You didn't speak to her."

"No. But that's when she told me about the list."

"Glad you let me know."

The pieces churned inside him, knowledge and safety and facts and opinions. If he could get up and pace, they'd come together faster. He pounded his fist against his good leg. Helplessness sawed through him.

"What're you thinking?" Walt said.

Dang it, I don't know.

"Marcus?"

"Maybe I'm supposed to talk to her. Anonymously."

"She doesn't know your name?"

"She does."

"There's no guarantee she wouldn't use it."

"If I do nothing." He stretched his good leg and swiveled on the bench to face Walt head-on. "If I say nothing. It won't make me safe. They'll send another agent after me now that Jason's dead. And even if they don't, what about the others? What about Austin, if they make him number sixteen on that list? And who says where it stops? In a year there could be hundreds, getting picked off one by one, taken back and locked up, and Texas doing nothing."

If stopping them meant risking his identity with Nicole Stopczy, then . . . He pictured the betrayal in print, his name, his description, his Kearby address somehow dug up by her or maybe she'd follow him out to his house. He pictured stepping outside one morning and seeing the Constabulary agent's car parked under a tree across the street. Being tackled again, handcuffed again.

"I never expected you to do something like this," Walt said. "Not you, after all the wrangling we've done."

"If you've got a better plan . . ." One that didn't involve any talking by Marcus. To anybody.

"I can't ask you to risk yourself with the press."

"No. Tell me straight, like I'm anybody else. If somebody on the list talks to her, if she publishes it — would it make a difference?"

Walt gazed out on the park, then turned to Marcus. "I believe it would."

Ten minutes later, they left the park, after Walt had extracted a promise from Marcus that he wouldn't talk to Nicole Stopczy till Walt "looked into" her. Marcus got into Millie's car and sat staring at his phone. *Man up and make the call.*

"Good morning, Platt Orthopedic Center."

"I'm a patient of Dr. Platt's, and I . . ." Acid rose in his throat. "I need an appointment. Whenever you have something open. He hasn't seen me in a couple months. Marcus Brenner."

"B-R-E-N-N-E-R?"

"Yeah."

"Can you confirm your date of birth, please?"

He did, and the woman paused a moment. He squeezed the steering wheel with one hand while he waited.

"Would you be available June nineteenth? That's a Wednesday."

Over a month. He closed his eyes, and the breath shuddered from his lungs. "Is there anything . . . sooner? Please?"

"Not at this time, but if a cancellation happens, we can call you."

"Yeah. Okay."

He scheduled the appointment and lowered his forehead to the wheel. He could make it until June nineteenth. He'd be okay. He sat there awhile, sun streaming in his windshield, while people passed him, entering the park.

His phone vibrated, still in his hand. Dr. Platt's office.

"Hello."

"This is Tracie calling from Platt Orthopedics for Marcus Brenner."

"Yeah. That's me." Hope swelled in his chest.

"Hold for Dr. Platt, please."

Only a minute, and then the doctor's husky tone came over the line. "Marcus?"

"Yeah."

"You didn't tell my receptionist why you wanted an appointment."

The acid taste filled his mouth. He'd told the detectives everything yesterday. Medical staff should be easy to talk to, in comparison. *And you think you can talk to a reporter?* Well, he'd deal with that later.

Dr. Platt knew who Jason was and what he'd done. Knew about the four-month hole in Marcus's life that would be dark forever.

So Marcus could tell him this. "Knee's been bad."

"Did you reinjure it?"

"I think so."

"Have you been walking on it?"

"Yeah."

"With the brace?"

He gritted his teeth. The brace hadn't been optional the first few months. But it was too thick to wear under the leg of his jeans. He had to wear it on the outside. Visible. He might as well walk with a cane, if he was going to start advertising his injuries. And how would the knee strengthen if he continued coddling it?

"No," he said.

"Right." No doubt Dr. Platt was shaking his head. "Can you be here before noon, by chance? Or are you working?"

"I'm not."

"You might have a wait. My schedule's booked. But if you come in, I'll see you."

"Thanks."

"I'm glad you called."

Dr. Platt knew too how hard it was to call. At his first appointment, Marcus had frozen on the exam table. Brain blacked out. Stiff with panic. When he came back to himself, Dr. Platt sat in a chair across the room and talked to him. Just talked, for long minutes he didn't have, until Marcus could nod permission for the knee to be examined.

He drove to the clinic, limped into the waiting room, signed his name on the clipboard, where the receptionist promptly blacked it out. He waited an hour in the waiting room chair while throbbing radiated up and down his leg, the knee a white-hot epicenter so intense he couldn't read the covers of the magazines spread on the table to his left. Then one of the medical assistants called him back, and he followed her down the corridor to the only exam room with a window. Another kindness, one more thing nobody in this office knew but Dr. Platt.

He came in ten minutes later, white coat, white wreath of hair, eyes the color of faded denim.

"Well then," Dr. Platt said, "how long have you been tolerating it this time?"

"A few days."

"And you already called me? Good job." He smiled. "Now let's get you back on your feet."

After an X-ray to verify he hadn't injured the bone, Marcus hoisted himself onto the table and braced himself on the arms of the chair, curling his hands around them. He nodded that he was ready, and Dr. Platt took the knee between his hands and examined it. Marcus kept his lips sealed tight, tried to keep any sound from seeping through them. Didn't always succeed.

"Definitely sprained the MCL again," Dr. Platt said a few minutes later. "This ligament sure knows how to give you trouble. It probably happened during a quick change of direction or if you slipped at all lately. Remember anything like that?"

"No." But that didn't mean it hadn't happened.

As Dr. Platt circled codes on the exam sheet, Marcus loosened his grip on the arms of the chair and cleared his throat. Dr. Platt looked up.

"You know that shooting on Third Street . . . the Constabulary agent."

White eyebrows shot up. "Named Mayweather, I think."

"It was him."

Dr. Platt set his clipboard on the counter beside the sink, then dropped down onto his rolling chair. "Were you there?"

Marcus nodded.

"And how are you doing with all that?"

Marcus kneaded the muscles above his

knee, aching but less tender than the knee itself. "A lot of scenarios used to go through my head. Being taken again, going to prison, him tracking me down and shooting me. But this never did. Him being dead. I never thought what it would mean or — or change."

"What did it change?"

"Well. I'm safer with him dead."

"But?"

"Nothing he did got erased. It's not that I thought it would. But I . . ." He shook his head. His own thoughts were confusing.

"You don't have the closure you expected," Dr. Platt said.

"If one of us was going to get killed, it was going to be me. So I don't know what this looks like. Me the one still alive."

Dr. Platt exhaled a long breath and studied him. After a few seconds, Marcus fidgeted on the table. The man's blue eyes were almost as searching as Pete's, and all the decades of his life creased around them and seemed to shine from them.

"Give yourself time to sort it out. You can do it."

He could. With God's help and Pete's. And the other people who stuck by him.

"It might take longer for you than for somebody else. Living with pain changes the equations."

The old defenses rose up inside him — not in pain, okay, always okay. But they were lies. Every day, he measured pain in degrees to be ignored, forgotten, unnoticed. And the strongest thing he could do was be honest. Like Sheriff Brody, do the thing that scared him. He shut his eyes and saw himself punching through the lies and facing the truth.

"Yeah," he said.

"You'll get there, Marcus."

Pete had told him that for the first time when Marcus was still pushing back at everybody, even Lee. When he was barking at people and breaking things in spurts of anger he didn't recognize in himself. He was learning, but some days hearing the words again were what he needed most.

"Thanks," he said.

"Sure thing." Dr. Platt tapped his pen on his thigh. "Now, one way to get you there is to deal with the physical issues. So let's talk about that brace."

Marcus left the office wearing a new brace. On Dr. Platt's orders, he made a follow-up appointment for two weeks from today, warned by the receptionist that the doctor's schedule was already full. Marcus told her he'd wait as long as necessary.

He should have gone back to the brace days ago. It helped with the pain more than he'd expected, and the knee no longer threatened to buckle with every step. Dr. Platt had told him to wear it at night, too, at least until his next appointment. If it would make him better, he'd do it.

Lee would be at his house in a few hours. Maybe he'd go home and sleep.

Maybe he'd call Nicole Stopczy and ask to talk with her. Not an interview. Just talking.

No. Give Walt time to check her out first.

He drove back to Kearby thinking about Lee. Picturing her at work, wearing scrubs and hurrying down a hospital corridor alongside a gurney, keeping somebody alive.

After working all day, she wanted to serve him dinner. That wasn't right. Especially when he *hadn't* worked today. He called and waited for her voice mail.

"Please leave a message," said an automated voice.

"Hi," he said. "That spontaneous thing? Forget it. Dinner's on me. Just come over. I'll have everything ready."

He'd been so concerned with taking things at her pace, not crowding her. It had been too long since he showed her the gift she was to him. Time to fix that.

26

To Lee's knowledge, the only food preparation Marcus had ever mastered was eggs and sausage, and his idea of making an edible egg was flipping it once in the skillet and delivering it onto a plate, the yolk ready to bleed at the first poke of a fork. If he offered her breakfast for dinner, she would . . .

She would eat it gratefully. Too tired to do otherwise. But she did hope he'd gotten takeout.

Something had been morphing inside her, so slowly she hadn't noticed until now. She'd always wanted solitude when she arrived home after a shift. Silence. A good book. Violet had learned to give Lee her space at the end of the day, at least for an hour (preferably longer, though Lee had never told her that). Yet here she was, leaving the hospital and driving straight to Marcus, anticipating his voice.

He had become part of her space.

She knocked on the orange front door, then tried the knob. Locked, of course. After a minute, he opened it, dressed in jeans and an olive Henley that put a hint of ginger into the waves of his hair. He was barefoot, and for some reason that observation took Lee an extra moment to look away from. The smells of refried beans and seasoned beef drifted out to her, and she was tempted to thank God for Rosita's.

His eyes crinkled first, and then the smile found his mouth. The warmth of it traveled all the way to Lee's toes.

"Hi." He stepped back to let her inside.

He shut and relocked the door, and her eyes traveled him again. The cowlick at the base of his neck. The rest of him.

"You're wearing your knee brace."

"Yeah." He turned to face her. "I saw Dr. Platt today."

"Good." Days late, but at least he'd gone.

He sighed, stepped close to her, and took her hand. "I'll fill you in on the drive to the hospital — and yeah, I'm still driving. But right now, we're having dinner."

He led her to the kitchen without releasing her hand. He'd done the best he could with one chair and no table. A clean white drop cloth draped his monstrous metal toolbox, the chair pulled up to it. Marcus motioned her to sit and brought her a paper plate of chips and two small plastic containers of salsa. She smiled. One would be medium, one absurdly hot. Marcus kept the latter cup in his hand and snagged a few chips. He ate leaning his lower back against the counter, weight off his leg.

"Please sit," she said.

"In a minute."

"I can eat standing."

He finished the chips in his hand and stole a few more. "You've been standing all day. Sit and — and rest."

They finished the salsa in silence, and then he threw away the plates and brought two more. Hers was heavy with steaming enchiladas. Her favorite.

He set down a side of sour cream and smiled. "Forget anything?"

"Not a thing."

They drank bottled water from the stock she and Violet had bought. Dinner passed as quietly as the appetizer. Lee sank into the ease of it, and only as she was finishing her last bites did she understand. He'd been silent for her sake. With her, serving her, letting her recharge.

He finished his burrito and again cleared the plates. When he rounded the counter, his hand braced on it. Only a flash of movement, and then he was standing unsupported again, but if he thought he'd get away with knowing her better than she knew him . . . She stood.

"Your turn." She gestured to the chair.

His jaw clenched. He stood there like a mule planting its hooves.

"Thank you for all of this. I needed it. Today was long. Now please sit."

When he dropped into the chair, a fire in his eyes banked low. Too low. He stared at his hands in his lap. He didn't think she could see the defeat. From others, he masked things well, but they didn't look at him closely enough.

She startled at the image in her mind — the rest of a lifetime with him, reading his tells as astutely as he read hers.

She softened her voice and stood between him and the toolbox. "Marcus."

"I . . . I wanted to give you dinner. And space. I wasn't going to talk about anything tonight."

"Is there something we need to discuss?"

His eyes met hers, steady, resolute. "Yeah."

Lee backed up to the counter and hoisted herself onto it. He angled in the chair to face her. Whatever was churning in his head, if it was something about them, something wrong and he'd delayed telling her to spare her feelings . . . Lee crossed her ankles and tucked her hands under her thighs. The counter was cool under her palms.

"Say it, please," she said. "I'm prepared."

His brow furrowed. "Okay." He glanced away, then back to her. "In movies, you know those guys who tell the woman to be with somebody else. For their own good."

A giant fist constricted her breath. He couldn't think . . . yes, he could. He was Marcus. But no matter, she wouldn't listen. She would fight for him. For them. She held his gaze with hers, open, hearing what he had to say, every nuance of it, so she could disprove it all.

He was waiting for an answer.

"Yes," she said.

"They're morons."

Her breath left her in a rush. She let her ankles uncross, her legs dangle free. "Yes."

"I don't want you with some other guy. Any other guy."

Again, he waited. Again, she nodded.

"I want you with me. But . . . the me . . . before." He tucked his chin to his chest as his shoulders caved in. "There's so much, Lee."

She waited for clarification of the last part. He knew she needed more than that, and he'd say it when he could.

He lifted his head. "You already know. Some of it."

In the following quiet, Brody padded over to Marcus and nudged his arm. Marcus petted the dog's head, but his eyes didn't leave Lee's.

"We don't talk about it. But I know sometimes you still . . ." His mouth pinched a little. "You keep an eye on me. Looking for anything that could be . . . wrong. Or . . . or hurting."

"That's true." A part of her, the part that had absorbed emotional blows in the beginning of his recovery, couldn't help remembering how he'd treated this subject in the past. His voice now wasn't taut, storming with helplessness. He'd come too far for that.

"I . . ." He gave Lee a smile that strained not to become a frown. "You're doing it now."

"Yes," she said.

"I hate it."

Lee took his words with a slow blink and tried to seal them inside her, somewhere they couldn't hurt.

"Six months, I shouldn't need it anymore. The watching."

The quiet held cracks. Perhaps only Lee felt them, and perhaps they weren't fair.

Marcus wasn't yelling, wasn't pounding his fists on the nearest surface. He was putting those things into words instead.

"But . . ." His next breath seemed to labor.

Something elemental pulled her. She dropped off the counter and went to his side.

His voice dropped. "But there's so much still wrong. With me."

"Marcus." Her fingers grazed his shoulder, and some flicker deep in her needed to be closer than this.

The contact of her hand seemed to break something in him. His hand caught hers and gripped hard. "I want to be . . . I want . . . but . . . it's like . . . like I'm full of holes."

"Holes that are mending," she said.

"I know. But I don't know when."

This was what he wanted her to know. Nothing to do with expectations of her — rather the expectations he'd set on himself. Lee stood close to him, kept his hand securely in hers, and brushed her other hand through his hair. Again, the contact sent a shudder through him. He was close to tears. Closer than she'd seen him since the only time he'd ever cried in front of her. The day she accepted God's salvation. But whatever was fighting to come out of him now wasn't relief, wasn't gratitude. It quaked inside him, tightened his grip on her hand. It needed release.

"Marcus." Lee drew him to her, his cheek pressed into her shirt, below her breastbone. "You haven't expected me to heal within a certain timeframe. I won't expect it of you."

His arms wrapped around her waist. He held on a long minute, and then a sigh poured from him.

"You need to remember the distance you've come."

"I do."

"I don't mean only physically. I'm talking about your expectations for yourself. Your emotional health. You were . . . Marcus, you were . . ." She blinked against the memories. "Every hour you were awake, you were finding ways to push yourself too hard. You convalesced for what felt like five minutes and then you decided you should be functioning at one hundred percent."

Marcus pressed his hand to her back, his cheek to her shirt. He seemed to be absorbing both her words and her touch.

"During my first session with Hannah, I told her, he's never been able to accept limitations, and he'll disregard them now, too. He'll do more damage to his body than is already there, and I don't know how to prevent him from doing it. And . . . Marcus, you didn't see yourself. How angry you were."

"I remember," he said.

He'd lived it from the inside, yes, but that couldn't give him the same perspective. "I was afraid for you."

He released a long breath and sat back in the chair, eyes fixed on her face, posture straight. Everything about him was listening. Lee took his hand between hers.

"You had no concept of getting well. You expected to *be* well all at once."

"Yeah."

"There you are, then. See how far you've come. How many holes have mended already. And I don't need you to be the man you were a year ago. I love the man you are today, this minute."

He pushed to his feet. "What . . . did you say?"

"I said you don't need to be —"

"No. Not that part."

She had said it. Unplanned up to the moment it left her mouth — no, even past that moment.

He stood still, a small crease between his eyes. Uncertainty.

She took his other hand. "I love you."

Light filled his eyes until not a shadow remained. The crinkles she loved formed around them, and then he was smiling. "You love me."

"Yes."

"You. Love me."

He was letting this be about her words, knowing what words meant to her, but for Marcus she could do better than words. She brought his left hand up to her lips and kissed the scars on his knuckles, then lifted her head.

"I love you," she said, because she owed him several years of the phrase.

"Lee."

They stepped into each other's arms at the same time. His hand cupped the back of her head, fingers threading through her hair. She tilted her lips up to his, and he took her mouth and somehow gave her the wholeness of what they were together. Even with his kiss, he took care of her.

The kiss was careful and slow, but when she pulled back from it, his eyes weren't careful at all, didn't want slow. He kissed her forehead, and she could have laughed and cried at his determination, honoring her boundaries. She came up on tiptoes and whispered close to his ear.

"Show me how."

"How . . ." She'd never seen his eyes burn quite like this. *Smolder,* a word Juana used about her romance novel heroes, and laughter bubbled in Lee again. *Joy.* A word from Hannah. This might be it.

"Your experience well outranks mine."

"Well?"

She shrugged. "The girls in high school. And the other one, when you were twenty-two."

"You make me sound like a . . ." He shook his head, but amusement tilted his mouth.

"Compared to a woman whose only crush never progressed beyond hand-holding . . ."

"Does it count as a crush when you're five?"

"I'm sure we thought so."

He traced his thumb over her cheekbone. "Lee."

He'd waited so long without hope that she'd ever say yes. She shook her head and eased back.

He let her go. "You okay?"

"Fine. Only . . . sorry, I suppose. For the lost time."

"No," he said. "It was God's time. For both of us."

She rested her hand on his chest. Took another step closer and pressed her cheek against the beat of his heart. His arms encircled her again. He kissed her hair. She looked up into his eyes, showed him how sure she was, how safe she felt, and kissed him again.

27

Lee loved him.

He'd known she cared. He'd known she trusted him. A friendship like theirs, lasting through so much conflict — that was care and trust on both their parts. And Lee wouldn't have been ready to kiss him before if she hadn't felt something more than what they'd had for the last ten years. Still, if somebody had asked him, point-blank, *Does she love you?* he couldn't have answered for sure. Till now.

How does that feel? The question came in Pete's voice. Marcus smiled. Knowing Lee loved him felt like an endless sunny day. More light than he could ever take in.

But he had to focus. The drive to the hospital gave him time to tell Lee what she needed to know. The knee sprain. The conversation with Austin. And finally, all Marcus's thoughts in the last twenty-four hours involving Nicole Stopczy. Whether or not to talk to her. How much to say. How to ensure his anonymity when she already knew his name and the town he lived in. Lee was quiet awhile, watching out the side window while the highway rolled away under the tires and the flat Texas land stretched out alongside. He had to keep from looking at her while he drove. Lee. The woman who loved him.

"You believe this could help Austin as well as yourself."

"Yeah. And the rest of the people on that list."

"Walt agrees?"

"That it could make a difference, yeah. That I should do it . . ." He shrugged.

His pulse notched up a little when they arrived at the hospital and crossed the parking lot where the reporters had stood yesterday. Nobody here today, though.

When the elevator opened on Heath's floor, they were met by a few church people, leaving for the day.

"Have you seen the news?" said a man Marcus didn't know. "The US is claiming that Mayweather guy was an exemplary agent, here on a mission of diplomacy."

The comment passed as he and the others got on the elevator. Everybody said their *see-you-later*s as its doors slid shut. Marcus blinked away the image of Jason's body.

As they approached Heath's room, Gloria came toward them from the other end of the hallway. Marcus and Lee said hello, and Gloria waved them toward the room with a smile. "The morphine makes him slightly more direct than usual."

Lee arched her eyebrows at Marcus. *Go ahead.* As hemmed in as Gloria had been the last twenty-four hours, this was a good time for Lee to talk to her. Make sure she was really okay.

In the doorway of Heath's room, Marcus stopped. Monitors still beeped beside the bed. An IV line snaked from Heath's hand. The white sheet and blanket were pulled to his chest, and he lay reclined, eyes closed.

The first twenty-four hours had passed. Somewhere, probably from Lee, Marcus had heard the first twenty-four hours were important.

"Good to see you, brother." Heath's voice carried less strength than usual, but the smile didn't seem strained.

"You, too." Marcus entered the room and stood next to the bed.

There must be things he wanted to say, things you said when your friend got shot and almost died in front of you. He cast his gaze around the room. On the far wall hung a white board bearing the printing of at least two different people. One of them was more of a scrawl.

"What's it say?" Heath said. "I forgot to ask Gloria."

Maybe Heath was trying to give Marcus a conversation topic. Or that handwriting was too hard to read on pain meds. "Um, your nurse's name is Holly. Your doctor is Dr. Stamos."

"What about the rest of it?"

"Well, the faces are a pain scale."

"I figured that."

Heath seemed to be waiting for more. "In the corner, it says, um, 'If you sense a noticeable change in your loved one or your medical condition, call your nurse immediately.' And in the other corner, 'Patient Goals and Questions.' "

Heath's mouth twitched. "Goal is to get out of here."

Couldn't blame him for that. The smells, the sounds, the stark white of everything — worst, Heath was trapped in a bed with a needle in his arm. A shudder ran through Marcus, but Heath didn't seem edgy or even frustrated.

"What about the header at the top? Is it my name and room number or something?"

"And the date."

"Thanks. It was starting to bug me. Morphine and dyslexia are a terrible combination."

Morphine and . . . "What?"

Heath's eyelids started to droop, then lifted again as confusion wrinkled between them. "Sorry. A little foggy. I guess I've never told you that."

"No." Marcus crossed the room in a few steps and sank into the bedside chair.

Heath's smile was a shadow of itself, as if his body lacked energy for the real thing. Memories of him tumbled around Marcus's mind, reframing and redefining. He shook his head.

"You read Greek."

"Very slowly."

"Heath, you read all the time."

No response this time, but Heath's eyes were steady on his. No wonder he memorized his sermons instead of preaching from notes. But as the sifting of new and old knowledge settled, Marcus couldn't find any more *aha* moments. Heath functioned seamlessly.

There had to be a cost. In frustration, if nothing else. A pastor with dyslexia was like . . .

Like a contractor with a bad knee.

A frown crimped Heath's face, as if he

couldn't quite grasp a memory. "What?"

"Not now." Marcus shifted in the chair, feet wanting to pace.

"Why not?"

"You're . . ." Marcus jerked a hand toward the bed, the IV line, the monitors. If they were going to talk, it should be about this.

"Oh." Heath's dismissing gesture barely raised his hand from the bed. "Nothing to say."

"Why'd he grab you?"

A dying hostage. Marcus had wrestled with the logic of it last night, lying stiff on his mattress with Brody's warmth and dog-smell beside him. The only conclusion was that Jason didn't care whether his hostage lived or died — a random person, innocent as far as Jason knew. Expendable anyway.

"You were right about him," Heath said. "The impulsivity."

"Did he know I was inside?"

"I don't think so. I think he was covering bases, asking around. But at the time, I wasn't sure. I approached him, and he wanted to scare me off, I think, but . . . I don't know what happened. Don't even know what I was doing, really, but I knew you were inside and . . ." Heath shut his eyes.

The last of the pieces fell into place with a

solidness that fell on Marcus's shoulders and tried to crush him. Heath had nearly died, trying to have his back.

"Next thing I remember is being in the car with him. And then I was in the ambulance. Don't remember getting put in there. Is he in custody?"

"Jason's dead."

The words fell into the room before Marcus could consider them. Heath's eyes opened, studied him. Marcus pushed to his feet and paced, grateful for the knee brace. No way he could sit still another second.

"The US will use this. Somehow. They're calling him a fallen hero."

Heath stirred under the blanket, winced with a hand to his side. "Texas won't call him that."

"It won't matter, if they don't push back." Hard. Refuse to give the US its way in anything else. Marcus dug his knuckles into the ache in his neck. If people knew who Jason was, what he'd done . . . Would it matter?

"Would you talk to Walt?" Heath's words slurred. Sleep was trying to claim him, but he was keeping it at bay.

Marcus should leave him alone. "About what?"

"About Mayweather. We have to make

them acknowledge they sent a man like that into our country on a kill mission."

It was like Heath knew, had read his mind. Or listened in on him and Walt at the park.

"You're not a threat — not to innocent people, not to national security. You're just a person trying to start over here. A . . . a civilian person."

Heath pronounced his words clearly, but the rambling betrayed him. Marcus crossed to the chair and dropped into it.

"Go to sleep, Heath."

"Have a plan?"

"Maybe."

Starting to drift, Heath frowned too hard, like a little kid trying to dramatize his point.

"I'll tell you later."

"God's with you, brother."

"I know."

Marcus stood as Heath's breathing evened and his hand relaxed, still resting on his side. He headed to the door. Lee would be disappointed not to see Heath awake.

"Marcus."

He turned. Heath was watching him, eyes alert again.

"If He's asking you to do something, He's also promising to go with you. You know that."

Before, the image would have been strange

to Marcus — Jesus walking beside him into Nicole Stopczy's office. But Jesus hadn't left him in four months of darkness, in six months of growing stronger inside and out. He wouldn't leave Marcus now.

Still, the thought of what He might be asking Marcus to do — it made him want to grab Lee, grab his dog, grab his toolbox, get in his truck and drive somewhere nobody would ever find them. Not the US government, not Texas, not reporters, not Constabulary agents. He grasped for the certainty he'd had before. *Not supposed to run.*

He stared at Heath, not really seeing him, till the man's eyes closed and sleep overcame stubbornness. Marcus left the room and went to find Gloria and Lee.

Gloria smiled as he approached. Lee stood from the waiting room chair beside her.

"Is he sleeping?"

Marcus nodded.

"Good," Gloria said. "When I told him y'all were coming, he said he'd keep himself awake for you."

So many reasons to stay. Heath and Gloria. Violet and Austin. The half dozen families who gathered around Charlie's tables on Sunday afternoons. His clients who trusted him to do good work. Even the streets of Kearby, fringed with magnolia and live oak and sweetgum trees.

And if Texas turns you over?

Nicole Stopczy's knowing already — it wasn't coincidence. He couldn't ignore it. He couldn't protect himself at the expense of so many.

"Marcus?"

Gloria and Lee both studied him. He rubbed his neck and sighed. "There's something I've got to do."

Gloria cocked her head, waiting for details, but Lee's expression smoothed into knowing trepidation.

"Yeah," he said to her.

"All right," she said.

Gloria looked from Marcus to Lee and back again. "Fill me in?"

28

Voices drifted from the living room as Lee toed off her tennis shoes. She shrank back against the door and gripped her keys to mute them, pointless reflexes. Whoever was in her apartment, they'd heard the door open. The place was less than a thousand square feet.

"Lee?"

Violet. Lee expelled her pent breath and walked through the kitchen, setting her purse and keys on the counter. "Do we have company?"

"Just Austin." Violet's voice broke on his name, and a male voice said something too low for Lee to hear. Violet's laugh broke too.

Lee found them in the living room, sitting on the couch, shoulder to shoulder, leg to leg. Closer than expected, given Violet's impassioned speech at the clinic two days ago. Across the room, a suitcase and duffel sat against the wall. One look at Austin's face confirmed the reason for his visit.

He was wasting no time.

"Marcus spoke to me," Lee said before he could launch into an explanation.

Austin nodded.

"There has to be another way," Violet said.

His eyes cast to one side.

"Lee, tell him."

The choice was his. Perhaps Lee should leave them alone to sort things out. But Austin looked up at her, blue eyes asking a question . . . or a favor. As if they shared something Violet couldn't understand, and maybe they did. They'd both come here for someone else. Embracing faith had changed everything for Lee, but she could imagine herself in Austin's place — a place in which nothing had changed at all.

Nothing but the bullet that had killed his former boss.

Lee perched on the ottoman — not claiming a place in this discussion, ready to leave if Violet or Austin seemed to prefer that. Her hands settled on her knees, and she let silence be her answer.

Violet looked from her to Austin and back again. "Really? You're going to let him go off to Canada without a fight?"

"Canada?"

Austin shrugged. "I'd rather see Australia, but not until I can relocate my sisters, too. Canada would only be an hour away, if I had to get to them."

Sensible. When Lee nodded, he gave a small sigh. Somehow her approval mattered.

"This isn't just about the shooting." Violet's right thumb rubbed her left wrist.

Austin glanced down at her hands, and a smile flitted over his face, then faded as his Adam's apple bobbed.

Violet's eyes welled, and she looked at Lee. "I thought — I wanted us to be friends. I wanted it to work."

"That may not be best for everyone," Lee said.

"Of course it's best. We belong together. All four of us. That's — that's how it's supposed to be."

Austin set his hand on her knee. "No, babe."

"Don't call me that." Her spine curved as she leaned forward and hid her face in her hands. "I can't believe this is happening. I thought Walt would make everything okay."

"Walt's the reason I can go."

"That's not making everything okay!"

He glanced at Lee again, his expression brimming with things he wanted to say. Needed to say. To Violet. "Lee, if you don't mind . . ."

Lee rose and stepped back, and gratitude eased his posture. "Will I see you after tonight?"

"I hope so," he said.

Violet covered her mouth with her hand, and her shoulders shook. Austin stood.

A hug would be appropriate, but neither Lee nor Austin moved forward for one. Just as well. Lee laced her fingers behind her back and thought about the hole Austin would leave behind, a square torn from their four-square quilt. She hoped Marcus had told him he mattered to them. She hoped Austin believed him.

No, that wasn't enough.

"You will be missed." The words were like an unsalted cracker in her mouth. *Try harder.* "You've been a friend to us. To me. Thank you for coming with us when you didn't wish to, and for . . ."

He nodded with a little smile. He was telling her she didn't have to verbalize it. But she did.

"Thank you for saving Marcus's life. I hope you'll return to us in time."

"Maybe I will," Austin said. "Thanks for wanting me to."

Tears dripped down Violet's face, one after another, no pause between them. Lee reached down and squeezed her shoulder, and Violet let out a sob.

Nothing else to say, to do. Lee left them in the dimly lit living room, padded through the kitchen, past Violet's room, where the empty aquarium bubbled. In her room at the end of the hall, Lee put on a tank top and pajama pants and sat on her bed. She selected a book from her nightstand. *Fahrenheit 451,* an old favorite whose corners she'd worn and whose spine she'd creased. Down the hall, quiet reigned for a few minutes, and then voices slowly rose until Austin's pierced the apartment.

"Not like this!"

Their voices dropped again.

In half an hour, the front door opened. Ten minutes later, it closed. A soft wail tore the silence.

Lee set Montag aside and got out of bed. Halfway down the hall, Violet appeared at its end, stared at her for a moment, and rushed into Lee's arms before she thought to lift them. Violet held onto her and cried into her shoulder.

"I knew the whole time. I knew I wouldn't talk him out of it. I was praying so hard, Lee, for God to keep him here with me, but I knew He wouldn't do it. I knew."

"Perhaps he needs this. Time, space —"

"I'm so selfish, asking him to stay when we can't be together. But I couldn't help it."

"I doubt he'll hold that against you." She withdrew and turned to shepherd Violet, one hand on her back, to Lee's room.

They sat on the bed together, legs drawn up like children. Violet's tears kept flowing. Nothing Lee could say would help this hurt. She sat silently until Violet sniffed and met Lee's eyes, the lamplight shining in her tears.

"I didn't even see it coming."

"I'm sorry."

"And of all the days . . . I — I was going to tell him today —" Tears fractured her words, and she swiped at her cheeks. "My paperwork's all finalized. I got my driver's license today, my Texas driver's license. I became a citizen the day he left."

Lee waited for the tears to flow afresh, but those words seemed to bolster Violet instead. She wiped her palms over cheeks again and drew in a shaky breath.

"It has to be more than a coincidence, right? It means God's doing something big."

Did it mean that?

"Anyway, I have to toughen up. Like you would do."

"Like . . . me?"

"Good grief, Lee, you have no idea how many times I've wished . . ." Violet smiled and repositioned to kneel on her hands. "I don't want to *be* you, I want to be me. But yeah. A slightly more Lee-like version of me. You're . . . cool."

More like icy. Lee's throat constricted around every memory of her fellow nurses calling her Spock.

Violet's forehead furrowed. "That's a compliment."

"Violet, I've often wished to emulate . . . you. Your warmth, your ease with people."

Violet went still, not a blink, not a breath, and then she shook her head. "If you saw inside my head, you'd never say that."

"If you saw inside mine, I doubt we would remain friends."

A grin spread over her face. "Let's just be us, then."

"All right."

"And thanks for listening to me cry over my boyfriend."

Not ex. Lee smiled.

29

Mid-morning, Walt called Marcus with information: Nicole Stopczy was exactly who she claimed to be. A human interest reporter trying to become an investigative reporter. A skilled writer who hadn't made any obvious enemies, but Walt added that if she broke the story of Jason Mayweather, that would change.

"You're going to do it, aren't you," he said.

"I have to."

"Anonymously?"

"Yeah." Of course.

Silence.

"Walt."

"Hear me out. If you spend fifteen minutes in the public eye, it'll be a heck of a lot harder to assassinate you quietly."

"You're kidding."

"Not a bit."

That ended their phone call, and Marcus drove to the park and made his way to the nearest sidewalk. He passed a few people, mostly moms with kids. He pictured Aubrey here with Elliott, then Pamela Mayweather with her boys, and the images pierced in different ways.

He passed the play scape and stopped where picnic tables scattered over a wide grassy area open to the sunshine. The nature path was the best place to pray. Trees filtered half the sunlight and let the rest pour down on him. Birdsongs and insect hums would keep him company. But walking on the uneven wood chips today wouldn't be smart.

He claimed a picnic table and sat awhile. He waited for God to lift the burden from his shoulders. To show him an alternative. Couldn't Becca tell her story? She'd been grabbed by an agent right here in Texas, shoved into the trunk of a car. She would want to speak about it, if she knew what he knew. And she'd speak better.

Anybody would speak better than Marcus.

"Please, Jesus," he said. "I don't know if I can."

Calm sank into him like a seed and grew. He felt his Father's hand again, this time in the center of his back, nudging him forward.

His hands trembled as he held his phone.

"Will You strengthen me, like that Philippians verse?"

He dialed the number from the business card she'd given him, days that felt like months ago. His chest tightened while the line rang.

"Stopczy," she said, sounding like a detective, and he almost hung up. "Hello?"

"It's Marcus Brenner. I'll meet you."

In the pause, paper rustled. "Name the time."

"Now."

"Umm." Another pause, and then a half laugh, and for some reason he pictured her grinning while she shook her head. If she didn't agree, he'd work with her. But the longer he anticipated what he had to say, the harder the saying would become. "Do you have something to write with? I'll give you my office address and you can come right over."

He couldn't talk to her caged in by four walls. He pushed knuckles against his chest. "The park in Kearby. That's where I'll be."

This pause was the longest. Then she sighed. "I want this story, Mr. Brenner."

"Meet me at Kearby Park, whenever you can get there."

"An hour?"

"Okay."

"Thanks for calling." She hung up.

He could see the parking lot from here, and the places the sidewalk began. He propped up his leg on the picnic bench and watched. Dog walkers, more moms and kids, a few people in workout gear. Running. Loss ached in him.

Nicole Stopczy arrived about fifty minutes later, dressed in a navy skirt suit and heels. She carried a messenger bag and an iced coffee, and she walked as if the park were her office. Good. He hadn't wanted his time and place demands to intimidate her. Really, she wasn't that smart, meeting a strange man here by herself, but it was public enough to reduce risk. Still, he wouldn't want Lee to do what this woman was doing.

He swung his leg down from the bench. When her gaze traveled the picnic area, he lifted his hand to shoulder level. She headed in his direction.

What was he thinking, talking about this in public? Talking about this at all? He should have told Pete what he was going to do. Pete might have ideas to help him.

God. The reporter was almost close enough to hear him if he prayed aloud. Definitely would see his lips move. *Strengthen me, because I can't do this.*

"Hello," she said. Slid onto the bench across from him and set her messenger bag on the picnic table.

He nodded. Already lost to words.

"Thanks for getting me out of the office into the sunshine." She smiled. "Although a little more notice next time would be helpful."

No need to apologize. She'd have met him at midnight, he was pretty sure. Marcus waited for her to say something he had to answer. He wouldn't pretend to like her. Or trust her.

She unzipped her bag and pulled out . . . a voice recorder. "Do I have your permission to — ?"

"No."

Surprise lifted her eyebrows for only a moment before a frown took over her face. "Recording an interview is standard procedure, Mr. Brenner. I don't mean anything underhanded by it."

Tension gripped his shoulders until they ached. Every stammer, every pause for words, every tremor in his voice — a permanent record in her possession. And if adrenaline clobbered him midinterview, the shortness of his breath would be recorded too.

"No," he said.

"Okay." But she didn't put the recorder

away. "So you're aware, if I don't have a recording to refer back to, I'll have to check with you as I write the article. Multiple times in the next week or so."

Heck no. He gripped his neck and glared at the picnic table, at flaking red paint and gouged initials — *S.R.N.*

"Accuracy is my job."

Sure. He got that. Their eyes met across the table, and while he was still searching for words, she tugged a red spiral-bound notebook from her bag and flipped to the middle of it, pages zipping by, filled with writing in different colors — green ink, blue, purple, pink. From the bottom of the bag, she grabbed a pen.

"I can't make promises about what this will accomplish, Mr. Brenner, but I believe you and I want the same things for Texas and for the refugees coming here."

"Who told you about the list?" Might as well ask.

"I can't tell you that. It would jeopardize someone like you — someone who is trying to stay safe in an unpredictable environment. Fair enough?"

"Yeah." Walt would have to find out on his own.

"And if you allow me to record the interview, you can tell me to stop at any point."

He'd come to her. He'd decided to make a difference. This was part of the cost, the risk. He nodded.

"Okay." She pressed a button on the side of the device, and a red light lit up. "May sixteenth, interview with Marcus Brenner. Thanks for agreeing to this interview, Mr. Brenner."

She was going to drive him crazy with that. "Just Marcus."

She smiled. "Then please call me Nicole."

Well, so far he hadn't called her anything, but he gave another nod, and this one felt less stiff than the last one.

"You're not a native of Texas," Nicole said, as if his accent didn't make that obvious. "When did you emigrate here?"

"October."

"This past October?"

He nodded.

"Please voice your responses." Another smile, warm, nothing condescending in it.

Heat rose in his cheeks. "Sorry. Yeah, this past October."

"How's our new country been for you so far?"

Possible responses pinged through his brain. Weather — how he'd missed snow but loved their spring, so full of sunshine. Food — he'd loved Cajun at his first bite, but unlike Violet he still didn't get the obsession with salsa. People — straightforward, no-nonsense, generous and friendly.

Nicole tipped her head. Probably thinking, *This isn't even one of the hard questions.* Her strategy was obvious — start with the easy ones, get him to relax. But that wasn't why he'd come here.

"I want to stay," he said.

Now her eyes narrowed, studying. "Your phrasing doesn't sound sure. Have you applied for citizenship?"

He planted his fists on the table. "Turn it off."

At the bite in his tone, Nicole jerked back a little on the picnic bench, then shut off the recorder. "I don't understand. Hundreds of people apply for citizenship here every day. I don't know the exact numbers. It's a fair question, isn't it?"

She didn't know as much about this situation as she thought she did. Not her fault. Up to him to explain. He drew in a tight breath and pressed his palms to the rough wood.

"Fair. Yeah. But it isn't safe."

Nicole shut her notebook and set the pen on top. "Off the record, then. Help me understand."

"This can't go in the article."

"That's what *off the record* means."

He glared at her, but she stared him down. Okay, then. "You guessed right, at the hospital. I'm on the list."

Muscles pulled in her face, smoothed it out, widened her eyes, as if she were talking to — not a celebrity, not somebody merely famous, but somebody important. Respected. It was a quick expression, too quick to be put on, but when it faded, the respect in her eyes stayed.

"You weren't only part of a resistance movement," she said. "You led one."

He nodded. This part of the story couldn't endanger anybody, not even him.

"Tell me what you did. How you joined. The barest details, if you prefer, but I'd love to know. And maybe we can find a way to inform readers, too. Knowing this will make them care about you personally, and that's what we want."

Barest details. That was safe enough. "I hid people, moved them, helped them start life over. I was the — the middle man. The contact."

"Contact for whom?"

Everybody. Marcus shrugged. "Michigan to Ohio. Fugitives to havens. People to their families sometimes, if they were separated."

"So there *are* states cooperating. How did Michigan get word to Ohio?"

"Michigan didn't. I did."

Nicole stared at him a long moment. "May I take notes on this?"

Marcus nodded, and she flipped her notebook back open.

"You're on the list because you were the leader of the Michigan resistance. You started it, didn't you?"

"Yeah." Though he hadn't known at the time how it would grow, who would join him, how many people would come to him, hiding under porches and decks and in garden sheds until he could get to them and take them to a haven. He hadn't known how powerful word of mouth could be.

"Anyway," he said. They were detouring from his point. "Citizenship documents include your address. If the Constabulary find out those documents exist for me . . ."

Nicole's lips set in a firm line. "They could show up at your door."

"Texas isn't going to protect my information."

"I had no idea . . ." She shook her head, distant for a moment, then blinked and seemed to refocus. "I don't think any of my other questions pose a danger to you, but if I'm wrong, let me know."

They talked a minute more about how much of his anti-Constabulary activities was safe to reveal. Nicole turned the recorder back on and asked questions repeating bits of what he'd told her, zeroing in on the fact he'd reunited families. She winked when she asked about it, and Marcus frowned at her, which she ignored.

Oh, right. Make readers care. He huffed, and Nicole's grin made him wonder how young she was.

"We've talked about your work in Michigan. Now let's talk about the circumstances that caused you to leave."

His stomach knotted. She didn't know what she was asking. *This is what you're here to talk about. So talk.* He balled his hands on his knees.

"Did they suspect you? Question you, threaten you?"

"No." The word strangled a little.

Nicole didn't notice or pretended not to. "Was the environment growing more dangerous, politically or — ?"

"No."

She looked up from her notes. And waited.

"They arrested me."

Her mouth formed an O. Her pen hovered motionless over the page.

"I was . . ." He looked past her shoulder

for a minute, counted the sparrows hopping over the grass behind her. One, two, three, four, five. "I was held illegally by an agent who knew me. We weren't friends, but . . . acquaintances, I guess. When he found out I was leading the resistance, it . . . it was personal to him. Messed with his head. Re-education was too good for me."

As were a lot of other things. Food, water, sunlight . . . death.

She set down her pen. "Held illegally? You mean secretly? No records?"

"Right."

"No one discovered this?"

"Somebody did. Got me out. Brought me here."

"Brought you?"

"I was hurt. Sick. I . . . I would've died."

Her fingers curled around the pen again and began to scrawl ink over the page, faster and faster. "Was it the woman you were with at the hospital? Did she come with you to Texas?"

"Yeah." He wouldn't bring Austin into this, no matter what she asked him, and he couldn't find a reason to include Violet, either. He let Nicole write another line or two and tried to choose his next words.

"This story — okay, please forgive me for how I'm about to describe this, Marcus. I understand it's your life we're talking about, but if you can picture with me for a minute — a Texan who's reading this story, who's on the fence about all of this going on in our government, should we deal with the US or shouldn't we . . ."

Her words trailed off as she continued to scribble words onto the page. Well, quiet could only help him. He breathed in, focused on his senses. The sweetness of Texas spring air, the song of a mockingbird.

"Your story is going to capture people. The — sorry, but the drama of it. I hope you know what I'm trying to say. I can't thank you enough for calling me. For sharing this with my readers."

Time for the last puzzle piece. He cleared his throat. "You know about the shooting. About Jason Mayweather."

"Of course," she said, pen poised. Her eyes grew their widest yet. "He was your acquaintance? The one who . . . ?"

A memory flashed, not Jason's lifeless eyes this time but the sparkling, trusting eyes of Jason's son. The weight of J.R. on Marcus's shoulders while he stood in a department store, while both of them watched through the window as Jason handcuffed an old man who'd found God and wanted to preach about Him to everyone walking out of that store.

"The US spokespeople are saying he was here on a mission of diplomacy. They're saying he was killed to sabotage Texas/US relations."

A breeze swept over the clearing, and Nicole pushed her hair back from her face. Stared at Marcus. "Were you there at the shooting?"

Nod.

She forgot to remind him to speak for the recorder. Her voice hushed a little. "He was sent here to work the list. Or . . . maybe he wasn't assigned the entire list. Do you know how it works? Do you have someone keeping you informed?"

"It's not been proved yet." His voice steadied. "But yeah. He was here for me. The shooter was protecting people at the scene. People Jason was threatening."

"Including you."

"Yeah."

"And to confirm for the recording, you were there."

"Yeah."

"The United States is lying. They sent agents here to . . . Was he here to kill you?"

"I think he was supposed to take me back."

But it wouldn't have gone down that way. Marcus, if nobody else in the world, knew that. His escape to Texas, Jason seeing him again here, healthy, standing on his feet, muscled and strong again — it would have been enough for Jason finally to put a bullet in Marcus's head. Too easy or not. Cheating or not.

"You said he was threatening people. Other immigrants like yourself, I assume?"

"The man in the hospital is a Texan."

Her head jerked up. "Hold on. Agent Mayweather shot a Texas citizen?"

"Yeah."

She scribbled a note. "I can't believe this. A Texas citizen gets shot by the Constabulary and it doesn't get reported."

"Politics."

"Please don't think I'm saying his life is worth more than yours."

"No, I get it."

Nicole popped the top off the back of her pen and pushed it back on. "Okay, you're not going to like my next question."

"Go on."

"May I please have permission to use your name in this article?"

He was shaking his head before she finished, but it was a reflex, a reaction. A shiver crept over his arms. No, she couldn't use his name. But if he let himself consider it . . .

"The details you've given me, Marcus — you're not who I thought you were. You're not a random fighter in the resistance. If I go public with this story, you'll be a nameless stranger to your potential allies. But your enemies are going to know exactly who gave this to me. That's the opposite of what we want."

"I don't want to be found," he said quietly. The possibility was heavy on his chest.

"I understand. And you deserve anonymity, you really do, but you're not going to get it. Not if I print this about Agent Mayweather, and that — that's the fulcrum of the lever that's going to sway public opinion to your side. Exposure of the lies about him, exposure of what he did and what he was sent here to do."

If he was wrong about staying in Kearby, if he and Lee were supposed to leave, say good-bye to Grace Bible Church, disappear and start over somewhere south . . .

No.

"While you think on that, let's talk about this rescue. Was your friend working with the resistance, too? Did they — ?"

"What if I say no, you can't use my name?"

Nicole studied him. The red light on the

386

recorder seemed to do the same, an unblinking eye. "I'll abide by your wishes. Anything else would be unprofessional."

The edge in her voice might be insult, but he had to ask. He swallowed an apology. Professional, not personal. That's what this was to her. Had to be the same to him.

"And . . ." She shrugged, spun her pen where it rested on the notebook page. "I'll pray for you."

The recorder light was still on. Risk buzzed in Marcus's brain, an old reflex he might never get over. They'd been talking about this stuff for an hour, and still, her admission elevated his pulse a notch. Something in him wanted to warn her.

"I'm not just saying that." She must have misread his expression. "I'm a Christian."

So easy, those three words. Easy because they were safe here. But . . . he fidgeted again, and the stiffness in his knee gave a different kind of caution. If he didn't stretch it, he might not be able to get up in another hour. He pushed to his feet, stepped away from the picnic table, and paced the length of the bench. If she thought he was restless, fine. Every stride worked more motion into the knee. The brace kept it stable. He thanked God for Dr. Platt and then focused on what he'd been about to ask.

"You're a Christian reporter?"

"That's right." She smiled.

"How'd you get a job like that?"

"I hear you. And yes, my colleagues know about my faith. They hired me anyway because I'm a decent writer."

She must be better than decent. He shook his head. "Good for you."

"Thanks." Another smile.

She knew what she'd achieved, but she hadn't brought it up till now, hadn't pushed her faith in his face even knowing he shared it. Restraint. It would be a good quality for a journalist. Especially one who wanted investigative work.

His neck muscles tightened, and an old knife pricked at his center. She was a Christian. Asking for information that could get him locked up again. Asking him to trust her.

Like you trusted Clay.

No. It wasn't the same. Was it? Walt had told him the same thing: publicizing Marcus's name could protect him. And he did trust Walt. With his life.

Like you trusted Clay.

The four words hammered his brain. He stretched the knee one more time, settled back onto the picnic bench, and looked at the little red light. He prayed the Philippians verse. *Strengthen me please.*

Nicole said something to him, but the warring in his head was too loud. And then a new thought came, so quiet it drowned out the rest. *Heath.*

Heath. Praying for him, opening his home, walking alongside him even on tough roads. Stepping between him and Jason. They were brothers. Heath had proven it with blood.

Marcus lifted his head. Nicole's face held no confusion, no concern. Only a second must have passed.

"Okay," he said.

"Okay?"

"My name. You can use it."

30

"I'm not human interest anymore. I'm news."

Marcus's voice, quoting that journalist woman, cycled in Lee's head as she pulled up the *Decatur Clarion*'s website on her phone. Eight in the morning might be too early to check, but she had to know the hour it was up. The minute, if possible. The journalist had told Marcus yesterday that she hoped to break the story today. Timing was vital. The entire country of Texas was reporting not only the shooting, but also Jason's identity as provided by the US spokespeople.

The debate, the unrest, were happening now. Marcus's story couldn't wait.

The page loaded, video feed at the top, articles below the menu bar — a center splash and a column to the right of it. The main article featured a picture of the Capitol building, the headline the largest text on the page: *"Embargos Lifted, Prices Lower-*

ing." The column beside it had no photograph at all, but the headline was enough to still her breath.

"*Immigrant from Michigan Says Constabulary Agent Jason Mayweather Held Him Illegally.*"

Lee swallowed twice, trying to restore her voice. "Violet."

Violet's barefoot steps came from the kitchen, nearer, and then her voice was over Lee's shoulder. "They printed it?"

Lee angled the phone to show her.

"Wow," Violet said. "I didn't really believe they would."

They read the article together. The words volleyed around Lee's head like the pellets of a shotgun blast. Marcus's name, age, occupation, and then . . . the story.

This Nicole Stopczy was good. She told facts and only facts, but her goal glimmered between the lines, in her careful word choice. She started by explaining how she'd found Marcus and used the flash flood to introduce him as an everyman hero. Then she painted him in more remarkable but still accurate colors: a hero who resisted religious tyranny and protected others from it, a hero who'd been not arrested and imprisoned but abducted and . . .

The word *torture* wasn't used. That was a

surprise; it was the kind of vivid language the article favored. The details of his physical condition were given only a vague mention — that Marcus had reached Texas "badly beaten and suffering from pneumonia." Nothing about the near-starvation. For some reason, that piece of his ordeal remained deeply personal to him, maybe more so than the damage to his knee, though that detail wasn't included either.

"Lee?"

She blinked. Looked back at Violet.

"Scroll down?"

The words were soft. Lee forced her attention back to the article and tapped to view the rest of it. Marcus's account of the shooting. And then . . . the list. The danger he courted by coming forward.

In the final paragraph, Stopczy wrote that she'd asked him during the interview how he felt about the country of Texas. Lee could hear him speaking the quote: *"I want to stay."* And the last sentence ventured from old-fashioned fact telling to the new breed of journalism, betraying the writer's opinion in barely subtle terms: *"Time will tell whether the New Republic of Texas proves itself a haven for Marcus Brenner and the other people on the list of freedom fighters."*

"What's it going to mean?" Violet whispered.

"I don't know."

But Lord Christ, let it mean something. Please. Marcus had hollowed himself out for this. She had to talk to him.

Violet went to the kitchen and unplugged her phone from its charger. "I want to see what else is in the news. If any of it looks connected."

Lee closed the article to dial his number. No. It wasn't eight-thirty yet, and he wasn't working. She wouldn't risk waking him for this. She sent a text instead. *Call me when you're available.*

From across the apartment, Violet still stood in the same place, scrolling on her phone. She jolted, phone slipping in her hand but not dropping. "Omygosh. Lee."

A cold finger traced Lee's neck. She hurried over. "What is it?"

"This article posted twenty-seven minutes ago, and it has ninety-six comments. And . . . good grief, Lee. Read them. It's a battle zone."

Lee returned her phone's browser to the article. The comments sorted to newest first. Outrage, all of it — but the target varied.

If this is for real, where are the other people on the list? Why aren't they speaking out too?

She clicked on the link to replies and read down the thread.

If the Stab were after you, would you go public? I bet you wouldn't.

So why is this guy doing it then? Why risk this if he's telling the truth?

It's called fifteen minutes of fame, you idiots.

Spot on. People will do anything for the spotlight. I'd like to see some proof the dude's even from Michigan.

The next reply lightened the weight on Lee's chest.

You're all stupid if you can't figure this out. If this list is real, then our government's turned its back on this guy and he has no hope but that we the people will stand up for him. What if he'd never given this story to the media at all? Sounds like he would have disappeared one day and we the people wouldn't ever even know this crap was going on. I say hats off to Mr. Brenner from Michigan and let's stand with him and tell Gov. Catalano to burn that list.

She couldn't stop scrolling and reading. All ninety-six comments, various levels of support that buoyed and animosity that boiled. By the time she reached the bottom of the thread, refreshing brought up twenty-two new ones.

"I went to their social media," Violet said from across the room. "Two hundred thirty-one comments. But some of them . . ."

Lee looked up. "Yes?"

"I hope Marcus doesn't read them all." A frown pinched her face. "People are mean."

"Show me." Surely no meaner than the fifteen-minutes-of-fame imbecile. Violet handed her phone over.

"The ones being voted most helpful are good," Violet said. "It's just those few toward the bottom."

Lee scrolled to the bottom.

So it's not enough that we're letting refugees mess with our economy etc. Now we're supposed to admire the criminal element among them? If this guy broke the law, he gets what he gets. Very disappointed, *Clarion.* Thought there was more common sense in your reporting than this.

Her fingers grew tighter on the phone with every reply she read.

You do realize ALL Christians in the US have broken the law and can go to "re-education" a.k.a. prison? Or maybe you haven't been paying attention to the news for the last seven years?

He's not talking about Christians in general. He's talking about the "resistance" people. The felons. This guy is admitting to being one of them and yet he's whining about the danger. It's ludicrous. I mean, he knew the risks when he decided to defy his state government, right?

You folks are acting like this guy robbed a store and is complaining that he got arrested. The "crimes" Marcus Brenner committed wouldn't be crimes in a free country (like ours, if you forgot) and yet he was treated awfully by the Stab, maybe worse than what's in the story. You don't typically get pneumonia unless your body's been compromised in other ways first. Can't believe the lack of support from some of you folks. Wow.

I am thankful to God every day for the resistance fighters. Without them, I would have given birth in prison and my baby would have been taken from me. Because of the resistance network in my state, I reached Texas a week before her birth. She is five months old now and I'm raising her in freedom. Thank you, resistance fighters of Illinois, and thank you, Mr. Brenner.

Yes! Thanks for speaking up, Jessica from Illinois! And thank you to all the resistance and thank you to Marcus Brenner and I hope he is well recovered and stays safe and free here in Texas!

Lee pressed the phone to her stomach and hunched in a kitchen chair. She closed her eyes. Opened them. She tried to pray, tried to process, but the comments drew her eyes back. She needed to know every word written about Marcus. Everything that could be read and debated.

Before she could, her phone began buzzing in her other hand. A phone call replaced the browser screen. Marcus. She accepted the call and handed Violet's back.

"Lee." His voice was slow and blunt. Sleepy.

"Are you awake?"

"Mm-hm."

He might have lain awake all night, only fallen asleep a few hours ago. "Go back to sleep, Marcus."

"You texted me."

"If it were an emergency, I would have called."

"What's going on?" Fabric rustled, as if he'd rolled over in bed, still under the covers. The image spread warmth through her middle.

"You won't sleep again even if I hang up."

"I got four hours straight," he said as if it were all the sleep he needed. "What is it?"

"The article's online. And in print, I'm sure."

He was quiet a moment. "Is it good?"

It was generating more comments than she could keep up with reading. Did that make it good?

"Lee?" Marcus's voice turned brusque with wakefulness.

"It's well written and . . . honest."

"Good."

"It seems to be stirring up a . . . a fair amount of response online."

"Well." Caution tinged his voice, reflecting hers. "That's good. That's the point."

"Yes."

"Lee?"

Of course he'd read her even over the phone. "I don't suppose I can convince you not to read it all."

"I wasn't going to read anything but the article."

He wasn't?

"There's people saying they want me turned over to Michigan."

"Then you did read — ?"

"No. It's just what some people are going to say. I knew that."

"Marcus, I . . ." Emotion clogged her chest. She propped her forehead in her hand, her elbow on the table.

"It's okay," he said.

"You revealed so much. You opened yourself to them, and they . . ." She shook her head as if she could rid it of their words. Their scorn.

"Lee. Stop reading it."

"But I need to be aware of —"

"No. Stop."

Her breath shuddered out.

"Listen. Those people don't know me. They're not . . . betraying me. Or anything. There's only one thing that matters. Whether Texas will end the deal with the US and protect the people on the list. Okay?"

No, it wasn't. Her lungs weren't functioning right. "And if they don't? Your connection to Jason makes finding you that much easier."

"I know."

"They'll look in the town where he was killed." Her voice strained, rose in pitch. She had to level it, had to calm herself. She'd known all this before, but it was hitting her like new information.

Violet had set her phone down on the table. Lee picked it up and hit refresh on the article. Two-hundred-ninety–seven comments. That was sixty-six new comments since Marcus had called, and they'd been talking less than ten minutes.

What if all sixty-six of them were against him? What if public opinion helped the Constabulary agents find and apprehend him?

"We should have run." Her breath came short. "We should have disappeared."

"No."

"Why?"

"Not again."

"Marcus, starting over would be preferable to . . ." She couldn't voice it.

"I told you." A long sigh poured into her ear. Fabric moved again, and he sucked in a breath. The knee, the first time he'd stretched it this morning. She knew as certainly as if she'd been in the room with him.

He didn't speak for a minute. He also didn't mute the phone. A few more breaths, in and out, a small huff as she pictured him leveraging to his feet. Shuffling to the kitchen in a T-shirt with seams that stretched at the shoulders, drawstring pants that rode his hips. Her face heated, but the desire to be near him wasn't only physical. She needed to look into his face and find any hurt hiding behind his eyes, to touch his shoulder and gauge the tension in his muscles. She needed to stand close to him and know he was well, safe, strong.

Please, Lord Christ, guard him. Please.

"What I said before at Heath and Gloria's. Running would be wrong."

"How do you know that?"

"I was supposed to talk to Nicole. Lee, I . . . I couldn't have. God was there. Strengthening. Or I couldn't have."

She wanted to hold him, as she had two days ago. The steadiness in his voice was not effortless.

"And He's not done. I don't know how to say it, but I know there's more. And I know He's with us."

"Will you speak to the church tomorrow

during the service?"

"Walt and some other elders called a meeting for today at five. They sent out an email to all the members."

On a Saturday, people would come? Interrupt their day off? "All right."

"Heath talked to me last night. Called me from the phone in his room. Walt had been by and told him. I . . . I wasn't going to bother him with this. But he prayed for us, Lee. Both of us. He prayed and . . . I felt it. I'm not ready. But I have to be. For whatever it is."

No. Not more. *Let him rest now.* But one thing she'd learned of God: His timetable was His Own, and Lee could not dictate it.

"Dinner tonight," he said. "After the meeting."

"Yes."

Quiet again, and Lee nearly told him good-bye, but after a moment, he gave a soft sigh.

"Whatever's next," he said, "Jesus is walking with us."

She knew. But she wished she could feel it the way he did.

31

The moment he stepped into the church, eyes drilled him. Every person he passed in the halls stopped and stared without trying to mask it. Marcus's gut balled up. These weren't faceless strangers. Spiteful comments online? Easily ignored. Those people didn't matter to his heart, so their words couldn't either. These people, though . . . his family. They occupied a large space inside him. He'd thought it would be easier, letting them read the basics first, filling in the blanks now. But some of the stares were wary.

Betrayed? The last thing he'd wanted. He ducked his head as he neared the sanctuary.

I'm sorry. He had to start there.

If he was going to stay here, be a part of the body and not run from it, then he couldn't be anything other than real. And the real him was the one in danger. The one who'd committed felonies. The one who'd gotten their pastor shot.

One minute he was ready to tell them everything. The next it hit him again, icy, heavy fear, digging into the marrow of his bones. He read Nicole's story this morning and saw how much his church knew about him from a source other than his own mouth. He had found the strength to tell strangers before family. That wasn't right.

"Marcus."

He looked up. Becca Roddy barreled toward him and threw her arms around him. Marcus froze. She'd never hugged him before.

"Why didn't you tell me?"

Of course, Becca would ask aloud what others only asked with their eyes. She dropped her arms before he could hug her back.

"It's not like I didn't know something happened," she said. "You disappeared. Your end of the network basically collapsed. And then, when we first met up here and I saw you — that vague 'health crisis but now I'm getting better' thing only worked because these people didn't know you before. I knew the con-cops had done that to you, and I kept waiting for you to bring it up, but I never dreamed . . ." She blinked away tears.

"I'm okay." The words sounded flat, avoiding, even to him. He tried again. "I'm sorry."

"I want to talk to her. That reporter. The only way this works is if more people stand up. I was rescued last week by cops and Rangers. And if they're willing to rescue me, they've got to do the same for you."

No, they didn't. But he set a hand on Becca's shoulder. "You want her number?"

"You have it with you?"

He dug out his phone and pulled up Nicole Stopczy's contact information. Becca was still sniffing back tears when she walked away minutes later.

He entered the sanctuary at the back, walked up the aisle, and sat in the fourth pew from the front. More stares. All these people sitting in the pews around Marcus, listening to Benjamin Schneider call to order the emergency meeting — if they belonged to Jesus, they were family.

Family turns you over.

No. Not real family. Heath had shown him real family.

Shakes your hand and walks away.

No.

Leads the Constabulary to you and leaves you. Handcuffed. Helpless.

He bent over the back of the pew in front of him, hands clasped at his forehead. More stares, boring into his back. Silent prayer wasn't enough, not while his thoughts lurched like this. He felt battered, the way he had for those few seconds at the park, before the peace came. He barely let the whisper out into the room. Nobody could hear him over Benjamin anyway.

"Jesus, I need strengthening again."

The room around him seemed less cold. He kept his head down. Lee had said she'd come. She'd find him when she got here. But he couldn't lean on her tonight. He lifted his head enough to look around. A few people smiled when he caught their eyes.

Am I safe, Jesus?

Benjamin stood behind the oak podium in his customary T-shirt, shorts, and sandals, sorting through his notes while a few murmurs drifted from the group. Lee slid into the pew beside Marcus and set her hand on his arm, fingers light as flower petals, maybe braving physical touch in public only because she knew he needed it. He covered her hand with his.

They had a quorum tonight. Marcus had asked Heath and the rest of the staff to put his continued presence to an official vote. They'd unanimously told him he was being ridiculous. There'd be no voting tonight, only information.

"Y'all probably weren't expecting that mass email," Benjamin said. "But you can understand why a meeting was needed."

Marcus's mouth filled with sawdust.

"There's been a news story about one of our members today. I'm sure y'all have seen it. The original article has almost three thousand comments."

Original article — there were more? And . . . three thousand? He glanced at Lee. She shook her head, lips parted with surprise. She'd listened to him, then. Stopped reading them.

"I don't have to tell you, there's potential danger for this brother now that he's told his story. But he was in danger before too. God willing, his decision to speak about it will make him safer, but he's here today either way. Ready to talk to us. It wouldn't be safe to bring this up tomorrow morning, where visitors could be on the lookout for him. So this is how we chose to handle it, and . . . here he is. We're all yours, Marcus."

Benjamin beckoned with one hand and offered the cordless microphone with the other.

Talk. To all these people. About Jason.

Lee squeezed his arm. A warm, gentle pressure that shored him up. He braced his hand on the back of the pew and pushed to his feet.

He gritted his teeth for each of the three steps up to the platform. He should have worn the brace, but he couldn't look weak and say what he had to say. He took the microphone from Benjamin and held it under his chin and turned to face them all. Two hundred people or more. Looking at him. Waiting for him to talk.

He cleared his throat, and the mic picked up the sound, and heat flooded his face. His fingers tingled. Too much adrenaline. Where was Lee? If he could just find Lee in the ocean of faces — there. He let her gray eyes anchor him. She was with him.

And, safe or not, God was with him.

The silence had grown too long. People were shifting in their pews, embarrassed for him before he spoke a word. He held the mic down and cleared his throat again, then brought the mic back up.

"I . . . um, I don't . . . there's a lot of you."

A few quiet laughs. He found Walt in the crowd. Wished, for a selfish moment, that Gloria and Heath were out there too. But he couldn't lean. On anybody. He had to be strong enough on his own. About time.

"You know now . . . the things Walt told you about. The wanted list and the Constabulary agents hunting here. That was about me. I started the resistance in Michigan, the southeast network. I worked with Ohio, sometimes Indiana. They sent people to me. I sent people to them. You know now — in Michigan, I'm not just a fugitive. I'm a felon."

More nods. Some of these people, he knew better than others. A few of them had been part of resistance movements too.

"You know Texas isn't giving me sanctuary anymore," Marcus said.

Murmurs began. Some people looked confused, whispered to others. Most met his gaze with grim frankness. Marcus took the moment to breathe. The words he'd already said were the easiest ones.

"You know about the Constabulary agent who was shot three days ago. Who shot Heath. That agent would have killed me or taken me. Heath got in the way. He —"

Blood on his hands. The crack of the gunshot that obliterated the back of Jason's skull. Marcus lowered the microphone and sucked in a breath. *Get a grip. Not done yet.* Lee sat forward, hands on the back of the pew in front of her. Her eyes were fastened to him as if she could pour strength and steadiness into him.

"Heath had my back. He probably saved

my life."

The group of people could have been a single sculpture. None of them seemed to be breathing.

"I don't know what else to tell you." Marcus shut his eyes against the images, but that only brought them out in more detail. He looked out on the people. "Walt said you might have questions."

He found Walt in the crowd. *Did I cover everything?*

Walt gave him a quick salute.

"So . . . if you do, I'll answer them."

Silence roared in the sanctuary. A woman in the back raised her hand, then stood up to be heard. "You took this information to the media first."

A challenge. He nodded.

"I guess I'd like to understand why." She sat back down.

The one question he couldn't answer.

Heath's voice, *"A body doesn't amputate pieces of itself."* And Pete's, *"Every Christian you meet is not Clay Hansen."*

Did he have to tell them? *Jesus, help me, if that's what You want.* A cloak of warmth spread over his shoulders. His bones thawed a little.

"I . . ." He met the eyes of the woman

410

who'd asked the question. No blame in her eyes, but she wasn't backing down, either.

"You didn't trust us," she said.

"No," he said. "I didn't."

A faint stirring drifted up from the group, nothing so blunt as whispers, but shifting in seats, intakes of breath. Disappointment, maybe. He couldn't tell.

"This isn't in the news story." His voice rasped. Without the mic, nobody would have heard him. "But I . . . I was . . ."

He held the mic down for a few seconds, waiting, but words didn't come together in his head. Maybe he was supposed to battle through it. He lifted the mic again and looked out at all of them.

"I was . . . traded . . . turned over. And I . . . for a while, I didn't. Trust you. But I think I'm supposed to stay here, and if I do, then I've got to . . . learn how."

The same woman stood back up. The lights made a halo above her blonde hair. "What do you mean, traded? Who would do that?"

"A . . ." Brother? Friend?

"Not other Christians," she said.

"One. Yeah."

The stir among the crowd gave way to something else, something he couldn't read, but it held understanding.

The rest of the questions were about what they could do. How they could help. A man Marcus knew only as Eli, around Walt's age, stood up after the people's comments had dwindled. The lights reflected on his shaved head, and he wore a tan corduroy jacket that was too hot for the weather, even in air-conditioning. Either age had chilled his blood, or he was carrying. Marcus wouldn't bet against either.

"So this agent's no longer a threat. But now that your story is out there, other agents will be after you unless Texas throws them out."

Marcus nodded.

"You need protection."

What? "That's not what this meeting's about. You need to know what's happening. That's all."

"Where are you staying, Marcus?" piped a woman from the back.

From the pew behind Lee, Walt stood up. "With me until a few days ago. Now he's got his own place."

"Alone?" the woman said. "How do you sleep at night with all of this?"

An honest answer would only fuel them, but in his silence, they read everything anyway.

Benjamin stepped up to the front of the

room. "We'll work in shifts. If the Constabulary comes for Marcus again, they'll have to go through us."

This was getting out of control. Marcus had to clarify. Get them to back off. He'd been using the big oak podium as a buffer, but maybe standing up here, removed from them, was deadening his point. He forced a strong stride as he started down the three steps. One. Two —

The knee gave out.

No catching himself. His left foot tried, but the reflexive hop only pitched him over the edge of the stair and missed the bottom one. He dropped the microphone. The blue carpet rushed up at his face, bit into his palms. Both knees hit the floor. The breath burst out of him, along with a weak sound that made his face burn.

Before he could try to rise, an arm looped under each of his. Lifted him from the floor. He looked to his right — Benjamin. To his left — Eli. They helped him to the front pew, then stepped back. Eli returned to his seat. Benjamin picked up the fallen mic and tapped it with a little smile.

Rows back, Lee was sitting forward, both hands gripping the pew in front of her. Marcus gave her a single nod.

Deeper than he could reach inside himself,

something cracked open. The humiliation in his gut throbbed harder than his knee, but as he darted a glance around the room, men and women met his eyes. No pity. No derision. Not even awkwardness. Just a steady acceptance.

"Okay?" Benjamin's smile was easy, as if church members fell off the stage every week. Marcus nodded.

He'd chosen not to wear the brace. God hadn't pushed him down the steps to teach him something. Yet he'd thought only a few minutes ago about not leaning on people, and here he was, collapsing in front of the whole family. And God was near him, as always. Not a cruel sense of humor, but a patient hand on his shoulder. His Father's hand.

Benjamin was talking, but Marcus bowed his head and closed his eyes. *I've got a lot to learn, don't I, Jesus?*

32

Lee had expected dinner conversation to revolve around the meeting — or more specifically, around the response of the church to Marcus. Several people agreed he needed some kind of protection. Before they adjourned, Eli Whitaker, Walt, and several others were creating a rotation of bodyguards to watch his house at night. One man had asked Marcus how to find out who else was on the Constabulary's list, and after a quick glance at Walt that only Lee could have noticed, he said he didn't know. No one wanted to leave it at that, but Marcus kept firm.

Crowds didn't exhaust him the way they did Lee, but speaking in front of so many, not far from panic the whole time, left Marcus quiet while they waited for their food. By the end of dinner, he seemed reenergized, the process complete when Lee told him about Violet's new standing as a citizen of Texas.

The crinkle-eyed smile took over his whole face. "She's safe."

"Yes."

"She can take the GED."

Lee forked a bite of Greek chicken salad. "I know she intended to tell you sooner."

"There's been a lot." A wince drew his eyebrows together, but then his face smoothed again. "We should do something for her. To celebrate."

"I'm picking her up from work in an hour."

"What would she like?"

The answer came with only a moment's consideration. "Fish."

He grinned. "There's a huge pet store in Decatur. I drive by it all the time. There's this long window with pictures of fish."

They left Millie's car at his place, and Marcus offered to drive. Lee had never understood the way driving relaxed him, but she shrugged her agreement. One of them might as well benefit from it, and she didn't care either way.

Violet darted out of the store precisely on time and ran to Lee's car with a grin that evaporated when she saw Marcus.

"Why're you both here? Is everything okay?"

As Violet climbed into the back, Lee turned to meet her eyes. She caught the nearness of Marcus's woodsy aftershave and . . . wanted to kiss him. The strength of the desire left her wordless.

"You guys?" Violet stared from one of them to the other, a frown crimping between her eyes.

"You're a Texan," Marcus said, eyes on the rearview mirror.

"I meant to tell you. But then Pastor Heath and . . . it wasn't ever a good time."

"Well. It is now."

"And that's . . . why you came to pick me up?"

"We're going to the pet store." Marcus put the car in gear and started driving.

Violet bounced on the seat. "To buy fish for my tank?"

He nodded.

"Really, you guys? But I — I'm still saving up for them."

"No," Marcus said. "It'll be a welcome home present. Like you got me."

"Marcus, really, you don't have to —"

He shot her a look that silenced her.

Violet leaned forward between the seats and caught his gaze away from the road. "Thanks."

A soft contentment filled the spaces,

flavored with Violet's anticipation. After the strain of the church meeting, Lee let their ease with one another soak into her. She tipped her head back and closed her eyes. If they were in Marcus's truck, she could have slid to the middle and leaned on him.

What were these new thoughts? Kissing him, resting against him? She shook her head, but she didn't try to push the thoughts away. They were pleasant and right.

Marcus set his right hand on the console between them, palm up. An invitation. Had he read her mind? She drew a circle on his palm and linked her fingers in his. Glanced at him. He didn't look away from the road, but crinkles formed around his eyes.

When they pulled into the parking lot of the pet store, Violet's tiny squeal bounced around the cab.

"You guys are the best. Seriously. I can't even believe it. Look how big the store is!" She rushed from the car and all but skipped toward the door.

Lee waited while Marcus emerged more slowly. He had resumed wearing the brace as soon as they left church. She'd stood watching him strap it in place, trying to decide whether to say something about his stupidity, until he looked up at her and said, *"I know"* with an expression that actually did.

Inside the store, Marcus took her hand and held it. They walked down the open main aisle with shelving units on one side and the two cash registers on the other. The section dedicated to everything aquatic was located at the back of the store. Bubbling tanks, the distinct yet not unpleasant smell of fish-dwelt water, lower lights to enhance the view of colorful fins under fluorescence. Violet already bent with her face to the glass of one tank.

As they approached, she glanced up at them long enough to note the lack of space between them. One blonde eyebrow tilted, and a grin stole onto her face.

"Hi," she said.

Lee waited for Marcus to step away from her, but of course he wouldn't. He smiled. "Hi."

Violet looked ready to dance and squeal, so Lee took one step to the side. "Have you chosen any yet?"

"Oh, not these." Violet waved a hand at the tank she'd been gazing at. "These guys will kill each other if you put the wrong species together. We can't afford that, plus I don't understand why you'd want to choose the best fish you can, take them home, and wake up to find half of them bullied to death."

"Do you have an idea what you want?" If not, they'd be here until the store closed. The selection spanned a whole wall.

"Tropical and peaceful. Do you guys mind if I browse a little? I used to have a marine tank, before. I haven't had freshwater fish since seventh grade. I don't know exactly what I want."

"Of course."

Violet was rarely absorbed by anything the way she was by fish shopping. She watched them swim for long minutes, an unconscious smile teasing her lips.

After a minute of watching Violet study her purchasing possibilities, Marcus joined her at a tank that had captured her attention. "Well?"

"I'm thinking gouramis, two or four. See these ones here, the way the blue shimmers on them? They're males. The female's in the back, by the heater. See her?"

"The brownish one?"

"That's her."

He trailed behind Violet as she browsed, asking questions that she answered with a grin. By the time they were ready to choose fish, Violet's face glowed at Marcus's interest. As the kid in the store-logo shirt swept his net around the tank, Violet swung Marcus's hand beside her like a little girl.

"I'm so excited," she said to all of them, as if it needed saying.

Lee seemed to be the only one who noticed when a couple a little older than she and Marcus entered the fish room. Violet was watching the netting of her fish, and Marcus stood behind her, one hand braced on a post of the aquarium shelves. The couple bumped each other's shoulders when they disagreed about which plants to put in their aquarium. They laughed louder than necessary. They squabbled over one fish species and then another. They appeared untouched by trauma, untouched by anything. Perhaps they weren't, but if not, how could the woman pout and the man sulk, even for thirty seconds, over aquarium fish?

She and Marcus would never be casual to that degree, not even outwardly. But Lee wouldn't want to be.

They left with eight fish. Any more would be too many to start with, Violet said, but too few wouldn't be an accurate gauge of whether the tank was healthy if they all happened to die.

"This is complicated," Marcus said.

Violet missed the tease in his smile. "Yup. That's why it's so awesome when you finally get an aquarium that lives and lasts. It's an accomplishment."

She kept up chatter about her old saltwater fish for the twenty-five-minute drive back to Kearby. They parked. Got out. Entered the apartment lobby. At the stairs, Marcus stopped.

So did Violet. "Hold on. Let me set the fish down at the door."

Without pausing for confirmation, she darted up the stairs, two ballooned bags in each hand, careful not to bump them in her haste. Then she scampered back down and came to stand on Marcus's left.

"Now we can both take some of your weight."

"How did you . . . ?" Marcus frowned.

"You thought I didn't notice? I figured you wouldn't want me to make a big deal of it."

He sighed, closed his eyes. "Violet."

"Come on. You bought them, you have to see them swimming around their new home."

He looked up the long flight and gripped the railing. "Okay. I can make it."

"No, Marcus," Lee said.

She draped his right arm over her shoulders and wrapped her left around his back. As if they'd scripted this, Violet was already in action, doing the same with his left arm and her right. For a moment, all three of them had to adapt to the distribution of his weight. He eased off his right leg with a quiet sigh.

His voice was quiet, too. "Thanks. This will help."

"That's what I said." Violet nudged him without threatening anyone's balance. "Macho man."

By the time they reached the top, Marcus was breathing hard but steady on his feet. He rested against them for a few seconds, and then they supported him down the corridor to Lee's door. Not once did he try to pull away from them.

"Let's see them swim around," he said as Lee unlocked the door, and Violet bounced through the doorway first, bags in hand.

Lee made coffee while Violet floated the bags of fish in the top of the aquarium to acclimate them to the tank's water temperature. When the pot started to brew, Lee ventured to Violet's bedroom and found her and Marcus sitting on her bed, watching the fish poke at the bags and nudge themselves into motion over the top of the water.

"Ten minutes and we can let them out," Violet said.

Lee left them to their fish gazing and returned to the kitchen. She hadn't looked at the news story since this morning. Benjamin had said there were over three thousand comments, so she couldn't read them all, regardless. But she could look at the most popular ones. Determine if public opinion were swaying for him or against him, if his vulnerability had accomplished anything at all.

She stood beside the coffeemaker, back against the counter, and navigated to the news site.

Top Stories. His was still there. And . . . *Breaking: Protests Growing as Many Call for Answers from Governor Catalano.* She tapped the link. Protesters demanded a response to the stories of Marcus and others. Others? While the coffee steamed and gurgled into the pot beside her, she scanned multiple articles, all centering around the same topic: Marcus. On the whole, the people of Texas wanted the Constabulary out of their country. And they were walking the streets of Dallas and Austin with signs saying so.

When the coffee was done, Lee poured a mug and took it and her phone to Violet's room. She handed the coffee to Marcus, and he breathed in the scent of it before taking his first sip.

"Thanks."

She couldn't find a transition. "There are protesters in Dallas and Austin."

He went motionless, the mug wrapped in both hands. Violet straightened up from her study of the fish.

"They're demanding the Constabulary be forcefully ousted from the country. They say allowing the Constabulary any room to work here is undermining the sovereignty of Texas and violating the principles on which the country was built less than a year ago."

Violet looked from Marcus to Lee, and her thumb rubbed at her wrist. "That's awesome. That's what we hoped would happen."

"Yes," Lee said.

"But?"

She couldn't explain it and doubted Marcus could either. Inside her, hope struggled to breathe, but if she let it and this meant nothing, if the protesters and Marcus and the others now telling their stories all achieved nothing . . .

"Let's pray," Violet said.

"I am." Marcus's voice was hushed.

"But that two-or-more thing. Let's pray together."

Perhaps it was selfish to pray for freedom, but they did. Marcus's prayer was for everyone's protection, not his own, so Lee added a specific petition for him. Afterward, she set her phone aside again.

Violet watched the fish for a moment, then turned to both of them. "I wanted to ask you guys something."

"Of course," Lee said.

Marcus waited, quiet, still. Someday she'd be acclimated to that. He'd been so full of motion. He'd be pacing, if this were before. Six months, and she didn't know if this new stillness came from the limits of his body or from somewhere deeper. Lately she would choose the second possibility.

"I've been trying to figure out what to do," Violet said. "With my life, after high school. I want to go to college, and now that I'm a citizen I can probably get some grants and scholarships. But I'm willing to get loans too. I really want to do this."

"Of course," Lee said. Violet would thrive in school as she thrived everywhere else.

"But I didn't know what to study. For a while, I thought, I like fish. I'll study fish. I'll work in a lab or something and make discoveries about them. I don't know, it was all kind of vague, but I figured it's what I would do. Except . . ."

She watched the fish for a minute. A blush had seeped into her face. What was she trying to say?

426

"Don't take this wrong, okay?"

"We won't." Marcus's voice had softened. "It's okay, Violet."

"I love you guys. And I love seeing you — especially you" — she looked at Marcus — "getting better. Stronger inside. Not so hurt."

He held her eyes, steady, and nodded.

"I want to be a counselor. Like Hannah and Pete. I want to help people like — like you — who need help." Her thumb kneaded her wrist, and she fidgeted beside him on the bed. "Do you . . . do you think I'd be any good at it, though?"

Lee didn't have to strain to imagine it. Violet, kind but honest. Peacemaking but not a pushover. "I think you'd be very good."

Violet smiled. "Yeah?"

"Definitely."

She turned to Marcus, and he nodded. "You pay attention to people. You see them."

"I want to talk to Hannah and see what advice she has."

"Do it," Marcus said.

Violet grinned as her phone began to chime like an old clock tower. "Oh, time to let them out!"

Lee watched from her perch on the foot of the bed while Violet and Marcus freed the fish. He held the net steady over one of Lee's mixing bowls, and Violet poured the bag — water and fish — through the net. Then she took the net from him and dashed the few steps across the room to the tank and plunged the net inside. As she shook it inside out, the fish swam away to explore their new home. Twenty gallons and four glass walls, all the freedom a fish needed.

33

He stayed late. Didn't want to leave. And it had nothing to do with avoiding a trek down the stairs. Down was easier than up, and anyway, Lee and Violet would help him. Strange how little he'd minded being carried between them. Pete would call that a big step.

He reminded Lee she had to drive him home, and she shrugged and said she didn't have a shift tomorrow and could stay awake indefinitely. So Marcus stayed. Violet had grown quiet while they sat around the living room, him with his coffee, Lee with tea, Violet munching on warmed-up nachos that were starting to lose their crisp. When he asked if she was okay, Violet's smile held sadness.

"Austin should be here."

The kid would come back. Had to.

Lee didn't own a TV, but she did own Scrabble. Her entertainment priorities would always baffle him. The three of them played two full games, and Marcus placed last both times by at least a hundred points. He couldn't seem to make a word with more than four letters. Every time Violet peered around his arm to help him, Lee called it cheating. As if even the two of them paired up could beat Lee. Halfway through the second game, they quit keeping score.

It was almost eleven. They should start back to his place. Watching Lee tonight in the pet store as she watched that couple . . . watching her purse her lips while she reordered her Scrabble letters, triple-score words filling her head . . . watching her now while she carried his mug to the kitchen sink so he didn't have to get up. He wanted to hold her. He wanted to kiss her. He wanted more than that.

Waiting was killing him.

He pushed to his feet and started for the door. "We should go."

Violet sprang up from the couch to hug him. "Thank you so much for my fish."

"Sure."

She held on another second and then let go, told him good night, and headed to her room. Always wanting to give him and Lee time to themselves. He had to thank her for that sometime. By the time he walked with

Lee to the stairs, Violet was rocketing down the corridor after them.

"Sorry, I forgot!"

He started to tell her to go back to bed. That he could make it down on his own. He could if he had to, but . . . he didn't have to. He lifted his arms and braced them over Lee's and Violet's shoulders, and the three of them made it down as they'd made it up. Together.

They stopped at the doors. Violet said good night a final time and darted back up to the apartment.

Lee crossed the foyer toward the doors.

Ask her.

He couldn't get on one knee. He didn't even have a ring.

"Marcus?" She tipped her head toward him, waiting.

Blood thrummed through his body. He took her hands in each of his. Drew them to his chest. His heart pounded. Last time, she said no. She said not if he were the last man on earth. But they were in their twenties then. And Lee loved him now.

Still. She might not say yes.

She stepped closer, tightened her grip on his hands. "What is it?"

"Lee . . ." He brought her hands to his lips, one after the other. Soft, even her

431

knuckles, and he looked into the gray depths of her eyes, smart and determined and beautiful and willing to accept everything she saw in him, which was pretty much everything in him.

Her lips parted with curiosity. Maybe invitation.

"I want to marry you," he said.

She stood there. The silence lasted years.

"You want to marry me," she whispered. Her eyes shone with so many things, he had no idea what they were.

Maybe he hadn't said it right. "Will you? Marry me?"

Lee closed the small space between them, let go of his hands, and curled both of hers into his shirt. She pressed her face to his chest. He wrapped her up and pressed her even closer. He buried his face in her hair, his heartbeat calming. He'd said it, and this was her *yes*. How wrong and right, Marcus saying the words and Lee answering with her touch.

She turned her face to the side without drawing away from him. "Marcus."

He rested his cheek on the top of her head. He was going to kiss her but not yet. For now he would hold her.

"Yes," Lee said.

"I know."

A small laugh ran through her. "Well, then, I suppose —"

She lifted her head, and he claimed her mouth with his, and they kissed until both of them were out of breath. He drew back and kept her face between his palms, stroked her cheekbone and her lips. Lee shivered.

"I love you," he said.

"One would hope so." Her lips curved under his thumb.

He kissed her again, held her some more. His limbs felt so light, and Lee's eyes were like sunshine, and he wanted to pick her up and spin her around the lobby, but that would end with both of them in a heap. He could have growled, but . . . no. For this moment, it didn't matter that he was still mending. Lee would be beside him, and they'd keep doing what they'd always done. Seeing the pieces and accepting them all, and helping each other mend. *Jesus, she said yes! But You knew she would.* He felt as if a sun beamed from inside him.

"You love me." He linked his hands behind her waist.

"I love you."

"Let's tell Violet."

She glanced back at the stairs. "I could text her to come down."

"Okay."

Lee sent the text. Less than a minute later, the door upstairs opened and shut too loudly. Violet remembered to quiet her steps on the stairs.

"What in the world, you guys?"

Lee turned to him. He took her hand, turned to Violet. "We're getting married."

The shriek bounced off the foyer walls. Violet danced in place, hand over her mouth. She grabbed them both and hauled them outside so she could shriek again. She hugged Marcus, then Lee, then both of them at the same time. When she withdrew, she was crying.

"Finally! I feel like I've been waiting for years!"

A small, fragile laugh came from Lee. "You've known us less than that."

Violet grabbed her in another hug. "It doesn't feel like it. Omygosh, you guys, I'm so happy, I can't . . . This is the best day."

Yeah, it might be. He squeezed Lee's hand, and she squeezed back, and their message was more than *I see you*. It had become *I see you and I belong to you*. He knew now what people meant when they said their hearts swelled. His was like a helium balloon, straining the confines of his chest, ready to burst with more feelings than he knew how to hold.

"So." Violet swiped her tears away. "When?"

"Um," he said.

Lee squeezed his hand again. "Legally speaking, it might be prudent to wait and see what transpires in the next few months."

"I guess." Violet sighed, then perked up. "What if you had a secret wedding? A *Braveheart* wedding?"

"I don't recall that one ending well," Lee said.

"We're having a church wedding," he said. He hadn't thought about it before, the wedding itself. He'd only thought of being Lee's husband. Of Lee being his wife. But yeah. Heath would marry them. The family would be there.

Lee was nodding slowly. Her voice softened. "I would like that as well."

Violet grabbed both of Lee's hands and swung them. "Then I promise to be the best wedding planner ever."

34

Somebody was watching his house.

He coasted Lee's car past the red truck parked across from his place, and the street-light shone through the window on a dome of shaved head. His eyes caught the driver's, and his shoulders sagged. Not Constabulary.

"It's Eli Whitaker," he said.

Lee sighed.

Marcus pulled into the driveway and got out of the car. Lee walked around the back, eyeing Eli's pickup, and slid behind the wheel.

"I'll see you tomorrow," she said.

"Yeah." He leaned into the car and kissed her — a quick good night, nothing more, especially not with an audience. But she'd said she would marry him. He had to force himself to pull back.

"Good night." Lee held his eyes a moment, smiled with no idea what she did to him. She shut her door.

Marcus waited for her car to pull away. Then he crossed the street to the red truck.

Eli's window was rolled down. "You weren't expecting me."

"No."

"We said we were going to watch your house at night."

"Yeah. But I didn't . . ." Marcus shook his head. What, he hadn't believed them? "You're going to sleep out here?"

"Wouldn't be much good to you if I fell asleep."

He couldn't let them do this. He huffed, rubbed the back of his neck, found no words.

"Honestly, Marcus, I don't think we'll need to do this long. I think Texas is going to make the right decision, and you'll be safe in a week or two. But as long as one of my brothers is at risk of disappearing by unlawful arrest, I'm not going to sleep in my bed and say a prayer for you as I drift off."

The force of his words, the intensity in his eyes — Marcus wouldn't argue with him and win. Didn't want to. He'd only be insulting this man. This brother.

Family. Body of Christ. Heath would smile if he could see that thought. This body was losing sleep to keep from losing Marcus.

Opposite of amputation. He pressed his lips tight.

Eli rubbed a palm over the crown of his head. "Anyway, that's how it is."

"Okay."

The man peered at Marcus's house, at his neighbor's place, then turned his head ninety degrees to scan the street.

"Are you a cop? A soldier?"

"Both. Army first, then state police. But that list of guards we compiled tonight has a few teachers on it, too. A mechanic, an insurance rep . . . Not everyone's equipped to engage someone if they show up here, but we can all keep watch and make a phone call. We can all make it clear if they try anything, they'll have a witness."

"Okay." All Marcus could say.

"Do you have a weapon in your house?"

"Walt was willing to teach me. We talked it over and I told him no, and he agreed."

Eli's gaze strayed to him, ticked him off like an item on a checklist and kept going. Studying the house again. "Why's that?"

Marcus rubbed his neck. Honesty. This guy was sure earning it. "Panic attacks. Getting better. I'm not going to black out and shoot somebody, or anything like that. But I didn't feel right about it, learning to use a gun for the first time, with my head still . . .

like this."

"Good call. And good for me to know. Thanks."

"You ever work with Walt?"

"Met him later, while we were both acclimating to retired life. Civilian life. Our wives are grateful we found each other." Another smile, easy, watchful but not watching Marcus.

"Thanks for . . . what you're doing."

"You're welcome, brother."

Marcus went inside, wrestling himself. Figured he'd never sleep, but with Brody beside him, he didn't wake up until his phone alarm went off. He checked through the blinds at the front of the house, and the red truck was still there. Eli shadowed him to church and gave him a salute as they walked through the doors together, then took different paths through the lobby.

As Marcus entered the sanctuary, churchgoers watched him. They needed to stop doing that. He was the same person he'd been before they knew about Jason. Well, he'd keep being that person. Eventually they'd be easy with him again.

He looked for Lee and Violet, made his way to them, halfway to the front of the church. Lee liked to sit in the balcony, but she wouldn't until his knee improved. He sat beside her, and she angled a smile at him.

"Good morning."

"Hi."

"Sleep well?"

"Yeah, actually." Not even a nightmare.

She leaned closer to him as Benjamin began the announcements. "Violet kept me up half the night looking at flower arrangements on her phone and asking about my dress."

Her dress. He grinned. That's right, Lee would have to wear a dress. He caught Violet's eye from the other side of Lee, and she gave him a thumbs-up.

Lee arched an eyebrow at both of them. "Perhaps a *Braveheart* wedding is in order."

"No," Marcus said.

Her mouth curved. "I'm told most men don't care about the ceremony."

"Just the church part."

Then he turned his thoughts away from the image of Lee in white and listened to the announcements. There was no mention of Marcus, as agreed on at yesterday's meeting. Walt, Eli, and the rest of the church's security team were keeping eyes open for suspicious visitors that could be Constabulary agents. But there was no guaranteed way to spot them, no guaranteed way to know church was safe. The new reality weighted the mood in the room.

Maybe he should have stayed away, just for a while. But even now, that thought rubbed against him like rough wood leaving splinters.

A woman named Brooke updated them all on Heath's condition. He'd had a calm night, and Gloria was back at the hospital, both things Marcus knew from Gloria's text this morning. Brooke and Benjamin led the prayer time for Heath, in which multiple people called out their prayers.

The sermon was given by an elder named Bob, who Marcus didn't know. Galatians, one of the mostly pink books in his Bible. Violet leaned forward to catch his eye and sigh at the highlighted pages, and they shared a smile. When everyone stood for the closing hymn, Lee sang with her eyes closed. Her focus on the music was always intense, as if it connected her to God like nothing else did.

Marcus and Lee were nearly to the doors when Walt intercepted them, followed by a man about their age. His sandy hair was receding, and his dark brown eyes ignored Lee to focus on Marcus. He was one of the only men in the church wearing a suit jacket and was built the way Marcus used to be —

tough to knock over. Marcus edged forward as Walt made the introductions, not blocking Lee but close enough to step in front of her if he had to.

Hypervigilance. Calm down. Walt was introducing the guy. Everything was fine.

"Lee Vaughn, Marcus Brenner, this is Dan Sobczek. Seems he knows you from Michigan, Marcus."

By the time Walt had finished speaking, Dan's posture had tensed. Marcus edged over a step, his body half blocking Lee's.

"What're you trying to do here, man? What's in this for you?"

Marcus shook his head. "I don't know what you're —"

"Did you give the *Clarion* that story?"

Marcus nodded.

"Are you a Constabulary plant? Are you — I can't figure it out, but I won't let you get away with this — this posing."

Marcus opened his mouth, but words wouldn't come.

Walt stood to one side, arms hanging easy at his sides, looking from Dan to Marcus and back again. Assessing. Marcus had seen that look enough to know.

"I've met the real Marcus Brenner, and you're not him, buddy."

None of this made sense. Why would

somebody pretend to be Marcus?

Wait. Sobczek. "Elliott."

The man's fists balled. "What?"

"You — you took Elliott. The baby."

"You leave my son out of this."

Sparking in the man's eyes was more fear than anger. Of course, fear, because Elliott hadn't always been his son, and nobody was supposed to know that but Marcus Brenner, and his image of Marcus was . . .

"You're right," Marcus said. "It wasn't me. That brought him. It was —" Not a friend. Not a brother. "I was in Ohio the night you were leaving. The night I was supposed to bring the baby. I thought I could get back in time, but there were agents. We were pinned down for a while."

Dan shifted from one foot to the other, still looking like a boxer waiting for the bell.

"I called somebody — somebody I trusted. I told him you'd probably assume he was me. He brought Elliott to you."

"You know how this sounds?"

He needed something else. A detail. Marcus thought back to the baby. Aubrey's son. Small and fragile in the crook of his arm, screaming in protest while Aubrey tried to make eggs instead of holding him, and she broke all the yolks. . . .

Lee's hand settled on his left arm, the

place Elliott had fit though she couldn't know that. Marcus forced his focus to now, here in the lobby of Grace Bible Church with people milling around them, droning voices, sun glaring through the tall glass windows.

"Elliott's deaf."

Dan blinked.

"I sent him with a letter. So he'd know about his mom. I initialed it. I told him . . . I told him she'd be happy if he liked to read."

A long sigh poured out of Dan. His hands opened. His eyes filled, and he lowered his head, pinched the bridge of his nose, looked back up. "Marcus Brenner."

"Yeah."

"You're him."

Marcus nodded.

Dan stepped forward and clasped Marcus's hand. "Sir, we — my wife and I, we've said so many times that if we could only thank you again for what you did. And come to find out, we never thanked *you* at all."

Marcus matched his grip, firm but not a challenge. "How is he? The baby?"

"Come with me, please. My wife's outside . . ."

Walt took his leave with a clap on Marcus's shoulder, gone too quickly for Marcus to say what he needed to say. But maybe it didn't need saying. Walt knew.

Lee followed close as Dan Sobczek led them out the doors, off the walkway onto the patch of grass that sprawled parallel with the south parking lot. They walked under the branches of a live oak, over grass dappled with shadows.

"Ruthie? Honey?"

A woman rose from where she'd been kneeling in the grass, a slight redhead in a yellow sundress. She came to them, balancing a toddler on her hip. "Dan . . ."

"I know, but this is him. Marcus Brenner, the real one. He's the one who did it, who got us Elliott."

Elliott. Wispy oak-colored hair like his mom's. Blue eyes. A gummy grin. He looked right at Marcus.

"Elliott?" Marcus said. Lee slipped her hand into his.

Elliott waved at them.

"So who was the man who brought our son to us, if he wasn't you?" Ruthie's other arm circled Elliott.

"He worked with me for a little while." Only once, really.

"And what was his name?"

"Clay."

Lee's hand was going to squeeze the blood

out of his fingers.

"Well, he let us think he was you."

"I didn't tell him not to. There was a lot going on. I was supposed to be the one you met that night, but I couldn't be there."

"If you're still in contact with him, would you thank him for us too?"

"I'm not."

Ruthie handed Elliott over to her husband and shook Marcus's hand, a timid grasp, quickly withdrawn, but her eyes held warmth. "He's seen a few doctors, in Ohio and Texas. The hearing loss is profound, but they're optimistic about a hearing aid. We've all been learning sign language, and he's getting his first hearing aid next week. Our son will get to hear our voices."

She swiped at sudden tears. Looked from Dan to Marcus, then to Lee as if seeing her for the first time.

"I'm sorry, would you be Mrs. Brenner?"

Not yet.

"Lee Vaughn." She held out her hand, releasing Marcus's, and the loss of contact left him hollower than it should have. "Pleased to meet you."

"Likewise." But she refocused on Marcus. "We owe you so much."

"No," he said.

"Did Dan tell you? We live an hour south,

have a church home there. But when the story released and we recognized your name, we thought, this is our chance. To find you, say thanks, let you see that Elliott's healthy and happy."

He couldn't say anything to that. He kept looking at Elliott, trying to compare this boy who bounced on Ruthie's arm with his last mental image of the baby, crawling across Chuck and Belinda's floor. This Elliott could clearly walk and run. Might even know a few words, despite the deafness.

"The news story," Ruthie said, and her voice quieted. "That's all true? What happened to you?"

Nod. But inside, he was closing in on himself. Couldn't stop it.

"Then you have even more gratitude from us. I know it's only words, but we . . . we had to try to find you. After what you went through for helping us and people like us. We couldn't not try."

Nod.

They shook his hand again, both of them. They said thank you one last time. Then they walked away. They didn't look back, but over Dan's shoulder, Elliott waved.

Marcus ducked his head, chin to chest. Go somewhere. Private. Get a grip. Eyes on the ground, he set out for the clearing on the north end of the property. The grass nobody cut, the old stumps left rooted in the ground. He could talk to God there. He could stay a few minutes till the heaviness lifted from his chest.

Almost there.

A cool hand caught his. Lee's thumb ran over his knuckles. She kept pace with his forward march.

"No," he said.

She didn't answer. Her hand didn't pull away.

"I've got to . . . by myself."

She squeezed his hand. They kept walking. Side by side. Through the knee-high grass, silencing locusts as they passed, cicadas still rasping no matter how near they came. He tried to keep going, but the first tree stump that blocked his path seemed to snap something inside, and he collapsed onto it, his right leg stretched in front of him, so much weight on his chest he was losing his breath. Elliott. He should have told them how Aubrey tried to give herself up for her baby. How much Aubrey had loved him.

They'd come here to thank Clay. Clay had held Aubrey's baby last, after Marcus, after Chuck, after Belinda, and all these months he'd wondered if Clay was working for the Constabulary the whole time, had never delivered Elliott to his new family at all but instead took him to state foster care. Marcus never would have known. Never would have voiced the fear — what good would it have done, no fixing it — but Clay hadn't done that. Elliott was safe. If only Aubrey could know.

He was doubled over, sitting on the stump, gasping as weight fell off him. As something else cracked in him from the core outward. Aubrey's cold body in his arms. Clay's handshake. Jason's boots breaking his ribs, striking the knee again and again. Hunger and filth and darkness and hurt and Sam finding him there. Sam lifting Marcus into his arms and carrying him into sunlight that hurt his eyes.

It was too much. He couldn't let it happen. Or he'd drown in it.

But Clay hadn't given the baby to the Constabulary. He'd given them only Marcus.

"Marcus."

"Why? Why did he do that to me?"

Lee's hand in his hair. Massaging his neck. Her other hand on his arm. She'd said she would marry him. Focus on that. On thankfulness.

"Shh." Lee, so gentle he couldn't take it. He hid his face against his good knee.

"Marcus, I know what you're doing." She rubbed a circle on his back. "Stop fighting it. Stop."

His hands came up to his face. He had to keep from breaking. He had to prove he wasn't broken.

But he was.

35

A wild shake of his head, and then Marcus was weeping, too lost in the tears to try to stop them. A pang seized Lee at her deepest center. These tears were not the kind she discovered after she'd finished speaking her first prayer, with him beside her. These tears were not quiet, were not contained. They came from his gut, wracked his whole body. They were grief. He needed her close, but there wasn't room on the stump for both of them. She lifted him from the bent pose and sat across his lap, drew him to her until his head rested on her chest. He turned his face and wept into her shoulder, sobs coming harder when she kissed the top of his head.

For over an hour, the tears ebbed at times but didn't stop. When he was finally quiet, Lee brushed her fingers through his hair. He rested against her, spent.

After a few minutes, his arms loosened around her. He lifted his head from her shoulder and seemed surprised to find her sitting there. Perhaps she was too. He looked around the lot, taking it all in.

"Lee." His voice was hoarse from weeping.

"I'm here."

Her phone buzzed against her thigh. Not for the first time, now that she thought about it. She ignored it. Marcus swiped his palms over his cheeks and looked down at them, as if the tears puzzled him. He drew in a breath that shook, let it out and rested his forehead against her collarbone.

"It was a while, wasn't it," he said.

"No longer than you needed."

"We should be driving to the hospital."

They should be there. But she wouldn't move until he did.

"I knew there was a lot. But . . . there was more than . . ." He reached out blindly, and Lee caught his hand. He clung. "You'll tell me not to apologize."

"That's right." She rubbed his back, the slow circle that seemed to steady him when he was brittle. His breathing strengthened, in and out.

"Why? Why am I still . . . so . . . ?"

She couldn't answer that. She asked the same question of herself. Asked why she could kiss Marcus, yet a strange man stepping into her path made her want to vomit. Asked why she trusted Marcus with her life yet quaked at the thought of their wedding night, not because she didn't want him, but because he might finally find something he didn't want of her.

He flexed his knee and let out a hard breath.

"Stiff?" She stood and took his hand in a firmer grip.

"Wait. A minute. Please." He closed his eyes and worked the knee through a few stretches, breathing tightly controlled, then let her help him up.

Lee's phone buzzed again.

"Probably Violet," Marcus said.

"I imagine so." She tugged it from her pocket. "Hello, Violet."

A sob burst over the line.

"Violet?"

"Oh, Jesus, God, thank You — Lee, is he with you? Tell me he's with you."

Her heart constricted with understanding. Of course. She hadn't thought. "Marcus is here. We're both fine."

Quiet crying, nothing held back.

"Violet, I'm so sorry."

"I th-thought — you were here and then . . . I've been trying to f-find you —"

"Where are you?"

"In the sanctuary. I was praying."

Marcus kept pace with her, wading back through the grass, rushing up the walkway, inside, through the propped-open doors. Violet sat in the front pew, drying tears on her sleeve. She stood and ran to them.

She hugged them both. "This is not a great time to go off somewhere and . . ." She pulled back from Marcus's hug. "What happened?"

He shook his head. "I . . . I can't right now."

Violet hugged him again, longer this time. When they stepped apart, she looked at Lee, questioning.

"There's no bad news," Lee said.

"Let's go see Heath." Marcus led them outside.

Yes, Gloria would be wondering. But Marcus needed time. Perhaps not time alone — he wasn't like Lee in that — but surely some reprieve before being with Heath and Gloria. His eyes were still red, his voice too quiet.

Her uncertainty blistered as she drove, Marcus beside her and Violet in the back. They used Millie's car as infrequently as possible, but Marcus didn't volunteer to drive Lee's this time. She kept her hand on his arm the entire way, and he covered it with his own. What she needed, however, wasn't touch. She needed a solitary place to process his tearstains on her shirt. To process the ache in her that existed because Marcus was aching. The volume of his tears, the enormity of his hurt — she hadn't expected it, which had to be some level of failure, except focusing on her failure was focusing on herself. She had to focus on him. *Lord Christ, show me how best to help him.*

She drove ten minutes before Violet broke the silence that pressed in on all of them.

"Is it always going to be like this?"

Marcus glanced at her in the rearview mirror. "It might be."

Violet hunched in her seat. "I know we have to trust God, but I thought He was giving us Texas for our haven. Like the news story said at the end."

"No."

Lee watched him. He seemed steadier than he had been minutes ago.

"No, you think He won't give us Texas?" Violet straightened, interest overcoming emotion.

"He might. But if He does. Or doesn't." He looked out the window at the highway and the plain blurring past, then found her in the mirror again. "Violet, there's only one haven. Him."

The fact of it sank into Lee but didn't loosen her grip on the things she wanted, Marcus's safety at the head of the list and Texas one line beneath it.

At the hospital, she searched out the open lot for a parking space. Marcus looked to the north entrance, the closest to post-op recovery, and his hands clenched. Lee parked and followed his gaze.

The reporters from Wednesday had multiplied. Close to twenty of them milled around the hospital, Nicole Stopczy not among them. Lee turned to Marcus in time to see his Adam's apple dip to the collar of his T-shirt.

"Should we return later?"

"No," he said. As they got out of the car, his voice gained an edge of quiet command. "Go inside and don't stop. Even if I do."

"You plan to talk to them?"

"No."

Lee nearly forgot the cooler in the back of her car. She'd written her name on several blank lines of the sign-up sheet at church — *Dinners for Heath and Gloria* — but those weren't due for a few weeks. Gloria was likely to have a full fridge of casseroles by now. Lunches were another matter, though, especially with Gloria spending most of her days here. Lee had made chicken salad sandwiches, cold food easier to keep than warm. She'd included an apple, a banana, and half a dozen peanut butter cookies that were Gloria's favorite, warm or not. Perhaps soon, she could bring food for Heath as well.

Marcus led them to the sidewalk that nearly circled the hospital and approached the entrance without a glance toward the reporters, as if they couldn't possibly be concerned with him. Lee and Violet followed one pace back. The taste of sawdust filled Lee's mouth as they neared the doors. Perhaps no one would bother them. Perhaps . . .

"That's him."

The triumphant words came from the reporter who had pursued them last time, the man who'd stood down when Marcus refused to. But that was four days and forever ago, before the news story.

Marcus was shielding her and Violet from the onslaught when two hours ago he'd been weeping for things these people wanted to put on parade. Lee clasped his hand and stepped up beside him, and the instant press of people sped her pulse. No, she didn't want to face them. But she wouldn't escape into the building while they harassed Marcus.

"A few words, Mr. Brenner?" The tall man's voice was less patronizing this time, but he continued before Marcus could answer. "We know you're here to visit a friend. We want to know your thoughts on the release of the list."

The freeze that traveled Lee's limbs seemed to seize Marcus as well.

"Do you know any of the others? Have you been in contact before or since their names were released?"

Marcus drew her hand closer, pressed it to the outside of his thigh. He shook his head.

"I'm sure you have an opinion on how this is being handled," the man said.

"I didn't know," Marcus said.

"Really? The news broke almost four hours ago."

So fast. Two days ago no one had known about Marcus. Two days before that, Jason had been alive, hunting him.

"I haven't looked at the news since earlier this morning," he said.

"Must have been at church, then." The reporter leaned closer, into Marcus's space. "Grace Bible Church, isn't it?"

One of them must have been there. Heard the announcement of Heath's progress. Heard that the church had a guest preacher while their pastor was recovering in Decatur General Hospital. Lee couldn't move, but Marcus tugged her toward the hospital doors and kept the reporters at bay with his other arm, his elbow a right angle, his hand a fist. No one ventured near again, though their voices came as the heavy glass door shut after him.

"Please consider —"

"Good luck with everything —"

At least someone had extended more than an interrogation.

The elevator took them up alone.

"If that's true," Violet said, "it means Texas is listening. Not just the people, but the government."

Marcus nodded as they stepped onto Heath's floor. He didn't release Lee's hand, so she didn't release his.

Violet trailed behind them a few steps. "When do you think we'll know? What they're going to do?"

"It might be very soon," Lee said. "I believe all of this is progressing more quickly than Walt anticipated."

"Yeah." Marcus pointed. "There's Gloria."

Shadows lurked under Gloria's eyes, but she smiled and rushed forward when she saw them. She wore a fresh shirt, red-and-blue paisley print, and jeans with a broad red belt. Someone from the church had brought clothes for her.

"Good news from every source," Gloria said. "The fever's down again, he's ravenous, and the wound is looking good."

Lee offered the cooler. "An alternative to a fast food lunch."

"Really?" Gloria took it and popped open the lid. "My word, this looks delicious, Lee. I'll have to hide it from Heath. He'll throw his applesauce."

"Is he awake?" Marcus looked toward the room.

"He is. Prayer requests currently are for continued healing and pain relief. The more aware he is, the more he hurts. But he'll be happy to see you."

Violet led them into the room and stood in a corner, as if she didn't want to intrude. Cards lined the bedside table, and a stuffed bear sat in Gloria's reclining chair in the corner, its belly embroidered with the words *Get Well Soon.* Heath had the TV on, studying the news with a frown of concentration. He saw them and gestured at the screen.

"You did it," he said.

They watched without speaking. In the twenty-eight hours since the release of Marcus's story, four others had come forward, claiming they'd known for the last week of their place on the list and felt they were powerless to change it.

"I can't exactly say Marcus Brenner gave me hope," one woman was quoted by the news anchor, "but I feel like I can come forward now that I'm not the only one."

No photographs, no video, only written interviews like Marcus's and one voice interview — a man with a New York accent. But the media didn't allow these limitations to reduce the drama.

"And we have the latest development," the onscreen reporter said. This had been a news recap, showing events leading to the breaking story. "In an act of support for these individuals and defiance against what was supposed to be a covert negotiation, Governor Catalano has released the Constabulary's full wanted list. He's holding a press conference in ten minutes, and we're reasonably certain his actions will include ending negotiations with the Constabulary for any refugees currently in Texas, whether or not they've achieved legal citizenship at this time."

Marcus leaned against the wall, legs half folding before he pushed himself back up.

"You did it, brother," Heath said.

"Not me."

"You started a fire that caught faster than

anyone could have hoped. Texas is standing with you."

"We don't know yet," Marcus said.

Heath shook his head. "I'm a Texan. I know."

"So Gloria filled you in?"

"She read me your interview. I asked her how come I didn't know you were doing this, and she said it's my just recompense for getting shot."

Lee flinched. Humor in the face of difficulty would never make sense.

"That doesn't sound like her," Marcus said.

"It does if you're married to her."

A current passed between Lee and Marcus, so alive Heath had to feel it too. But his attention turned back to the news. Violet, however, watched them both from her corner. Her eyes sparkled.

Lee arched her eyebrows at Marcus, and he smiled.

Another man might have tried to make it witty. *"Actually, Heath, I'm engaged to somebody else."* But he was Marcus, so he said, "We're getting married," exactly the same way he'd said it to Violet, none of the joy diminished from the three words. He took Lee's hand, and she didn't try to squelch her smile.

Heath tossed the remote high enough to flip it in his hands and gave a *whoop* that had to be born of pain medication.

Marcus laughed.

She hadn't heard that sound in a year. She blinked hard against the burning in her eyes.

"So when are we doing this thing?" Heath said.

Marcus looked at the TV, images of protesters with signs, some of which bore his name. "Soon."

Yes. For today, at least, Lee was ready too.

36

The setup was so obvious, Marcus felt like a character in a movie. After about fifteen minutes of talk about the news and updates on Heath's condition, Gloria invited Lee and Violet down to the cafeteria with her. When the women were gone, Marcus leaned against the wall and folded his arms.

"Was she trying to be subtle?"

"The opposite." Heath stretched and winced, then elevated the bed until he was sitting upright. "Gloria doesn't believe in setting people up to talk unless she lets them know she's doing it."

"Okay."

"I'm too drugged up to find a roundabout way into the topic."

"Sure." He didn't want roundabout, anyway.

"I've been meaning to have some kind of conversation with you. About our respective thorns."

Thorns? He cocked his head.

"Thorns in the flesh. Have you read about Paul's yet?"

The phrase was familiar but not in a biblical context. Marcus shook his head.

"Paul prayed three times for God to remove his thorn in the flesh, and God said no. Said, 'My grace is sufficient.' Scholars aren't sure what the thorn was, probably a physical ailment of some kind."

God said no to Paul. Marcus wouldn't have expected that, but it proved what he was learning. Paul must have felt the hands of God on him, too, when he hurt. Maybe God showed him the reason for his thorn, or maybe he accepted it without knowing the reason.

"I was too drugged for a real conversation last time. And I'd guess you were too shaken up."

"Well, you were bleeding out on the concrete."

Heath made a vague gesture that didn't rise as far as he wanted it to.

"You don't remember. But you were."

Heath studied Marcus, was still studying him when his voice came more quietly, more serious than he'd been since their group arrived. "It's been, what, four days?"

"Yeah."

"That curtain." Heath jerked his chin toward the fabric drape between his room and the next one. "Every time somebody snaps it open or closed, I jump a mile."

If Heath needed to say it, Marcus would hear him.

"It's not like a curtain snapping has any resemblance to a gunshot."

"You're not expecting it," Marcus said. "Anything you don't expect is a threat."

"I don't know. It seems extreme."

"Getting shot is extreme."

Heath sighed. He muted the TV, then shifted in the bed and pressed a hand to his side. "That thorn is feeling pretty literal."

"Do you need anything?"

"You could sit. Might make me feel less like an invalid here."

Marcus shifted his weight against the wall. Besides Gloria's chair, the only one in the room was on wheels. Probably intended for the doctor, and rolling chairs never seemed reliable when his knee was bad. "No. Thanks."

"Feel free to move the bear." Heath grinned. "A present from my second-grade niece."

That explained it. Well, okay. Marcus's mouth tugged as he set the bear at Heath's feet. He eased into Gloria's chair.

"So you know I'm dyslexic."

Marcus nodded.

"I've talked to men before, and I do think God used me to help some of them. Men with major sports injuries, early onset arthritis, injuries from car accidents . . . I knew you faced different things than those guys. But I didn't understand. I still don't. Maybe I'm a tenth closer today than I was before this week."

"Heath." He had to say something. He rubbed the back of his neck.

"I'm not comparing. This" — he gestured at the white walls, the white curtain, the white sheets — "this doesn't compare to four months. I know that."

Marcus pressed into the chair. "Pete says trauma's trauma."

"Sure it is, but four months, brother. Yet you're functioning. No, more than that. You're growing nearer to Him. I see it. Someday you'll be the one talking guys through their stuff."

Marcus scrubbed a hand over his face. He could do only so much talking.

Sure, Heath was on pain meds, saying what came to him. But Marcus couldn't shut down the chain reaction in his head — inwardly stumbling into the raw hole of the last few hours, a hole that welled with everything that had poured out of him while he sat with Lee in the church clearing. If Heath knew about that, he'd never suggest this.

"What would you have told me?" he said.

Heath frowned. "About me?"

"Yeah. Before this happened."

He looked toward the nurse's whiteboard he couldn't read. "I wanted you to know I wasn't comparing. But also that you weren't alone."

"So I'm alone now because you understand more?"

"Of course not." His eyes flickered to Marcus's, then back to the board. "I would have said I get the frustration. Loving what you do yet being limited at it. Yes, I read Greek. I also pop a lot of NSAIDs when I'm studying and keep an ice pack ready for times the pills don't kick the headache. Gloria says my stomach lining and my liver are probably those of an eighty-year-old. But it's that or the sermon doesn't get written."

"Do most people know?"

"Not most, I guess. Some. If it comes up naturally, I let it." A smile twitched the corner of Heath's mouth. "Eating out at ethnic restaurants is a humbling experience. Gloria reads the menu to me."

"Not at Rosita's."

"Yankee. Tex-Mex isn't ethnic."

Marcus ducked his head to hide his smile. He propped his leg on the recliner's footrest.

"Besides, I've got Rosita's menu memorized. But we go out for Italian, and all that *zuppa* and *insalata* in script fonts . . . I'm hopeless."

"Fluorescent bulbs make me sweat." He looked up. Hadn't meant to say that. But Heath was waiting, listening. "When they're starting to go bad, and they buzz. It's . . . it's not the same pitch as a Taser, but it trips my brain up anyway."

Heath hadn't known about the tasing. Nobody knew that one but Lee and the doctors. Heath's face had gone still. Maybe Marcus had wrecked it, pulling their conversation from restaurant menus to flashback triggers. Maybe he should shut up.

"I knew there had to be some reason you couldn't escape." Heath's voice was tense but not with judgment.

"I tried." Too many times to count. Even knowing the Taser would get him, that Jason would shock him at least once more after he was down.

Heath passed the TV remote from one hand to the other. "I got pretty angry with God in seminary. Not how it's supposed to work, I guess, but people had tossed me some platitudes over the years. God doesn't call the equipped; he equips the called. God doesn't ask you to do anything you can't handle with His help. So there I was studying to spread His Word and demanding He fix what was wrong with me. Surely He couldn't expect this of me unless He made it easier. I mean, that's what 'equipping the called' must mean, right? I dropped out at one point, and a few people in my life encouraged me. Said I had misheard God's call, He wouldn't expect scholarship from a guy who read at the pace of a second grader."

He stopped. Waited. And Marcus got it. *My turn.*

"Sometimes . . ." Marcus hunched over on the chair but held Heath's eyes even as his chest constricted. He drew a hard breath. "Sometimes I'm doing something random. Working. Anything. And my heart starts pounding. No reason for it. But my skin prickles and burns like . . . like any second, something's going to attack me."

This was ridiculous. Talking to Heath like this. Trading vulnerabilities, showing them like trophies. Heath could blame the meds. Marcus could only blame the seeping scab from the last few hours.

"Sometimes I still ask God what the point of it is," Heath said. "Tilt my head back in my office chair and holler at Him through the ceiling."

There was one thing left. One piece he didn't want out there in words, especially to a guy like Heath, strong and whole, but . . . *Weren't you listening?* The strength had holes in it. Like Marcus's. Like Paul's. Maybe every guy who ever served God had this in common.

"Sometimes." Marcus swallowed hard and clamped his hand above the knee brace. "Sometimes I get tired, Heath."

"Of living?" Heath's gaze sharpened.

"No. Just tired."

Heath's thumb and fingers rubbed his temples. He took a long breath. "I hear you, brother."

Whatever Heath's road looked like ahead, he'd make it. And Marcus would have his back the whole way. He reached over the bedrail and clasped Heath's hand, and Heath's grip was firm.

"Stay the course," Heath said.

"You too."

37

As Marcus turned the corner from the main parking lot, Violet lifted her head. She was sitting on the curb, knees almost to her chin. She clutched her phone in one hand, probably praying for Austin's name to light up her screen. But nobody had heard from Austin since he'd confirmed safe arrival in Ontario. Marcus coasted the truck to the curb and stopped next to her.

He rested his arm on the window frame. "Get in."

She pushed to her feet and hooked her purse strap over her shoulder. "You got your truck back."

"Yeah."

"Going to get it fixed?"

"Soon." He didn't want to see the reminder every day, but he didn't have the money for a cosmetic repair.

"Okay. Um. Thanks for coming."

"You're going to tell me why now."

Violet got in and shut the door. "I promised Lee I'd put gas in her car."

"Okay." And what, she needed money? He had a little cash, but asking wasn't like her.

Violet pulled in a deep breath and faced him across the worn vinyl seat. "We're not that far from Austin's apartment. Like, six minutes, tops. When the car needs gas, he drives over, leaves his car here, and we drive Lee's car to a gas station and fill it up. Then I bring him back here and we both drive home."

All this time . . . ? Marcus flexed his left hand. "Okay."

"I'm really sorry."

"Why?"

"I shouldn't have called you. Not for something stupid like this. And I do know it's stupid."

"It's not."

"It happened eight months ago. I should be over it. I know I should."

"What happens when you're at a gas station?"

She pressed her fingers to her eyelids. "The first week we were in Texas, I pulled up to the pump, freaked out, and drove off. I must have looked crazy. A mile down the road I realized I was speeding. Like, fifteen over."

He couldn't hold in the sigh, not with that picture of her behind his eyes. How had he not known about this? "What about now?"

"I've gotten so much better. I can do all of it by myself. But I haven't tried it alone yet. I'm scared I'll go back to square one and run away."

"Lee doesn't know?" he said.

"She'd tell me to be a responsible adult and pump my own gas."

"Not if you explain."

She shook her head.

"Violet."

"She was there too. And she's never run for her life from a gas station."

"She wasn't the one held at gunpoint."

She folded her arms, more defense than defiance.

"Okay," he said. "We'll put gas in her car. But you need to tell her."

She didn't say a word while he drove three blocks west to the gas station. He pulled Lee's car up to one of the pumps, parked, and shut it off. Violet stared through the windshield, at the little building that sat a few hundred feet away. Wide windows painted with milk and beer prices, the door that rang a tinkling bell when you opened it, the guy standing behind the counter, in charge of the milk and the liquor and the gas receipts and the cash in the register.

"Hey," Marcus said.

She jolted.

"Okay?"

She tugged the door handle, and it slipped in her grip, but she held on. "Let's do it."

"You can stay in the car."

"Nope. Way past that. You stay here and I do everything." She opened the door and got out.

She pumped the gas, walked into the store, and Marcus kept an eye on her while she stood in line and paid. She left the store at a measured walk, the receipt crinkling between her fingers.

She got all the way to Lee's car before she trembled. Not surprising. This was when it had happened before. She turned a full circle, eyes darting for danger.

"Hey," Marcus said out the window. "Still okay?"

"Uh-huh."

She scampered inside the car and didn't duck. Her head hit the doorframe, and the impact had to hurt, but she didn't seem to notice.

She barely whispered. "Leave now, okay?"

He turned the key, and the engine started, a little too loud, like always. Maybe it would help remind her. Yeah, that's what he had to do.

"Hear that?" He motioned to the dashboard.

"Engine?"

"Right. Lee's car. Not the truck from before."

"I know."

"Different car. Different place. Different day."

"Please, can we leave?"

"Did you buy gas?"

She gave him an eye roll. "Of course I did."

"And paid for it."

"Yeah."

"And walked back to the car and got inside."

"Yeah."

"Did anybody hurt us?"

"N-no."

"Did anybody try?"

"No."

"Was there anybody with a gun?"

"No."

"Okay. Good." He put the car in drive and didn't look at Violet again as he drove back to the store. When he pulled Lee's car into the parking space next to his truck, she didn't move.

"How's your head?" He motioned to his head where she'd bumped hers.

Her face flushed. "Fine. Um, thanks."

"Sure."

She smiled, and the accomplishment in her eyes didn't need explaining. She'd faced them both — the real gas station and the one in her memory. And neither one had hurt her. Did she have to remind herself of that every time she pumped gas?

"I bet I can go next time on my own."

"No," he said. "Call me. We'll go together a few more times. Until you're sure you're okay."

Her eyes welled up, overflowed.

"Violet?"

"Don't say what we're going to do."

"I don't mind." But something was happening here.

"You don't know what we're going to do. You don't know we're going to do anything."

He tried to turn toward her, but the car left no room to maneuver, and a knife twisted in his knee when he tried. He got out and walked around, opened her door. She stared up at him.

Marcus took her hand and tugged, and she got out and followed him over to the curb. A bench was bolted into the cement

477

against the wall of the store, and Marcus sat. Tugged her down next to him and put his arm around her shoulders. Violet shook her head.

"Stop being nice to me. I'm being stupid."

"Violet." He waited for eye contact. "Tell me."

"It's just . . . what if . . . ?" She sniffed and swiped at her cheeks. "I know Texas is on your side now. But they might turn again. Next month or next week or tomorrow. We don't know."

"No. We don't."

"You might leave Lee's one night and I say good night to you, and you drive home, and — and I know those guys from church are going to keeping watching your house for a while, but there could still be a concop waiting to ambush you or — or —" The tears flowed again. "Or shoot you — and that's it, you're dead for real, or you disappear, and I never see you again."

He couldn't deny any of that. He shifted on the bench, searching for what he could say.

"I think about it every day," Violet whispered. "I probably could have got gas by myself today. I've been doing a lot better even in the last month. But then I thought, what if Marcus is supposed to be with you, and because you don't ask, he's somewhere else, and the con-cops take him, and you could have saved him if you'd asked him to come?"

He tugged her close to his side, and she hid her face against his arm. Tears seeped into his shirt.

"How long have you had thoughts like that?"

"A month or two, I guess, but then Walt told us about the wanted list, and I got . . . um, kind of terrified."

Kind of. He stretched his leg. Tried to think.

"I don't want to have no one left."

"Violet. Look at me."

She lifted her head.

"You'll never have nobody left. Not as long as you're God's."

"So I can't have anybody else?" Tears dried as she frowned at him.

"That's not what I said."

Violet burrowed against his shoulder like a little kid. "I really want to keep you. And Lee."

"Well, I want that too."

He closed his eyes as something prodded him from the inside. Not heavy like Violet's fear, but decisive. Needed. He kept his arm around Violet's shoulders and kept his eyes closed.

"God, You're here with us." Words stalled. He kept going, not planning them, just talking to the One Whose hands rested on him. "Please let Violet know You're with her. Please strengthen her. Take away the thoughts that make her terrified. Thank You for making us family. Amen."

They sat for long minutes while Violet's breathing evened until he thought she was asleep against him. Then she stirred and sat up.

"Okay?" he said.

"A lot better."

"Good."

"Some counselor I'll be." She sighed.

"You think counselors don't have their own things?" That was ridiculous. Pete was just a guy.

"I guess they do." Her face reddened, and she turned away from him, facing the parking lot that emptied and refilled while they sat here, shoppers coming and going.

"What?" he said.

"I wasn't going to dump all this on you. The last week, I've really been trying to handle it myself."

And she'd done so well at that, he hadn't seen anything different in her. Maybe she

480

was trying to distance herself to prepare for him being gone. The thought worked a dull ache in his stomach.

"Why?" he said.

"Because."

"Violet."

"I'll do better at telling you stuff, okay?"

"No."

She fidgeted on the bench and waited for a few kids to run past on the sidewalk. Then she faced him. "Because you've got your own stuff. Okay? And your stuff is bigger than some angsty fear of being left alone that I don't even know where it came from."

The ache grew, spread up into his chest. "You thought . . . because of my . . . things . . . you thought I wouldn't care about yours?"

"Good grief, Marcus." She rolled her eyes. "I knew you *would* care. Because you care about everything. And I didn't want to add to your stuff."

He hugged her. Violet hugged him back, the kind of hug only she gave, with the tiny *you're awesome* squeeze before she let go. They sat side by side for a minute.

"I don't know where we'll end up, Violet."

She turned her head to look at him.

"If we have to run, me and Lee, we won't leave you here. But . . ." He gripped the back of his neck. "If the Constabulary does get to me. Or if I get pneumonia again and die. Or whatever."

She shuddered beside him.

"I'm not your haven. Okay?"

She sighed. *Duh.* "You're not a place."

"Well, Lee was mine for years."

Violet was still.

"But I'm telling you this. Because I've been . . . four months, I've been . . ." Still hard to say, even now that the entire state of Texas knew the facts. Maybe the words would never be easy; maybe they shouldn't be. "There was nobody. Except God. And I'm telling you. If you let Him hold you, He's enough. And you can't lose Him."

"Okay," Violet whispered.

"But while I'm here, you can come to me. Always. With anything."

Violet leaned her head on his shoulder. "Best big brother a girl could ask for."

38

There could be no pretending anymore. Lee braved the long hallway, past the windows that looked out on the fountain and the garden, the place she'd surrendered to God. She turned left toward the adult classrooms. Kept her eyes straight ahead as people passed, eyeing her without greeting. She sensed no judgment, only uncertainty in how to approach her. She might be responsible for that.

She'd found safety too long in wearing the cloak of collectedness. She couldn't face these people now that they knew — Marcus wasn't fine, she likely wasn't either — unless she was willing to remove that cloak. She stood out of sight past the doorway of the fireside room and listened to the women's chatter, to the creak of a couch as someone sat down.

Did she want this?

Tonight, she would decide.

483

She stepped into the room.

A few of the conversations continued, but several drifted to silence. Juana stood from the couch in the far corner and came to her, no hesitation in her steps or her smile.

"You came," she said for Lee's ears only. "Good job."

Lee tried to unlace her hands behind her back, but her shoulders had turned to steel, her spine to a ramrod. How pathetic if her very presence was an achievement. She shuffled to the couch and sat beside Juana.

For another five minutes, chatting reigned. Lee listened while the cluster of women around her gushed about a concert several of them had been to. She imagined them dancing under oscillating lights, feeling the bass in their sternums, but then Monique mentioned the artist, a solo violinist who had been touring for years. Whom Lee had always wanted to see. Hollowness ached in her stomach. But of course they hadn't asked her to come. They didn't know she loved music.

Ruby waited until seven o'clock before suggesting they get started with prayer requests. They began on the far side of the room and worked their way toward her, an undertow, and she the lone swimmer in their sea. Beside her, Juana asked for prayer that she would be a godly mother to Damien, "even when he makes me crazy." On Lee's other side, farther from her personal space border, Monique asked for prayer for herself.

"For my heart," she said after a pause. "Sometimes it knows right and doesn't want to do it."

"Hear that," said someone, and another chimed, "For sure."

Monique knew how to be transparent. They all knew.

Lee wanted to know.

She looked up from the fingers clenched together in her lap. Every other woman in the room had either spoken a request or smiled and waved the invisible baton onward, *nothing to add tonight.* Now the baton hovered in front of Lee.

"I do have a request," she said. A ball of ice rolled from one shoulder to the other, made her shiver. "You're aware of the rapid news developments since Saturday."

Nods around the room. Smiles from the women who met her eyes. Encouragement.

"I suppose the first thing would be a . . . a praise. For Texas and its decision to reject the Constabulary's wanted list."

The nods gained enthusiasm.

"But this doesn't repair everything." She

turned the weave of her fingers inside out but kept her gaze above her lap. "We don't know the Constabulary will go quietly. We don't know Texas won't remove this protection at a later date."

She waited for someone to fill her pause, to move them on, but no one did. She'd said all there was to say. They understood why this situation needed prayer. But something nudged her to continue.

"I would like to request God's protection and also His peace. Marcus . . ." Several women seemed to lean closer as her voice failed. "Marcus has been through a great deal. He's healing, but it has been difficult for him."

"We'll pray for both of you," Monique said. Her eyes held nothing but compassion.

"Thank you." Another nudge from deep inside. Her gaze strayed to her hands again. She looked up.

They all still watched her, as if they could see the tug-of-war between speaking and silence.

"I was not a Christian when we arrived here in October. I became one shortly after our arrival."

Only as she informed them did she realize they hadn't known.

"I am still learning how to . . . how to have faith. And peace."

"It's not easy," Ruby said.

Lee shook her head before she could hold back the reflex. Enough transparency. But she was made of fault lines, and the shifting of one created a quake that crumbled all of her. Her mouth pulled down and her throat constricted in an attempt to hold the cracks together.

"What, Lee?" Monique said.

"You are able to trust. Even in difficulty, you don't doubt or question God."

Monique was shaking her head before Lee finished. "If you think we never doubt or question God, then you haven't been listening to us."

Lee looked around at all of them. Juana gave her a little nod.

"And we're delighted to pray for you," Ruby said. "We hope you pray for us, too."

"I do," Lee said.

Ruby paused a moment, assuring Lee was finished speaking. She'd said enough for a month of Wednesday nights, yet the words didn't want to stop.

"I would also like to . . . praise . . . that . . ." What was she doing? "Marcus and I are engaged."

"Congratulations!" The word burst over

the group in multiple voices.

Juana stared at her. "When did this happen?"

"Saturday night," Lee said.

"Four whole days, and no text? No phone call? No let's-go-to-coffee-so-I-can-share-my-news?"

"I would have told you at coffee tomorrow."

Juana shook her head, and a flicker of disappointment surfaced behind the playfulness.

When their evening ended, Lee waited for Juana outside the doors. As others left, they paused to congratulate her again and reiterate that she and Marcus were "in their prayers." Juana was one of the last to leave. Lee stood in front of her and rubbed her thumb over the strap of her purse. "I wanted to apologize."

"It's fine." But Juana looked away.

"I should have thought to tell you."

"I shouldn't expect so much."

In general, or from her? The cold caught Lee again. "I am sorry."

"No, Lee, really. The more I find out about you — sorry, I don't mean that like it sounds — I mean, on top of what you've told me, you didn't come here in some planned escape. I can read between the lines of Marcus's article. Y'all were running for your lives."

Dramatic phrasing, yet . . . "I suppose we were."

"Well, don't worry about me." The smile seemed real.

"Juana, I would have said this tomorrow as well, but now seems an appropriate time."

"Okay."

"Violet will be my maid of honor. I'd like you to be my bridesmaid."

They might not know one another well enough. Asking Juana to commit her time, to purchase a dress . . . Lee laced her fingers in front of her and tried not to school her face. Tried not to hide.

"Oh, Lee." Juana's hand pressed her heart. "I'd love to."

A breath gusted out of her, and Juana laughed.

"You thought I'd say no?"

"I thought it might not be a fair request."

"It's an honor." Juana hugged her. After a moment, Lee hugged back. "So, what colors?"

Women always cared about the most absurd details. "Violet suggested a muted pink. She said it would complement your coloring as well as hers."

"You want your girls wearing pink?"

"I don't have an opinion."

"Of course you do. Do you like pink, yes or no?"

Lee sighed. "I'm not fond of it."

"Then we're not going to wear pink. What's your favorite color? Please tell me you have one."

"It's your dress. Why would I make you wear my favorite color?"

"It's called bride's privilege."

Sudden bravery gripped Lee, nudged her toward the stairs. "Do you have a minute to come to my car?"

"Sure."

By the time they got there, bravery had fled. Her stomach knotted as she unlocked her car. Juana might find this silly. Or insulting. Lee had to be sure she explained properly. She leaned in and withdrew the boxed casserole dish.

"I know I can't replace something with sentimental value, but I saw this, and I thought of you, and . . ." She let the words trail as Juana opened the box.

Cradling it, Juana sat on the curb, purse set beside her. She trailed her fingers over the stenciling of delicate tree branches in the bottom of the dish. She drew it out of the box and looked it over from every angle.

"Lee, this is beautiful."

"I thought so." Lee sat next to her.

"But you know I'm not holding a grudge about the other one?"

"I know. But this seemed to . . . belong with you." Now she did sound absurd.

"Thank you. It's really beautiful." She settled it back into the cardboard packing corners and looked sidelong at Lee. "This is kind of weird, but yesterday I saw something and thought of you. And I bought it. And then I thought about taking it back."

"Why?"

"Because . . . it might not be my business."

Lee arched an eyebrow at her.

Juana laughed. "I guess I've never let that stop me before."

"I'd like to see it." She tried to imagine what it could be. Juana didn't know about her lost library. It must be something musical.

Juana set the casserole dish on the curb next to her and pulled her purse into her lap. She dug into a side pocket and drew out a tiny gift bag. Her smile looked nervous as she handed it to Lee.

Lee pulled the tissue paper from the top of the bag. The item inside was wrapped as well, the tissue paper held with a gold sticker that said *Fragile*. Lee tore it carefully, and the paper rustled.

It was some kind of ornament, hung on a thin plastic wire. Lee lifted the wire, and the ornament rose from the paper. A crystal teardrop. It cast rainbows on the pavement in front of her. It turned in her hand. On one side had been etched a cursive L.

"I was going to get a G." Juana's voice was soft. "For grace. But an L felt right. For love and life. And Lee, I guess. It's . . . I got it for your baby. I thought you probably don't have anything to remember her by."

Lee's hand trembled, and the teardrop spun and swayed. She took it in her other hand and let go of the wire. She held the teardrop to her chest. She lowered her forehead to her knees. She remembered something Marcus had said once. God's gifts. Juana was one. And this piece of cut glass was another. Love and life. And . . .

"Lee?"

She lifted her head. "I named her Lacey."

Juana's lips parted. She sat like a statue.

"But a few months later, I decided I had no right to give her a name. I no longer called her anything, in my head."

Juana cradled Lee's hands, the empty one and the one holding tight to the teardrop. "Oh, friend."

Lee's eyes welled. Twin tears blotted the tissue paper in her lap.

Juana closed her eyes and whispered, "Lord," and Lee's soul agreed. She bowed her head, and a few more tears fell. A long breath filled her. In a little while, she tucked the crystal teardrop into its bag. Juana picked up her dish.

Somehow there was no strain between them.

For once, Juana waited for Lee to speak first, but she couldn't express what had happened. Some old lesion had been excised and bandaged, deep inside her. She could see Lacey, alive before the face of God.

"Thank you," she said.

"Ditto."

Lee should have felt weighted and tired. But she got up from the curb ready for the rest of the day, ready for tomorrow. She set the gift bag on the passenger seat of her car and trailed one finger over the ribbon handles before she shut the door. If she had to put a word on this feeling, as Hannah had taught her to do, it would be *clean*.

Juana smiled. "Now that we've cried on each other . . . do you and your fiancé have plans tonight?"

"He found an old-fashioned ice-cream shop in Decatur. He wants to try it."

She could hardly point out the breach of health rules in eating dessert after eight-thirty, not when his eyes had held that rare boyish twinkle at the idea. She headed back toward the church, and Juana walked with her, still cradling the casserole dish in the crook of one arm.

"By the way, we never got around to your favorite color."

Lee let her eyes travel the dispersing crowd for Marcus. "Teal."

"Well, fortunately for you, my skin tone is great with teal. And as a blonde, Violet will look fabulous in it too."

"All right."

"You're going to be the most easygoing bride of all time. Have you set a date?"

"Not yet."

"Better get on that, girl."

From across the foyer, Marcus spotted them. His slow smile ignited something in Lee's belly, and more heat seeped into her cheeks.

Juana followed her gaze to Marcus as he threaded around groups of people toward them. "You're head over heels, my friend."

"I believe so." The heat deepened.

Juana hugged her again, lingering this time. "Go enjoy time with your man."

"Thank you."

She met Marcus halfway, and their hands found one another without conscious thought, at least on her part. They didn't speak as they walked to the doors, then out into the parking lot. Still didn't speak as they climbed into his truck. He started to drive and rolled down the windows, and the wind ruffled the waves of his hair. Lee stayed in the passenger seat despite an urge to slide over and twirl her fingers where the wind played.

"They're open till ten," he said after a few minutes.

"Perfect."

"Surprised you said yes."

Her heartbeat stuttered. Of course she'd said yes.

"We're breaking your no-food-after-whenever thing."

"Ah, that."

His eyes darted to hers, then settled back on the road. The drive was already working into his tensions and loosening them. Cares around his eyes were smoothing away. "You thought I meant the proposal?"

Curse the ease with which he read her. But it warmed her too. She nestled against the seat. No answer necessary.

"It did go through my head," he said after a moment. "What if you said no."

"Not for weeks, I hope."

His grin flashed. "Seconds."

39

Marcus opened the door of the ice-cream shop and followed Lee inside. She went directly to the counter for a cardboard cup, but Marcus paused a moment to appreciate the design of the place. It was small with dark wood trim and a real wood floor, the kind that was so old it couldn't help bowing. Five round tables stood around the shop, clean white surfaces and dark wooden legs. It might have been cozy, if it weren't cold. The wall to the right of the entrance was white tile, soft-serve dispensers built in and chilling the air more thoroughly than air-conditioning. Ten different flavors of ice cream. The toppings bar spread out along the back, open on both sides.

This was going to be fun.

He and Lee took their bowls to the dispensers. She got vanilla without even looking at the other options. Marcus chose brownie batter. At the toppings bar, he set to work. He'd never seen such a variety. Half of them were fruit — blueberries, strawberries, banana slices — so he ignored those as well as the sprinkles. They had that chocolate shell stuff, but that only got in the way. He found his faithful favorites and spooned on chopped peanuts, Oreo crumbles, brownie bits, chocolate chips, and finally crumbled peanut butter cups for something new. Oh, and here were M&Ms. Might as well. He doused the whole thing in fudge syrup and looked back at Lee.

And shook his head. Her vanilla ice cream was decorated with all the berries, bananas, almonds, and what looked like one quick squirt of strawberry syrup.

Lee was staring at his bowl. "I don't believe I'll ever get used to that."

"Well. I'll never get used to *that.*" He jerked a nod at hers.

Marcus paid for them both and had to grin at the difference in bowl weight. His was almost double the price.

After nine o'clock, the shop was empty except for a few college-age kids. He and Lee claimed a table at the front, next to the window. She let him take the chair that faced the door. Then, as if this were some sort of ceremony, she waited for him to take the first bite.

Chocolate, crunch, sweet, nutty — the flavors burst in his mouth together, so rich they made their own rush, forget sugar in the bloodstream. He rolled the bite around on his tongue. Tasted each piece and the whole. For a moment, the patient hand on his shoulder seemed to squeeze with satisfaction, affection. *Thanks for taste buds, Jesus. And for . . .* He ducked his head. He was going to cry over ice cream.

"Marcus?"

He swiped at his face. "Just . . . good to be . . . here."

She reached across the table. Her hand, chilled by her spoon, rested on his arm and stayed there.

After a minute, he wasn't so quivery. He dug back into his sundae with his left hand, but Lee's stayed on his right arm, even while she took a few more bites.

"Juana says we should set a date," she said halfway through her bowl, the banana slices all gone and only berries remaining.

"Okay."

"Are you thinking this year?"

His head jerked up. It was only May.

Her mouth curved, continued to inch upward until her teeth nearly showed. "I suppose that answers the question."

"When are you thinking?" he said.

"I'm ready."

"Not scared?"

She set down her spoon, withdrew her hand from his arm, but the gesture was unconscious, not a deliberate pulling away. "I'm not afraid to kiss you."

Yeah, she'd proved that. He wanted to grin, but her tone was somber.

"However, the other aspects of . . . I don't know what will . . ." She closed her eyes a moment, opened them. "I'm concerned you will blame yourself. If it takes time for me."

"No," he said.

"You can't know that until we're . . . in the situation."

"Lee, if you need to wait, I told you we can."

"I don't want to wait."

"Okay."

"But we need to be cautious. Marriage requires legal paperwork. I don't know if Juana's right about committing to a date."

The common sense of that made him want to growl. He hid his expression with a bite of sundae.

"I know," she said.

"If Texas stays free for the next two months, we apply for a marriage license."

"Two months isn't very long."

"Yeah, it is." His mouth twitched.

Lee blushed to the roots of her hair. She reached across the table again. He offered his open hand, and she traced the lines of his palm. He remembered her lips on his knuckles and wanted to take her out of this shop somewhere solitary and kiss her mouth and her fingers and her eyelids and then her mouth again. He sighed and leaned back in the chair. *Chill, man.*

"Two months," Lee said.

"July."

"We could get married on Independence Day."

He cocked his head at her, and she smirked. Okay, good.

He finished his sundae before it could turn to soup, a few more gobbled bites that he held in his mouth until the ice cream melted and the toppings all crunched over his tongue. He pushed the bowl away. Lee finished hers more slowly, and their silence was punctuated by laughter and voices from the kids at the far table, clinking silverware and dishes from the back, and a speaker over their heads playing oldies at a low volume.

When Lee's sundae was gone, she looked up at him, rawness in her eyes that turned their gray color to a storm. "If you marry me, and I'm not . . . suitable . . . it will be forever. You don't quit. Even when you should."

The table between them was too much of a barrier. Marcus got up and slid his chair close to hers and took her hands. They were still cold. She bowed her head, staring at their hands, and a breath shuddered into her and didn't exhale.

"Lee," he said.

She looked up at him. Her eyes were shiny.

"Unless you want me alone for the rest of my life," he said into her ear, "you've got to marry me."

A silent laugh shook her, and then a little sob.

He kissed her temple. "Okay?"

She rested her head on his shoulder. They sat awhile, until the college kids filed out and the manager turned the sign from Open to Closed. Lee would have leaped up to go if she'd seen, but her back faced the doors. Marcus hoped she would stir on her own in a minute. He met the manager's eyes with a silent apology, and the man waved a *no problem* gesture.

"I wish . . ." Her words barely reached him. She pulled his hand into her lap and cradled it in both of hers. "I wish there was at least the possibility of . . . my giving you a child."

He'd given that up so long ago, it didn't sting anymore. But it would be different for a woman, maybe. She hadn't talked about this for months, but that might not mean she was past it. He shifted, working stiffness from the knee. He wouldn't have brought up his recent idea so soon, but maybe she needed to hear it, though it was new to him, too.

"We could have kids," he said. "Adopted kids. Like Elliott."

She went still.

"Not soon. Parents have to be ready. To take care of a person all the time. I'm still . . ." He sighed. "I could be home with a kid and have a panic attack. Or something."

Lee was quiet.

"But in a year or two. If you want."

"Yes." Her voice was fragile. She drew back to look at him. "I would like to investigate that possibility. With you."

"Good." He lifted her hand and kissed the palm. "Ready to go?"

She nodded, and he took her hand.

They walked under glittering stars to his truck. He'd had to park across the street. The night air had cooled only a few degrees, much warmer than the shop had been. In the dark neighborhood, a canopy of tree branches rustled over their heads as they made their way down the sidewalk. They crossed the street, reached the truck, and Marcus dug out his keys, opened the passenger door.

"Have you ever sensed God?" Lee said.

"Yeah."

"Sensed He was molding a specific piece of your life into something new, something you thought would always be . . . old."

He had so many examples of that in the last year, he couldn't count them all. "Yeah."

"I believe I felt that today."

"Want to talk about it?"

"Yes."

Marcus turned. She tilted her face up to him, lit and shadowed by the streetlights. He shut the truck door.

"A little later," she said.

He cradled the back of her head. He kissed her. But not the way he'd wanted to in the ice-cream shop. He made this kiss as soft as he could. Filled it with all the things that made them who they were, all the things that made him sure of them. It lasted, and she returned it, angling her head to take and give more. When they pulled back, it was only by inches. His fingers twined in her hair, and she rested her hand on his chest.

They held each other. Around them, the trees whispered.

Epilogue

A gentle piano melody began, and the guests rose from their pews. Austin glanced at the groom. Crinkles nearly hid Marcus's eyes, and his smile carved deeply into his face. On Austin's other side, the lone groomsman, Walt, watched the back of the church to see the bride. Austin should do the same, yet his eyes strayed across the altar to Violet. The teal gown complemented her curves and ended below her knees. Her blonde hair swept up to one side, but a few curls spilled over one bare shoulder. A single pearl on a teal ribbon nestled at her throat. She was smiling bigger than he'd ever seen, while beside her, Juana looked ready to cry.

Austin forced his gaze to the back of the church.

Lee stepped into view, and Marcus's breath caught audibly. She approached them slowly, the white linen sheath fitted to her height and slimness, brushing the floor behind her. The straps were wide over her shoulders and the neck dipped enough to show a white-ribbon-and-pearl necklace. Gathered in along her waist, more pearls were woven into the dress, and some kind of pearl net covered her hair. Austin had never seen her wear makeup before, but today a dusky color accented her eyelids, and her lips were glossed. Violet's doing, or Juana's.

Lee stopped in front of Heath Carter, and as rehearsed, he took her hand and joined it to Marcus's. Lee had been firm that since Sam Stiles wasn't here to walk her down the aisle, she would walk alone.

Heath spoke to them about marriage, what it meant to a Christian. A picture of Christ and the church. Austin kept himself from fidgeting at that but couldn't prevent his gaze from finding Violet. Would he be able to love her that way? Could he ever deserve submission? Did he want it? Mom had submitted to Dad since Austin was born, and look how that turned out.

The ring in Austin's palm was small — Lee's fingers were narrower than Violet's — a thin band of white gold inlaid with a tiny diamond that winked in the lights. Austin didn't know any other woman, even Violet, who would choose something so unimpressive, but he also couldn't imagine anything larger on Lee's finger.

When he handed the ring to Marcus, the man's trembling hand nearly dropped it. Austin met his eyes, and the depth of emotion in them caught him in the chest. Marcus wasn't afraid or even unsure. The thing that overwhelmed him was joy. He slid the ring onto Lee's finger with a steadier hand.

They spoke traditional vows. Lit a candle, something Austin had never seen done before but knew was a tradition from eras bygone. A woman named Monique, whom Austin had met yesterday when he flew in for the rehearsal, sang an old-sounding melody. The lyrics were based on 1 Corinthians 13.

Before long Heath was saying, "By the power vested in me, I now pronounce you man and wife. Marcus, you may kiss your bride."

A breath passed over the sanctuary as Marcus didn't move, stood looking into Lee's eyes, and then he wrapped both arms around her. Their lips met gently.

Grinning, Heath motioned for them to turn and face the guests. "Ladies and gentlemen, it is my honor and joy to present to you for the very first time: Mr. and Mrs. Marcus Brenner."

Violet might have squealed, but she was drowned out as the church erupted. Applause. Cheers. Whistles. More noise than Austin would have thought possible from this group of a hundred or so. They kept it up while, hand in hand, Marcus and Lee descended the platform steps and walked out the wide doors. A few random claps and whoops continued as Austin linked Violet's arm through his and escorted her down the aisle and out into the foyer.

Less than ten paces out of sight, the bride and groom were clinging to each other. Not a kiss of passion, not a kiss at all. They held each other as if they couldn't get close enough.

"Guys?" Violet whispered.

Marcus lifted his head. Unshed tears shone. "We're okay."

Lee pulled his head down to bring their lips together, kept both her hands in his hair while the kiss lasted. She didn't seem to care about witnesses as Juana and Walt exited into the foyer and stopped beside Violet and Austin.

"Congratulations," Juana said with a hint of mischief.

They pulled back, and Lee's eyes were glistening too. "Thank you."

"You're Mrs. Brenner." Violet threw her

arms around Lee and didn't let go. "Wow, Lee."

"Yes." Lee hugged her back, hands pressing Violet's shoulders.

Austin stepped up and shook Marcus's hand, and the man's grip was firm and steady. "Congratulations."

"Thanks."

"Ready for the reception?" Juana grinned.

Violet bounced once in her high heels. "Yes, please."

But first came the receiving line and the pictures. Nothing zany — Walt and Austin certainly didn't pose with Lee lounging across their arms — but Violet asked for a "jump shot," and Lee and Marcus leaped into the air along with the rest of them. In the July heat, everyone's faces were rosy. A few beads of sweat trickled from Austin's neck into his collar as they all headed to the cars, ready to join the reception.

The hall was decorated in teal and white, the food served buffet-style — simple but delicious. Violet sobbed her way through the maid of honor's toast and Austin made the best man's as short as he could at Marcus's private request. Out of deference to the groom, the wedding party toasted with bubbling white grape juice instead of champagne.

Marcus and Lee fed each other cake, and then it was time for dancing. Marcus and Lee's first dance was to a nineties country ballad Austin wouldn't expect either of them to know. Even more wondrously, the two of them danced to it — not swaying but dancing, a simple step but a step nonetheless.

"Lessons," Walt said with a wink, and Austin closed his mouth.

"Marcus took dancing lessons."

"From yours truly, he sure did."

Okay, that was different, but . . . still. Austin looked down the table, and with the bride and groom's seats vacated, his view to Violet was unobstructed. Her attention didn't waver from Marcus and Lee. Tears streamed down her face and caught in the corners of her smile. Juana leaned in to say something, and Violet laughed and then cried harder.

He thought he'd never get to talk to her. But when the dance floor opened up, Austin slid down two chairs.

"May I have this dance?"

Violet's smile caught the rotating lights on the dance floor. "Okay."

Holding her in his arms was everything he'd remembered. But talking wasn't going to be easy. He searched for a neutral topic to start as they swayed to Sinatra.

"You must be feeling pretty good about your citizenship."

She grinned. "So far, so good."

The music swelled, and he lifted his arm. Violet twirled beneath it, her skirt a gentle whirl. Back in his arms, her face creased with pensiveness, and he waited. She had more to say.

"It's been less than ninety days. If Texas was a new employee somewhere, they'd still be on probation."

A chuckle shook him.

"Walt's optimistic, though," she said. "He won't talk about it, but I can tell. And that helps."

Less than forty-eight hours after his flight touched down, he couldn't really complain that he and Walt hadn't spoken yet about work. He pressed his shoulders back and tried to relax. Let himself take in Violet's light perfume, a scent of vanilla and oranges.

How are you? Really? Not time yet for that one.

"Marcus is a citizen now too," she said. "And Lee isn't processed yet, but we're hoping marrying him will move her up the line."

Austin looked past her, over the dance floor. Marcus's broad shoulders and Lee's

512

white dress were equally easy to spot.

"How are they?" he said. He hadn't expected to care so much about the answer.

Violet danced and watched his face. Wondering how much she should say, how much he was still privileged to know? Almost three months away. Hardly any contact. Maybe he'd forfeited a few things while he was gone.

"They're doing really well," Violet said, and it didn't sound like a brush-off. "Still dealing with a lot. But dealing."

Even if she gave him details later, nothing would change that he hadn't been here. He'd gone to Canada partly based on Walt's advice, but Violet knew there were other factors in the decision.

"Don't you want to stay here?"

"Not like this!"

He blinked. "That's good."

Violet nodded in their direction. "He sprained his knee again about three weeks ago. Lee told me his doctor mentioned surgery this time."

Austin tried to picture Marcus agreeing to be laid up that long. Not likely after the recovery he'd already gone through. "If it would help long term, he ought to consider it."

"I think he was going to. But when general

513

anesthesia came up, he freaked out. 'Nobody's cutting me open while I'm asleep.' He thinks the topic's closed, but we both know Lee better than that." She twirled under his arm again almost before he had time to raise it, then settled back in.

Everybody had something. That was life. Austin was still hitting the gun range once a week to improve not only his skill but also his tolerance for the occasional flashback. Jason's empty eyes filled his head less often, but they weren't gone yet. Violet pressed closer to him, appropriate as the song changed to a true waltz, but her nearness raised his awareness of his own pulse.

"So how are you? You've been here two days and haven't told me."

Of course he hadn't. It was up to her to ask. He wouldn't assume she wanted to know. He rested his chin in her hair as they continued swaying; neither of them knew the traditional step.

"I invited Esther to come with me," he said. "Here, to the wedding. I figured Marcus and Lee wouldn't mind."

She drew back enough to meet his eyes. "They'd have liked to meet her."

"She wouldn't leave Olivia, even for a weekend." That, or she hadn't wanted to taste freedom knowing she'd have to return to the cell block of their parents' house for another two years.

"Have you seen your dad?"

"Don't plan to." Ever. One edge in him that might never dull.

"But you've seen them, your sisters, since you went to Canada?"

"Once."

"And they're okay? I pray for them all the time."

If *okay* only meant they hadn't been physically hurt. If *okay* didn't include being stressed and silenced every day. "They need to be out of that house."

As Carole King began to sing about the earth moving under her feet and the dancers around them began to enliven their moves, Austin backed toward the edge of the floor.

"Can I . . . show you something?"

Violet frowned but nodded. Followed him to the hallway. From out here, Carole King was still audible as he led her toward the double doors to the parking lot. Violet stopped.

"Where are you going?"

"To my car," he said. Shoot, this all sounded underhanded, but he hoped she trusted him more than that. He couldn't explain without the item in his hands. He might not be able to explain with it.

Violet glanced back at the closed doors, then sighed. "Okay. Just for a minute."

The night's heat hit them as they stepped outside, along with a sweet fragrance, something like honeysuckle. Austin stripped off his suit jacket and hung it over his arm. Violet stood a few feet from the rental car as he unlocked it and scrounged through his suitcase in the back.

"You brought a lot of luggage for one weekend," she said. "I mean, for a guy."

Good observation. He found the leather-bound book under his clothes and tugged it out, rezipped the case and relocked the car. And . . . he was an idiot. Talking to her, really talking to her, out here in the parking lot. Forcing topics he should have faced tomorrow. But he couldn't wait to know what she thought. How she felt.

"I have to ask you something first," he said.

Violet's heels tapped the asphalt as she approached him. "You've got your scholar face on."

He choked on the laugh. Still his Violet. Unless she wasn't. His lips froze.

"Are you going to ask me if I'm with somebody?"

So much for guarding his expression. His

mouth dried.

She tilted her head. "Have I been dancing with you like I'm with somebody else?"

Not exactly a *no*. But pretty close. He swallowed. "You could be embracing the festive mood."

"I was embracing *you*. And I wouldn't be, if I had somebody else."

He exhaled. "Okay."

"For the record, I haven't dated anybody since you."

He took her hand. Led her to a wooden bench set outside the hall entrance. Violet sat and smoothed her skirt over her knees, and Austin dropped next to her. Handed her the journal.

"I was mad when I left," he said.

"I know." Her voice dropped. "I wasn't fair."

No, she hadn't been. But she'd also been conflicted, and he hadn't done much to convince her he was worth a second chance.

"Well, anyway." No sense rehashing. "I didn't stay mad. And Marcus said something the last time I talked to him. I tried to ignore it, but he was right. So in Toronto, I went to a shady little bookstore in the lower level of a pub, and I bought a Bible."

Her breath caught. She lifted her head. "And?"

"And I read a lot of it. It ticked me off, so I'd quit reading, but then I'd keep thinking it over and . . ." He'd been like a man with an addiction, never staying clean long enough to detox. After two days of ignoring the book on his nightstand, he'd have to open it again and read more of the red letters that ticked him off.

Violet was sitting as still as he knew she would, absorbing his every word with light in her eyes.

"Listen, babe, I'm not convinced it's anything more than a historical document. I'm not convinced God showed up in the flesh to let us murder Him. Okay? You need to know that."

A crimp between her eyebrows, but she nodded.

"I haven't thrown the book in the trash yet either. I'm not saying I won't. It's all . . ." Epic and stirring in the most ironic, eloquent ways. Strange and sensible at the same time. He shook his head. Enough of the talking in circles. He handed her the book.

"I took notes. And I railed a little. Wasn't planning for anyone but me to see it."

Violet took it in both hands as if he'd offered her something living and fragile. She didn't look up.

"By the end, it turned into kind of a journal. Then it turned into a few letters. To you. Some of them are about God. Some of them are about us."

Now she met his eyes.

"I'd like you to read it all. If you want to, maybe we could talk about it. My notes and . . . the rest of it."

If she handed it back to him, he didn't know what he'd do. Yes, he did. He'd get on the next plane for Ontario. But he'd have to find a new apartment. He gritted his teeth. What was this root that had been growing in him the last month, wanting to understand, wanting to feel what faith must be like? It had wrapped so many tendrils around him, he'd come to Texas hoping.

"I'll read it," Violet said. And smiled.

"Thank you."

"Will you want it back before you fly out?"

He had to clear his throat. This was it. The last thing he should have told her tomorrow. "I'm not flying out."

"Wh-what?" Her voice fell to a whisper. Her hands tightened on the journal.

"I talked to Walt a few weeks ago, after Marcus asked me to be his best man. My old job's still available. I'm figuring Rosita's got a new cook, but Walt offered —"

She threw her arms around him, the

journal sliding forward in her lap. "Oh, Austin."

"Yeah?" He stroked curls that had loosened from their pins.

She pulled back, and he waited for the frustration to ignite in his chest, make his hands clench. It barely flickered. For tonight, anyway.

"I'm going to be a counselor," she said. "I'm going to school in the fall with financial aid and maybe some scholarships. I have fish. You can meet them if you want. I have friends. I'm sharing an apartment with Alexis. I'm happy. I pray for you every day. And I have days when I'm scared this is all a dream and I'll wake up in Lee's apartment in Michigan and she'll still be throwing up all the time and Marcus will still be dead."

He couldn't help it. He pushed her curls back over her shoulder. "Quite a torrent there."

"You told me about you. I wanted to tell you about me."

That revealed more than she knew. Or maybe she did know. He exerted all his willpower not to kiss her and drew her to her feet instead. "We'd better rejoin the party."

"She's Lee Brenner now. It sounds great

together."

He laughed. "Okay."

Violet stowed the journal in the old silver car she'd inherited from Lee. Back inside the hall, the dance floor was full, everybody — even the pastor and his wife — line dancing to one of those inane club numbers. The bride and groom had retreated to the wedding party's table, and Marcus was pouring two goblets of sparkling grape juice. His eyes smiled when he saw Violet and Austin.

He gestured to his right leg, stretched out under the table. "I'm done."

"As am I," Lee said.

"The noise?" Violet claimed the chair next to Lee.

"Precisely."

"One more hour?" But Marcus didn't look committed to his suggestion.

"I'm quite sure they can continue their revelry without us."

Violet laughed. "Lee, only you can make a party sound horrible."

A corner of Lee's mouth lifted. She and Marcus toasted each other and sipped their juice.

Violet rolled her eyes. "You're like two old people already."

Austin fidgeted on his feet. The three of them had kept their friendship growing. He didn't regret the time and space away. He'd needed it. Sorted out a lot. Worked through things he hadn't known needed working through. But if there was no catching up to them, if he'd always be standing outside their team that had crossed a country together . . . It had been his choice. He couldn't blame them for it.

Marcus caught his eye and nodded to the next empty chair. Austin hung his suit jacket over the back and sat down.

"How long will you be staying?" Lee said.

"Awhile, I think." The pleasure in her smile was real, but tonight was about them. He would not waylay that. "Tell me about you guys."

For the next hour, they did. They'd already made the greeting rounds, fulfilled courtesy's demands, and while a few people waved at them to come dance, only Juana left the group to try to persuade them. When Lee gave her a pointed look, Juana retreated with a good-natured sigh, and Marcus, Lee, Violet, and Austin continued to talk.

They told Austin how Marcus's fifteen minutes of fame actually lasted about three weeks, until enough other refugees began telling their stories too, emboldened first by him and then by others who spoke out. How the media left him alone now, but the people of Texas hadn't forgotten him. How restaurant servers who saw the name on his debit card sometimes got permission from their managers to discount the bill and didn't let Marcus refuse. They talked about the surprise bridal shower Violet and Juana had organized, never expecting the church to pull together and give everything from gift cards to gently used furniture. The people Violet invited told others who told others, until even those who didn't show up contributed to the furnishing of Marcus's empty house.

Finally, Marcus looked to Lee. "We could disappear."

"No, you cannot." Violet sprang to her feet and marched over to the DJ.

"What is she . . . ?" Lee looked ready to bolt.

"Announcing your departure," Austin said.

"Is that necessary?"

"It's your wedding, Lee. It's tradition."

Lee tucked her hands between her knees, hiding them in a fold of her dress. Marcus pushed to his feet and held out his hand, and she stood to take it.

The music faded, and the dancers drifted to a standstill. Instead of the DJ's voice, Violet's sounded over the PA.

"Hi, everybody. It's time for our sendoff of Mr. and Mrs. Brenner."

A few cheers. And then, as if by instinct, the crowd on the dance floor parted down the middle.

"Great!" Violet's smile was audible. "Okay, we didn't have rice or anything at the church, so imagine your voices are the rice as Marcus and Lee make their grand exit. Let them know how much we love them."

More cheers.

"No, not yet," Violet said, and laughter filled the room.

Marcus leaned down for a kiss, and Lee obliged, and the laughter was replaced with applause. Then he tugged her by the hand out onto the floor. Side by side, they jogged down the center path everyone had opened for them. The noise crescendoed — applause from every pair of hands, cheers from every voice, whistles and foot stomping. Somebody hurried ahead and held open one of the doors, and Marcus and Lee ducked through it, both waving as they disappeared. The noise continued for a full minute.

A touch on his arm. Austin turned. Violet didn't say anything, didn't meet his eyes, but she stood beside him as the music started up again mid-song and everybody milled around and resumed their dancing.

Maybe that would be him and Violet someday, a suit and a white dress, running into life together. No way to know, for now. But he'd stick around long enough to find out.

ACKNOWLEDGMENTS

So it's October, a month of melancholy change, of good-bye to summer (or at least, autumn has always been these things to me). Appropriate that I'm sending off the final Haven Seekers novel now, the one that chooses a place to stop telling the story of Marcus, Lee, Austin, and Violet. It's been a whirlwind — four books released in seventeen months — and I could never have stayed upright in the storm without help, support, love, and belief from many people. Thank you . . .

To every single person who read this series. (Yes, you!) Double gratitude if you have written a review of any of my books.

To my advance reviewers and my coworkers, who keep asking me when the fourth book will be out, who have shared their personal reading experiences in encouraging detail — what made them laugh, cry, and think. An author could ask for no bet-

527

ter tribe than all of you.

To Dave Dunham and Denise Hardy, for informative and engaging Biblical counseling electives at church. A lot of my note-taking was related to these fictional people. And especially to Denise, for answering my questions about counselor protocol and how to help someone like Marcus.

To Michelle Lim, for asking me (a few years ago now) what I wanted more: to see my name in print, or to see Marcus and Lee in print? My answer surprised both of us, I think, but it centered me and pushed me forward on the Haven Seekers path.

To Jordyn Redwood, for information on Heath's injury/surgery, and even more for your constant willingness to answer yet another medical question.

To Jocelyn Floyd, for friendship through all the history between us and for giving away all those paperbacks and for telling everyone you've ever met that they should read this series. (I might not even be exaggerating there.) Oh and, of course, for the meteors.

To Andrea Taft, for friendship, for my favorite mug and sun catcher, for being the first person to tell me this was not a terrible book, and for reading the revisions faster than I'd hoped and telling me I really had "fixed all of it."

To Melodie Lange, for demanding I now write Marcus and Lee's newlywed story, and for a constantly open door of friendship.

To Jess Keller, for tough feedback I needed to hear, for factual corrections regarding crime scene and police procedure, and for the umbrella of grace.

To Charity Tinnin, for more tough feedback I needed to hear, for getting through that edit though it wasn't an easy season for you, and for friendship.

To Jessica Kirkland, agent and friend, for showing me your beautiful state of Texas and letting me lean out of your car taking pictures of small towns, for believing in me and in this series, and for your enthusiasm about my "next thing."

To Nick Lee, designer of the original publisher's editions, for some of the most beautiful covers in the history of publishing. I do not take them for granted.

To Jon Woodhams for editing savvy, for encouragement, and for trying to teach me about that comma rule I still mess up.

To David C Cook for saying yes to Haven Seekers.

To my family, as always: Joshua, Emily, Andrew, Emma, Mom, and Dad. You know why by now.

To my faithful God Who holds me even though I'm prone to wander, Who uses me despite the cracks in this jar of clay, Who has redeemed my life story with His blood and, I pray, will place the story of Marcus's and Lee's redemption where He wants it to be, for His glory alone.

ABOUT THE AUTHOR

As a child, **Amanda G. Stevens** disparaged *Mary Poppins* and *Stuart Little* because they could never happen. Now, she writes speculative fiction. Holding a Bachelor of Science degree in English, she has taught literature and composition to home-school students. She lives in Michigan and loves books, film, music, and white cheddar popcorn.